DEBORAH SWIFT is a USA TODAY bestselling author of historical fiction, a genre she loves. As a child she enjoyed reading the Victorian classics such as *Jane Eyre, Little Women, Lorna Doone* and *Wuthering Heights*. She has been reading historical novels ever since; though she's a bookaholic and reads widely – contemporary and classic fiction.

In the past, Deborah used to work as a set and costume designer for theatre and TV, so enjoys the research aspect of creating historical fiction, something she was familiar with as a scenographer. More details of her research and writing process can be found on her website www.deborahswift.com

Deborah likes to write about extraordinary characters set against the background of real historical events.

The Silk Code

DEBORAH SWIFT

ONE PLACE. MANY STORIES

HQ
An imprint of HarperCollins*Publishers* Ltd
1 London Bridge Street
London SE1 9GF

www.harpercollins.co.uk

HarperCollins*Publishers*
Macken House, 39/40 Mayor Street Upper,
Dublin 1 D01 C9W8
Ireland

This paperback edition 2023

1
First published in Great Britain by
HQ, an imprint of HarperCollins*Publishers* Ltd 2023

Copyright © Deborah Swift 2023

Deborah Swift asserts the moral right to be
identified as the author of this work.
A catalogue record for this book is
available from the British Library.

ISBN: 9780008586829

MIX
Paper | Supporting
responsible forestry
FSC
www.fsc.org   FSC™ C007454

This book is produced from independently certified FSC™ paper
to ensure responsible forest management.

For more information visit: www.harpercollins.co.uk/green

Printed and Bound in the UK using
100% Renewable Electricity at CPI Group (UK) Ltd

For John, the eggman

PART ONE

PART ONE

Chapter 1

Scotland

February 1943

Nancy blew her nose. Tears would be no use for what lay ahead. They'd no telephone at the manse, and the public one was miles away, so she'd have to walk over to Stranraven House to have it out with Andrew. Now Kitty had told her the truth, she'd have to confront him in person, while she was still angry enough to want to see him squirm. She guessed he'd try to talk her round, and the thought of this unsavoury conversation filled her with dread.

The weather was still foul, so she pulled her knitted beret further down over her wavy hair and buttoned up her mackintosh as she trudged across the fields. Stranraven House was a large granite building sunk in the valley, beneath the scree and the pines. Before today, its stark turreted outline had always given her a kind of romantic pleasure, but now she was furious that she would never dance a ceilidh in its great hall, or dine in its wood-panelled dining-room. And Andrew's parents would be

1

so hurt. She'd come to think of them as relations, and she liked them both, his slightly scatty mother and his old-school father.

Andrew's new motorcar, a Humber – his pride and joy – was parked outside on the drive. He was definitely in. She wondered bitterly if Audrey had been treated to his little tour of the nearby lochs and glens in his new toy, just as she had. Whether they had kissed in 'their' favourite picnic spot next to Loch Earn. The thought re-fuelled her anger, as she marched across the field in her wellington boots, not caring as she squelched through the mud, her hair whipping across her face as it escaped her hat. Up past the staring herd of Highland cows, feet scrunching up the gravel to the front door. She tugged hard on the bell pull, hearing it clang inside the door.

Mrs Havers, the housekeeper, opened it. The familiarity of the hall, with its ticking grandfather clock, almost derailed her resolve.

'Ah, Nancy, how are you, my dear?' Mrs Havers smiled benignly at her as if she were still five years old. She'd have no idea why she was there. Nor, for that matter, would Andrew.

Nancy steeled herself. 'Is Andrew in?'

'Down in the drawing room, dear, with the paper. He's finished his rounds with Dr Barker now.' Andrew was a junior doctor, and exempt from army service.

Nancy headed down the corridor, her cheeks hot and heart thumping. Of course, Hamish and Hector, the two gundogs, leapt up to greet her exactly as usual and she had to fuss them. After all, none of this was their fault.

'Hello, Nance,' Andrew said, standing up with a smile and approaching her with arms out for his usual kiss.

She backed away. 'Keep your hands off me.' Her voice was tight and small.

He frowned. He was wearing that brown cardigan she hated too. 'What's the matter?'

'Don't pretend you don't know. Audrey Hamilton is what's the matter.'

His face took on a stiff expression. 'What's she got to do with anything?'

'Kitty McIntyre told me you've been seeing her.'

'No, that's rubbish. We chat sometimes, like friends do.'

'Don't lie to me, Andrew. I've just been with Kitty on the bus, and I know she's right. She saw you and Audrey kissing on Stirling high street. And besides, I've been friends with Audrey since school and the last few weeks she's been distinctly "off" with me. How could you?'

'I haven't done anything,' he said bullishly. 'You'd believe Kitty over me?'

'Audrey's my best friend. Or was.' Nancy found that her throat seemed to have closed so it was hard to speak. She took a deep gulp of air. 'You've not only spoiled things between us, but also between me and Audrey. I wondered what on earth was the matter with her last week at the WRVS; when I started going on about her being a bridesmaid at our wedding and she just looked so miserable, and I couldn't work out why and—'

'Audrey and Kitty are just jealous,' Andrew said, as if he was diagnosing an awkward patient and had just solved the problem. 'That's what all this is about.'

'So now it's their fault? Nothing to do with you, I suppose. Kitty saw you. You were right under her nose.'

'That was ages ago. I might have had the odd dalliance with Audrey once, but it's over, been over for ages—'

Nancy stared. So now he was trying to make out it was something old. 'I'll tell you what's over, Andrew. We are over.' She pulled off her engagement ring and placed it on the sideboard. 'I wouldn't marry you now if you were the last man on earth. You and Audrey are welcome to each other.'

She turned and headed for the door.

'Wait, Nancy! Don't go—' He grabbed her by the shoulder but she twisted away.

She looked up into his face. A face that made her mind swim

3

with a hundred memories that would never happen again. 'No, Andrew. I trusted you and you broke my trust.' She swallowed back the lump in her throat. 'What kind of man betrays his fiancée with her best friend? And then, worse, tells a pack of lies about it?' The humiliation of it burned deep. 'I will never trust you again. It's over.'

'Aw, Nance. I never meant it to go this far. It was just a little dalliance, that's all.'

'And how far is "this far", Andrew?'

He shrugged. 'I like Audrey. She's a live spark, she's a wee bit outspoken but she's got "get-up-and-go". She doesn't spend all day mooning over furniture catalogues.'

'What? Is that what you think I do?'

'Audrey's ambitious, she's applied for the WAAF. She's actually going to do something, not sit around here like you do, winding up bandages and gossiping like an old woman.'

'I don't!' she said. 'That's unfair. It was you who persuaded me to do it! When I told you they needed girls at the munitions factory at Bandeath and I wanted to go, you told me you didn't want a wife of yours working. You said it wouldn't look good, that it would look like you couldn't support me. You said I'd be better off volunteering. You know you did! You said I'd meet a better class of person.'

He let out a sigh. 'You should've fought for it. Audrey would have.'

'Oh, the saintly Audrey, who can do no wrong. Well, you're welcome to each other. At least now I know you're nothing but a two-timing swine.' She blundered from the hall, with the dogs following, tails wagging, at her heels.

Andrew's mother must have heard the raised voices and she came to see what was going on. 'Nancy, what's . . .?'

'Ask Andrew,' she said with venom. 'Goodbye, Mrs Fraser.' She barged past as fast as she could and out of sight into the scrubby woodland and the path by the loch. She was aware with a hollow sinking sensation that Andrew hadn't tried to follow her.

She sat on a rock on the rough pebble shoreline and stared at the dark water. The rain was still pelting down and made concentric ripples eddying towards the shore. As she watched, pulling her mackintosh closer over her chest, a salmon leapt from the water, a sudden flash of silver, it landed with barely a splash.

There are plenty more fish in the sea, people always said.

Except in Glenkyle, where everyone knew everyone else.

She couldn't stay here. Not with the date of the wedding coming in only a few months – the wedding that was no longer going to happen. How could she bear it? The pitying looks of the neighbours and friends, who all knew she'd been taken for a fool. The feeling of everyone staring. Worst of all she wouldn't be able to swallow her mother's sympathy or her father's 'let it blow over, boys will be boys' attitude.

No. She needed to get right away. But where?

She thrust away the thoughts of the comfortable, spacious Stranraven House, and all the plans she'd had for redecorating the lodge, the visions of paddocks for ponies for the children she would never have. The loss of it all caught in her throat like a wire.

She choked back the tears and instead looked hard at her life. There was a grain of truth in what Andrew had said, and that's what hurt. Though, of course, he'd twisted it, to make excuses for his affair with Audrey.

There was a war on. Here in Scotland, they hadn't seen much of it though, and she winced at the thought that all she'd done was knit and fold bandages for the WRVS. It seemed paltry when people all over Europe were struggling, persecuted by the Nazi regime, and her problems seemed petty in comparison to the people in France or Poland. With guilt she remembered her mother's white face on hearing of the devastating blitz on her home town of Rotterdam, and how it had left a lasting scar.

She'd show Andrew Fraser who had 'get-up-and-go'. She'd contact her brother, Neil. He worked in London for something called the Inter-Services Research Bureau. Maybe he'd have some work she could do. She could type, after all. Anything, anything at all, to get away from here.

Chapter 2

The train was draughty and full of rowdy troops, but Nancy managed to squeeze herself into a compartment with only two WAAFs. The train limped and clanked along with much hissing of steam, signal failures, and extra stops for loading and unloading harassed-looking men from airfields and army bases. A weary conductor stamped her travel permit several times on her long journey from Scotland to London, and at one point the train stopped at a small station and one of the desperate WAAFs risked missing the train to run and fetch them all mugs of tea. They had to drink them scalding hot and return the mugs before the train departed again.

Nancy relished the bustle and activity, despite the stops and starts. It took her mind off Andrew. She was still bitter. Fancy him blaming her for his own insistence that she shouldn't work. No doubt he'd imagined her in the manor house, standing beside him flanked by his two dogs, with her like the extra dog, quiet and obedient. Now, suddenly, he wanted her to be different. Well, she'd show him.

It was evening by the time the train creaked into King's Cross, and a cold March fog had set in. Nancy scanned the people on the platform for Neil, her eyes trawling over the damp sea of

7

trilby hats, mackintoshes and umbrellas. He hadn't wanted to put her up – it had taken a stiff letter from Father to persuade him. When Father gave orders, everyone had to jump to them.

All at once she spotted Neil, his fair hair hidden under the obligatory hat, but she'd know him anywhere by his slightly worried, buttoned-up expression, and his limp as he hurried towards her. He was anxiously beckoning a porter to follow.

To her relief, his face split into a smile. 'Sis!' He embraced her with a perfunctory hug.

'It's all right,' she said, 'I don't need a porter. I've only one case and this bag.' She indicated the cloth bag slung over one arm.

Neil dragged the case from the luggage van and heaved it down. 'Good Lord!' he said. 'What have you got in here, bricks?'

'Books. And Mother insisted on woollen vests. I'll throw them away once we get to your flat. The vests, not the books.'

She hurried after him as he wove through the crowded concourse, past the news stall with the headlines chalked above it: *French revenge after British destroyer HMS* Harvester *sunk!* Neil didn't even glance at it as they passed out of the dimly lit station and into the dark. She hadn't realised what it would be like in a blacked-out city. Every window was taped with a cross against bomb damage. No lights shone anywhere. In the distance, stripes of searchlights swept the sky, presumably looking for enemy aircraft.

They huddled at a dingy brick bus shelter with a long queue of people, mostly factory workers by the look of their cloth caps, and when the bus arrived, they crowded on board. Neil bought both tickets, put the case on the luggage rack and ushered Nancy to the back of the bus. A strong smell of damp wool and tobacco pervaded the air, and Nancy rubbed the steamed-up window as they moved off.

'This area was hit pretty badly,' Neil said as the bus slowed. 'For a few days last week nothing could get through. They've cleared it quickly though.'

8

She peered out. Whole facades of buildings were missing; sudden spaces hacked into the cityscape. More heaps of rubble as the bus veered, bumping over potholes.

The bus conductress clipped their tickets and said, 'If you're going to Kilburn, you'll need to get off the stop before and walk. Yesterday's raid means we can't go via Elgin Avenue because of an unexploded bomb.'

'I read it in the paper this morning,' Neil said. 'More than thirty dead across London. Women, children, just eating dinner when the bombers struck.'

'Awful,' Nancy said. The reality of life in wartime London was beginning to bite.

Sombre now, they disembarked early and Neil insisted on lugging her suitcase the extra half-mile to his flat in Princess Road, Kilburn. Despite his limp, he could get along at quite a pace. Neil lived on the first floor of an old Victorian terrace that had been divided up. His set of stairs were dank and lightless, and after he'd unlocked the door he closed the blackout blinds, and at the click of a switch, a garish bulb with no shade lit up the room.

'Home sweet home,' he said.

She glanced around, trying not to be appalled at the dingy condition of the walls and the threadbare sofa.

'I've only got one bedroom,' he said, 'and a box room. You won't mind, will you?'

'No,' she said, heart sinking. He took her case to a small room little more than six feet end to end, with ancient flowered wallpaper. It was obviously never used. She squeezed in next to an iron bedstead and a small chest of drawers as Neil heaved her case onto the bed.

'Cosy,' she said, doing her best not to show her disappointment. She turned to him. 'Thank you for putting me up. I really couldn't have stood it in Glenkyle with Audrey Hamilton lording it over me. Did you know, she's joining the WAAFs?'

'It won't last. Audrey'll see straight through him.'

9

'And I didn't?'

'Andrew Fraser needs his head examining.' Neil patted the bed. 'Sorry it's a bit spartan. I don't go in for much in the way of décor. Never get time. You'll soon get on your feet though, and once you're working you'll be able to afford your own place with some other girls.'

She nodded. 'It's good to see you. We'll be able to catch up.' The last time she'd seen him was two years ago when he'd come home for Christmas. Since then, the worry lines around his eyes had increased, and his face looked thinner. Wartime made it hard to travel around, and anyway she guessed he didn't cook much. She tried to inject a bit of cheer. 'And while I'm here, I'd like to cook. I'm not bad at eking out our rations. And I'm really grateful you got me the interview at your office. I'll try not to mess it up.'

He grunted noncommittally as he led her back to the living room and slumped onto the sofa.

'Is there anything I need to know before I go in?'

'I don't have much to do with the interviewing process,' Neil said. 'I guess it's probably straightforward for secretarial work. Major Stanley can be rather intimidating, but I don't suppose you'll get him. And anyway, he's no worse than Father. But you could do better than work for us, it's really quite dull. Father's a fool to insist on it. You'd have more fun working at a Lyons' Corner House or being a nurse in the FANYs.'

'I don't mind. I thought it might be rather nice for us to be working in the same place. We can travel to work together, and I can make our lunches.'

He smiled, but the smile seemed forced.

'Are you all right, Neil?'

'Fine, just tired. This damned war. It gets to me, that's all.' He recited the words as if he said them often, as if they had no meaning.

* * *

10

The next morning, Nancy dressed in a neat skirt and a blouse that had been freshly pressed before she left for London. Her mackintosh and soft felt hat completed the outfit. She applied lipstick in a colour that wasn't too fierce and hoped she looked as if she was secretary material. The feeling in the pit of her stomach, the gaping hole left by Andrew Fraser, had been replaced by an unwelcome flutter of nerves. 'Brace up,' she said to herself. 'Go knock 'em dead.'

The offices were upstairs in a building called Orchard Court, an imposing stone edifice under a hideous wrought-iron archway. When she arrived three other young women were waiting. All had faces that were fully made-up and hair tamed into fearsome rolls. Just the sight of them, their obvious 'cityness', was intimidating. They exchanged wary smiles and began a conversation about where they were from. When she said Scotland, the other girls expressed surprise that she didn't have a Scottish accent.

'I was at boarding school in England,' she said.

'Ooh, posh,' the blonde one said, and the two other women exchanged meaningful looks and rolled their eyes. It sapped Nancy's confidence even more, but she was determined not to let it show, and she kept quiet as the other girls exchanged their work backgrounds. All of them had worked as secretaries before.

'What about you?' the blonde asked Nancy. 'Where did you work before?'

'Nowhere,' Nancy confessed. 'I mean, it was a small village. Just voluntary work with the WRVS.'

Again, she saw the women smirk.

Just then the door opened, and a stiff-chested man filled the doorway. He had a face that looked like it had been scrubbed with a scourer, and a pencil line of a moustache. 'Stand up.'

They all shot to their feet.

'Major Stanley.' His introduction was curt. 'I'm sorry to say you've all failed the first test,' he said, ignoring their wide-eyed expressions. 'Follow me.'

Chastened, but confused, they trooped after him down three flights of stairs into the cellar. There, in the dusty darkness, they were told to stand still while he clicked the 'play' button on a tape recorder.

'The room was bugged,' he said, 'and you have just revealed enough personal information about yourselves to be easily identified by the Germans.'

The reels turned and hissed and their conversation was replayed in all its embarrassing triviality through a speaker in the machine.

'First rule for any employee in this office,' the major said, 'is watch your mouth. Keep your lips firmly sealed at all times. The second rule is, no fraternisation. If a stranger approaches you and wants to engage you in conversation, you move away. Got it?'

His serious expression was alarming, and hearing their inane conversation had filled her with embarrassment. She had no idea her voice sounded so upper crust. Neil had never said anything about all this tape-recording palaver. She thought she was to be interviewed for a nice quiet desk job.

They trooped back upstairs in the major's wake, and he called them one by one for interview in a whitewashed featureless office. It had no pictures on the walls and a bare light bulb in the ceiling.

'You are Neil Callaghan's sister, is that right?' Major Stanley sifted through a pile of papers from a brown folder. Nancy was about to answer, but he cut her off. 'And I believe you have the same facility with languages, yes? You speak Dutch and German? A little French?'

'Yes, I do speak French,' she replied, 'but better Dutch. My mother's Dutch, so I speak that pretty well. She met my father in Rotterdam at the Scottish church, after the first war.'

'So I understand. And German?'

'My German's okay, because we used to holiday in Austria with an Austrian family. We swapped skiing seasons. In the winter they'd come to Scotland for the skiing, and in the spring, we'd

12

go to them. Neil was a keen skier, until he broke his leg so badly he couldn't do it anymore.'

'I see. And I've been looking at your school certificates, and I see you enjoyed mathematics?'

'Gosh, that's a long time ago, and I can't say I enjoyed it exactly, but I seemed to get on okay.'

'Your results say so. Has Neil told you what we do here?'

She wanted to appear informed, so she said, 'Yes, we discussed it.'

A frown. 'What did he tell you?'

Now she was uncomfortable under his stare. She recrossed her legs and tried to remember. 'Only that the Inter-Services Research Bureau takes messages between all the different wartime departments,' she said. 'He said you were looking for more women in secretarial roles. I can type – fifty-six words a minute – and I'm good at organising. I organised the women's voluntary services back home.'

He seemed to exhale. 'He didn't tell you anything else?'

'No.'

'Well, what we have in mind for you carries a great deal more responsibility than the WRVS. We need more women in the coding department, and although your brother only put you forward as a shorthand typist, we think we could usefully employ you as a decoder. Do you know what that is?'

He didn't wait for an answer but went on to explain that it was to do with messages from agents in the field, but it was a lot to take in and she was still a little surprised he hadn't asked about her shorthand. 'Are you willing to give it a try?' he asked, finally.

She was put on the spot. It sounded exciting, and she was slightly insulted that Neil thought her only fit for the most menial of tasks. Her decision was made in an instant. 'Yes, please.'

'Then you will need to sign this.' He pushed an official-looking wodge of paper across the desk towards her and handed her a pen.

Official Secrets Act 1939. At the top, a crest with the words 'HM Government'.

Was this right? She'd never expected this. She looked up to see he had a slight smile under his moustache. 'Take your time to read it. It's a long document and not something to be taken lightly. I'll leave you to it and be back in about twenty minutes. If you feel you can't sign, then I'm sure we can find you alternative employment elsewhere.' He turned to go.

'Tell me one thing,' Nancy said. 'Has my brother signed this?'

'Let's put it this way, if you sign, you'll be making it a family tradition.' He gave a small chuckle as he left.

She pulled the sheets towards her and took her time to read them through. So much official language. And all this talk of espionage, spies and secrets. And Neil was part of it all. No wonder he'd been so evasive, and that must be why he looked so tired. He was doing vital war work and couldn't tell anyone. If only she could tell her parents; they'd be so proud. Father might finally give him the respect he deserved, instead of the usual barrage of criticism. Father had what he called 'Standards', with a capital 'S' – rules that seemed only known to him, and no matter what Neil did, he never seemed to be on the right side of them. She felt sorry for him; her father didn't expect so much of her.

She read each section carefully. Once signed, she'd have to be careful. No more idle gossip in case she let something slip. And decoding, well it sounded more interesting work than just typing. She needed something really challenging to get her teeth into, something to quell the pangs of homesickness and the yawning hole in the pit of her stomach caused by that swine Andrew Fraser. She picked up the pen and unscrewed the top.

With a flourish, she signed her full name, Agnes Margaret Callaghan, and dated it March 12th 1943. Just wait until she told Neil; he'd be thrilled for her.

'Why on earth didn't you tell me you were in intelligence?' she said to Neil that evening as she peeled a bowl of wrinkled potatoes. 'I felt like a real idiot.'

'I couldn't. The SOE would've burst a blood vessel if I'd told you anything about what I do.'

'SOE? I thought you worked for the Inter-Services people?'

He sighed. 'The Inter-Services Research Bureau is just a cover name for the Special Operations Executive.' He hovered at her shoulder watching her cook. 'Did they make you sign?'

'The Official Secrets Act? Yes, I've signed. They put me on coding.' She threw the potatoes into a pan and turned on the gas for the kettle.

He groaned. 'But that's my department.'

'Is it?' She turned. 'I was never sure what you did.'

'I'm in charge of the main-line code room in N Section. The Netherlands. Under Beauclerk and Blunt. We communicate with base stations in Holland and Belgium. But Beauclerk told me last week they're bringing in a hot cryptographer to try to speed up traffic. I don't know how he thinks we'll manage if it gets any quicker; we can barely cope with the speed it's at now.' A sigh. 'Just don't expect me to help you out. You'll have to fend for yourself, I'm afraid.'

'Fine, I'll keep out of your hair. It's such a shame you can't tell Mother, you know how she is about the Dutch royal family, especially now they're here in London. She'd be thrilled to think you're in touch with Holland.'

'I'm not in touch with Holland. I just do administration.'

'You make it sound dull.'

'It *is* dull. Just paperwork and minutes.'

That night, she wondered why Neil had been less than enthusiastic. Whatever it was, she wasn't going to let him put her off. This was serious stuff, and signing the Official Secrets Act had made her proud. It was the kind of moment that sticks in your mind. She was honoured that Major Stanley had enough confidence in her to trust her with the responsibility.

Glenkyle seemed an awful long way away. She wished Andrew Fraser could have seen her sign.

Chapter 3

In the training room in Baker Street, a room furnished like school – rows of wooden desks with inkwells, and the iron smell of ink – Nancy joined twelve other girls. Thank goodness, none of them were the girls she'd met at the interview.

She shuffled into a space next to one of the others just as Major Stanley arrived. Another younger man hurried in after him, tall and dark, with intense eyes behind his dark-rimmed glasses. The younger man scanned the room with lively interest.

'This is Mr Lockwood,' the major said. 'He'll be training you. I know some of you have had training before in the FANYs, but this is new. Mr Lockwood's from our coding centre in Buckinghamshire, and he's a bit of a coding expert. He'll be supporting Mr Marks in the cryptography department.' Neil had told her last night that Mr Marks was the man in charge of decoding. 'Mr Lockwood's going to teach you the latest methods, but don't forget our tried and tested coding systems are always there to fall back on. And may I remind you all, nothing that goes on in this room ever goes outside this door.'

Mr Lockwood smiled at him pleasantly. 'Thank you, Major.'

'Okay, I'll leave you to it.' As the major went, a flutter went around the girls as Mr Lockwood shut the door behind him.

'Now,' Mr Lockwood said, perching himself on the edge of the desk at the front, 'I want you to imagine you are an agent in occupied France. The Nazis are circling the building, looking for your transmitter, and you have to send us a vital message. What's the last thing you want to do?' He didn't wait for an answer. 'Send that transmission twice, right? Sending it once is risky, but twice is suicidal.' He glanced around the room, making sure he had their attention. 'So it's vital that the message is decoded, and decoded quickly. That's where you come in.' He stood up and went round the desks to hand out papers.

A grid of numbers, like some sort of arithmetic test. It made Nancy immediately apprehensive.

'I've prepped some test codes, and I'll explain the method we currently use to decode them.' Mr Lockwood bounded over to the blackboard and rapidly chalked up the ciphers of letters and numbers.

Nancy liked the way he moved, not stiffly like her brother, but with fluid movements and a light of enthusiasm in his eyes. She glanced around the room and saw all the women hanging on his every word, including the dark-haired woman next to her. She resolved there and then that she would never be part of the Mr Lockwood appreciation society. She thought of Andrew back in Scotland, his flop of sandy hair and self-assured smile, and it gave her a fresh bolt of fury. She bet Audrey Hamilton would be planning her trousseau and talking to her mother about bridesmaids now.

Don't be so fatalistic. She dragged her thoughts back to the numbers on the blackboard and pinned her attention on the methods Lockwood was describing.

After about fifteen minutes, he handed out a coding cipher – a pad with a set of random letters, and a sheet of paper bearing a coded message, also random letters. 'I'll give you an hour,' he said, 'as it's your first time. Don't forget, if you can't break it, it means the agent might have to send it again. And that's a risk he

17

doesn't want to take. Bear in mind he's doing this in the dark and under pressure, with a Nazi breathing down his neck, and there may be errors. Use your intuition as well as the codes.'

All was quiet then, except for the sound of scribbling pencils and crossings-out, and the clock's loud tick. Nancy thought she'd understood the method, complex as it was. She had to use the random alphabet key to decode the letters by transposing the letters to another position, then numbering them on a grid. Frustratingly, she couldn't get the letters in the message to make any logical sense. Mr Lockwood paced about the room, full of impatience, hardly able to be still. Just as the time was about to be up, Nancy suddenly saw a pattern.

One of the letters had been repeated, and if she removed it then it changed the grid and everything lined up differently. A message emerged from the jumble of random letters. It said, *'This is the easiest code you will ever be sent.'* She smothered a laugh, and Mr Lockwood walked over to read her workings-out over her shoulder.

Her eyes met his and she grinned up at him. He tapped his long fingers on the desk and gave a wink in a kind of affirmation. 'Five more minutes,' he called to the rest. He fished in his pocket and brought out a scruffy piece of paper with a coded message in numbers on it, and then hastily scribbled out a poem with each letter numbered. 'Try this poem code,' he said to her, slapping it down on the desk. 'After you've transposed the letters, follow the same grid method you've just used'

She recognized the poem – the last verse of *Invictus* by William Ernest Henley.

It matters not how strait the gate,
How charged with punishments the scroll,
I am the master of my fate,
I am the captain of my soul.

As she wrestled with the new coding, Nancy threw surreptitious glances at Mr Lockwood. He was tidily dressed in a way that didn't stand out. A plain suit, white shirt and grey knitted tie. Understated, not like Andrew's flashy ties and expensive brogues, but unlike Andrew, Mr Lockwood seemed to be possessed of so much restless energy it almost made him crackle.

'Time,' Mr Lockwood called. 'Put down your papers.'

She blew out a sigh. She'd made no headway at all with the second message. The random letters bore no relation to the agent's poem. Even when she moved the letters along the grid, she couldn't make it make sense.

He explained then about how they were the first of a new team whose only task was to tackle what he called the 'indecipherables' – the messages like this one that arrived too scrambled to read.

'And this girl here' – he tapped a hand lightly on Nancy's shoulder – 'realised that the agent had written one of the numbers twice, and although some words repeat letters it's not common. Sometimes an agent will miss a letter, or misspell, or add an extra letter. Your job is to keep your eyes open for these anomalies.'

So that was it; that was the job. Nancy couldn't help being a little disappointed. For the foreseeable future she was going to be stuck in this cipher room with dozens of these baffling messages every day.

'And just in case you're in any doubt,' Lockwood said, as if to read their minds, 'it might not look exciting, but your work will save lives. Decoding these messages is life or death for the agent. You have to understand – you are literally his lifeline, his link to home. And if I have my way, we'll make sure no agent's message is ever written off as indecipherable. They are doing their part in the worst of circumstances and we must never, ever let them down.'

After class was dismissed, and Nancy was putting away her

pencils into her bag, Mr Lockwood bounced over to her again. 'Any luck with the second code I gave you?'

'Sorry,' Nancy said. 'I'd barely got started. Do they all have poems as their code?'

'They do now.' He perched his hip on a desk, one leg swinging. 'Some idea of Mr Marks and the Signals Office. They think pieces of paper too risky, that they could fall into enemy hands. So they have every agent memorise a poem instead.'

'So what happens if the agent gets captured?' she asked. 'If the Germans know they've memorised a poem, won't they try to beat it out of them?'

'Exactly. That's precisely the situation we're in, not to mention the fact they kept on giving agents the same obvious poems – one man even got the national anthem! Easy to break, or what? Of course, the advantage is that the agent can remember it easily, but the disadvantage is that it doesn't take much digging for the Germans to find the poem if it's a well-known one, and then a whole network can go down the pan. So Mr Marks soon scotched that, and now we've started using our own poems.'

Now she was interested. 'I love poetry. Who writes them?'

He looked down, embarrassed. 'Mr Marks does. And actually . . . I do. Well, sometimes. Or the men themselves, but they're not always proper poems – frankly, most of them are terrible doggerel not fit for a lady's ears. The bluer they are, the easier the men find they are to remember.' She laughed along with him. 'Unfortunately, I expect you'll come across one or two, and then you'll have to try not to be too shocked.'

'I'm not easily shockable,' she said.

'Good. You'll do well here then. What's your name?'

'Nancy. Nancy Callaghan.'

'Nice to meet you, Nancy. I'm Tom.' He shot her a sudden smile and swept the codes from her desk into the wastepaper basket. 'Make sure you don't leave anything lying around. They do snap inspections. One of the senior officers forgot once, and he had his lunch box blown up; they thought it was a booby trap.'

And with this astonishing fact, he went out, leaving her alone in the room.

'That new coding expert you were talking about,' Nancy said to Neil as she pushed two tiny pork chops under the grill, 'I think I've met him. Tom Lockwood.'

Neil looked taken aback. 'That's him. Where did you meet him?'

'He was teaching us coding this afternoon. Young chap, very intense.'

'Major Blunt's daft idea. Blunt's a bit of a worrier and he's in charge of the Dutch lines. He keeps wanting to change things, and Beauclerk and I keep telling him we don't need some new whizz-kid in our offices.'

'Who's Beauclerk?'

'He's in charge of the whole shebang. F Section, N Section, all the offshore stuff. He agrees with me; we were managing perfectly well before, and new methods just lead to more confusion. And haven't our boys got enough to cope with without the damned coding changing every five minutes?'

'It does seem pretty complicated.' She drew a spill from the spill box and lit the gas. 'You go and sit down; supper'll be twenty minutes or so.' The kitchen was small and Neil was just getting in the way, moving things around on the counter in the maddening way he had of setting everything straight.

He didn't take the hint. 'What was he like, this Lockwood?'

'Energetic. Pleasant manner, but can't sit still for two minutes. Sounds like he knows his stuff.'

'And you'd know, would you, having spent all of six hours working for the SOE?'

She flushed. 'No need to be so tetchy.'

He went then, and she saw him slump onto the sofa and open his briefcase and draw out some tightly typed papers, which he

21

was careful to keep out of her view. She turned back to the meat she'd put under the grill. Neil seemed tense, unlike the mild-natured older brother she used to idolise as a kid. She supposed this sort of responsibility made him stressed. So much secrecy. Living with him was not going to be easy.

When everything was cooked, she plated it up and put it out on the table with the cruet and the HP sauce. The sight of the food seemed to cheer him.

'I've got a meeting later,' he said through mouthfuls of mashed potato and turnip, 'so I'll have to go out. You'll be all right on your own, won't you?'

'I expect I'll have an early night. There was a lot to take in and I'm whacked. Where's your meeting?'

'At The Cavendish. A hotel close to Piccadilly. It's all hush-hush, so I can't tell you anything.' He scraped the meagre remains of the mash onto his fork.

'Gosh, I never thought we'd really do anything like this. Remember when we used to play at spying? And you had that old telescope of Father's?'

A look almost like pain shadowed across his face. 'It's nothing like that. We're not in some game of the three musketeers now. For someone supposedly so intelligent, sometimes you can be incredibly stupid.'

An awkward silence. She let it pass. It was wartime, and it made everything different. Starker somehow.

'Sorry, Nance.' He reached to pat her hand. 'It's been a long day, and the last thing I feel like doing is going out in the cold again. If the siren goes, your nearest shelter is the Underground station – out the door, turn left, first street on your left. Kilburn Park. Don't forget to lock up; spare key's on a string by the door.'

He got up and shoved the papers back in his briefcase. Moments later he was gone.

Nancy cleared and washed the plates before making herself a hot drink. Camp coffee with powdered milk. As she passed into the living room, she noticed Neil's desk diary by the telephone. She looked down at it to see all his appointments for the week in his tidy handwriting. She saw Sunday's '*collect Nance station 5.45*' entry, and various meetings, '*Beauclerk 9.30*' and '*Pay Milk Bill*'. Today's read '*8pm Cavendish O.J.*'

It was unusual to have a telephone, so Neil must be quite high up in the SOE. And especially if he was having hush-hush meetings in the evenings. She was glad of the telephone though. Perhaps she'd be able to arrange to talk to Mother by telephone one night, if Mother could get to the post office. She still felt guilty about abandoning her to the flak from all the relations about the cancelled wedding.

Unable to settle, she prowled the flat with her coffee cup in hand. There was a bookshelf full of her brother's favourite type of books, cheap science fiction with shouty covers, and a pile from the London Library on the Duke of Wellington. She peeked in his bedroom to see his cello, still in its dusty case, and a table covered in soldiers laid out in military formation. From their uniforms, they looked Napoleonic, like something from the Battle of Waterloo. He'd always loved these, right from a kid. Loved laying them all out in order of attack. God alive, war was easier then. No bombs, no tanks, no bullets from the sky.

Crammed in the shelf was a burgundy photograph album like the ones on her mother's shelf at home. Curious, she set down her coffee cup and pulled it out. She settled down on the sofa with it on her lap.

As she'd thought, it was one of Mother's family albums – photos of one of their skiing trips to Austria, before Neil's accident. They'd all lived for skiing then, and exchanged visits with an Austrian family, the Hefners. She turned the pages, instantly transported back. There were Mother and Father leaning on the balcony next to Frau and Herr Hefner, with the stark Austrian peaks behind. Another shot showed her and Neil grinning at the side of the ski slope in their knitted hats and jerseys. Shame the photos could never be in colour. She remembered that jersey, knitted in Fair Isle by her mother in a lovely petrol blue. The next page showed one of Otto and Neil, skiing downhill. Otto, the Hefners' son was a year older than Neil, and the two were inseparable.

She slid the photograph out of its mount and peered at the picture. Otto was out in front as usual, snow whooshing up from his skis. At least she thought it was Otto, or it could have been Neil. In those days they looked so alike, both tall, fair and with the same straight-nosed good looks. But probably Otto; he could never bear to lose. Even at draughts, he'd play like it was life and death.

Happy days. Of course, her parents hadn't heard from the Hefners now for years.. It felt strange to hear nothing after the families had been so close, but of course Hitler had changed everything. The Nazis had trampled over half of Europe, and her mother was still mourning the loss of her country to an enemy force. It would have felt traitorous now to be fraternising with the enemy. Hadn't Churchill said that *Any man or state who marches with Hitler is our foe?*

She replaced the photograph and closed the book, overcome by a sour wave of nostalgia for earlier times.

A piercing wail broke into her thoughts. Air-raid siren. Panicked, she grabbed her coat and hat and the spare key, and flung herself downstairs, bumping into the woman from the upstairs flat. After hurried apologies, together they ran for the Underground.

The all-clear sounded at 3 a.m., and when Nancy and the neighbour emerged it was to a smell of cordite and masonry dust lingering in the damp air. In the morning, the bell on her alarm clock had her shooting out of bed in a panic, until bleary-eyed, she realised it wasn't another air raid.

Neil was already up and dressed, and a pot of watery tea stood under the tea cosy. 'What were you doing with my photo album?' he asked, before Nancy even had time to sit down.

'Nothing,' she said. 'I was just glancing through it when the siren went.'

'I don't like you snooping through my things.'

'Honestly, Neil, I wasn't snooping. I just saw it was one of Mother's albums and fancied looking at some holiday snaps.'

'I borrowed it the last time I was home,' he said. 'I wanted some pictures of the family – and that was the last time I could ski properly. My damn leg put paid to all that.'

'Does it still ache?'

'No. Only in very cold weather. I've got used to it now and it hardly bothers me.' He paused. 'Funny, I can still remember the feeling, the cold air and the skis silently gliding downhill through the drifts, and everything so white . . .' He sighed.

She poured a cup of tea. 'And do you still keep in touch with Otto? When we stopped going to Austria, I know Mother used to write to Frau Hefner. And did you see much of him at Oxford?'

'No.' A pause. 'He was the year above me. And since the war started, I've lost touch with him. Hardly surprising, really. I expect he went home to Austria.'

'It's a shame. When you followed him to Oxford, I always thought you'd end up in the same law practice.'

'I didn't "follow him" to Oxford. That was Father's idea, not mine.'

'Still, you were such good friends when you were younger.'

'Yes.' He looked down at his tea cup and stirred the tea round and round.

'You'll wear out the bottom of that cup.'

'Hurry up, we need to get a move on.' Neil lurched out of the chair. 'Beauclerk has asked to see me first thing.'

The spring sun had come out, and Nancy was thrilled to be an official employee at Baker Street. Once inside, she was issued with an official pass which she must carry at all times, then told to go to room 4a. The stairs were a crush of men and women rushing about carrying files or briefcases, and it was like some sort of crazy obstacle course to squeeze past them all.

Once Nancy had found her way, one of the women, a short plump girl, with hair tied improbably in two plaits, grinned and introduced herself as Daisy, and pointed to the desk next to hers. They'd no time after that to even share a few words as there were already messages on the desks, and Nancy got stuck in straight away, trying to fathom out their meanings. Every now and then a boyish chap in rolled-up shirt sleeves hurried through with another message, and a copy was distributed to all of them to try to unravel it.

Tom Lockwood's words had stuck in her mind, that each of these transcripts was from an agent in the field who could be in acute danger. It was sobering, and she scrutinised every letter. She hadn't bargained on the tension in the air, and by lunchtime her shoulders were stiff as a stone.

Late in the afternoon, Tom Lockwood himself appeared, brandishing another sheaf of teleprinted messages. The SOE occupied several buildings in Baker Street, and apparently the telex department occupied a mews building round the back of St Michael House, further along Baker Street, which was why the person bringing the coded messages always seemed out of breath.

'This one's important,' Mr Lockwood said. 'It's from a Dutch agent, and I'm afraid it's probably suffering from mutilated Morse code. Added to which, this particular agent had to wait a long time before being sent out. He's probably forgotten every bally thing he learnt in coding school.' He gave her and Daisy a copy. 'I've tried for six hours and got precisely nowhere. I need more brains on it. See what you girls can do with it, would you?'

Nancy took the paper and set to work. By now, she was tired, and the numbers and letters shimmied before her eyes. All these alien letters that should make up a scheduled message, or 'sked', meant something but somehow didn't. Every sheet began to look the same; inner resistance had set in. She leant back on the chair and closed her eyes. She'd only been here one day and already she was jaded. How was she going to stand it? She should be at home, looking out over greening pastures, with the distant mountains rising through unrolling mist.

She'd wanted war work, hadn't she? Well, this was it. So what if it was hard? It had to be a darn sight easier than being on a battlefield. She gritted her teeth and applied herself to the problem. By the end of the day, she was no nearer to solving the code and her desk was full of wastepaper and failed attempts, just like the others.

'Any luck, Miss Callaghan?' Tom Lockwood appeared by her desk. His expression was hopeful.

'No. I'm missing something, but I don't know what. It's just gibberish at the moment.'

'Glad it's not just me. This message could be vital. He's important to us because he's to set up a whole network of agents in Holland. Churchill's calling it his Secret Army, and according to Churchill they're supposed to *set Europe ablaze*.' He gave a dry laugh. 'We've been forced to ask the agent to send his sked again, but no reply has come, and we're worried he's been caught.'

The thought that what was in her hands could be the agent's last message struck a chill. 'Let's hope we hear from him soon.'

'Don't repeat any of what I just said,' he said. 'We should only tell you anything on a strictly "need-to-know" basis.'

She looked up at Tom Lockwood and he pressed his lips together in a worried smile. He really cared; you could see it in his face. It wasn't just a job – these agents relied on him.

'My lips are sealed,' she said.

She watched him collecting the wastepapers ready for incineration. He was rather nice; there was something appealing about his earnestness. She spoke sharply to herself: *Oh no you don't.* She wasn't going to get involved with any man. Not after Andrew. She'd learned her lesson. She picked up her handbag and umbrella and headed for the door.

On the way out, Jimmy the doorman searched her handbag before letting her go. 'Standard procedure,' he said. 'And you'll need your brolly.'

Sunshine and showers, typical March weather. Nancy put her head down against the rain. She hadn't seen Neil all day, but then again, she'd been too busy to miss him. At the back of the bus her mind still whirred over the codes. She uncapped her fountain pen, took the blue bus ticket out of her handbag and printed the letters of the last code in tiny writing. She hoped she'd remembered it properly and would be able to double transpose it. The ink bled and blurred because the paper quality was poor, but she carried on working on it as the bus juddered and creaked down the rain-soaked streets.

She looked up to glance out of the steamy window. She was passing a cinema that had suffered bomb damage. It was dark, and some of its letters were dangling off. That was it.

Misplaced letters again. Worth a try. She removed a couple of duplicate letters and began to run through possible anagrams. Thank goodness for her passion for crosswords. At last, she had it. A full deciphered message stared back at her from the back of the bus ticket. She wanted to whoop.

'You getting off or what?' The bus conductress, a wide-mouthed cockney, was beckoning to her.

She shoved the ticket in her pocket and leapt to her feet. She'd missed her stop. It was the end of the line. But the thought of telling Mr Lockwood she'd solved it gave her a thrill of anticipation.

Chapter 4

The next morning Nancy asked Jimmy the doorman where Tom Lockwood's office was.

'Up the stairs, second on the right,' he whispered. 'But don't tell anyone I told you. We're not supposed to know. Security, you know.' She smiled. Security. It was all anybody talked about.

She hurried up the stairs and knocked on the door. No answer. Gingerly, she pushed at it, and it opened. The room was small, like a broom cupboard, and tidy. Next to the desk a window with opaque glass gave a milky light, and an upright metal heater was plugged into a socket. She reached out a hand – still cold. Next to the blotter, pens and pencils bristled from a glass tumbler in front of a leather volume of the *Oxford English Dictionary*, and Wordsworth's thick blue hardback edition of *The Book of a Thousand Poems*.

She'd written out the decoded message again neatly and she was putting it on the desk when a sharp voice behind her said, 'Hello?'

She turned in panic.

Tom Lockwood was staring down at her with an expression of hostile incredulity. 'What are you doing in my office?'

'Sorry. I just wanted to leave you this,' she said, feeling her face grow hot. She stabbed a finger at the paper before him. 'I solved it last night on the bus home.'

He paled. 'You took some of our coding home? Don't you know anything? What a damn foolish thing to do! Nothing of our work should ever leave this building, I thought I'd made that perfectly—'

'But I—'

'Don't you understand? Lives are at risk and—'

'I didn't take anything out of the building,' she said. 'I swear! I remembered it and I just wanted to solve it. I thought I was helping.'

He pushed past her to look at the papers on the desk. He bent over the words she'd written down and the missing letters she'd underlined. He ran a hand through his hair, his face a study in concentration. 'Of course. It's blindingly obvious once you see it.' He raised his eyes. 'Miss Callaghan, if you didn't take the papers home, how did you work on the coding?'

'I wrote the letters out on a bus ticket. And I was glad to read the agent was alive.' She took the crumpled ink-stained ticket out and held it out like an offering.

'But I don't get it.' He was frowning. 'How could you possibly solve it without the coding key?'

'I remembered what was on it. But I remembered it wrong. I'd added an extra 'L' and it put everything in the wrong column. That's how I managed to solve it. The agent must have made a mistake remembering as well, because he added an extra letter too.'

'What an idiot. I should have seen that straightaway. Sometimes you just get addled, or complacent, or both.'

'I was just lucky.'

'You must have an elephant's memory to remember all that.'

'I'd just spent more than two hours staring at it, remember?'

He smiled, and it was a huge relief.

'I promise I didn't take anything home,' she said shyly. 'Only what was in my head.'

'You can't be too careful. Secrecy is drummed into us here but it's a slippery thing that's difficult to maintain. Not so much

30

outside our work here, but within it too, because we all think we can trust one another, and a casual slip-up is so easy. And you're new; I should have made allowances. Sorry I was so hard on you. Can I buy you a coffee in the canteen?' he said. 'I feel like I owe you an apology for ranting at you like that.'

She was torn. He was nice, but she'd sworn to keep away from men. They were only trouble. 'Sorry, I can't. I always meet my brother for breakfast.' A white lie. She rambled on. 'Neil Callaghan. He's across the road in the other building.'

'Maybe another time then,' Mr Lockwood said. His eyes held hers.

Somewhat flustered she muttered, 'Better get on,' bid him a polite goodbye, and hurried away. On the way past the ladies' lavatory, she nipped in and splashed cold water over her flaming face.

He was right of course. She'd been carried away with the idea of impressing him, and what had seemed harmless could have easily turned into something else. What if she'd dropped that bus ticket? Anyone could have picked it up. It would be the last time, she vowed. From now on, she'd be the model of discretion.

Tom Lockwood turned over the extraordinary bus ticket in front of him and marvelled at the tiny letters and figures. Nancy Callaghan was obviously a woman with brains and initiative, even if she was a bit hot-headed coming to his office like that. He'd liked the look of her straightaway, her shiny auburn hair and neat figure, and she'd stood out in that first coding class as someone who could be useful. She was pretty, but with none of that primping and preening the other girls did.

And how she'd remembered all that code, he'd no idea. She must have a lightning good memory. He groaned aloud. How idiotic to suggest the canteen like that. The poor woman; she'd run off like a startled deer. It was one of the things you weren't supposed to do; it was frowned on by the higher-ups to have an affair with a work colleague. It could compromise secrecy, and the SOE prided itself on being so tightly nailed up against leaks that nobody dared even tell someone else what they'd had for breakfast.

And wasn't Nancy Callaghan the sister of Callaghan from N Section? One of the die-hards who'd made it perfectly clear that they weren't going to change anything? Even if men were dying because of SOE inefficiency, the pen-pushers would have to be obeyed. What an utter shambles.

He got on the telephone to head office and sent in the message that Nancy had decoded. Now he could report that agent Chess had arrived safely in the Netherlands, and his message had all the requisite checks. Later this morning, he and Leo Marks, his coding boss, had to carry on training two more SOE agents in coding. Duffers both of them, and it had taken some doing last time to make them understand it couldn't be rushed. They were destined for France, and the French were always a little more impatient than those going to the Netherlands.

He glanced at his watch. Time was shooting by, and he still had to prepare for his appointment with Beauclerk next week. Only fifteen minutes left before Mr Marks would expect him, to give him more instructions, so he'd better get a move on. He grabbed a notepad and began to write down the points he needed to make.

Beauclerk's office in Baker Street was furnished comfortably with a leather-topped desk that looked as if it had come from a country estate, and the room reeked of expensive pipe tobacco. Tom, who had spent a week preparing his pitch, was shown into this sacred enclave by Beryl, Beauclerk's wooden-faced secretary.

He launched into his request. 'I've an idea that could save a few lives,' Tom said. 'And Mr Marks is keen to implement it.'

'Go on.' Beauclerk, a lugubrious bespectacled man in a shabby suit, seemed more interested in his pipe than in hearing anything Tom had to say. He was engrossed in tamping the tobacco down with a small silver pick.

'At the moment,' Tom said, 'if a poem code's broken by the Germans, then anyone else using that poem code is vulnerable, and what's worse, the Boche will then have our entire method, one that can be applied to any other poem.'

'That's always been the case,' Beauclerk said. 'Not much we can do about that.'

'But think of the advantages of a unique code that could be destroyed message by message. Then each cipher code, or key, would be unique and there'd be no chance of the Germans working out the code.'

A sigh. 'Marks tried it.'

'No, bear with me. Each agent would have a pad, for one-time use only, and he would tear off the bottom part each time and destroy it.'

'Far too cumbersome. We've tried one-time-use pads before and they're too hard to disguise and far too easy for the Gestapo to find if the agent's captured. Even if they're printed really small, then that causes more problems, because how can an agent see something so minute? Especially in the dark, when he's panicked and under pressure. No, I think Mr Marks's poem idea fits the bill, so why not stick with that?'

A rapid knock and the door swung open. Neil Callaghan came in bearing a brown file.

'Ah, Callaghan, just the man. Lockwood thinks we should try one-time-use pads again.'

'We already did it,' Callaghan said, sliding the file onto Beauclerk's desk. 'It was hopeless. Agents lost their pads, or they got wet and couldn't be used. Or worse, the Germans got hold of them and used them pretending to be our chaps.' He eased himself down onto the other chair. 'And it was massively time-consuming to produce them if we wanted each one to be different. We ended up doing them in batches.'

A silence.

'You mean the one-time-use pads were used for more than one

agent?' Tom was horrified. It would mean if one was caught the others were dead meat too. Callaghan and Beauclerk exchanged glances.

'It was standard practice,' Beauclerk said huffily.

'A practice that should be outlawed,' Tom said. 'While we're sitting here in these stuffy offices, our men are out there – out there in enemy territory with Nazis breathing down their necks. They're risking their lives and trusting in our coding system. We lost a wireless operator last week, and why? Because he had to send his message twice and the second time he got picked up. It makes me ashamed. We've got to do better. I just want permission to try some new coding pads, that's all. I ran it past Mr Marks and he's all in favour.'

'But what about the costs?' Callaghan said. 'Paper's scarce, and ink. Everything's in short supply.'

'Our agents will be in short supply unless we can keep them safe,' Tom said sharply. 'And if this department can't see the importance of what I'm saying, then I really do despair.'

'All right. Keep your hair on. We'll see what we can do. Make up a prototype and then I'll see what Requisitions say.'

Tom's heart sank. He knew this was fobbing him off, but what could he do? He decided to be polite. 'Thank you, sir. You won't regret it.' Tom leant over the desk to shake hands, gave a nod to Callaghan and went out of the door.

Outside he took a deep, frustrated breath. If nothing was done, he'd keep on at them over and over until it was.

'He's bloody insistent,' Beauclerk said to Neil once the door had shut.

'Just because he's come from the hallowed Bletchley Park, he thinks he can throw his weight around,' Neil said. 'We're always going to lose agents, everyone knows that. They're all told the survival rate before we parachute them in. And wireless ops never last more than six weeks, six months if they're very lucky. It's part of the job.'

'Take a look at the figures though,' Beauclerk said. 'I thought we'd be losing less since Marks introduced the poem code, but we still seem to be haemorrhaging agents.'

'The Nazis have got more vigilant,' Neil said. 'That's all. Before, they were too busy posturing and declaring total war on the Allies.'

'Could be you're right. But get me those figures anyway, would you, Neil? I'd like to check them out, and at the very least if Lockwood comes back, I'd like to have some convincing data to throw back at him.'

Once outside the office, Neil went to wait for the lift. His leg ached and he didn't want to take the stairs. There was no way he'd take the figures to Beauclerk. If he did, Beauclerk would see how many planes they'd lost on the return leg from Holland and start digging a bit too deeply. No, he'd forget for as long as possible. Then, maybe the figures could get lost somehow. The lift arrived, and he pulled back the concertina grill with a squeak and a rattle, and stepped in.

Two other men were already in there, going down. Fawn macs, trilbies, black umbrellas, nondescript. Deliberately forgettable. He didn't know their names and they merely nodded to him. He wondered what was going on inside their heads. Each man here was like a microfilm, walking about stuffed with things they could tell no one. He had a crazy urge to slit them open, see everything spill out like stuffing.

He shuddered. That's probably what the Gestapo did if they caught you.

Chapter 5

Nancy ran down the stairs anxious to get some fresh air after another morning cooped up in the cipher room. She'd been working nearly a month now, and despite the blustery Spring weather she decided she'd brave the cold and eat her beetroot sandwich in the park.

She was just turning at the bottom of the stairs when she bumped into another woman hurrying up.

'Excuse me, I don't suppose you know where I can find Tom Lockwood, do you? I've got an appointment with him.' The woman was sharp-featured, petite and dark-haired, dressed in a tweed skirt and jumper under her beige swing coat.

Nancy paused. 'Didn't our security man at the door tell you where his office is?'

'I didn't think to ask.'

'You'd better follow me then, it's like a warren in here.' She hoped Mr Lockwood wouldn't bite her head off again.

'Oh, thanks, that's really good of you.'

Nancy registered that the woman had a slight accent like her mother's. She bet she was Dutch. 'This way.' She led her upstairs to the office and knocked, but there was no answer. 'Guess he might have gone for lunch. We could try the canteen.'

They were just on their way down the stairs again when they met Mr Lockwood coming up. 'This lady's looking for you,' Nancy said. She turned to her. 'Sorry, I don't know your name.'

'Best not to,' she said. 'They call me Fenna. I'm reporting for training.'

Unusual name, thought Nancy. *But probably not her real name.*

'Thanks, Miss Callaghan,' Tom said. He turned back to Fenna with a smile. 'Sorry I'm late, I got held up in a meeting. It's this way.'

And he sped away back up the stairs with Fenna clattering after him on her high heels. Nancy watched them go with a pang in her heart. *Don't be ridiculous*, she thought. *He doesn't mean anything to you. You're just on the rebound, that's all.*

Still, she couldn't help wondering what Fenna was there for, and whether it was something else secret. Another girl for code breaking perhaps?

She didn't have to wait long to find out, for that afternoon in the coding room, Mr Lockwood suddenly appeared. 'Another batch from N Section,' he said, slapping a sheaf of papers on the table. 'Try to get these done quick as you can. We've lost too many agents already in the Netherlands, so much so that now we're sending out women. Women just like you. In fact, I've just been teaching one of them coding.'

A rustle of interest went around the room. In truth, none of them had thought the agents might be women. They'd just assumed they'd all be men.

'Do they do the same things as the men?' Daisy blurted the question they all wanted to ask.

'Yes. In fact, women are better at surviving. They blend in more naturally, carrying shopping or laundry back and forth. In occupied countries, men stand out because they should be fighting for their country, or working for the Germans. A young man is an object of suspicion unless we can supply him with a really good cover story.'

37

Mr Lockwood took around the batch of coding, and the chatter stopped. Now they knew these could be messages from women as well as men, they were sombre. Nancy couldn't get the face of the woman called Fenna from her mind. The woman was so slight, as if a puff of wind might blow her over, yet she was tough enough to be dropped into enemy country, her only means of communication – the radio. She couldn't help a tingle of admiration.

At the end of the afternoon, she'd made scant progress with the indecipherable, but Daisy had managed to make some sort of sense of the message, and Nancy gave her the thumbs-up. Nancy deliberately took her time getting her things together, until she and Tom were the only ones left in the room.

'That woman I met, Fenna,' she asked him, 'will they parachute her into Holland?'

'Holland?'

'She had an accent like my mother's. She's Dutch.'

'So we have a Sherlock Holmes among us.' He grinned at her. 'I'm saying nothing. But now we're sending women overseas, I can't help wishing we had a better system of coding.' He sighed in frustration. 'Beauclerk's a bit of a dinosaur – seems to think that it's the calibre of the agent that matters, that the braver you are, the more likely you are to survive. He thinks it's all about derring-do. But actually, evidence shows the reverse is true. Excellent coding skills plus a cool head and a degree of caution, they're what matter much more in the field, not gung-ho tactics.'

'They'll have trained her though, won't they?' She slipped on her coat and began to button it.

A nod. 'Doesn't stop me feeling guilty though every time I send someone out with a poem they have to remember. It seems so much to ask when their heads are already spinning with the actual coding.'

'So what's the answer?' she asked.

He rumpled his hands through his hair until it stuck up like a brush. 'Lord only knows. We tried disposable pads, but they're just too bulky, and Beauclerk says they don't work – too easy for the Germans to find. But it gets to me every time we hear another poor sod has been captured and shot.' He lowered his voice. 'I can't help feeling we should be doing more somehow; it's all so amateur.' He shook his head. 'Sorry to go on. It's a bugbear of mine.' He picked up his briefcase and clicked it shut.

'No, it's interesting,' Nancy said. 'I want to know everything about everything, but I keep hitting a brick wall whenever I ask.'

'And I had the nerve to call you out for loose talk when I'm just as bad.' He glanced at his watch. 'I say, have you got time now for that coffee?'

'If it's quick,' she said on impulse. 'I've half an hour to spare before my bus.' Why had she said that? It was something about his openness that had got under her skin. Now, somewhat embarrassed, she listened to him impressing on her again to forget everything he'd just said, as they went over to the canteen, her hop-stepping to keep up with his long, determined stride. He ordered them coffee and two rock buns and insisted on paying.

'You must call me Tom,' he said as they sat down. They were the only two people left at this end of the canteen; nearly everyone else seemed to have gone home.

They grimaced at each other across the table when they discovered the coffee was grey as dishwater.

'They should issue these as grenades,' Tom said, holding up one of the rock buns, which was rigid under its thin scrape of margarine.

Nancy laughed and only then noticed Daisy and some of the other girls coming in and taking another table. She was aware of them nudging each other and shooting glances their way. She ignored them but was disconcerted to feel herself blush.

Tom leant in and lowered his voice. 'As we're in the same department, I don't think I'm breaking any secrecy rules if I tell you this,' Tom said. 'The difficulty is, what agents need for the coding is something small and light to carry,' Tom explained, 'but it has to be something indestructible.'

39

'Like these rock buns?' she quipped.

'If only. No, something that can't be easily destroyed by wet weather. But then it has to be able to be destroyed by the agent once the code is sent.'

'I see your problem. Indestructible but easily destroyed.'

He stirred his coffee round and round. 'I know. Crazy.' He was silent a moment. 'Have you ever wondered what would happen if Nazis infiltrated our agents' networks and started sending us messages pretending to be them?' He was looking at her with a peculiar intensity.

'It would be a disaster.'

'But not easy to spot. Say you got messages that look okay, but something about them stinks?'

'You'd have to tell someone.'

He shook his head. 'What if they don't listen?' His face was suddenly older, more serious.

'This isn't hypothetical, is it?' she said.

A shake of the head. 'I took it up with Beauclerk last week, the fact that some of the messages seem just . . . too tidy. There are no indecipherables from N Section. Poor man, he must be sick of the sight of me. But he won't have it there's anything wrong. He just wants to bury his head in the sand.' He clammed up as one of the canteen women came to take their empty plates.

'I know you've signed up with the Firm, so I know I can trust you not to repeat it.' He fiddled with his teaspoon. 'Enough of all this. Tell me a bit about yourself, where you're from. I can detect a trace of an accent.'

'It's not supposed to show. My father sent me to school in England to get rid of it.'

'Why? I think it's nice. Scottish, right?'

'Yes. A small village called Glenkyle. My brother got me a foot in the door here. But we're not supposed to talk about ourselves either, are we? Major Stanley was really hot on that when I arrived.'

'Put the wind up you, did he? He does that to all the new recruits. It was just to scare you into seeing how serious it all is. A few months ago, one of the new girls was claustrophobic, couldn't bear the cellar and screamed the place down.'

'Good grief. At least I didn't do that!'

'Where's Glenkyle?'

She told him about the village and her parents, and before long they were talking away. Or rather she was . . . he was a good listener. She was so engrossed that she didn't notice Neil approach until she heard his voice. 'Hello, Sis. Daisy told me you were in here.' He didn't look pleased.

She glanced at Daisy's table to see it was empty and the others had all gone.

'Ready?' Neil said tersely, obviously expecting her to go with him.

'Yes, I'm coming,' she said, embarrassed, gathering up her things. She threw on her scarf, jammed her beret on her head and gave a smile to Tom, who lifted a hand in farewell.

Neil ignored Tom and shepherded Nancy out with a hand at her back.

On the bus he turned to her. 'You're not getting involved with that Tom Lockwood, are you?'

'No. Of course not. It was just a coffee while I killed time waiting for the bus.'

'I thought you were still cut up about Andrew Fraser?'

'I am. I was just killing time,' she repeated. She looked resolutely out of the window.

'Lockwood's a pain,' Neil said. 'He's only been here a few weeks and he keeps wanting to stir things up.'

She lowered her voice, though the seats around them were empty. 'I think he just wants to make sure our people have the best chance they can.'

'Damn it, don't we all! But we can't keep changing things every few minutes. There's enough to do without his mad ideas.'

41

She dare say nothing else while they were in a public place. But when they got into the flat, she said, 'Look, Neil, I had a good chat with Tom Lockwood, and his only concern is agents' safety. He told me. He says he's worried in case one of the networks gets infiltrated by the Germans.'

Neil's face froze.

'I know,' she said. 'It's too terrible to even think of it. That they—'

'What makes him think that?'

She explained about the messages being too tidy.

'Rank nonsense. He's seeing phantoms where none exist. We're getting better at training people, that's all. And don't go repeating this stuff, hear me?'

'I thought it would be okay with you. Can't I even have a conversation with my own brother?'

'No. Not about this. You signed the act. The part that says "not even with your family members"? You signed it, Nancy. You've been here only a few weeks and it's rank stupidity to go discussing these things when you've not been here long enough to know what's really going on. If they catch you talking out of turn it'll be a prison sentence before you've even begun. For God's sake just keep your head down and do the job you're supposed to do.'

'Okay, okay. But Tom seemed pretty heartfelt about it. And it can't hurt to check it, can it?'

'And how would we do that? Send a message to the agents asking if any of them is a Nazi?'

'Now you're being deliberately obstructive.'

Neil sighed heavily. 'I guarantee, it'll be a figment of Lockwood's overactive imagination. He's only been here five minutes and the man wears us all out. Why Marks took him on, I've no idea.'

She didn't raise the subject again, but she was surprised at how passionately she'd wanted to defend Tom. And she hated it when Neil got all overprotective about the men she dated. Not that Tom Lockwood was a date of course.

Once they'd got over the prickly subject of Tom Lockwood, Neil unwound a little and they had a pleasant evening sparring over the crossword in the *Standard*. Because of the blackout there was not much nightlife in London, and Nancy was content to turn in and get an early night.

She opened her suitcase, which she still hadn't had the time or inclination to unpack, and drew out the woollen vests that Mother had insisted she brought, and smiling, she piled them neatly on one side. Ugly things. But she baulked at getting rid of them. So many years of wartime had made her thrifty. Maybe she could convert them into something else.

She brought out two more blouses, but beneath those lay a set of delicate silk camiknickers and a silk camisole, originally made for her wedding night. Their pearly lustre made her stop and stare. Why had she brought them with her? It was a foolish idea. She stroked them, marvelling at their cool slipperiness.

They were the single bit of luxury that made her still feel she might be a desirable woman. She swallowed hard. She'd never have the chance to wear them now. What a waste. Mother had saved so many coupons, made endless enquiries by letter to find these offcuts of silk, and then she'd sewn them late into the night, embellishing the edges with lace – lace unpicked from her own wedding dress of thirty years before. Nancy slid the delicate fabric over her hands, reining in the feelings of loss and hurt that the sight of them brought.

She folded the undergarments together into a tiny square and thrust them back under her other clothes.

A moment later she pulled them out again. Silk. That was it.

That was something that could be easily compressed and hidden, something tough but light. What if agents' codes could be printed on silk? Was it possible? Maybe Tom Lockwood would have thought of it already. But she stifled a laugh – she couldn't show him this, her underwear. Perish the thought.

Chapter 6

Tom arrived at his desk early. He'd two more agents to brief on coding today, and he was still trying to work out how many of the incoming Dutch messages were too neat. He arranged all the recent Dutch messages in a row on his desk and stood contemplating them. All perfect. It really raised his hackles.

A rap at the door.

'Come in!' he shouted, expecting to see Mr Marks or another courier from the Morse room with a batch of messages to decode. Instead, it was Nancy Callaghan again, cheeks pink and eyes sparkling from the cold, still in her trench mac and felt hat.

His mood changed instantly and he couldn't help smiling. 'Don't tell me, you've got another bus ticket for me,' he said.

'Ha ha.' She took a deep breath and launched in. 'No, actually, I've been thinking about what you said yesterday, in the canteen. And I know you've probably already rejected the idea, but I wondered if the codes could be printed on silk.'

'Silk?'

'Just an idea,' she said, her face getting pinker. 'I've got to go now, or I'll be late.'

'Wait!' he called, but she was in too much of a fluster to hear him; she'd shot away and back down the stairs before he could say any more.

Silk. They were already printing agents' maps on silk. So why had he not thought of it before? Tom began to sketch out random figures and numbers on his blotter, before grabbing a sheaf of foolscap and writing more urgently. What if he used strips of silk? With the coding numbers randomly printed on each one?

No. Too fiddly.

Or even better, a handkerchief where a strip could be cut off after each transmission? Nancy Callaghan could be on to something. He grabbed a sheet of numbers, bounded out of his office and up the stairs two at a time to the printing department. An older balding man in navy-blue overalls looked askance at him as he burst in through the door.

'Can I have a look at one of your maps, one that's printed on silk?' Tom said, shouting over the noise of the clunking machinery.

'Maybe. Who wants to know?'

'Oh, sorry. Yes, I'm Tom Lockwood. I work in coding, under Leo Marks and Major Beauclerk.'

'Papers? I need authorisation.'

Tom hurriedly fished in his jacket pocket and brought out his pass.

'Henry Napier at your service,' the man in overalls said, examining the pass with black-stained fingers. The noisy machine stopped its racket. 'Which map do you want? You'll need the proper signature, the information's classified.'

'I'm not interested in the maps. I just want to see how you print on silk.'

'Why?' Napier was curious now.

'In case we can print codes on them too.'

Napier seemed to defrost and walked to a plan chest with many slim drawers. 'I shouldn't be doing this,' he said, but nevertheless, he drew out a piece of silk and brought it over.

Tom knew as soon as he got hold of the delicate fabric that this was the answer. So light, it could easily be sewn into a collar or cuff. 'Does it burn?' he asked.

'I'll say. But slowly. It sort of shrinks from the flame.'

'Have you a spare piece you can show me?'

'Now you're asking,' Henry said, pursing his lips. 'I suppose we might have an offcut somewhere.' He rummaged in another drawer and brought out a thin sliver of silk.

Tom took out his Zippo lighter and ignited it, holding the flame to the silk, which flared briefly then shrivelled to a black, hollow bead. He rubbed the bead between his fingers and it disintegrated instantly to a greyish dust. He sniffed. Only a faint smell like singed hair. Untraceable.

'Perfect,' he said. He unfolded the printed paper he'd stuffed in his pocket. 'Can you print this onto it?' he asked Henry, handing it over.

Henry glanced at it. 'Easy,' he said. 'Compared to maps it'll be no problem. I'll get our graphics man on to it.'

'Splendid stuff. I'll need to talk to Beauclerk, but I expect he'll want to requisition a batch straight away. Meanwhile, can you print me just one, as a sample?'

Henry gave an audible groan. 'It'll mean setting up a whole new machine.'

'It'll save lives. Go on, it would be a huge favour if you would.'

Henry sighed, rolled his eyes and said, 'Come back in three days and I'll see what I can do.'

'Two days. An agent's life may depend on it.'

Henry shook his head, but a twitch of amusement showed he'd been persuaded.

Two days later, Nancy was just about to walk out of the building to go home when a voice called out, 'Nancy!'

She turned to see Tom Lockwood hurrying towards her.

He drew her to one side. 'That idea you had. I've got

something to show you. Can you spare a few minutes before you go home?'

She paused. The bus was due in five minutes. But Neil was out this evening, meeting his contact from the government, Oliver Johnson. So she saw no reason why she should hurry home. She could always get a later bus. 'All right,' she said.

'Better be in my office,' Tom said. 'I don't want to let it out of my sight right now.'

Once closeted in his tiny office, he opened a locked drawer and brought out a silk handkerchief printed with numbers. After he'd explained how it worked – that each row of figures was a 'one-time-use' cipher, and that it would then be cut off and destroyed – he placed it on the desk in front of her.

'It's what we call a WOK,' he said. 'It's short for Worked-out Keys, which are pre-arranged transposition keys. They make all the business of learning poems unnecessary.' He looked up to check she was following. 'And it's so obvious. They use silk for maps already, but somehow we had our heads fixed on paper and pencil. That's coders for you – blinkered. What on earth made you think of it?'

She flushed. 'I had some underwear made of silk and noticed how small it packed.' She tried to hold his gaze without flinching.

He seemed to see nothing amiss, didn't make any sort of ribald comment. 'It's a genius idea,' he said. 'Can I buy you dinner? It feels like we should celebrate.'

'Okay.' She tried to keep her reply low-key, but she was thrilled to be asked.

'I'm afraid it's only the Lyons' Corner House,' Tom said, 'but they do shepherd's pie on a Tuesday and I'm rather partial to it.'

Their meal lasted far longer than either of them intended, and neither of them could stop talking. She told him how she'd loved the mountain slopes in winter and how, as children, she and Neil had loved to ski.

'I was never one of those outdoor types,' Tom said. 'As a child I used to sit for hours just reading the encyclopedia,' he confessed. 'I started at 'A' and went through the lot.'

'You too? Seriously? I thought I was the only one!'

'You're kidding me.' His eyes were very bright.

'Ours was green. *The Encyclopaedia Britannica.*'

'With twenty-four volumes!' he said, delighted. 'Was yours like something from the Dark Ages with hardly any pictures?'

'That's the one,' she said. 'It's turned me into a mine of useless information.'

'In that case we're stuck in the same mine.'

They both laughed. Nancy found Tom's lack of pretension refreshing.

When Nancy left a little of her shepherd's pie on her plate, he said, 'D'you mind if I finish it? Shame for it to go to waste.'

'Help yourself,' she said. 'I don't think there's much shepherd in it though, it seems to be ninety per cent peas.'

It was enjoyable to see him polish it off. She reckoned his long legs would take some filling. Afterwards, he said, 'I really enjoyed this evening. Can we do it again? I mean if you're not dating anyone else . . .'

She hesitated. 'I'm not seeing anyone at the moment, but I was engaged to be married to someone back home and it didn't work out. I'm still licking my wounds, if you must know.'

'Ah.' He smiled sympathetically but didn't make any other comment.

She rushed in to fill the gap, and before she knew it, she'd told him the whole story.

'You had a lucky escape then,' Tom said. 'Imagine if you'd found out about his shenanigans after you were married!'

'I suppose that's true. I never thought of it like that.'

'Still, it must have hurt. How about we meet just as friends,' he said. 'See how it goes.'

'I'd like that,' she said.

'Same time here next week then?'

'Are you sure it's not just the second portion of shepherd's pie you're after?'

He laughed. 'Well, yes, it does have some bearing on it. But not quite as much as the very well-read girl sitting opposite me.'

Chapter 7

As time went on, Nancy occasionally glimpsed Neil rushing past on the stairs, or buzzing by with arms full of papers. He was often out in the evenings, meeting his government contact, Oliver Johnson, at The Cavendish, and his eyes had taken on an even more strained look.

That night as she served up the cheese and onion pie that was more flour and water than cheese, she asked him what was going on. 'You seem busier. It can't be good for you to be working all these hours. Shall we take a night off to go and see a film?'

'Can't. I've another meeting with Johnson.'

'Again? Is there something big going on?'

He thought a moment, then said, 'We're trying to set everything up ready for the Allied invasion. I can't tell you any specifics, but I'm in charge of sorting out the Dutch contingent: sabotage of industrial targets.' He paused for another mouthful of pie. 'And the Dutch are vital because their agents can easily travel overland to France. They're a key communication hub; we need them to organise resistance from within and help destabilise the Nazi response to the Allied attack.'

'When will the Allied invasion happen?'

'Anyone's guess. Classified, of course. So not a dicky bird about any of it to anyone, not even Lockwood. But soon, I hope, I can't bear all this waiting. Tell you what, though, if you like, we could go to the cinema tomorrow instead.'

She shook her head. 'Sorry, I've said I'll meet Tom at the Corner House.'

Her brother's tight-lipped silence showed his disapproval. He put his knife and fork together and headed for the coat stand behind the door.

'Don't wait up,' he said, picking up his briefcase.

Later that night, she heard him come in very late, caught the whiff of smoke and alcohol on the landing as she went to the shared bathroom. So whatever meeting he was having with Mr Johnson involved drinks. She wished he'd get a few early nights; he looked exhausted.

'I'm telling you, sir, the messages we're getting are too clean,' Tom said, as he stood once more before Beauclerk's imposing desk. He was annoyed to find Neil Callaghan had been invited to their meeting, and it seemed unfair, two against one.

'Our agents are efficient, I don't see the problem,' Beauclerk said, aiming a glance at Callaghan to get his support. 'Besides, there are five networks running in N Section. You can't tell me they've all been compromised.'

Tom pressed on. 'I talked it over with Mr Marks, and he agrees – doesn't it strike you as odd, sir, that whenever we drop someone, the plane gets hardly any flak on the way in, but then on the way out it's bombarded by Messerschmitts?'

Callaghan shrugged. 'It takes time for the Germans to realise we're in their airspace, that's all. Like it takes time here for our people to register theirs. I think you're worrying unnecessarily. Some of our best men are in that network, and there's never been any suggestion that they are not receiving the armaments the Dutch Resistance ask for.'

'That's not the point! We could be sending arms straight to the Nazis. You don't see the messages like I do – some of the messages clearly show the duress code. The agents are asked to always put in two false letters, and if these are omitted, it's a sign they could be operating under duress. In other words, the Nazis could have infiltrated the network. Two more messages came in on Tuesday without those letters, yet nobody queried it.'

'But isn't it true that the duress could be that our men simply panicked, or that under pressure they've forgotten the proper procedure?' Beauclerk asked.

'Maybe on one or two occasions, but nearly every time?'

Callaghan weighed in. 'I'm in Major Blunt's team, and we've seen nothing unusual. And even if it were true, what could we do about it?' he said. 'Cease supplying agents and arms? What would that do to the morale of the Dutch Resistance, or even the confidence of our own agencies at home?'

'Agencies at home? Oh, you mean MI6,' Tom said. 'It baffles me, this foolish competition for us to look better than MI6. You'd all rather risk men's lives by ignoring our problems, than risk losing face.' Tom was outraged. 'If I prove to you that I'm right, and the Netherlands is controlled by the Nazis, I'll make you eat your words.'

'And if we are proved right, which is more than likely, will you apologise for that unnecessary outburst?' Beauclerk said. 'I won't be shouted at in my own office.'

'You can have your apology now,' Tom said. 'As long as you promise to stop sending agents to the Netherlands like sitting ducks. At least until we know one way or the other.'

Beauclerk sighed and tapped his fingers on the desk.

'All right. I'll ask Major Blunt to look into it again,' Callaghan said, holding open the door, 'though I think it's a waste of time when we could be doing something more useful.'

Tom shook his head as he passed. He didn't dare open his mouth again in case he swore.

He caught sight of Callaghan exchanging a sidelong glance with Beauclerk, and it made him want to punch him. He knew his type; he'd come across them before. Callaghan was a stick-in-the-mud, always in favour of doing nothing, always wanting to preserve the status quo. His too-tightly knotted tie irritated him to death. How could a spineless man like that possibly be the brother of someone as bright as Nancy?

When Tom had gone, Neil exhaled. 'Lot of fuss over nothing,' he said to Beauclerk. 'I'd ignore it.'

'I had a stupid argument with Beauclerk,' Tom said to Nancy as they walked home from the Corner House.

'What about?' Nancy asked. She liked the way Tom held her arm lightly to guide her. Fog hung like a grey blanket in front of them, and in the blackout the pavements were full of hidden obstacles, so she was glad of the support to guide her. Also, she liked his gentle protectiveness, found it charming. Andrew would have been much more controlling.

Tom glanced into the fog to see if anyone could hear them, but then said, 'You know I can't tell you. But the fact we argued could be why I can't get our new idea signed off for printing. I had a memo telling me that the in-house printers are too busy, and if I want it done, I must find somewhere else.'

'You think it's sour grapes? Did Beauclerk give you any leads about who to ask?'

'Ssh. Don't say his name. No. The whole Firm is so damn inefficient.' He stopped, looked over his shoulder, and drew her into a shop doorway so he could whisper. 'A female agent is due to go out on the next full moon and I wanted to have time to train her in the new method with the silks, but now they won't be printed in time and—'

'Fenna?'

He nodded, and she shivered. He drew her closer. 'You're cold.'

'No, it just felt as if something "passed over". That's what my mother used to say if she had a foreboding about something.'

Above them, searchlight beams cut across the sky. In the

distance, there was the faint metallic 'crump' of an explosion. She looked up at Tom's face and saw him take his glasses off and put them in his pocket.

He's going to kiss me, she thought.

He rested both hands gently on her shoulders. 'I'd never hurt you,' he said. 'I want to kiss you, but I think it's too soon.' He pulled her into a fierce embrace instead.

All her senses longed for that kiss. She gripped him tightly around the waist, clinging on, hoping he might relent. Finally, he pushed her gently away, linked his arm in hers and set off again.

Nancy's legs were weak, her stomach alive with strange trembling sensations. Andrew and Scotland seemed a million miles away from this new dangerous world of agents and codes. And a million miles away from her dangerous feelings for Tom.

They walked silently, the space between them seemed alive with longing. When they got to the house, Tom kissed her on the cheek but gripped her hand as if he couldn't let it go. When he finally detached himself, he hurried away with his head down, as if afraid someone might be looking.

The next day, Tom pushed his papers away from him and stood up. He was like a man on fire, restless and taut with nerves. He needed another excuse to visit the decoding room. He was surprised how soon he had fallen for Nancy Callaghan. He could imagine her flying down the slopes on skis, her cheeks pink with cold and her hair flying. And yet she was as bookish as he was. It was a tantalising combination. Her ex-fiancé sounded like a proper bounder; an aristocrat born with a silver spoon in his mouth and a sense of entitlement that meant he felt he could ride roughshod over the women in his life.

The messenger boy knocked and handed over a batch of N Section messages from the teleprinter. No indecipherables again. It annoyed him for two reasons: one; that he had no excuse to take it to the girls working on the indecipherables and get a glimpse of Nancy, and two, it just confirmed his suspicions that the Dutch were really puppets of the Nazis.

He had to do something. If he could only send some sort of message through the Dutch lines to try to catch out the Germans. The stakes were high. If he was right in his suspicions, Churchill's much-lauded Secret Army in the Netherlands was all German. But if he was to send a message and it somehow signalled to the Nazis that the game was up, who knew what they'd do. He'd heard tales of atrocities. They might execute all the British agents.

Tom wrestled with it, doodling on his blotter until the scratching and hatching itself looked like a battlefield. Did he dare risk it? Did he dare risk them?

After everyone from N Section had left, Tom crept up the stairs to the fourth floor, to Blunt's office. He hoped Blunt had gone home and wasn't lurking somewhere in the building. A faint haze of cigar smoke in the corridor seemed to indicate he wasn't long gone. Tom paused outside the door, listening. Tonight, he was going to get the incontrovertible proof he needed that the N Section cells had been compromised. To his relief, like all the offices, Blunt's was open so that the overnight cleaning and inspection staff could do their work. Tom creaked open the door and clicked the switch for the light.

Tom had been there only once before, but it had stuck in his mind because Blunt's lair was even more like a gentleman's club than Beauclerk's, with a leather and gilt topped desk and deep buttoned chair. A half-full whisky decanter stood on the filing cabinet alongside a cut-glass tumbler. Blunt obviously liked his little luxuries.

Tom hurried to the filing cabinet. The thought that he was even in here at all caused his stomach to twist. He'd heard from his coding staff that one of the Dutch messages had been rescinded. Message number 243. And a cancelled message was just what he needed to implement his plan. A plan so simple it would fool the Boche, who would readily believe the English were that stupid.

Instead of that cancelled message, he had to send one that was indecipherable. Of course, transmitting without authorisation was an offence for which at best he could be sacked, and at worst executed as some kind of traitor.

He extracted the grey folder of messages and flipped through until he found message 243, with a rubber-stamped '*cancelled*'. It detailed the time of an agent and arms drop, a schedule that the Germans, if they were waiting for it, would be salivating to get. Even better, it asked for confirmation in terms of a reply.

Tom sat down, took paper from Blunt's in-tray and began to recode the message, inserting several mathematical errors that he knew would make it difficult, but not completely impossible, to decode. None of the Dutch agents he'd taught would have the skills to decode it. So if he received a reply, it would be because the Nazis were so avid for English information they'd employed a cryptographer to help them.

An indecipherable cunningly constructed to need an expert.

Tom was halfway through the coding when heavy footsteps echoed in the corridor. On instinct, he grabbed the papers and ducked down behind the desk. From the kneehole he could see nothing, but he recognised the wheezing of Jimmy's breath as he did his usual night patrol. A moment later, the light snapped off and the door clicked shut.

Don't lock it, Tom prayed. *Please, don't lock it.*

Once the footsteps had faded, Tom let out his breath. A close shave. How the heck could he explain what he was doing?

He unwound himself back to his full height and dashed to the door. Thank God it was still open. But his hammering heart told him it definitely wasn't a good idea to stay long in Blunt's office. As quickly as he could, he copied out the rest of his coded message, shoved his workings-out into his briefcase, and replaced the original back in Blunt's folder.

It took only a few minutes for Tom to bound down the stairs and in to Maureen, the night shift supervisor in the Signals Office, where he gave her indecipherable message 243, told her it was urgent, and that it must be teleprinted straight away for the next scheduled contact with the Dutch agent Kers.

'Very good, Tom, I'll get on to it.' Maureen, a solidly built woman in her forties, seemed to notice nothing amiss, though he was sure his agitation must show from the sheen of sweat on his brow.

As soon as he handed it over, his mouth turned dry and he wanted to recall it.

Maureen buttoned up her coat over her stout figure, ready to go across the road to the teleprinter but he couldn't bear to watch her send it. Instead, he lurched out of the door and down the stairs, and out past Jimmy who was back at his desk by the door.

It was done. But he was on a knife-edge, knowing his actions would either save hundreds of lives or risk them.

To stop himself thinking, he counted lampposts as he walked home, skirting along the Thames, trying not to trip over anything in the blackout. Before he got home to his bedsitting room in his lodgings, the air-raid siren went, and he was forced to scurry into the nearest shelter along with everyone else. It struck him that Hitler was like the Pied Piper, and they were the children hurrying out of Hamelin and into the cave. He wrapped his overcoat around his knees and huddled on the dank platform with the rest of the Londoners who'd been dragged from their houses in the dark.

God help them all. He prayed his ruse would work and help bring down part of Hitler's empire. If it didn't . . . well, he couldn't even articulate the words. It was unthinkable.

Chapter 8

Grateful for the warmth inside the Regal Cinema, Nancy settled back as Tom shoved his coat and hat under the seat next to her. He'd steered her to a seat in the back row, and her stomach, knowing what that meant, gave a flip in anticipation.

The lights dimmed. In the row in front of them, a man lit a cigarette, and in the brief flare of light Tom caught Nancy's eye and smiled, placing his hand over hers. She turned her palm over and squeezed, and their hands remained clasped as the opening credits came up.

The film was *Above Suspicion*, an American spy film starring Joan Crawford, but it could have been Mickey Mouse for all Nancy cared. She was intensely aware of Tom's presence and of his warm hand interlaced in her hers. As far as she could tell, the convoluted plot was several shades away from any possible reality. A newlywed couple had decided to use their honeymoon to uncover a Nazi plot.

After about fifteen minutes Tom turned to her and rolled his eyes. She leant over and said, 'It's a bit daft, isn't it?'

He stroked her hair and turned her face to his. She let her eyes close and felt his lips find hers. The kiss was deep and long, and his grip on her hand tightened.

When he eventually released her, she felt as if she'd been at sea. Wobbly, disorientated, but exultant.

Tom was grinning. He whispered in her ear, 'I've been wanting to do that for ages.'

'Me too.' Before long they were kissing again.

As the final credits rolled, the lights suddenly came on, and they all had to stand for the national anthem. Nancy shot to her feet, her face flushed and dishevelled. Together they bawled out the words, holding hands like children at a party.

By the time they came out of the cinema, Tom had hold of her around the waist. 'What terrible tripe! Did you understand what was going on?' he asked.

'No idea,' she said, leaning her head on his shoulder. 'But it was a very good way to spend an evening.'

He laughed and squeezed her harder.

While Nancy and Tom were at the Regal, Neil shook the freezing rain off his shoulders and pushed through the revolving door of The Cavendish Hotel, where he immediately headed for the bar. He hated these meetings, but every time he decided not to come, he weighed up the consequences, and the nauseous feeling in the pit of his stomach left him little choice. This evening, Otto was already there, an elbow leant on the counter, a pint of English beer in front of him, half full.

Neil took in the fact that beneath his dark wool overcoat Otto was impeccably attired as usual, in a crisp shirt and with a tightly knotted tie, a neat triangle of handkerchief in his upper pocket. He sported a thick pair of glasses that not only disguised him, but gave him the perfect excuse, along with false papers, for not being conscripted.

Though the British Union of Fascists was banned, and Mosley and his most senior lackeys had been imprisoned, it had never stopped people like Otto. He had a kind of upper class glamour with his clipped Oxford accent, and he moved in circles that included right-wing Lords and peers of the realm. Of course, Neil had to be careful not to call him Otto in public – he'd got false papers with British nationality and he was Oliver now. Oliver Johnson.

Otto turned and nodded an acknowledgement as Neil arrived, but drained the last of his tankard. 'Right, we'll go out,' he said.

This was a familiar pattern, so Neil didn't even bother to take off his raincoat. He simply watched Otto throw a few coins down on the bar and stub out his cigarette in the metal ashtray, before following him out onto the street. Otto unfurled his umbrella with a snap but didn't offer to share it. They walked in silence, sloshing through the puddles on the pavement, and stepping aside every time a car went past in case they got showered by a wash of filthy water.

Otto headed for Kensington Gardens, now stripped of its metal railings, leading the way past the section that was now growing wartime vegetables, and onto a long broad pavement by the pond.

There, Otto stopped, glanced around, and stared out at the rain on the black water, before wiping a sleeve across his glasses. 'Blasted things,' he said, removing the spectacles with his free hand and shoving them in his overcoat pocket. 'Can't see a bloody yard in this rain.' He turned to face Neil. 'I haven't had a good week. First, a friend of mine was killed by your RAF raid on Berlin, which nobody knew was coming. Then, the last time we picked up an agent,' he said, 'we couldn't break the code. I'm not a happy man. What's going on? Has the encryption changed?'

'There's a new chap, Lockwood. He's a coding expert, here to take the pressure off Marks, and he's made everyone learn new poems. Not existing ones, but ones made up specially for each man.'

'You can get me these poems?'

'No chance,' Neil said. 'Marks or Lockwood devise them on the spot with only the agent present. Of course, the decoder for the agent's schedule knows the code, but they've been made to swear secrecy.'

60

'Then you must persuade one of them to talk, heh?'

'Look, Otto, I can't. I've done enough. You've had as much information as I can give you. I just want out. I don't want to do this anymore. My sister's here in London now and I don't want her involved.'

'Nancy?' Otto stepped nearer and his open umbrella nearly caught Neil in the eye. His stare intensified. 'She was just a kid the last time I saw her. You haven't told her anything about me, have you? She doesn't know I'm in London?'

'Of course not. What d'you take me for?'

The stare was replaced by a shrug. 'As for giving up . . . you know quite well that if you let us down there might be' – he paused – 'an unfortunate accident.' His eyes held Neil's, but they were unreadable.

Neil made one last appeal. 'I'm asking you as a friend, Otto. As someone who ate my mother's food and slept in our spare bedroom with our dog on the foot of your bed.' He drew out a photograph from his pocket and held it out. It was a photograph of them on the porch of the house the last time they holidayed. The two mothers were arm in arm, the children in knitted hats grinning shyly beneath. 'Remember your red bobble hat?'

Otto was silent a moment, chewing his lip.

Neil shook the photograph at him, and finally Otto handed him his umbrella and took it. Neil watched his face soften and then his lips tighten back into a hard line.

'As a friend,' Otto said, with a brittle smile, 'I will forget you asked.' He tore the photograph into shreds and tossed it into the water. 'You will persuade one of the decoders to give you the poem codes. I don't mind how you do it.'

'That was mine! Why did you do that?' Neil was filled with a raw sense of impotence. He hurried to the pond but the pieces were already half-submerged by the rain. He rounded on Otto, his voice choked. 'Look, the game will be blown soon anyway. The Dutch messages are too clean, and people are starting to notice.

There are not enough errors in the transmission. It's making Lockwood suspicious. It's only a matter of time.'

Otto stepped closer, grabbed his umbrella and closed it. He was the same height as Neil, but his expression held an undertow of menace. 'So you're telling me we need to make more errors, like the English.'

'We don't get any indecipherables from the Dutch agents and it looks odd.'

'Then it's simple. I'll take that report back to Jack King, who'll send it to Giskes in the *Abwehr* and arrange for more errors. We will pretend to be stupid Englishmen, heh? It's essential this *Englandspiel* is not compromised.'

The English Game. But it was only a game on one side. Giskes, the head of German Intelligence must be loving it. Neil looked down at his wet shoes. He didn't know how to answer the threats and bullying. He never had. His father had bullied him all his life. Now Otto, Oliver, was doing the same. Once the Nazis finally arrived and took over Britain, it would probably be worse.

Otto stepped nearer and put the tip of the umbrella to Neil's chest. Neil backed away involuntarily, until he was right on the edge of the pond.

'Your last agent caused Giskes' men a lot of trouble,' Otto said, finally releasing the pressure. 'The English don't seem to understand what makes a man. They think resisting is brave. But the best agents die quickly. They accept that death is coming anyway and volunteer for a quick death by suicide pill or by telling us all we need to know. Then their death is merciful: a quick shot in the head. The weak ones are the ones that will suffer. The ones that fail to see that their time has come and try to cheat death. They are the ones that are tortured and have to dig their own graves.' He gave a bark of a laugh. 'You should tell them.'

Neil was frozen, stunned by Otto's words.

'I want the new poem codes,' Otto said. 'When you have them, telephone to leave me a message at reception at The Cavendish.

Say, "Your dry cleaning is ready" and give a time when we can meet. I'll see you in the lobby of the London Library.'

Otto's cover story was that he was working at the London Library, shelving books and supposedly with eyesight too bad to go to war. A sudden rattle of anti-aircraft fire made Neil glance up. The succession of flashes blasted the sky from black to blue. He blinked, but by the time he looked back, Otto was already putting up his umbrella as he strode away.

Neil's shoulders slumped. He set off in the opposite direction, the rain, heavier now, splattering over his shoulders and back. If only he had never gone to Oxford. He'd hated the easy camaraderie of his peers, the whole confusing mess of student life. He'd been young and foolish. It had been a mad idea to ask Otto to cheat for him. He thought he'd get away with it, that Otto, a year older and on the same course, should take his finals for him because they looked so alike. He'd been so scared of failing and what Father might say.

And they had got away with it. Until the war came; until the day Otto had found his London address and turned up on the doorstep. Those first few moments when he grinned and told him how good it was to see an old friend were still indelibly etched into Neil's brain. He'd been so gullible.

Otto had threatened to send an anonymous letter to the SOE denouncing him as a cheat, and a person who hadn't earned his qualification. It would have sunk his whole career. In a flat funk, and just to get rid of Otto, he'd agreed to copy one or two papers from Beauclerk's files. In return, Otto would keep quiet and he, Neil, would save his reputation. And, of course, that had been the thin edge of the wedge. And now he couldn't reconcile Otto, his childhood friend, with this cold, weasely man he hated with such a grim intensity.

As Neil hurried towards the Underground station, the dirty rain hammered down, soaking through his raincoat. Neil felt his insides shrivel. If only the Nazis would hurry up and win, then there'd be no need for the SOE, and he could go back to a nice safe law practice. Otto would stop tightening the screws on him, and be grateful instead, and no one need ever know how idiotic he'd been.

No. He had to stop thinking like that. He didn't want to live under German law either. And the irony of the whole thing was not once had anyone ever asked him for proof of his degree.

He crossed the road deep in thought until a screech of brakes made him leap for the pavement as a car with slit headlights swerved to avoid mowing him down.

Shaken, he paused on the kerb, rain dripping down his neck.

If he gave up the agents' poem codes, agents would die. It was as simple as that. He'd have to play for time. It was what he always did: put things off until he had no alternative but to act. Even now, he couldn't quite believe that what he was doing was treason.

As he rattled through the dark on the Underground, he replayed the conversation in a loop. In the dark carriage window, a double image stared back at him, a pale ghost-like figure with shifting hollow eyes. *How did I ever get like this?* he wondered.

He should never have told Otto that Nancy was in London – that was another mistake. What if Otto contacted her? He must get Nancy to move on to another job, somewhere else, somewhere well away from him and the SOE.

Once in the house, Neil took off his soaking clothes and hung them on the back of the door. His shirt was damp and stuck to his back. Anxious to check that nobody had been following him, he kept the lights off and lifted the corner of the blackout blind.

There, between the gateposts, he could just make out two shadowy figures kissing. But he'd know them anywhere. Nancy, and that know-it-all Tom Lockwood. Lockwood who was intent on uncovering everything Neil had taken such pains to cover up.

* * *

64

Nancy had barely got through the door when Neil accused her. 'I saw you, kissing on the doorstep.'

'So? It's not a crime, is it?' Nancy retorted, taking off her coat and hat.

Neil followed her as she went to sit down. 'I just want the best for you, Nance. I promised Mother I'd keep an eye on you and make sure you didn't get hurt again. I said I'd make sure you found someone suitable.'

'And why isn't Tom suitable?'

'You don't know anything about him. He's just another of those whizz-kids throwing his weight about.'

'He isn't. You know nothing about him. He's the youngest of three boys brought up in a perfectly respectable home in Chatham. He has a first-class mathematics degree from Cambridge. What's wrong with that?'

Neil pressed his lips together as if she'd hit a nerve. It was a moment before he answered. 'Just don't get too involved, that's all. After all, in a few weeks you might be ready to move on to some better sort of employment.'

'What are you talking about? I enjoy my work. It's good to do something worthwhile and feel I'm making a difference. And, anyway, I like him. Why can't you just be glad I've found someone I like?'

Neil didn't answer. Instead, he picked up the paper and shook it open, but she knew he wasn't really reading it.

Later that night, she lay in bed reliving the evening at the cinema. The thought of Tom made her shivery with suppressed excitement. So what if her brother didn't like Tom? Neil wasn't her keeper.

And her whole body pulsed at the thought of Tom; she couldn't wait to see him again. He was so unlike Andrew. If she'd married Andrew, she'd have been stuck in the gloomy edifice of Stranraven House, fixing Andrew his whisky, while he dictated in his self-satisfied way what she could and couldn't do.

Here, she'd felt a breath of freedom. Tom came from a world where women could do things – take risks. She thought of the agent Fenna. A woman could parachute into enemy territory, and nobody would stop her. It was a far cry from what Andrew had insisted she should do – village fetes and knitting for the WRVS whilst he kept another woman on the side. It was liberating, and she wasn't going to let her brother stand in the way of all that. For the first time, she felt as if women mattered, as if they could do something important, even momentous, against the Nazis.

Chapter 9

Neil followed Major Blunt into the meeting room, which was simply an empty room, dark because the windows had been painted out with blackboard paint, and furnished with an ancient boardroom table and uncomfortable rickety chairs. Beauclerk, along with his thickset secretary Beryl, was already there waiting for them. He was rocking back and forth on his heels in front of a lopsided portrait of the King.

Beauclerk dismissed Beryl as soon as the men arrived, and that forewarned Neil it was something important, or off the record, that was supposedly unfit for such lowly female ears. Beryl herself showed she resented it by letting out a heavy sigh of disdain as she went.

Neil sat down next to Major Blunt on the other side of the table, glad to get the weight off his bad leg. Meetings like this made his heart rate rise because Otto's demands always hovered in the forefront of his mind.

A few inane pleasantries followed before Beauclerk got to the nub of the matter. 'What do you think of this notion of Lockwood's that the Dutch lines have been infiltrated?' Beauclerk asked.

Neil tensed; his hands gripped the edge of the chair. *Relax*, he told himself.

'We've no real evidence of it,' Blunt said. 'None at all.'

'But I asked the girls in the coding room, and they're getting concerned; they tell me Lockwood's right,' Beauclerk insisted. 'There's no hiding it, the Dutch messages are always correctly coded, unlike those of the French, even though the agents have had exactly the same training.'

'An exaggeration,' Neil said. 'All our agents are well trained. They don't make many mistakes. And only this morning one came from N Section that had to go to the indecipherable room for decoding.' He felt himself flush at the lie. Fingers crossed it would soon be true.

'Why is Lockwood singling out N Section?' Blunt snapped, sounding rather aggrieved. 'The French are far more trouble than we are.'

Beauclerk looked uncomfortable. 'Look chaps, we need to get a handle on this ourselves. If MI6 catch wind of it then they'll want an investigation, and they might even decide to shut us down.'

'They won't do that. Far too much at stake,' Blunt said.

At this, Neil began to sense the germ of an idea. Perhaps he could pour some doubt on Lockwood's judgement. 'That pencil and notepad idea of Lockwood's never worked,' he said. 'Now he's trying to blame us for his own incompetence. And talking of closing things down, the bigger question is why is Lockwood trying to convince us to close down N Section?'

Silence as Blunt and Beauclerk exchanged worried glances. Beauclerk was the first to speak. 'He's not.' But then Neil saw Beauclerk tense as he considered the possibility. 'Surely you're not suggesting—'

Their reaction told Neil he'd hit a nerve and he pushed on, warming to his theme. 'Doesn't it strike you as faintly odd that Lockwood keeps trying to get us to shut down a whole operation?'

'Come on, Callaghan, he's just doing his job, as he sees it,' Beauclerk shook his head. 'Lockwood's not got much tact, and to him nothing moves fast enough. He wants everything done yesterday, that's all.'

'But N Section's a vital hub,' Neil said. 'The main communication point in Europe for Churchill's Secret Army. Just think how it would work to the enemy's advantage if it was to go.'

Beauclerk took out a cigarette and lit it, inhaling deeply. 'I hadn't thought of it that way.'

'From what I can see,' Blunt said, with the air of having the final word, 'Lockwood's just a bit of an amateur. Hasn't the first idea of protocol.'

'Imagine for a moment,' Neil said, beginning to sweat, 'if there was no N Section. No one to tell us where the Nazis were mobilizing next. It's their stronghold as well as ours.'

'Lockwood knows all that,' Beauclerk said, frustrated. 'It's why Marks said we need him. He's trying to make our coding department more efficient.'

'And is it more efficient since he came?' Neil pushed on. 'Or less?'

Beauclerk frowned and took another deep drag of his cigarette.

'And anyway, what do we know about him?' Neil said. 'He just appeared from nowhere. I think we should check him out.'

Beauclerk held up a restraining hand. 'Now just wait a minute—'

'Callaghan's got a point. We can't have this Lockwood character blundering about though. God knows what damage he could do. If it was F Section he was interfering with,' Blunt said, 'they'd make damn sure to follow him up, just in case.'

Neil's tension released. Blunt had taken the bait.

Beauclerk stubbed out his cigarette but it continued to smoulder in the ashtray. 'I'm sure you're overreacting, Callaghan, and there's nothing to worry about. But better safe than sorry, as you say. I'll have a word with Marks, get someone to check out Lockwood's credentials, and work out how best to deal with this.' He stood up and walked to stare at the portrait of George VI, as if the King could give some sort of answer. Smoke wreathed around Beauclerk's head. At last, he turned. 'We need to keep it quiet about Lockwood. If we find he's, God forbid, some sort of double agent, the fallout will be terrible. It has all sorts of conse-quences. Not just for our future in Europe, but for him. Spies are to be summarily executed – oh, in secret of course, in case it has an effect on the morale of the population. And it's the devil of a business, shooting one of your own.' He shuddered. 'No, we must tread with extreme caution, find someone to undertake some surveillance on him. Leave it to me.'

Neil nodded and rubbed his sweating palms down the creases of his trousers. It was obvious to anyone with half a brain that Germany would win this war. He didn't know why these people were even bothering with their foolish little maps. Anyone who ever met Otto would know he was hard and cold as iron, and they'd be dealing with thousands like him. All better informed, better equipped and better organised.

Summarily executed. The words reverberated, turning his guts to water. If he could just play for time, hope the inevitable invasion came soon. He'd be on the winning side then, for once in his life.

Tom hovered near the doorway of the decoding room. He'd been there on and off for over a week, waiting for the reply to message 243. The Germans were either having trouble with it, or he was wrong, and the lines were secure. Phyllis Hetherington, a brassy blonde, was the decoder for the Dutch agent Kers, to whom he'd sent the fake message, and every time a message was brought to her, he had to stop himself from leaping onto it.

What made it worse was that while checking the files in case he'd missed the reply, he'd caught sight of the coded memo which told him today was Wednesday, and the full moon. Tonight, agent Fenna and her suitcase of wireless kit would be making her drop into enemy territory in a brake of trees on an isolated farm just outside The Hague.

The junior clerk from the Morse room, where they transcribed the messages from Morse code, brought in another sheet of paper and headed for Phyllis's desk. 'Reply to message two forty-three,' he said, sliding it over to her. Phyllis barely looked up; she was engaged in decoding another message.

The back of Tom's neck prickled; he was at Phyllis's desk in one swift movement. 'I'll take that,' he said, 'as you're busy.'

'Thanks,' Phyllis said with a smile.

The reply took him less than fifteen minutes to decode as it was coded perfectly. They would expect the arms drop he'd suggested.

There was zero chance his agents could have decoded that themselves. Tom leapt up from his seat and slammed a punch into his desk. Christ, he'd make Beauclerk sit up and take notice now. He grabbed the telephone and dialled.

Beryl answered it. 'He's not available,' she said in her stolid, slightly nasal voice.

'Where is he? It's urgent.'

'In a meeting.'

'Where?'

A pause. 'If you'd like to make an appointment, he'll be free this afternoon after—'

Tom pressed the cradle and cut her off. He bet he was in his office having sixty winks. He'd go and find him. He swiped up the papers and was just about to rush out of the door, when the enormity of it hit him.

The Dutch network was all German. He sat down again to think it through. And Fenna was about to be dropped into a trap. It seemed to suck the air from his lungs. The very thought of it, that she might be dropped straight into Nazi hands, filled him with guilt.

He'd have to tell Beauclerk and Blunt, and they'd need to inform Churchill. And Lord knows what it would mean for the Secret Army idea. Maybe the whole thing would be abandoned and there'd be no work for agents anymore. And no work for him.

With these thoughts racing through his mind, he took a deep breath and set off back down the stairs to Beauclerk's office. In the room just outside, Beryl glared at him, pulling her hand-knitted cardigan tighter over her chest. 'You hung up on me. Politeness

71

costs nothing,' she said icily. 'He said he wasn't to be disturbed.'

'Sorry,' he said. 'It is urgent though.'

He strode past her and knocked at Beauclerk's door.

'Come . . .' Beauclerk's voice sounded irritable.

He was obviously expecting Beryl because he had his feet up on the desk and was reading a copy of *The Times*, a cup of coffee in front of him. He swung his legs down, frowning.

'You have to stop tonight's drop into The Hague,' Tom said, planting one hand on his desk. 'The Dutch network is all German, and someone here must be giving our codes to the enemy.'

Beauclerk raised his eyes, put down the newspaper and looked uncomfortable.

Tom slapped the papers down in front of him. 'Here's the proof.'

'Hang on, Lockwood, these are serious accusations.' Beauclerk held up a warning hand. 'I'm not doing anything at all until you tell me what all this agitation is about.'

'Just spare me half an hour,' Tom said. 'I promise, you need to hear this.'

And he began to explain what he'd done, to the increasingly wide-eyed horror of Beauclerk.

'You mean you sent a false message?'

'No, no,' Tom said, frustrated. 'Not a false message, just one coded differently. But it needed a coding expert to decode it, that's the point.' Tom rushed on. 'And guess what? It's come back as a perfect reply. Now will you believe me? You must stop all activity with the Dutch Resistance.'

Beauclerk still didn't seem to get it. He was looking at him strangely, as if examining some creature he'd never seen before.

Tom leant forward and put his hands on the desk. 'I'm sorry, but we have to shut down the whole network.'

Now Beauclerk snapped back to life. 'No. Do you know what you're asking? There'll be hell to pay! That network's our main hub of communication into occupied Europe. There must be another way.'

'What other way?' Tom said, whipping round from the desk and pacing in frustration. 'We've already lost too many agents. One of our female agents is going to be dropped today. Today! If you let the drop go ahead, she'll be falling right into enemy hands. All her messages from then on will be false. And God knows what they'll do to her.'

'Calm down. I'll need to consult with my colleagues. I was only talking to Blunt this morning, and he sees no problem at all with his section.'

'Aargh! Blunt just wants a quiet life! What will it take to convince you? Blood? The proof's right there on that table!'

'It all needs looking at properly. I've told you. We need to go through the proper channels. We'll have to arrange a section meeting. We can't make knee-jerk reactions without thinking it all through.'

Tom opened his mouth to speak but Beauclerk cut him off. 'Not another word. You can leave it with me. Don't make me have to call your position here into question.'

Tom went out of the door and pounded his fist on the corridor wall. He cursed the War Office, cursed the SOE and cursed Beauclerk. Blasted committees. Why was it every decision seemed to take so long?

A moment later, Beauclerk's head appeared out of the office door. 'Lockwood! You will say nothing – and I repeat nothing – to anyone else of this matter. It's highly sensitive, and I don't want you trampling all over it with your big feet.'

Incensed, Tom put together a written report to Beauclerk, Blunt and to Sir Charles Hambro, head of the SOE, about his suspicions that SOE agents in the Netherlands were now in German hands. Maybe if they had it in writing, someone, somewhere would do something.

Tom could tell none of this to Nancy, though he longed to. Breaking the Official Secrets Act was treason. But just the sight of her hopeful face made him forget all his problems, and over

73

the last few weeks, he'd arranged to see her more and more often, until he nearly always found her waiting for him at the end of her shift, hoping they could eat together.

Tonight, she was waiting as usual, her raincoat belted tight around her neat figure, her hat pulled down over her wavy hair. Her eyes were apologetic. 'Sorry, Tom, I can't come to the Corner House tonight, I promised to eat with Neil. I've been rather neglecting him.'

Tom couldn't help his face falling in disappointment. 'That's okay,' he said. 'We can do it another night.'

'To be honest, he thinks we're seeing too much of each other, and we got into another row about it.'

'And what do you think?'

'I always want to see you, of course I do! But when I invited myself to London, and landed myself at Neil's flat, part of the deal was that I might cook sometimes, and I feel guilty that I haven't had much time for it. And I'm worried about him. He looks strained all the time now, and he's got really snappy. I thought it might give me a chance to talk to him, to find out what's wrong.'

'Of course,' Tom said. 'It's fine. There'll be plenty of other nights. But I wish there was somewhere we could be together, just us. A chance to talk in private without someone else looking over our shoulders. It's no good at your flat if Neil doesn't approve, and my landlady, Mrs Biggins, is the landlady from hell. She'd have a fit if I brought a girl home; she polices our every movement, in case of what she calls "improprieties".'

They laughed. He took hold of her by the shoulders and risked a quick kiss, before anyone else should come along. 'I'll walk you to the bus,' he said. As soon as they were out of the door he kissed her again, enjoying the softness of her lips. Her hands twined around the back of his neck as she kissed him back. He could feel the warmth of her through his clothes and it made him ache to kiss her again.

By the time they got to the bus stop, he was breathless and taut with longing. As he waved to her through the window of the bus, he thought he'd never seen anyone look more beautiful, that girl in the maroon hat, staring wistfully through the misty window.

On the bus, Nancy rubbed at the window to wave to Tom. She saw him stare after the bus, and it tugged at her heart in a way nothing else ever had. She felt as if everything was running away from her too fast. She'd fallen for him, she realised. But did he feel the same way? She hoped so. The light in his eyes told her that he did, but she was wary. It was wartime and nothing was certain; nobody knew if promises could be kept. A grinding fear lay underneath everything. The bus veered past one of the bombsites, and she caught a brief glimpse of ARP wardens with hurricane lamps scrambling over the rubble. It made her even more insecure. Why love in wartime when you could wake up tomorrow and find your life blown to smithereens?

Chapter 10

Despite Nancy's efforts to cheer him, Neil prodded at the apple pie gloomily and took a spoonful. 'It's a bit tart,' he said.

'What d'you expect?' Nancy said, frustrated. 'I can't get sugar.'

'It's not like Mother's Dutch apple pie.'

'Of course it's not! We're in the middle of a war, or hadn't you noticed?'

'Don't lecture me!' he said. 'You have no idea.' And with that, he grabbed his coat and hat and slammed out.

Nancy could have wept. Neil was getting intolerable. The next morning, he was still frosty and she couldn't get him to say more than a few words as they caught the bus to Baker Street. Nancy had tried to get him to confide in her, but any questions about his work just made him even more clammed up and irritable.

As they bustled into Reception, shaking the rain off their umbrellas, Nancy was surprised to find a note waiting for her with Jimmy. She tore the envelope open, expecting Neil to wait, but he shot off without even a goodbye.

A single typed sheet, asking her to report to Beauclerk's office at ten o'clock sharp. What could he want? Had she done something wrong? Since the bus ticket incident, she thought she'd been extra careful about secrecy.

Rattled at this summons, she worried all morning. She took a deep breath to calm herself in the corridor before approaching Beryl, his rather intimidating secretary, to tell her she had an appointment.

When she was called in, she was startled to find Neil there in Beauclerk's office. But he didn't smile, just stared at the floor.

'Good morning,' Beauclerk said. She had only ever seen Beauclerk from a distance, and his tall figure and lugubrious manner were daunting. 'Do take a seat, Miss Callaghan.' He gestured to Neil, who was sitting off to one side of the desk, picking at the crease in his trousers, his face even more closed off. 'I asked your brother to join us because our request is rather unusual, and as you live in the same house, it would be hard for you to hide things from each other.'

She nodded expectantly, wondering what it could all be about. What were they not expected to hide from each other?

'What I am about to say must go no further than these doors. Am I clear?'

'Yes, sir,' she said, now even more curious.

'We have a difficulty. Occasionally, one of our employees gives us reason to suspect that they are in the pay of the enemy.'

She glanced to Neil, but he was still looking at his knees. Surely Beauclerk couldn't mean either of them? She swallowed, her throat suddenly tight.

Beauclerk was looking at her kindly. 'We are checking certain members of staff by putting them under surveillance. One of these men is Tom Lockwood.'

'Tom?' Her voice was incredulous. 'But that's impossible—'

'I know, the thought is not a pleasant one, but it's one we must nevertheless engage with, to find out if it's true. And you, Miss Callaghan, are in the best possible position to find this out for us. Neil tells us you and Lockwood are . . . how can I say? Close.'

All this time she'd had her gaze fixed on Neil. Now he looked up. *You toad. You knew about this, and you never said a thing.*

77

'Sorry, Nance,' Neil said. 'We've checked his background and it all looks above board, but you can never be too careful. We don't want to upset Marks, but Lockwood's a bit erratic, and he's asking us to take actions that seem, well, rather beneficial to the enemy. It rang alarm bells, so we just want to know a bit more about his contacts – who he sees outside working hours . . .'

'. . . whether he makes any telephone calls, and who to, that kind of thing,' Beauclerk added. 'And if you can wrangle a visit to his flat, and have a good look round—'

'You're asking me to spy on Tom? Tom Lockwood?'

Beauclerk gave a nod.

'But that's ludicrous.' She looked from one to the other. Now neither would meet her eyes. 'Tom's only trying to save lives. The agents in the field are his top priority, he's always saying it. He's a bit impetuous, that's all, but I know for a fact he could never be a traitor.' But even as she spoke the words she was already replaying conversations she'd had with him. *It couldn't be true. Could it?* 'It's a bit of a shock. Can I have a glass of water, please?' she asked.

'Of course, of course,' Beauclerk said. 'I'll get Beryl to fetch one.' And he hurried out of the door.

She swivelled to face Neil. 'Why didn't you tell me?' she hissed.

'I couldn't,' he said. 'You'd have thought it was some plot of mine to stop you seeing him.'

'And isn't it?' Her words were full of venom.

'Of course it isn't. This isn't about you courting, it's not about you and lover boy, it's about the safety of a concerted campaign to defeat Hitler. Beauclerk's asking you to do your duty for your country.'

'I can't do this to Tom! He trusts me.'

'I know. That's why you have to do it. And if you're right, there'll be nothing to find. We just want you to keep an eye on him for a week or two and then—'

Beauclerk returned with a glass of water and handed it to her. 'I know we can rely on you, Miss Callaghan. Your brother's been with us since the beginning, and he vouched for you.'

'But what shall I tell Tom?'

'You don't need to tell Mr Lockwood anything. You can just go on exactly as before, but we'll need you to fill in a confidential report card every day, in case we . . . well just in case. Can you do that?'

She took a sharp sip of cold water and it cleared her head. What was more important, defeating Hitler, or her relationship with Tom? She knew what the right answer was supposed to be, but it still hurt her to say it. She couldn't get the words out.

Beauclerk leant forward. In the background the clock ticked. 'Can we count on you, Miss Callaghan?'

'What happens if I refuse?'

'Oh, you don't want to do that.' Beauclerk smiled as if it were a joke. 'We'd have to find you some work away from here, at one of the wireless communication outposts perhaps.'

She weighed it up. If Tom was innocent, then it would be just a few weeks, and then they could carry on as before. She'd be able to clear his name. But still, the idea of it felt like a betrayal, and she had a strange sense of foreboding, as if she was outside herself looking down. Again, she felt as if her life was running away from her, out of control.

They were waiting for her answer.

'I don't have a choice, do I?'

She barely registered their smiles and congratulations, because the words still felt as if they were lodged in her throat.

79

Chapter 11

That night Nancy refused to speak to Neil, but instead she took herself into her bedroom and closed the door. She could hear Neil banging about the kitchen, the clang of pans in the sink and then the pungent smell of something burning. Toast? Whatever it was, she resolutely ignored it.

When he rapped on her door and asked if she wanted tea, she didn't answer, though she knew it was supposed to be some sort of peace offering.

'Oh suit yourself,' Neil shouted. 'Lock yourself in there for all I care. But it's a bit childish. You can't stay in there forever.'

She sighed. He was right, but she wasn't ready to concede the point. Instead, she lay down on the bed to try and think this whole thing through. It was cold, but being summer they had no paraffin for the stove, so she threw on her dressing gown and wrapped the counterpane over her bare legs. Everything had been going so well. Now this. It couldn't be true about Tom, could it? She'd always thought herself a great judge of character. But then she remembered how wrong she'd been about Andrew.

When she awoke about four hours later, she was stiff and shivering, and realised she must have fallen asleep in her clothes. Her skirt was creased like a dishrag. In the distance she could hear the dull thud of explosions, but no siren had gone so she got up and braved the toilet at the top of the stairs. She was surprised to see Neil's light was still on. Good. Serve him right. She hoped he was worrying about what a fix he'd put her in.

As she crossed back across the landing, his door opened, and he emerged in a red checked dressing gown under which his bare feet were bony and blue. 'Sorry, Sis,' he said. 'It was Beauclerk's idea and I had to go along with it. You do understand, don't you?' His face was all jutting bones in this half-light, his eyes guiltily searching hers.

'I came here to get away from Andrew, from all his lies and deception and to find something worthwhile, something I could put my heart into. And now what do I find? I'm in the middle of some even bigger deception where I'm supposed to be the one doing the deceiving.'

'But it's war work. It's what we signed the Official Secrets Act for. Think of—'

'I know, don't tell me. It's for the greater good . . . blah, blah, blah. But it still doesn't make *me* feel good.' Neil was biting a thumbnail again, staring past her into the living room. 'It's cheating, and you know how I've always hated any kind of cheating. That's why I couldn't stand to be with Andrew.'

Neil stepped back. 'Deception's necessary in war,' he flashed. 'What do you think our bloody agents are doing? Pretending to be French, having all the labels in their clothes made into French ones, walking around with a gun in their pocket?'

'Don't swear.'

'You drive me crazy. You know nothing about war work, nothing. Yet you try to take the high horse with me—'

'I'm not taking the high horse, just calm down.' He was red in the face now, and his eyes were glassy. She took a deep breath. 'Let's just agree not to talk about it. I'll report to Beauclerk like he asked me to. You need know nothing about it from now on. Now go back to bed. You look like you hardly ever sleep.'

And as she headed back to her room, she had only one thought – if she was going to do this, she'd do her damnedest to prove Beauclerk and her brother wrong about Tom once and for all.

The next day seemed to go on forever. The usual endless stream of indecipherable messages for them to tackle, sitting on the hard wooden chairs with their heads aching from constant frustration. By now Nancy had got used to the decoding techniques and was becoming more adept at finding the errors in the messages' construction. Still, she was only managing to decode a couple a day, and there were always many more that were just unbreakable. But it wasn't just the work, it was the fact that Tom would expect her to be waiting for him after her shift as usual, and she'd have to act normally, all the time knowing she'd have to write a report about it afterwards.

As he came rushing up the stairs, his face was all smiles.

'Do you like dancing?' he said. 'There's a workers dance on tonight at the Astoria. It's a May Ball in aid of the Lord Mayor's War Relief Fund. I need a partner.' His eyes sparkled with the invitation.

'Will I have to get dressed up?'

'No, long dresses aren't allowed, in case there's an air raid and we have to run for it. If you want, we can eat in the staff canteen and walk straight there.'

She grimaced. 'My shoes aren't very good for dancing in, and I can't do all this new American stuff. I wouldn't know a jitterbug if it bit me on the nose. I'm used to Scottish jigs and reels.'

'Then we'll be well suited,' Tom said with a grin. 'I can't dance either.'

That proved to be false, as she soon found out.

The room was pulsating with bodies, so much so that barely a square foot of floor was visible. They wove through waves of smoke and body odour as the big band hammered out Glenn Miller's 'American Patrol'. Tom took hold of her by the waist to steer her into the only available space. Though it was supposed to be a workers' and not a forces' dance, uniformed soldiers, sailors and airmen from all over the Commonwealth were showing off their moves. If I were on leave, she thought, I'd want to sample the bright lights and have some fun too.

Tom removed his glasses and curved his arms around her. His face suddenly looked naked, like a small boy. He smelt of soap and ink. She felt a wave of tenderness for him and leant closer, until his warmth seeped through her thin blouse, and his closeness made her light-headed. Over his shoulder an American GI was smooching with a pale-skinned woman in red. So many servicemen – it made her feel guilty. Was she dancing with a traitor? But she couldn't deny the tug of attraction to Tom, and when he leant down to kiss her, she let him, to wolf whistles from the men nearby. When she came up for air, she was dizzy.

'You look beautiful,' Tom said. He had to repeat it again, as the band was so loud she could hardly hear him for the wailing of the saxophone and the shuffling of hundreds of feet.

She held on to him tighter, shut out her doubts and let herself be swept into the rhythm of the dance. Eyes closed, she rested her head into his shoulder, and for a few minutes he steered her gently around, and it was as if they were part of the music. When she looked up again to catch his eye, he stroked her hair, and as they danced he didn't take his eyes off her face. At the end of the dance, she felt as if she was on fire.

Yet in the back of her mind lurked the cold, hard reality of Beauclerk asking if she could wrangle an invitation to get into Tom's lodgings and take a look around.

But what would Tom think? He'd think her too forward if she suddenly turned red hot like that. At the same time, she cursed Beauclerk for setting the idea in her head, because she had to admit, she longed to go home with Tom.

She agonised over it but knew she couldn't ask.

83

Her reputation would be like mud. She knew where it would lead, and she both longed for it and feared it. And how on earth could she then write a report on the evening? She wouldn't, she just wouldn't.

Two days later, Beauclerk summoned her in to his office again, his manner like a headmaster who expected absolute obedience. That, and the portrait of the King staring down at her, made her want to rebel.

'You haven't sent us any reports,' he said, 'and I hear you went dancing at the Astoria.'

Bloody Neil! He must have told Beauclerk she'd been out dancing with Tom. What could she have said in a report? That they'd eaten shepherd's pie, danced cheek to cheek, and held hands as they went home? That she was in love with him? It just seemed ludicrous.

'There was nothing to report,' she said, bracing her shoulders.

'Then you should have filled in the form to say so,' he said crisply. 'Sit down, Miss Callaghan.'

She sat down on the edge of the chair, feeling as if she was suddenly on trial for some sort of crime.

'What did you and Lockwood talk about that night?'

'Nothing much. The music was too loud to do much talking.' She cursed her turn of phrase as heat rose and she knew her cheeks must be flaring.

'What about afterwards then, on the way home?'

'Just small talk. I can't remember.'

'We are paying you to remember,' Beauclerk said. 'Now, think harder.'

'He commented about how drab London looks, with everything blacked out.'

'So he was criticising London?'

'No, not at all.' She sighed in frustration. 'He wasn't criticising, just lamenting that we couldn't have a good time like normal couples before the war, and I agreed with him. It was just chit-chat.'

'And he made no mention of our work here?'

'Of course not! I swear, there's nothing to tell you.'

'No need to get so het up, Miss Callaghan, but this is an official assignment, one that the whole department, including your brother, thinks is necessary. You have a job to do. If you are not up to the task then we can always find you work elsewhere, out of London.' Her shocked face must have had the desired effect, for he pushed another of the horrible white forms across the desk. 'I suggest you fill this out now,' he said.

Under his watchful eye, she filled in what she could remember, feeling close to tears. Writing it down in a report sucked all the magic from it.

When she pushed it back, he gave it a cursory glance, then said, 'You'll find more forms in your pigeonhole. Make sure they are dated and filled in every day.'

Another week passed by, but Nancy found nothing suspicious about Tom. They spent almost every night together, walking the streets arm in arm, looking at bomb sites and the parks turned to allotments, and talking about the things they'd do when the war was over. Travel, have a seaside holiday, eat real eggs and butter, get seats for the opera. The nippys at the Lyons' Corner House knew them and always took them to the same table in a private corner at the back of the restaurant. Nancy looked forward to this routine and to seeing Tom and his wide enthusiastic smile. She could think of nothing but when she'd see him again.

She wrote him a little note most mornings, wishing him a nice day in a simple code she'd devised as a joke. He'd got it straightaway, and he passed her his reply 'BEST GIRL IN THE WORLD' in among the items she was supposed to be decoding. It was illicit, but it made her heart thump, and the secrecy only added to its appeal. It was secret too, in that she never put these messages into the reports.

Naturally, she was curious about where Tom lived, but he apologised and said that he couldn't really invite her back there. 'Mrs Biggins would have me out on my ear. She's insistent that only "respectable young men" should lodge there. So far, there's a bus driver, a man who sells blackout material, and me. And because I'm always a bit evasive about my work, she thinks I'm the most dubious of the lot! I worry she thinks I'm a German spy or something.'

Nancy laughed, but it cut sharply too. And she did wonder, to her shame, if Tom's dragon landlady was just a bit of an excuse.

One night Tom had a meeting, and so Nancy agreed to join Neil on the bus home instead. For the sake of peace, they now treated each other with wary affection.

The bus was late. 'Let's go down the road a few stops,' Neil said, glancing at his watch. 'We can walk through the park where it's quiet.' He guided her past a cordoned-off area where debris from a bomb blast had made a crater in the road. Once they were out of earshot of any other pedestrians, he fell into lopsided step beside her. 'How's it going?' Neil asked.

'How d'you think?' Nancy said. 'It's bloody difficult. I feel awful spying on Tom.'

'That's the Firm for you. Should have stayed a secretary,' Neil said. 'Beauclerk was on my back today asking if I'd chivvy you along a bit. Have you written today's report yet?'

'There's nothing to report,' she said defensively. 'Like always. He comes to work, does his job, and goes back to his lodgings. And I can't follow him there, before you ask. I'm just not that kind of girl.'

They walked in stony silence for about fifteen minutes, then turned left down a row of terraces past blacked-out windows and unkempt gardens. A few had 'Paying Guests' signs in the window, but most had 'No Vacancies' pinned to the door. A woman with too much cleavage showing under her moth-eaten fox fur flashed a torch on to her legs as Neil passed. She was obviously a prostitute and he ignored her.

'About Tom,' he said. 'There's no smoke without fire, Nancy, you know that.'

'Don't be ridiculous. As far as I can see there's no smoke either,' she said, getting out her house key. 'You're all barking up the wrong tree. When I went up to Tom's office yesterday, his desk drawer was open and there was nothing in it except a paper punch – no files marked top secret, no swastikas or guns or hidden cameras.'

'Of course not. He knows security will search his desk.'

'Aargh! Next you'll be accusing him of owning too many pencils and rulers.' She unlocked the door and clicked on the light.

'We're just being careful,' Neil said as he clomped up the stairs behind her. 'If you can't go to his lodgings, what if Tom came home with us one night, so I could have a chat with him? Sound him out a bit.'

She opened up the flat and closed the door behind them, ignoring him.

Neil was at her shoulder. 'We want to know what he does with the poem codes, whether he takes them home. Does he ever show them to you?'

'No!' she protested. 'Of course he doesn't! Is this another of Beauclerk's stupid ideas? I don't know why he's got it in for Tom like this. The poem codes never get as far as his office, they stay with the agent he's training. Even I've never seen one. And anyway, Tom says they're mostly rather crude.'

'Like what?'

'Just bits of doggerel, he says, not fit for my delicate ears.' She whipped off her hat and jacket, and hung them up. 'Anyway, they're done up the road at Norgeby House, I don't have anything to do with them.'

'Oh.' Neil sounded disappointed at that. After a pause for thought he said, 'I'd like to meet Tom properly, find out a bit more about who my sister's dating. If Tom's just an innocent guy, then there's nothing to lose by bringing him home. I can have a heart-to-heart with him and then set Beauclerk's mind at rest.'

She paused in the act of hanging up her hat and coat. 'Really? Are you serious?'

'I can see you're taken with him. Invite him, and then we can put this whole thing to bed. I think it's a good idea.'

'Only if you take your disgusting shaving brush out of the bathroom and your socks off the fireguard.'

'I might consider it,' Neil said, 'if only to get a half-decent meal out of you.'

'Watch out, buster, or you won't get fed at all.' She paused, then said: 'Though I'd love to ask Tom over. Then you can tell Beauclerk he's wrong, and get him to leave Tom alone, once and for all. And it would be nice to cook for him. He lives on his own with a terrible harridan of a landlady.'

'You'll invite him, then?'

'I'll see when he's free.'

'Sooner the better,' Neil said. There was something strangely persistent in his tone.

For over a month Tom had checked his pigeonhole every day for a message from the higher-ups about the Dutch networks, but every day there was no reply to his letters. And for a month he'd fretted, having heard nothing at all from agent Fenna. When, finally, today, they received word from her, it was to find that it was perfectly coded. Instead of reassuring him, this made him even more on edge. After sending the message onward with the rest, he set a copy of it on his desk and stared at it. She hadn't been the most careful of coders in training, and had made some elementary errors through being in too much of a hurry, but she was fluent in Dutch and could take care of herself, and that was all that mattered to Blunt.

His instinct was telling him it was all wrong. Yet what could he do? He couldn't bother Mr Marks again; he was supposed to be easing his workload, not making it worse. And he definitely couldn't go to Beauclerk. Beauclerk had intimated that if he got any more grief from Tom about it, he'd be asked to leave. Politics, politics. That's what it was all about. Confessing failure would give MI6 a chance to gloat over the inefficiency and stupidity of what they called the 'Baker Street Irregulars', and Beauclerk just couldn't stomach it.

Tom didn't want to leave Baker Street – he enjoyed his work and enjoyed being in the thick of it in London. Bletchley had just been too damn quiet. He'd never been the type to join the army, but he still wanted to do his bit, and unfortunately his eyesight meant he was better suited to Baker Street than the front.

Besides, he didn't want to leave Nancy. There'd been another blitz on the East End last night. Every night he wasn't with her, he worried about the bombs.

A soft knock. He leapt up to open the office door.

She was right there on the threshold, a big smile on her face.

'I was just thinking of you,' he said, pulling her in and shutting the door.

They kissed. 'Thinking of me? Nothing bad, I hope. I just thought I'd ask if you'd like to come over to the flat for dinner tonight. I've got some sausage meat and I was going to do a sort of toad-in-the-hole. But it might be more hole than toad, I'm afraid.'

Tom was taken aback. She'd never invited him home before. 'I'd love to. Will it just be the two of us?'

She blushed. 'No. Neil will be in, but I thought it might be nice for you to get to know each other better.'

'Good idea,' he said, forcing more enthusiasm than he felt. The fact Neil would be there rather dampened the invitation. 'Will we travel back together?'

'Just call for me as usual, and you can get the bus home with both of us.'

Chapter 12

Nancy had tidied the flat to make it look like a home, yet she was still painfully aware of how shabby it looked. *Please, let it not put Tom off.* She took Tom's coat, scarf and hat and put them on the coat stand, tucking his briefcase underneath.

Better leave them to it, she thought, and went to do the cooking.

From the kitchen she could hear Tom and Neil talking. She winced. There were too many pauses in the conversation and not much flow. She worried about whether they were getting along.

When they got to the dinner table, the atmosphere was still strained. 'You were a lawyer before the war, Nancy tells me.' Tom was pushing Neil to talk, instead of the other way around. 'Were you in practice here in London?'

'Only a year,' Neil said. 'Then war came, I joined the Firm, and here I am.'

Neil tucked into the food, but he didn't answer any more of Tom's gentle questions except with monosyllables. So much for him trying to get to know Tom. It made Nancy's blood boil. Neil had asked Tom precisely nothing.

'Tom used to work in exports, didn't you?' she said, drawing Tom into the conversation. Tom smiled and talked a little about his mathematics degree, his previous job as a logistics analyst, and how he got into coding. Neil gave grunts as if he was listening, but did nothing to keep the chat going, and the conversation stalled.

To relieve the tension, Nancy used the silence as an excuse to fetch the dessert: stewed rhubarb and a 'custard' – white sauce with yellow food colouring. Eggs were rationed and what was left of their dried egg powder was in the batter for the toad-in-the-hole.

When they'd eaten, Neil suddenly became animated. 'Hey Tom, why don't you help Nancy with the washing up,' he said.

She glared at him. 'You should be the one doing that, and our guest should relax.'

But Tom leapt up full of enthusiasm. 'Good idea,' he said, 'where's the tea towel?'

Tom seemed glad to be doing something practical, and grabbed the plates almost as soon as she'd washed them. It was nice to have him by her side. With Neil in the next room, it was as if a weight had lifted.

'That was a lovely meal, Nancy,' Tom said.

'No it wasn't, but I do my best with what I can get. Wish I'd had more sugar for the rhubarb.' She turned to catch a glimpse through the half-open door of Neil bending down over Tom's open briefcase.

Horrified, and uncertain what to do, she hurriedly pulled the kitchen door shut. So that was why Neil wanted Tom here. It wasn't about meeting Tom at all, but about finding a way to search his things. Her face grew hot with shame.

Nothing bad will be in the briefcase, she told herself as she sloshed suds over the plates. At the same time, she knew Neil would be looking inside Tom's things, and the whole idea made her arms prickle with gooseflesh. What would Tom do if he caught him?

She slowed her washing speed and handed Tom the last saucepan to dry. He smiled down at her. 'We make a good team,' he said, before putting the pan in the cupboard.

Gingerly she opened the door. Neil was still on his hands and knees under the coat stand. She shot him a look of daggers.

He saw her and looked sheepish. She saw him stuff something into his pocket as she shut the door again and put her back against it.

'Thank you for helping,' she said to Tom, reaching out her arms.

She leant back against the door as they embraced, and he kissed her until she was breathless and tingles were shooting up her spine.

'You're beautiful, Nancy,' Tom whispered. He kissed her again, but her thoughts were all of Neil on the other side of the door.

'If this is what I get for drying up, I think I'll do it more often,' Tom murmured.

Gently, her shoulders tight, she extricated herself. 'We'd better go and be sociable,' she said loudly, and she opened the door to the living room.

To her relief, Neil was sitting on the sofa reading the paper. 'Some great pictures here of the United Nations Day Parade,' he said.

'Yes, there was quite a crush in central London,' Tom said. 'Good thing there were no raids. Would have wiped out our personnel in one fell swoop.'

They talked a little more, but Nancy was livid. She kept seeing Neil's furtive searching of Tom's briefcase in her mind's eye, and she was longing to confront him with it.

At last Tom said he must go, and Nancy had to hand him his coat and hat. She watched as he picked up his briefcase. He'd trusted her, and her damned brother had betrayed that trust. *And so have I.* The thought came unbidden.

'Thank you,' Tom said. 'A real treat. It was lovely to see where you live.' He gave a wave to Neil. 'Thanks again for inviting me.'

Neil raised a hand but didn't get up.

'Have a safe journey home, Tom,' she said. She saw him to the bottom of the stairs.

'I'll see you tomorrow,' he said, giving her a tight hug. His eyes were soft. 'Lovely evening.' Neither of them mentioned the fact it had been a bit of a disaster.

As soon as Tom was out of the door, she raced back up the stairs and was barely in the flat before she confronted Neil. 'What the hell did you think you were doing?'

Neil held up his hands. 'I had to know,' he said.

'What? What were you looking for?'

'Anything that looks like it might lead us to his German friends.'

'He hasn't got any German friends. Why won't you believe me?'

He drew out a piece of paper from his pocket. 'This is why. It was in his briefcase. It's a coded message sent to agent Kers in the Netherlands. Look – see this agent code at the top? That's Kers, I'm sure of it. He's one of our longest-running men in Amsterdam.' He stabbed a finger down on it. 'I'm going to check out this message first thing in the morning and get it decoded. You know as well as I do that no coded message should ever leave our building.'

'There'll be a good reason. He's a coding expert, for God's sake! Maybe he's trying to crack the code or something. Let me have a look at it. I might be able to decode it.'

Neil snatched it away from her. 'No. You'll only see what you want to see.'

She was stunned. 'Are you telling me you don't trust your own sister? What's happened to you, Neil? Are you ill? You're frightening me.'

'No. But your boyfriend seems to be ignoring security rules and I'll have to report him.'

'Don't do that! We don't know what the message is yet. It could be something entirely innocent. Please, Neil. Why are you doing this?'

'Because we need to know.'

Neil hadn't slept, and after a hasty bowl of cornflakes, he left Nancy a note saying he had an early meeting. He'd kept the sked from Kers deep in his trouser pocket where Nancy couldn't get to it. Last night, he'd gone through Lockwood's briefcase hoping to find a poem, something to appease Otto, but this was absolute gold. He'd take the coded sked to Beauclerk. It was forbidden to take work home and this would cast doubt on Lockwood at least. Probably a little innocent bending of the rules, the sort everyone did, but he'd make full use of it to take the heat off himself if he could.

As Neil limped to the Underground station, he found he was walking even more slowly. Everything around him was grey and grim. He longed for Scotland, for the whiteness of the slopes, for the tingle of crisp air and the feel of a nipping wind. Nancy had been barely able to be civil to him after last night's argument, and who could blame her? He hated the person he'd turned into. It hurt to argue with Nancy, and made a chasm in his chest, but he felt like he was pressed tight into a corner and he had to play for time. He glanced at the hacked-off railings by the station. London had been beautiful once, and these had been Victorian marvels of twining fruit and flowers. If only the war was over.

When he got to Baker Street, he flashed his pass at the almost comatose Jimmy, who was huddled by the front door, and hauled himself upstairs by the banister. A woman with a mop was swilling the corridor, but he breezed past her and into the N Section office, relieved that Major Blunt was nowhere to be seen. Neil slid out the metal filing cabinet drawer and located the ring binder with the N Section transcripts. It was jammed with a thick pad of typed-up messages, all in date and number order.

He soon found what he was looking for. Message 243 – a long message about a drop of arms and supplies outside Arnhem with the requisite time and coordinates. It was stamped: MESSAGE RESCINDED.

What? The message hadn't been sent? But then there was another note scrawled in red pencil beneath it.

Attention of Beauclerk.

Now he was curious. He flipped the page.

There was a reply. Reply?

MSSGE RECEIVED UNDERSTOOD STOP WILL MEET STOP BBC PERSONAL FRANK IS WELL STOP MSSGE OVER

The original message hadn't been sent, yet here was a clear indication that the BBC had to broadcast a personal message of 'Frank is Well'. Personal messages were only ever used by the BBC to signal that an operation between England and the Resistance was imminent. Neil snapped the folder shut and put it back in the cabinet.

What was Lockwood up to? He glanced at the coded message in his hand, the one that should never have been sent.

There were no further messages, so had the drop been made or not?

He tried to make sense of it as he headed back to his desk. Lockwood knew something was up and now he might really want the whole of the Dutch line closed down. The opposite of what Otto wanted.

Neil pushed the cabinet drawer shut. Blunt wouldn't care much if N Section folded under him as long as he could protect his own reputation. Blunt was strung out, going through a messy divorce and always on the telephone to his solicitor.

But if N Section folded, Otto would hold him, Neil, responsible – unless he could shift the blame somewhere else. Beauclerk must never find out that Neil was the man who was a best friend to Hefner – one of a small group of London-based fascists who reported to Giskes in German Intelligence.

If he could only lay the blame firmly at Lockwood's feet, persuade Beauclerk that Lockwood was the leak, then he'd be clear. He could blame Lockwood, no matter what happened next.

Neil grabbed the receiver on his desk and asked the switchboard for an internal line to Beauclerk. 'It's about Lockwood,' he said. 'I've found something odd.'

'I'm free now,' said Beauclerk's plummy voice, followed by a heavy sigh. 'You'd better come over.'

Neil sat himself opposite Beauclerk, thinking, *he looks tired.* Beauclerk's face was grey and there were dark circles under his eyes.

'What is it now?' Beauclerk asked.

'Lockwood and my sister are pretty serious.' Neil tried to quell his nerves with small talk.

'So?' Beauclerk frowned, impatient.

'Well, Lockwood was at our house yesterday, and given our suspicions, I searched his briefcase.'

Beauclerk's eyebrows raised. 'Go on.'

'I found a message from N Section. Number two forty-three. Sitting right there in his briefcase: about a drop of arms and supplies outside Arnhem. But when I looked it up in the file, it said this message was rescinded and never sent. Yet filed right next to it is the reply, all typed out. How can there be a reply if the message was never sent and it's still in Lockwood's briefcase?'

'Which message is it? What did it say?' Beauclerk was having trouble keeping up.

'This one.' Neil placed the transcript on the desk. Beauclerk suddenly seemed to click.

'Ah, yes. I know all about this. Lockwood told me, and I bawled him out about it. He sent it himself. Some scheme he'd devised to catch the Germans out. Still thinks the Nazis are controlling our lines in the Netherlands and wants me to shut them down. But what I don't get, Callaghan, is why he'd do that if he's our leak?'

'I keep telling you. It's a ruse to get our operations shut down. The Nazis don't want our networks in Holland at all. They're afraid of an English invasion with support from within.'

'But—'

'Look. No matter how great Marks thinks he is, Lockwood's meddling with genuine messages to our men. Blunt won't be happy about that sort of interference. And with all respect, sir, if he can do it once, he could do it again. All sanctioned by you.'

Beauclerk rubbed a hand over his forehead. 'I wish I could sleep.

It all goes round in my damned head every night. What do you think we should do?'

'Increase our watch on Lockwood. Find out what he's really up to. Give him access to classified information and then find out what he does with it.'

'I can't take those sort of risks. What if the information does get through to the *Abwehr*?'

'It won't. Not if we have a solid watch on him.'

'We already have your sister monitoring him. Do we really need someone else? We're wasting a lot of manpower—'

'Think how foolish it would look to MI6 if Lockwood got the Dutch lines shut down and the Allied invasion had no support.' Neil knew the mention of MI6 would do the trick.

'All right, all right. I'll devise something,' Beauclerk said. 'Now get out of my hair.'

A few days later, at the end of her shift, Nancy was waiting in the lobby of 64 Baker Street for Tom. She heard him coming down the stairs before she saw him; he was always in a hurry, always bounding from place to place.

'Good news,' Tom said, reaching out to give her a hug.

'What?' she asked once they were out of the door and into the evening sun.

'The silk printing I wanted – looks like Beauclerk is going to give it a go.'

'Really? What did he say?' Nancy asked warily.

'Tell you in a minute,' he said. Tom took her arm. 'Let's take a walk through the park and up Primrose Hill.'

He took hold of her hand and she hurried along beside him until they were beginning to climb up towards the gun battery. They passed allotments, with women digging for victory in the low light of the summer sun.

Finally they were able to turn and see Regent's Park and beyond it, the city. Either side of the railway lines were craters where bombs had been dropped. She couldn't help watching Tom and wondering. Was Neil right? Was Tom a security risk? Her brother had seemed so certain.

Tom turned to smile at her and it still churned up her insides, and when he caught her gaze, it made her heart leap just the same as always. But now she found she was listening out for any odd thing he might say. It was as if she was now two people, one her usual self and the other a watchful snooper.

'You're very quiet today,' he said. 'The work's not getting to you, is it?'

'A little. It's frustrating. We only solve four out of ten. Some days I just feel like I've achieved nothing.' It was a sound excuse.

'Don't,' he said, reaching for her hand and squeezing it. 'Just remember, every agent's message that you solve possibly saves a life.'

It sounded heartfelt enough, but was it all an act? *Don't think like that.* She gripped his hand back and caught his gaze. There was unmistakable desire mirrored there. She exhaled in relief.

It was warm and hazy when they reached the top of the hill, and they both took off their jackets.

She dropped hers on the grass and sat on it. 'Tell me about Beauclerk,' she said.

He joined her on the ground, his voice low. 'I tell you, I had a shock when I picked up the phone and it was actually him and not Beryl or one of his minions. Wonder of wonders, he said he thought the WOKs were worth a try and to get in touch with Section Fifteen – they're the camouflage unit. Said they might be able to help with the printing. He's asked them to give me all possible assistance.'

'Gosh, he's changed his tune.'

'Quite odd really, don't know what he's been taking, but he was actually reasonably pleasant for a change. Anyway, I rang them and I've got an appointment on Saturday. They'd never heard of WOKs, thought they were some sort of weapon! I had to explain it stood for Worked-out Keys. But they agreed to see me and it's a coup – Station Fifteen is normally totally off-limits to small fry like us. We never get to see inside. It's all top secret classified stuff.'

'Maybe he's realised how useful you are at last,' she said brightly, despite the uneasy feeling in the pit of her stomach.

'Huh. Fat chance. Station Fifteen's out near Borehamwood, and they're going to lend me a car. I wondered . . . and tell me if this is a stupid idea . . . if you'd fancy the trip?'

She fiddled with her blouse buttons, unsure what to say.

'Of course if you're busy . . .?' he tailed off.

'No, not busy.' She pulled herself together. 'I'd love to.'

'I've heard it's run by a kind of mad professor who makes exploding rats.'

She couldn't suppress a chuckle. 'Now you're making it sound even more tempting.'

He glanced around to check no one could overhear. 'It's called the Thatched Barn, and it's full of folk from the film studios – the effects makers and technicians. It might mean a few hours hanging around, but we could enjoy the drive, and it will be a breath of fresh air to be out of London. A change of scene.'

'It sounds lovely, apart from the rats. Not sure I fancy those.'

'It's got to be secret though. They'd skin me alive if they knew I'd told you about it. Fingers crossed for good weather, eh?'

When Nancy was summoned again to Beauclerk's office, she had an inkling it was to do with this trip to the Thatched Barn, and she was right.

'How do you feel about an out-of-hours outing with Tom Lockwood on Saturday?' Beauclerk asked. 'On our behalf.'

'Let me guess. To the Thatched Barn. He's already asked,' she said, determined not to be intimidated.

'He shouldn't even be telling you the name.' A sigh of annoyance. 'Still, no point worrying now. You'll need to be briefed because you'll be staying overnight.'

'Overnight?' The idea flabbergasted her. 'I'm sorry, but I'm not ready for that . . . for that sort of relationship.'

'You like him though?'

'Yes, but it puts me in a compromising position, you must see that.'

'England's in a compromising position. We never wanted to go to war, but here we are.' He looked her fiercely in the eye. 'We always have the choice. To do all we can to stop Hitler and his jackboot army ever reaching our shores. Or to give up and give in. You don't strike me as the type to give up, Miss Callaghan.'

There was no answer she could give, so she stayed silent.

'Make sure you stick with Lockwood at the Thatched Barn and make a note of anything that seems odd,' Beauclerk ordered. 'Particularly if he makes any telephone calls. Check his luggage for cameras or weapons, or anything else suspicious. We are sending you there on purpose because it will be tempting for anyone in the pay of the Nazis to convey information about the Thatched Barn to the Nazis. Obviously we don't want that to happen, so take this.' He held out a slip of paper. 'My emergency telephone number. Call me from anywhere and ask to reverse the charges. Remember, the slightest suspicion and you call.'

'What if there's nothing?'

'Then we'll all be very relieved. But I'll be expecting you to try to charm him, so he gives something away. I've made an appointment for you to meet with one of our espionage experts so he can go through your kit. Ten o'clock tomorrow at Norgeby House. You will be briefed on breaking and entering, and given some things to make your job easier.'

She shifted uncomfortably in her chair.

'Miss Callaghan – you do want to do all you can for England's war effort?'

She had to admit she was excited about the idea of espionage.

But she squirmed at the idea she would have to spy on Tom. And he wasn't stupid, he'd see through her if she tried to do anything different.

At the Norgeby House meeting she was briefed on how to use skeleton keys and an infra-red torch, which she must go and collect later in the week. She found the idea of breaking into Tom's room surreal, and difficult, and she was relieved to get back to the quiet scratching of the cipher room.

Just before lunch, Tom stuck his head around the door and said, 'Nancy, can I have a word?'

Her stomach flipped. He couldn't know anything, could he? All the other girls were staring, and no doubt wondering why she was being summoned. Embarrassed, she grabbed her handbag and followed Tom out. He took her down the corridor out of earshot.

'I couldn't wait to ask you,' he said, a glint in his eye. 'Beauclerk must be serious about our printing on silk. He just asked to see me, said he wanted to expedite it all, so I'm to stay overnight and bring a sample back. Mr Marks has okayed it and Beauclerk's given me vouchers to stay nearby at a hotel in Elstree. I wondered if you'd like an overnight stay.' She was about to object, when he added, 'In a separate room of course, I wouldn't presume . . .'

Conflicting thoughts ran through Nancy's mind as she tried to process it all. He'd asked her away for the weekend. She'd normally be thrilled and nervous and excited at the thought of the chance of such an intimate romantic date with Tom. But now the whole atmosphere of it would be ruined. How could she possibly relax, knowing they'd both been set up like puppets? Worse, now she really would have to do as Beauclerk asked and break into his room.

'Nobody from here need know,' he said, misinterpreting her hesitation and reaching for her hand.

Of course they'd know. Beauclerk must have dangled it like bait, and Tom had fallen for it and done exactly what they predicted.

'Sorry, Tom, but I need more time to think about it,' she said. She couldn't accept too quickly, or it would look strange and out of character.

'Of course,' he said, crestfallen. 'I don't want to rush you into anything. It's just it seemed like such a wonderful opportunity, and you know how I feel about you . . .' He pulled her closer and enveloped her in a hug.

'It just feels a bit soon,' she said, hugging him back but horrified to find her voice held an edge of tears. She knew she would have to go in the end, and had no choice in the matter, but she was determined to at least give the illusion of deciding, in case she should find nothing.

'Never mind. I don't want this to spoil things between us. I'll go anyway, even if you don't come with me. The coding silks are a priority.'

'I promise I'll think about it,' she said. 'But I'd better go, I think we're already the subject of gossip.'

'It would be so much nicer if we were there together,' he said.

'I'll let you know tomorrow,' she said, and tore herself out of his embrace. She tried to walk coolly back to the decoding room. Just outside the door she paused to smooth her hair and apply a veneer of calm, though she was well aware her cheeks were flaming.

Daisy turned to her with her eyebrows raised. 'What?'

'Nothing. Just a message coming later that's important.' She dipped her head and pretended to get involved with the work on her desk, but she could feel Daisy's gaze on the side of her cheek, before Daisy sighed and shook her head.

Before they left, Daisy said, 'You've got it bad, haven't you?'

'What do you mean?'

'You and Tom Lockwood. It's written all over your faces. When he comes in here, he never takes his eyes off you.' She shook her head. 'I'm not criticising. If I were in your shoes, I'd do the same. He's a bit of a catch, isn't he?'

'You won't tell anyone?'

Daisy rolled her eyes and snorted. 'Don't need to, it sticks out like a sore thumb! Everyone knows. And you're as bad as him – you'd have to be plain stupid not to see how it is between you two.'

Chapter 13

Nancy sat back nervously on the leather upholstery, as the car, a maroon-coloured Rover belonging to the Firm, ate up the miles. Tom was cheery and relaxed at the wheel as he told her about Captain Wills, the man in charge of the Thatched Barn. Nancy tried to pay attention, but her mind kept drifting back to the meeting with Beauclerk, and her instructions from Norgeby House.

She fixed her gaze on Tom's leather driving gloves as he steered the car through the suburbs of Finchley and down the Edgware Way towards Elstree. It should have been a thrill to escape the gloom and grime of London and breathe the air of the country-side – a world where it was hard to believe a war existed, where summer was in full burst, with horse chestnuts tipped with white candles and the verges fragrant with cow parsley. But Nancy couldn't relax; her handbag, nestled between her feet, contained a bunch of skeleton keys and Beauclerk's number. What if she couldn't do it? Or worse, found out something bad about Tom? The thought made her grip tightly to the car seat.

Tom pulled up on the gravel at the Thatched Barn alongside a line of other cars. She'd imagined something rustic, but the Thatched Barn was nothing like its name might suggest – a huge rambling, mock-Tudor building, with a medieval-style turret at one end.

'Gosh, what a place,' she said, trying to appear natural. 'It's vast!'

Tom held the passenger door open while she climbed out. They walked towards the main entrance.

'Used to be a luxury hotel,' he said. 'Billy Butlin owned it, but now the whole hotel's been taken over by the SOE.'

'I don't think I'd better come in with you,' she said. Maybe she could tell Beauclerk they'd turned her away.

'Come on,' Tom said encouragingly. 'I don't think they'll quibble if I say you're an SOE colleague. I'm hoping we'll get a tour.'

She tried to object again, but he insisted and she was forced to resign herself to it. They were signed in by a skinny clerk in a knitted sleeveless jumper, but before Tom had even finished filling in their names on the yellow form, a voice boomed from the lobby, 'Lockwood, I presume.' A scruffy-looking old chap with large deep-set eyes and a ragged moustache held out his hand.

This must be the Captain Wills that Tom had told her about on the way – the rather eccentric film director and RAF veteran who ran the place. His baggy suit was polished at the knees and elbows, and the lapels were threadbare.

'Captain Wills? This is my assistant, Miss Callaghan.' Tom shook hands. 'I'm excited to find out if you can help us.'

'Not much we can't do here,' said Captain Wills. 'I was told you need some printing. Our girls will soon sort you out. Follow me.'

He swung open a double door into what was once a lounge, judging by the elaborate plasterwork cornices, but it was now a blacked-out workshop full of trestle tables and men in overalls working on radio parts. There was the hiss and smell of solder, and a tapping of hammers. It seemed bizarre to see such industry under the twinkling chandeliers and in such sumptuous surroundings.

The captain stopped and picked up an olive oil tin with a hole cut in it. 'We disguise the radios and the radio parts in all sorts of ways. I believe you're in coding?' Wills said. 'Well, this is what your agents will be using when they transmit to you from Greece.'

Nancy was amazed. She counted twenty men working on dismantling these cans, and another ten adapting briefcases. Captain Wills told them these were to carry wireless components but still leave room for innocuous papers to be put on top. It reminded her of Tom's briefcase and she gave a shiver. Tom was listening intently to the captain's explanations.

Her blood ran cold. If Tom really was a German spy, then this was exactly the sort of information the Germans would need. No wonder Beauclerk was so keen to get her here. She forced herself to concentrate.

Captain Wills led them behind a glass screen by the hotel swimming pool. Two boffins in goggles and ear defenders were firing depth charges against miniature models of submarines. Even from behind the screen, the crack of the explosion was deafening, and the splash threw up metal debris and water, making her step back.

After this excitement it was an anticlimax to be led into what seemed to be a tailoring room, where four women were sitting quietly, making alterations to suits. 'They're making our English suits look French,' Captain Wills said. 'Changing the labels and sorting out the seams. It has to look like French tailoring, but we add a few extras. Hidden compartments in the collar and cuffs for maps, and a place under the arm for a Welrod,' said Captain Wills.

'A gun used by agents in the field,' explained Tom to Nancy. 'It has the advantage that it's virtually silent.'

Nancy nodded, but she immediately wondered guiltily how Tom knew about these guns.

One of the other girls was sorting postcards into piles of different images. Tom picked up one of them and showed it to Nancy. A black-and-white view of Birmingham Royal Hospital. He turned it over. Blank.

'These postcards are sent at regular intervals to the agent's friends and family,' the girl said. 'That way, the nearest and dearest are reassured and don't ask awkward questions. For the women, we pretend they're in the FANYs stationed in Birmingham – a nice big city. For the men, we pretend they're in an offshore signal unit. The agents write all the cards before they go into occupied territory and then they'll be posted home at regular intervals. These are for delivery to the various training centres.'

Nancy pictured some poor mother receiving these postcards while all the time the agent was in acute danger somewhere in occupied France. 'It doesn't seem fair,' she said, without thinking.

'Better than the families asking all sorts of awkward questions,' Captain Wills interrupted, as he leant over to one of the tailor's dummies to retrieve a roll of silk from under a lapel. He shook it out with a flourish, so it flapped open to reveal a map about two feet square. 'I take it something like this is what you're after,' the captain said with a wry smile.

Tom took hold of the map and examined it closely. 'Good grief! The level of detail is unbelievable.' Tom rummaged in his pocket and brought out the silk sample of code that Henry had made back in London. 'How soon can you get something like this done?'

After a discussion about sizes and that each one had to be different, with the columns of numbers shifted along each time, Captain Wills held up his hand. 'No problem.'

'And I'd like to take some back tomorrow, if possible,' Tom said. 'I've got the originals here in my briefcase. Once you've printed them, I'll destroy the paper copies.'

'The documents will be safe in our hands,' Captain Wills said. 'Everyone here's been thoroughly checked. There are no leaks here at the Thatched Barn, you can be sure of that.'

Nancy smiled thinly. He shouldn't be so sure.

As they drove away, Tom fretted about Nancy. She'd been quiet all the way down in the car, and she'd looked positively worried when they toured the Thatched Barn. Once or twice, he'd caught her looking at him in a strange way, as if to study him. Was it

107

a mistake bringing her with him? He wondered what he'd done wrong. When he slipped his arm around her shoulders on the way out, she'd moved away. Perhaps she was nervous about being out of her usual milieu, and the prospect of being alone with him. He reminded himself that she'd been hurt the last time she'd been seeing someone. That damned Andrew Fraser had a lot to answer for.

He turned away from Borehamwood and slowed to let another car pass. It looked like the car he'd parked next to at the Thatched Barn. He waved the driver on, but the man, a stiff-looking gent in a homburg hat, didn't acknowledge him.

On the way to the hotel, he tried to engage Nancy in conversation, reliving aloud the gadgets they'd seen at the Thatched Barn, and exclaiming at the sheer number of people who worked there. Nancy nodded along, but he could tell there was something awkward in her responses. Still, he persevered, but it was like wading through mud.

'I'm rather disappointed we didn't see any exploding rats,' he said.

She gave a little laugh but it was half-hearted. He sucked in his breath. Maybe there'd be a better chance for a proper talk once they reached the hotel.

When he saw the hotel, his heart sank. Beauclerk was a cheapskate. He bet he'd never have to stay somewhere like this. The Welbank Hotel was pitifully small and shabby, and he got the impression it was a one-night stop-off used by travelling salesmen, but it had fallen into disuse during the war.

'Doesn't look too good,' he said.

'It might be better inside,' she said, but she didn't sound too certain.

A step through the door scotched that idea. The overweight and breathless proprietor, a Mrs Collins, wearing a stained and faded floral pinafore, led them up to the first floor and showed them to ill-furnished rooms next door to each other. Tom asked her about drinks and dinner, and she reeled off a list of dos and don'ts. 'Dinner's at seven o'clock,' she said. 'Latecomers won't be served.'

All this time Nancy was silent, unlike her usual self.

'Why don't you freshen up, and I'll see you downstairs at about six-thirty for a drink,' he said.

'Lovely,' she said, with a smile that didn't quite reach her eyes.

She was probably disappointed though, Tom thought. This place was a dump.

Within a few moments she'd gone into her room. A click clunk as she turned the key in the lock. This wasn't what he'd imagined at all. He slumped on the bed, perplexed. Nancy was right next door. He imagined her moving about the room, a room which must be almost identical to this one – a single bed and sash window with thin rose-patterned curtains over the ubiquitous blackout blind.

Restless, he had another shave and got out a clean white shirt and his favourite striped tie. To kill the time, he scribbled a few lines of a poem, one which included exploding bicycle pumps that he'd just seen with Captain Wills. It made him smile. He hoped it would fox the Nazis, were an agent ever to need a poem again – which, once they'd got WOKs on silk, he sincerely hoped they would not.

All the time he was aware of sounds from next door, of the sink running, of the scrape of the window being opened. Maybe Nancy was just tired?

Tom was early for their drink. Mrs Collins had told him to help himself from the bar, and she'd deduct it from the vouchers, so he made himself a whisky and soda and sat on the bar stool in the empty bar, feeling unaccountably on edge.

After what seemed an age, Nancy arrived. She was wearing a slim-fitting green dress that really suited her colouring. She was stunning.

'You look lovely,' he said, reaching out to embrace her.

She let him give her a hug. It was a far cry from how she'd been at the workers dance, when she was practically glued to him all night. 'Drink?' he asked.

'Nothing alcoholic. Just an orange juice or lemonade. Whatever they've got.'

'Lemonade.' When he poured the lemonade into the glass, he had to steady his hand. The girl had really got to him.

Once they were sitting down, he reached out to her, and this time she didn't pull away. 'Is something wrong?' he asked, caressing the back of her hand with his thumb.

'No, nothing,' she said. 'I think it just feels a bit strange being here. I'm not used to going to hotels, at least not like this . . .'

'Don't worry, there's hardly anyone else here,' he said. 'You know you're the best thing that's ever happened to me.'

She flushed. 'You're not so bad yourself, Tom.'

'So, let's forget the war for one night and just enjoy a good dinner together. Though I have to say, by the look of her, Mrs Collins probably doesn't go in for haute cuisine.'

She laughed then, and the old Nancy was back. They managed to have a giggle about the state of the hotel, and whether Beauclerk would ever stay anywhere like this. He leant to slide an arm around her shoulder and managed a kiss before Mrs Collins arrived at just the wrong moment to tell them dinner was served.

The dining room was cramped, with dark furniture huddled too close together, and there was only one other guest, an old gent of military bearing who smiled tersely at them before burying his nose in the *Evening Standard*. Tom stared at him. Was that the man who'd passed them in the car? He couldn't be sure.

He looked for a menu but was told there was no choice about the meal – they were served a brownish rabbit stew, but it came with a good dollop of potato and swede. Suddenly ravenous, Tom tucked in.

He'd eaten a good amount before he saw Nancy was hardly eating anything, just playing with her food. She was right; it didn't look very appetising, but at least it was hot. 'Come on, eat up,' he said. 'It's not at all bad, and I can't finish all that for you!' he joked.

'I just don't feel very hungry,' she said.

Tom tried to lighten the mood by telling her about various exploits he'd had as a student, and though to his ears it all sounded a little desperate, she did laugh and seem to loosen up a bit.

'Let's take a stroll,' he said once the meal was finished. He paced in the lobby while she fetched a coat and gloves, and then took her arm as they went out into the grounds and along a lane.

It was a relief to be out in the air, where the road was deserted and the only sound was a distant tractor engine. 'Can you believe it? We'll have a batch of silk codes to take back to Baker Street tomorrow!' he said.

'Will agents be using them straight away?' she asked.

'Yes. Gosh, you don't know what a relief it is to be out here and to be able to talk.'

'Yes, the Welbank's a bit stifling, isn't it? Do you think the Germans will find it harder to break the silk codes?'

'Dunno. It can never be a hundred per cent sure. Their cryptographers are as good as ours, but having randomly generated codes will help. And no more need to remember poems.'

'I rather liked the poems. I thought they sounded romantic.'

'Romantic?' He laughed bitterly. 'Not when you're in a torture chamber with the Gestapo and they're trying to beat it out of you.' A pause. 'Sorry. Let's not talk about that. What sort of poetry do you like?'

'The classics. Keats. Browning. And TS Eliot, though that takes a bit of work to get to grips with it.'

'"Oh, to be in England." Yes, I always liked Browning. He wrote another one, you know, as well as "Home-Thoughts, from Abroad". It was called "Home-Thoughts, from the Sea", but I can't remember how that goes.'

The conversation carried on for a little while about poetry and books before it died to silence. He was painfully aware of Nancy next to him, of the touch of her sleeve beneath his fingers; of the warmth of her beside him. He paused and wrapped his arms around her. She was tense as he kissed her, but then, all of a sudden, she was kissing him back with an intensity that was almost angry.

When he pushed her gently away, he could see a glimmer from her eyes; they were glistening as if she was about to cry. 'What is it, my love?' he asked.

'Nothing. Just a bit overwhelmed.'

He drew her to his chest again and encircled her tightly with his arms. He decided not to pry. Much as it was frustrating, he had to give her time.

As they stood there, clinging to each other, the rain started; a soft persistent drizzle.

'Wouldn't you just know it?' he said. 'We'd better get back, before you get soaked.'

They turned and headed back to the hotel.

He helped her out of her wet coat and shook it before handing it back to her. Gosh, she looked a stunner in that tight-fitting dress. He hoped for another more lingering kiss, but Nancy excused herself and said she was tired and would go straight to bed. In the resident's lounge, the military-looking man gave them a quick once over from above his paper.

Tom nodded to him and bid him 'goodnight' and reluctantly followed Nancy upstairs.

He couldn't work out what had gone wrong, how things had changed. He heard Nancy moving about in her room and weighed up knocking on her door and asking her if she wanted a nightcap, but in the end, he decided it might scare her off even more. And Mrs Collins might hear them.

Reluctantly, he undressed and got into bed. Maybe he'd read the signals wrong. The intense disappointment of this wasted opportunity made him want to smash something.

* * *

Sitting on the edge of the bed, Nancy kicked off her shoes and unrolled her stockings. Her insides were churning. She was useless at this business of being a spy. Tom was so damned handsome, and out in the lane she had almost given way and told him everything. Only the seriousness of the number of lives at stake made her stop. She was sure Tom couldn't be selling secrets to the Germans. Yet she'd have to check and do what Beauclerk asked her to do. She rubbed the back of her neck and waited until the noises from next door had ceased.

Every hour she glanced at her watch. Outside, an owl screeched its hunting cry. Three o'clock. He had to be asleep by now. She took the SOE issue red-beamed torch out of her handbag and crept the few steps to his door, letting her eyes accustom themselves to the dark. Hearing nothing from within, gently she turned the handle and pushed. The door opened a little, before it stuck on the linoleum. To her relief she didn't need the skeleton keys. She pushed a bit more and the door opened. She hesitated and listened. Tom appeared to be sound asleep.

Not contacting the Germans. Not doing anything suspicious.

She could hear his breathing and see the soft mound of bedclothes rising and falling. On bare feet she felt her way across the linoleum.

His briefcase stood by the bedside table, and she noticed he had put a glass of water there and his spectacle case. *Don't get distracted*, she told herself. She leant down slowly and pulled the briefcase inch by inch towards the door so the red beam of the torch wouldn't wake him.

She pushed away the image of Neil doing exactly this in their London flat.

A quick search revealed there was nothing in there except a rather rude poem about a bicycle pump. She had to stifle a snort of laughter. In an inside pocket, a paperback copy of *Scoop* by Evelyn Waugh, hardly opened by the look of it. His ration book. A change of underwear. Nothing else. And, of course, he'd handed over the code sheets to Captain Wills at the Thatched Barn. She felt all around the briefcase looking for a false pocket or hidden compartment, but zilch.

His jacket hung on the back of the chair by the dressing table. She switched off the beam and tiptoed over and found the trousers first so she could feel through the pockets. Only a pen and the car keys.

A creak from the bed.

She dropped down and froze. But it seemed he was just turning over. She waited in the dark until his breathing settled again. The jacket pockets held a few scraps of paper. She'd have to switch on the torch again to read them. Should she take them away to read them? If they were important he might notice they'd gone.

She turned to mask the light of the torch with her body and pressed the rubber switch. The papers were folded neatly into squares. She unfolded one.

Poems again. More poems.

'Nancy?' The voice was mild. 'What are you doing?'

She whipped around. Tom was sitting up in bed. He reached for his glasses. 'You were going through my pockets, weren't you?'

She thought quickly. 'No, I just thought you'd picked up my pen by mistake and I wanted to get it back.' *What a lame, idiotic excuse.*

'In the middle of the night?'

'I couldn't sleep.'

He got out of bed now and clicked on the light. She squinted in the harsh light. He was standing in his pyjamas, frowning, waiting for an answer. When none came, he said, 'Why are you so interested in my poems?'

She hesitated before she had a sudden stroke of inspiration. 'Someone told me you'd been seeing someone else.'

'Who? It's rubbish. So you thought you'd go through my pockets? What were you looking for? A love letter or what? Why not just ask me?'

114

'I didn't want you to make a fool of me. And I thought you might deny it all.' Painful memories of Andrew gave her voice a realistic choke.

'I knew it!' he said. 'I knew there was something wrong from the moment we set off. Who was it? Who'd make trouble between us? Oh, let me guess. Your brother—'

'Keep your voice down! You'll wake everyone up. It's got nothing to do with Neil.'

'Then who?' He paused a moment. An expression of incredulity spread over his face. 'You're working for someone.'

She was struck dumb.

'The Germans? Who?' In two strides he'd grabbed her by the arm.

'No, don't be stupid. Of course not.' But she couldn't look him in the eye.

'Our side?'

She squirmed to get free, still wouldn't meet his eye.

He threw her arm down as if it burned. 'I'm right, aren't I? Who put you up to it? Beauclerk?'

'I can't say anything, you know I can't.'

'So I'm right. Well, that says a lot about our relationship, doesn't it? I thought we had something good. Something that would last. But no, you have to spy on me.'

His words wounded because they were true.

He paced to the door and clicked it shut. 'For how long? Since the beginning?'

'No, of course not—'

'Why? That's what I don't get. What am I supposed to have done?'

'I can't . . . it's just . . . I'm under orders.' She threw down the torch and the papers on the bed, and crossed her arms in front of her chest. 'And I just had to be sure.'

'Sure? Of what?' He picked up his jacket and thrust it towards her. 'Go on then, go through it all, every pocket. Search the whole bloody room. You won't find anything.'

'No. I don't want to.' The humiliation burned, and she kept her arms firmly folded.

White with anger, he took out every piece of paper and laid them out on the dressing table. Took out everything from his pockets before turning them inside out. She was horrified to see a box of rubber condoms there.

It stared up at her as her face burned.

'There. Satisfied?'

'Tom— I . . .' but the words wouldn't come. What could she say? She wanted to reach out to him and say sorry, but this was a mess of her own making.

Her hesitation seemed to make up his mind. 'Go back to bed, Nancy. We can talk in the morning. If there's anything left to say.'

Back in her room Nancy cringed at what a complete disaster she'd made of that whole thing. The fact she'd hurt Tom made guilt gnaw at her heart, and the fact she couldn't put it right made it worse. What would he say tomorrow? It was clear she couldn't go on spying on him. He'd be on the alert now, and that stupid excuse about him being unfaithful – she must seem like a woman deranged with jealousy. Beauclerk wouldn't be at all pleased at the idea she'd been caught, and at the fact there'd been nothing at all to incriminate him. The sight of that condom box burned in her mind.

Bloody Beauclerk. It was all for nothing, and she'd never be able to look Tom in the face again.

Chapter 14

Nancy didn't sleep and breakfast was a miserable affair. Tom was studiously polite but distant, and it made Nancy retreat back into icy coolness herself. The breakfast was meagre, with only bread and margarine and sad-looking grey tea in chipped cups.

'I'll collect the stuff from the Thatched Barn after lunch,' Tom said. 'Then we go straight back to London. I understand now. This whole weekend was a farce, just designed to trap me into something. Well, I'll be speaking to Beauclerk and handing in my resignation.'

'No, you mustn't do that—'

'Don't you dare tell me what to do. There's nothing to say. We'll drive back this afternoon. Your time's your own until then.' He got up and strode away, and moments later she heard him check out and settle the bill, followed by the slam of the car door before a scrunch of gravel as he drove off.

She hadn't dared ask where he was going. It looked like it was over. She swallowed her pride. She'd been here before.

What a fool to get involved again so soon.

Determined to act as if she didn't care, she packed up her overnight case and took a walk to the village green, where she sat on a bench wishing she was back in the cipher room. At least there she'd been doing something useful. But if everything with

117

Tom was spoiled, then she couldn't imagine enjoying it anymore. If she saw him, it would give her such a pang. For the first time she realised how much a part of her life he'd become, and how much she'd miss him.

She walked back to the hotel in a sober mood. It didn't improve when Tom picked her up and was silent all the way to the Thatched Barn. There was no jubilation at the box of long-awaited printed codes.

'Are they done?' she asked.

'They'll do the job.' He simply put the cardboard box of silks in the back and set off with a roar of the accelerator. The traffic into town was appallingly bad because of bomb damage, and they had to sit in a jam for three-quarters of an hour.

Eventually she could stand the brittle atmosphere no more. 'Is this it, Tom? Are we finished?'

He sighed. 'What do you think? Would you go out with someone who doesn't trust you?' He didn't turn but kept staring at the road as he spoke. 'I was a fool. I thought I'd give you time, because you'd been treated shabbily by your ex. I thought the idea of trust was important to you. But I can see now, it's not. Better we go our separate ways.'

It pierced her. 'I'm sorry.' What else could she say? She couldn't tell him the whole truth, that they suspected him of being in league with the Germans, he'd be even angrier then. A weight seemed to be pressing on her chest. 'I'll miss you, Tom.'

A horn hooted, the traffic started up again, and he made it an excuse to put his foot down and not answer.

When Tom got back to London, he was frustrated to find Beauclerk out of his office. He told Beryl it was urgent and tried to get her to move an appointment so he could see him the next morning. She fobbed him off, but he was insistent. 'I'll be here tomorrow morning at nine, and if necessary, I'll wait right here in this chair until he agrees to see me.'

118

His whole world seemed to have collapsed inwards. He could have sworn Nancy liked him as much as he liked her. He'd been buoyed by her attentions, and now it was all spoiled. He went and hid in his office and doodled black jagged shapes on his blotter. Blow them all. Tomorrow he'd find out what was going on, then they wouldn't see him for dust.

The next morning, Tom was in front of Beauclerk's desk in one angry leap. 'I need to know why you sent Nancy Callaghan to spy on me,' he said without preamble.

'Okay, Lockwood,' Beauclerk said, holding up his hands as if to ward off the attack. 'But not here. Even walls have ears. Let's take a walk.'

Beauclerk grabbed his suit jacket and led the way out in the summer heat towards Regent's Park, now littered with rows of Nissen huts for the RAF encampments. Floating eerily above was one of the huge silver-coloured barrage balloons, cords straining in the summer breeze, its tail fins shearing away from the wind.

Beauclerk marched on, head bowed, his hands planted in his suit pockets. Finally, he stopped. 'They're filling it in with rubble now,' Beauclerk said, pointing to a rough stretch of uneven ground strewn with debris. 'Used to be beautiful – Regent's Park Basin.' He stopped, looked over his shoulder. There was no one in sight except a tipper lorry reversing, bearing more burst sandbags and rubble.

Finally, he turned to face Tom, and confessed, 'You can blame me. Someone thought it odd you were so keen to get N Section shut down.'

'Who? What bastard thought it was a good idea to spy on me?'

'I'm not at liberty to say. Only that it was I who asked Nancy Callaghan to investigate. If N Section's in the hands of the Nazis, then they must have had help. Help from an insider.'

'And you actually thought it was me?' The fact stung.

'You're new here. We didn't want to bother Mr Marks, but we had to be sure.'

119

How humiliating. 'Oh God. That man in the hotel, in the homburg hat. He was one of ours too, wasn't he?' Beauclerk didn't even need to answer. 'And what about Nancy? What did she tell you?'

'Nothing. Her report said there was nothing to tell. And we believe her, no reason not to.'

'So what does that mean? Am I in the clear, or what?'

'I've learned never to rush to conclusions.'

'You were quick enough to leap to a conclusion before, weren't you?' Tom said bitterly. 'You completely ruined it for me with Nancy.'

'Be careful.' Beauclerk's voice took on a steely tone. 'You know fraternising with other members of the Firm is highly undesirable. And the work we do must always come first. Above all else.'

'So what happens now?'

Beauclerk folded his arms. 'Nothing happens now. We carry on doing our job, just as we have been doing.'

'You mean that's it? You accuse me of being some sort of double agent and then just expect me to carry on as if nothing's happened?'

'That's exactly what we do expect. You're a good man and good at your job. You'd be hard to replace. We checked you out, and I think that perfectly acceptable in the circumstances.'

'If it's not me, then who is it?'

'No one. If there are irregularities in N Section, and I'm still not convinced there are, then I'm quite sure Blunt will ferret them out. And for your information your dismissal papers are already in my desk drawer. Don't make me have to sign them.' He paused, took a pack of Craven A from his pocket and tried to light one, but the breeze kept blowing out the match. Tom couldn't help noticing his hands were unsteady.

Tom cupped his hands around the flame to help him. After a few drags, Beauclerk looked Tom direct in the eye. 'See here, my best advice to you is to forget Nancy Callaghan, and just do your job and let me do mine.' He gestured around the park. 'I've got a bloody country to save.'

This was small comfort to Tom. He still couldn't fathom why Nancy hadn't just refused to do it. The fact she'd agreed, as if there might actually be truth in these accusations, still hurt.

Nancy's report to Beauclerk emphasised that Tom Lockwood seemed entirely above board. She'd done it straightaway, anxious to get rid of the taste of the whole disastrous weekend. She looked out for Tom, couldn't help it, hoped he'd be waiting for her the next day. But he'd avoided the cipher room, and there'd been no sign of him waiting for her after work, so she had to face the fact it was over. He hadn't resigned, for she caught glimpses of him in the canteen, but he cut her dead. It was as if a hole had been carved beneath her ribs. Should she write to him? But what could she say?

Neil asked her how the weekend had gone and she answered him in monosyllables before hiding out in her room. The next few days she pounced on the mail every day, but no letter came from Tom. In the daytime, Nancy kept on with her decoding work despite the fact she felt empty and everything seemed to have lost its colour. She was unsurprised when the summons came from Beauclerk. She had slept little for the fourth night running and wondered if she looked as exhausted as she felt.

'Thank you for your report,' Beauclerk said, tapping it where it lay on his desk. 'I believe you searched Lockwood's room and his effects thoroughly?'

'Yes, sir.' She hadn't confessed to the fact he'd driven off on his own for two hours – and he could have done anything in that time. 'I found nothing,' she insisted. 'No evidence at all of anything underhand. His briefcase was empty. If he's a spy then he's very careful and very well prepared, but I saw nothing to suggest he was anything but a person doing the job he was employed to do. He didn't call anyone. He took an interest in the

Thatched Barn – you'd have to be crazy not to be interested in what they do there – but he showed no desire to contact anyone afterwards. He seems totally committed to the SOE and the best way to support our agents abroad.'

'Yes, I was reassured and, I have to say, somewhat relieved by your report. And, of course, we had a man, Venner, stationed at the hotel too, to keep watch.'

She blinked. She hadn't noticed anyone.

'But Lockwood came to see me and wanted to hand in his notice. He'd obviously seen he was under surveillance and objected. I told him we had suspicions over why he wanted the N Section lines shut down, and as you can guess, he was not best pleased.'

She was aghast. 'Is he leaving?'

'No. I persuaded him to stay. Told him we were only acting in the best interests of security, and it was his patriotic duty to help our agents in the field. Flattered him a bit, said he was indispensable. Surprising how a bit of patriotic jingo can change people's minds.'

She frowned. She didn't like Beauclerk's manipulative manner. 'Did he say anything about how he knew he was being watched?'

'No details, except he'd seen Venner's car following him and noticed it was the same man in the hotel.'

So Tom hadn't told Beauclerk about their embarrassing little scene where he'd found her in his room. It made her feel even smaller. She'd had enough.

'I'd like to request to be stood down from these duties with Tom Lockwood.'

'Your brother tells me you are no longer seeing each other. Is that correct?'

Bloody Neil. Poking his nose in where it isn't wanted.

She didn't answer, and a lump seemed to have lodged in her throat, but Beauclerk seemed to take that as an assent. He steepled his hands and fixed her with a serious look. 'That being so, and in view of your report, we wondered if you'd like to take on special duties – a more active role in the SOE,' he said. When she didn't respond, he continued, 'We were impressed with how you conducted yourself, and would like to offer you the chance to volunteer for overseas duties.'

'Overseas?' At first the word was meaningless.

He helped her out. 'N Section, to be precise.'

'You mean to go into occupied Holland?'

'We don't ask everyone, but it seems you speak fluent Dutch and have the sort of coding skills we need, and we desperately need more women volunteers to act as wireless operators. Of course, you can say no, but we hope you'll consider it.'

'Does my brother know?'

'No. And you must tell no one, especially family members. It could put them, and you, at risk.'

Her palms were damp and she felt as if she were skewered to the chair. She struggled to find the right words. 'I heard some rumours, sir, that the Dutch Resistance lines have been compromised.'

Beauclerk gave a long-suffering sigh. 'And I can guess exactly where those rumours came from, but I can assure you they are totally without foundation. Of course there may be the occasional blown contact, that's to be expected, but we wouldn't be investing in such extensive training for our people if we thought there was any truth in the idea. Nevertheless, I can't beat about the bush; it isn't a task for the faint-hearted, and only the best and bravest are recruited. You understand the dangers?'

'Yes, sir. From our coding briefing.'

'So would you be prepared to give it a shot?'

Even though she knew the risks, for some reason, to be chosen for this job by Beauclerk felt like an accolade.

'We'll get you trained first, and then we'll see, shall we?'

'Yes, sir.' He'd assumed her agreement, and in some ways, it was a relief. She'd be away from here and away from her hurting heart.

'I'll contact the training centre in Guildford,' Beauclerk said, 'see if we can get you on the next course. It looks like you'll be going back to Scotland sooner than you thought. Agents go there for territorial training. You won't need an initial interview, as you've already proved your allegiance to our work.'

'Thank you, sir. I appreciate it.' Why was she thanking him?

'If anyone asks, you can tell them you're going to Birmingham to train with the FANYs as a nurse. We'll make you write a few postcards home to reassure your parents, and they'll be sent from there.'

She remembered the postcards at the Thatched Barn and it made her give a wry smile.

'What's funny?'

'Nothing, sir. Just I'd make a hopeless nurse. Can't stand the sight of blood.'

'Then you'll need to learn to, if you're to be any use to us.'

His eyes held not a shred of humour.

As she hurried along the top corridor from Beauclerk's office and rounded the corner to the stairs, she almost bumped straight into Tom. He had the cardboard box full of silk codes clasped to his chest and stopped dead when he saw her.

His face creased into an unhappy frown. 'About last weekend,' he said, 'I was angry and rude, and I overreacted. I've had a chat to Beauclerk, and I'm staying on. I'd like to be friends, if that's all right with you.' He shifted awkwardly from foot to foot. 'After all, we do have to work together.'

'Not for much longer,' she said, shielding her bruised heart with a matter-of-fact manner. 'I'm being transferred.'

Now his eyebrows shot up. 'Transferred? Where to?'

'I'm going to train with the FANYs. Drive an ambulance or something.'

'Where?' His expression was stricken.

'Don't know yet. But they need drivers and helpers, and I was never cut out for desk work.' She tossed her hair defiantly.

124

'But I thought you liked the work here?' he said. 'You were good at it, one of the best. You picked it up so quickly, you'll be wasted just driving a van.'

'Well, it will be good to have a change,' she said breezily, 'and Beauclerk says they need more staff there than here.' She suspected Beauclerk knew she was running away and was seizing this moment to strike. And he'd be right. She couldn't stand to see Tom every day while her heart ached so much, as if it had been crushed through a mangle. She turned to go down the stairs.

'Nancy? Have I done this?'

She paused. 'No,' she said breezily, not wanting to show how much he mattered. 'It was time for me to move on anyway.'

'When do you go?'

'I don't know exactly, but soon. Thanks for teaching me about coding, and . . .' She couldn't go on; emotion was choking her. 'Bye, Tom.' She fled down the stairs. At the bottom she glanced up to see him still leaning over the banister watching her go.

Chapter 15

Tom watched Nancy's back as she hurried away. He was pole-axed by her decision, and at the same time he knew it was probably his fault. She'd never mentioned any yearning to be a nurse before. He fiddled with his tie, wracked with guilt. He'd driven away a woman who was probably one of the greatest assets in the building. And the fact he'd never see her again was unthinkable.

He'd have to try to talk to her.

'You're in the way, Lockwood.' Beryl pushed past him.

'I was miles away. Sorry, I'm just on my way to see Beauclerk.'

'Have you an appointment?'

'Yes. Eleven o'clock.' He forced himself to forget Nancy and concentrate. His leg juddered up and down as he sat waiting in the lobby under Beryl's watchful eye. Finally, Beauclerk opened his door and summoned him inside with a crooked finger.

Immediately, he blurted, 'I saw Nancy Callaghan coming out of here a moment ago. She says she's being transferred. Did she give you any idea why?'

'Ah. I hear you've fallen out?'

'You made it impossible.' A sigh. 'I thought she was good at her job, so I wondered why she was leaving.'

'Yes, she told me you'd broken up. She wanted a change, I suppose.

That's women for you – fickle.' His gaze shifted away. 'Plenty more fish in the sea, eh, Lockwood?'

Tom bit back a retort. He was wretched. He doubted there'd be many like Nancy Callaghan.

Beauclerk shifted in his seat. 'Forget her. It's why we warn everyone not to fraternise – always causes hell. Have you got these new codes you've been hounding me about?'

With an effort, Tom pulled himself together. 'Like you suggested, I've brought you the new random code silks with the WOKs,' Tom said. 'With your permission, we'll begin using them right away.'

One of the sample silks had been rolled up in thin paper and slipped into a pack of Lucky Strike cigarettes. He shook the silk free. 'Once they've used the code, this is what they'll do. He took his penknife out and slit the bottom strip off the grid. Then he set fire to it and dropped the flaming residue into the ashtray.

'See? Gone.' Opening up a slit in his cuff, Tom pushed the remaining silk square back inside. 'Feel,' he said.

Beauclerk reached a tentative hand to Tom's sleeve. 'I see,' he said. 'Much less bulky than paper.' Beauclerk sat back and tapped his pen on his diary, seeming to stare into space. He looked gaunt; the fine lines around his eyes had deepened. 'All right,' he said, eventually. 'I'll sign it off. And Lockwood, take my word for it – there's nothing suspicious about the Dutch lines, hear me? We've got better things to do than go on some wild goose chase.'

Tom made no reply. He knew better than to spoil this moment. The fact he'd got the coding silks passed was a big achievement, and it would have to be reward enough for now. He'd tackle the Dutch lines next.

Neil and his colleagues leant over the map that was spread out on the table in the boardroom. It was a map of the Netherlands showing the border between Germany, Holland and Belgium. Their attention was centred on Arnhem and the Lek River and its meandering course towards Rotterdam. Major Blunt and Wing Commander Newsham from the Air Liaison section were deciding on the next drop point for British agents in the Netherlands.

Blunt favoured nearer to Rotterdam, and further from the German border.

'No,' said John Hancock, the geographer who'd brought the map from the foreign office. He traced his gangly finger over the red blob of the town. 'It's too hard to find a safe house in Rotterdam. The place has been flattened by German bombs and now their troops are demolishing the city centre. Except of course the Beurs Trade Centre, the City Hall and the post office, which are all hubs for the Gestapo and under strict Nazi control.'

'Then where?' Blunt asked, losing patience. 'Churchill wants us to prepare what he calls a "broad front" so when the Allies invade it will drive the German forces back into Germany.'

'If our troops ever invade,' Neil said gloomily under his breath.

Hancock ignored him with a roll of the eyes and stabbed a finger into a blank space. 'We have Resistance contacts here, here and here, from these small villages of Zetten, Opheusden and Doderwaard.'

And they're all controlled by Giskes, thought Neil.

'Agent Hockey tells us this place is a goer. It's agricultural land,' Hancock continued, 'so there are trees here, and there's a little cover and we can fly them in. Boat's too risky now they've started building the Atlantic Wall, and the coast is a literal minefield.'

'How many men?' Wing Commander Newsham of the RAF asked.

'No men for the air drop. They will all be women because of the *Arbeitseinsatz*. The Germans have drafted every single man over eighteen. More than three hundred thousand Dutch men are now working in German factories. Poor sods. Even worse, we keep bombing them. Women will be easier to camouflage.'

'So who'll be helping these women on the ground?' Newsham asked.

Hancock shrugged. 'Old men, farmers and those men who are allowed to stay. Doctors, essential workers. And some who refuse to work and are in hiding. It's dangerous work, and there are few volunteers. Without them though, we'd be sunk. We need these resistance cells to arrange collections of arms and supplies. Their task will be to coordinate a fighting force into units that will be able to support the Allies on demand.'

'Sounds like a thankless task. Half of Holland are Nazi sympathisers anyway,' Neil said.

'Thankless or not, those are our orders,' Blunt snapped.

More discussion ensued, including arguments about the best route to get downed airmen out of the Netherlands. The long route through Belgium and Switzerland, and over the Pyrenees south to a boat to Gibraltar would be the only feasible option, and this would have to be organised by the men or women on the ground.

Neil fidgeted during these painstaking plans. It was laughable. The chances of the airmen getting even as far as Belgium were remote. The Dutch lines were blown and the Waffen-SS was full of Dutch petty tyrants who'd seen a chance to grab some power. He rubbed his face; his chin had broken out in a rash of spots.

He waited for Newsham to decide on the drop zone, and took careful note of its co-ordinates. Otto would no doubt press him for these, and just the thought of it made him sweat. What would the Gestapo do to these women when they caught them? Could he fool Otto and pretend to know nothing?

He swallowed, stuck in a kind of nightmare. If the Germans found out afterwards he'd concealed this information, the outlook for him would be grim. A sense of despair gripped him. He couldn't go on. 'Excuse me,' he said. 'Out of ink.'

Barely seeing where he was going, he hurried out of the door and found his way back to his office, now mercifully empty. He sat down and put his head between his knees, staring at the bare floorboards.

The urge to tell someone, to confess it all was almost irresistible. But then he thought of Nancy and his mother and father.

What would it do to them to have to live with the humiliation? His name would be everywhere, and he'd only ever be remembered for his treachery. Not for the fact he was a skilled cellist, not for his voice in the university barbershop quartet, not for the fact he was the only one in the family whose knee their cat deigned to sit on.

He'd be the person they talked of with shame. If they ever remembered him at all.

He took a ragged breath and rubbed his hands over his face before wiping the sweat onto the knees of his trousers. He'd have to go back soon or it would look odd. He mentally packaged himself back into order and prepared to go back into the boardroom with a fresh pen. With luck they would have finished the meeting and he wouldn't have to hear anything else.

If only the war would end soon. But he knew from the desperate discussions they were having that the end of the war was nowhere in sight, and as he walked back, he fantasised about shooting Otto. The same fantasy he had day after day, in which he pulled the trigger and Otto fell.

But it was fantasy. Giskes and his Nazi friends would eliminate him if he did that.

Still, he knew where the guns were kept, and the keys to the locked gun cupboards.

Chapter 16

Neil had been summoned by Otto to The Cavendish. Unusually, today, Otto invited Neil up to his room. They went up the staff stairs at the back to avoid meeting anyone in the lift. Otto's room was the one closest to the stairs, so they saw no one. Obviously, Otto had thought all this out in case he needed a hasty getaway. Otto placed his revolver, complete with silencer, on the bedside table while he sat on the edge of the bed. It was there to make Neil sweat; he knew. If he had a gun too, he'd feel much safer.

'Did you get the poem codes?' Otto asked, as Neil sat stiffly in the chair near the window.

'No,' Neil said. 'But there's talk of a new method of coding anyway.'

'What new method?'

'I don't know. It's under wraps. I just heard a bit of a buzz about it from Blunt. He seems to think it will make agents' lives easier, but he won't tell me anything of course.'

'Then you need to make it your business to find out. Giskes won't be happy if his *Englandspiel* stops functioning. We closed down one of the Biesbosch escape routes only last week. A great success – fifteen arrests, though once the Gestapo start work, more will follow. We want to make sure that continues.'

So many. And all because one man had caved in to the Gestapo in the beginning. Otto had told Neil about that first man. His name was Lauwers and it was way back in 1941. Since then, every N Section message had been sent to England under Nazi instruction. What with Lauwers' information and Neil's from London, every agent, convinced the Nazis already knew everything, had caved in and told the enemy all their contacts.

The Nazis knew it all. Neil closed his mind to it. Focused on the lamp on the bedside table with its gold fringe and pleated shade.

Otto coolly adjusted his fake spectacles on his nose. 'Okay, Neil, here's the thing. You've been a little quiet lately and Giskes is getting antsy. Canaris, the head of *Abwehr* intelligence, is putting pressure on him, and in turn, he's leaning on our man, King. We need to know when and where the next drop will be in case it contains information about the Allies' invasion plans. N Section's gone quiet all of a sudden, and we know from other sources that the invasion's coming. Not that it will bother us, but best to lose as few men as possible.'

Neil's shirt was clammy under his suit jacket. 'It's not my fault. Tom Lockwood, the new coding man, is on to us. Right now, though, Beauclerk doesn't want to know because it's too awkward – he doesn't want to put the wind up his old buddy Blunt. Fortunately for us, Blunt's so pig-headed he can't see the wood for the trees – just wants to bury his head in the sand, and pretend his section's a roaring success.'

'So what's this about Lockwood and new coding methods?'

'Thing is, Lockwood was shouting his mouth off even before all this, about an N Section sked that had arrived without the transmission codes. That should be a red light to any decoder. You should tell your men to make sure they send them with the codes.'

'The men are not trained coders. They do their best. But yes, I'll tell them. Is London suspicious?'

'I think I managed to defuse the situation enough. And the ruse of adding some errors to the skeds is definitely working, so it took the heat off, and now Beauclerk's satisfied enough. But Lockwood's determined to update the system anyway.'

'Sounds like Lockwood's a problem.'

'He's like a terrier with a bone. He's convinced there's something going on, but I'm trying to hold him off.'

Otto sucked in his cheeks, ruminating. 'No chance he might be able to be persuaded to help us?'

Neil shook his head. 'Not a hope in hell.' This bald fact made him feel even smaller. The fact he himself had sold out to Otto was like a thorn in his chest. Instead of making him feel clever, it just made him feel ashamed.

'If he gets too vocal we might have to find a way to disable him,' Otto said.

Neil swallowed. He remembered another man who had had his knees broken and been found face down in the Thames. And he couldn't tell Otto he'd tried to push blame for the leak on to Lockwood because he knew they'd think he was a dangerous fool, drawing attention to the leak rather than hiding it. And he'd need to be on the right side of Otto after the Nazis took over.

'We've had intelligence that the invasion will come from the Pas-de-Calais. We expect you to get as much information to us about that as you can. Maps and so forth. We'll need to tighten up, close down the lines of escape so no one can get intelligence about our German troops back to England. All British agents will be eliminated from now on. We can't let any agents get through, it's too late in the game to create new agent networks even if we put them under Nazi control.' He handed over a small package in a leather case. 'A micro-camera, complete with microfilm. We expect you to use it. Poem codes, maps, whatever you can get us.'

Neil took it as if it burned his fingers. Words were one thing. Having hard evidence stowed about your person quite another. The new Treachery Act meant the death penalty for anyone aiding the enemy. Which was the better death? Killed by fascist sympathisers like Otto, or killed by your own countrymen? He hadn't got an answer.

Tom searched his pockets again before setting off for work. He'd mislaid the crucial message 243 he'd sent to the Dutch lines, and though he'd searched everywhere he hadn't found it. It worried him because coded messages were never supposed to leave the building, and hadn't he yelled at Nancy for exactly the same crime?

After braving the scurrying rush hour of bicycle bells and running feet, he stood in front of his pigeonhole and flicked through the internal memos. Still no reply to his urgent letters to head office about the N Section lines. But talks must be going on somewhere because the RAF had suddenly become reluctant to supply N Section with planes.

He'd bet his life they'd seen that the flights to the Netherlands always arrived without a hitch, and that there was never any trouble finding a suitable drop spot. On the other hand, planes were shot down all too often on their return trip to England. No less than twelve in the last year. Giving planes to N Section was getting too expensive.

Major Blunt, stubborn as usual, wouldn't give up. He was still trying to obtain planes, or so the messages to the agents in the Netherlands suggested. Tom hoped the RAF would hold out. He shoved the pile of telexed memos back into his pigeonhole and headed for the coding room to pick up any indecipherables.

When he'd dashed up the stairs with the latest batch, the buzz of conversation stopped as soon as he opened the door. The women in the decoding room were subdued. 'What's up?' he asked Daisy. 'You look like a wet weekend.'

She hesitated, looked around for reassurance. 'I just heard . . . agent Fenna didn't make it.'

'You're not supposed to gossip about individual agents. But

it's understandable I suppose that you'd take a special interest in the women.'

'They're saying it was an accident. A wound from a German bullet became infected, and she died in hospital.'

'How awful. Which hospital?' one of the girls asked.

'They didn't say,' Daisy said.

They never say, he thought. *The agent always has an accident and never makes it home.*

'Enough chat now,' he said. He sat down on one of the spare chairs and rubbed his forehead. Another life lost without reason. He longed to talk to Nancy, but he'd ruined that chance, and besides, today her desk was bare. He kept glancing at the empty chair.

'Is Nancy all right?' he asked Daisy. 'She's not at her desk today.'

'She's at home,' Daisy said, 'packing. She's going tomorrow morning. Neil says they're sending a car to take her to the station.'

Her sympathetic expression was hard to bear.

'You'll miss her,' Tom said to Daisy, knowing he really meant that he would.

'Just won't be the same without her,' Daisy said. 'Can't understand why she wants to leave,' she said, looking pointedly at him.

Tom left the pile of indecipherables on the desk. 'Get these done soon as you can,' he said, before he hurried out of the door.

Nancy was going tomorrow. He had to see her. Who knew when he'd get another chance? He leant against the stairwell wall and scribbled a pencil note for Beauclerk pretending he had an urgent meeting. He bounded downstairs, shoved the scrap of paper in Beauclerk's pigeonhole and set off by bus to Nancy's flat.

The wind was howling down the street, blowing a tin can, bomb debris and dust along the gutter. There was the rancid smell of old burning from the previous night's incendiaries. Bits of cloth curtain that looked as though they'd come from a bomb site were caught around the remains of the railings. He rang the doorbell and waited. Nobody answered. He rang again.

A clatter of shoes on the stairs, and the door opened.

Her face immediately flushed red, and her auburn hair blew wildly around her face. She pushed it out of her eyes.

'I had to see you,' he said. 'I don't want you to go until we've had a chance to talk.'

'There's nothing to say.'

'The coding room's not the same without you. Just give me five minutes.'

'I can't.' She was holding the door to stop it slamming in the wind. 'It's too late. I'm going away tomorrow.'

'I know. Daisy told me. Can I at least write to you?'

'Better not to,' she said. 'Better to have a clean break.'

'There's never been another woman,' he said. 'There's only ever been you.'

She lowered her eyes. 'I know.'

'Then what the heck is it all about? Why are you leaving Baker Street?'

'I can't tell you.'

'What do you mean, you can't tell me?'

She shook her head, but when she looked up, he could see some sort of conflict in her eyes.

'What's going on, Nancy?'

Again, she was silent. He wanted to shake her. 'Is it Neil?' No answer. 'Is it to do with the Firm?'

A flicker in her expression. He was right. He stepped back, reeling. Thoughts rampaged around his head.

'I'm sorry, Tom,' she said. 'Some things are more important than us.' Very slowly she shut the door and the Yale latch clicked into place.

He rang the doorbell again and again but she wouldn't answer.

Perplexed, he stared up at the flat as if the very windows might give him some answers. Something blew and clattered in the road behind him.

Her brother. Callaghan. He must have something to do with making her want to join the FANYs. A flame of anger made Tom

136

stride out down the road. He replayed the weekend when it had all started to go wrong.

Tom walked past the bus stop deep in thought. Who else had him on a list of suspicious employees? Blunt? Hambro? Where had the whole idea come from? God help him if Mr Marks ever found out. If someone was giving classified information to the Nazis, and it involved codes and coding, he needed to know. What he couldn't understand was why they ever let it pass? If he was them, he'd have made an arrest straightaway on the first suspicion.

Suddenly realising he'd gone past the bus stop, he stopped to orientate himself and turned off towards Kilburn Park Underground station. In the rattle of the train, he pondered over the fact that because agents' lives were so anonymous, the powers that be thought the SOE had an endless supply, and agent security could always wait. But he'd trained agent Fenna, seen her suck the end of her pencil as she wrestled with the transcription, seen her bitten fingernails and her determination to put her life at risk with a joke and a smile. It broke his heart. For him, every agent who'd crossed his path was personal.

When he got back to his tiny broom cupboard of an office, he stood and stared out of the window on to the brick wall behind. It had hit him hard that Nancy was leaving Baker Street. He bet Neil had something to do with it all. Right from the beginning, Neil seemed to be trying to set him and Nancy apart. Tom had tried to befriend him, but he could feel the antagonism coming off him from a mile off. He couldn't shake the idea that it was Callaghan who'd told Beauclerk he was a security risk. There was only one reason why Callaghan might do that, and that was to deflect the heat from himself.

Well, two could play at that game. If Neil was the leak in N Section, thought Tom, then he'd be the first to know. He'd keep tabs on Callaghan and see where he went.

Chapter 17

Nancy hugged Neil. 'I'll write,' she said, 'send you a postcard from Birmingham.' Last week she'd written the postcards that would go to family and friends on her close contacts list. Several with a picture of Birmingham General Hospital, and more of Victoria Square. All had general anodyne messages saying she was well and enjoying the work. She thrust the postcards out of her mind and clung to Neil a moment, painfully aware this might be the last time she would ever see him.

'Stay safe, Sis,' he said. 'You're better off out of London.'

Not true. Last week a German air raid killed a hundred children in a cinema in East Grinstead. They were watching a Hopalong Cassidy film when the bombers struck. But London was so much more of a target. She hoped Neil would be okay. Tears threatened. She swallowed them back.

'Hey, Nance?' he said. 'It's only Birmingham, not the end of the world!'

'I know,' she mumbled. 'Sorry, I'm being stupid. Don't work too hard.'

'I won't.' He seemed almost relieved to see her go, and quite cheerful. He helped load her bags into the car, driven by a woman in a FANY uniform, and slammed the door shut.

Once in the car, she wound down the window and waved at his lone figure on the doorstep, hoping her deception hadn't shown. She hadn't realised she'd feel so cut up about leaving him. Her big brother. *Keep him safe*, she prayed.

'All right?' the freckle-faced driver said, in broad cockney.

Nancy smiled wanly, turning her head for a last glimpse of Neil.

'I'm to take you to Waterloo, and your travel tickets for Guildford and permits are in my bag,' the woman said, efficiently accelerating away. 'Someone else will collect you at the other end.'

'Okay.' Nancy sat back as the woman drove. They skirted the Lyons' Corner House near Charing Cross and it made Nancy wince. She still couldn't get Tom Lockwood's face out of her mind. The thought that she should never have agreed to Beauclerk's demands. She'd betrayed Tom, and he must have been so hurt by the whole business. She sighed. It was too late to undo it all now. She was on her way.

Why was she such a disaster with men? This training was a chance to be a success at something. To be a vital part of the war effort. If she was to be some sort of spy, then she wanted to be spying on the enemy, not on her friends. But missing Tom was a pain she couldn't escape. She marvelled that her affair with Andrew had seemed thin in comparison with what she felt for Tom. She hoped one day Tom would understand her choices and forgive her. If they ever saw each other again.

PART TWO

Chapter 18

The military induction course lasted three weeks, during which time Nancy barely had a moment to breathe, let alone think of Tom. Winterfold House at Cranleigh was a dilapidated country mansion, so shabby and faded it was hard to believe anyone had actually existed there. Sleep was interrupted by the scurrying of mice, and all hope of it fled at the heart-stopping clangour of a fire alarm at 5.30 a.m. Of course, there was no fire. It was just to get them out of bed.

Shivering in shorts more suitable for a girl's PT lesson, she followed the rest for a punishing cross-country run, which finished at an assault course through freezing mud, specially hosed for the purpose. Determined to beat Iris, the only other female recruit, Nancy forced her burning thighs to push harder, until, weak from a scrambling ascent up what seemed to be a never-ending mountain of logs, she saw Iris already nimbly running back towards the finish, barely out of breath.

No concessions at all were made for the women, though she got the impression she was considered something of a nuisance by the male instructors, who sighed and shook their heads over their stopwatches every time Nancy came panting back, legs spattered with mud. Iris, of course, managed to make even PT uniform look like French chic, and raced through it all like a thoroughbred, earning many admiring glances from the men.

At the end of the course, she and Iris were whisked away by car to Hendon Aerodrome to board a plane for Scotland. Nancy had never been in a plane.

'Eh, best enjoy,' said Iris, in her heavy French accent. 'Next time they will be wanting us to jump out of him.'

It was a sobering thought, and the fact there was only a slice of tin between her and thin air gave her the jitters. With a judder they were up in the air, and two hours later, touched down with a bump. After a draughty ride in a freezing train and then a battered car, they arrived in the grounds of Arisaig House. Nancy's first impression, as she climbed from the car, was that it looked more like a haunted house from a film than a training camp – high forbidding stone walls and massive chimneys. The rain was lashing down.

'*Mon Dieu, quelle horreur,*' Iris said. 'Worse than Cranleigh.' They tramped across the field with their luggage, rain sluicing over them until they might as well have landed in the nearby loch.

Inside, the furniture was sparse and functional, and the place was ice-cold.

Iris complained about the state of her hair all the way up to their room, a spartan twin with creaking beds. Iris found a towel, but Nancy was so exhausted she threw off her clothes, pulled on damp pyjamas and fell asleep instantly. It was only the next day that she saw the view from the window. Her heart lifted. There was no mistaking the Scottish landscape – the heather-covered hills and rugged woods leading to flat meadows, the inevitable Scottish mist and drizzle softening the harsh outlines of the mountains. Nancy's first feeling was one of homecoming and relief; there was little sign of war here.

Or so she thought. Lessons in silent killing began the same morning, euphemistically entitled 'Unarmed Combat'. Nancy was sceptical when she saw their instructors – two mild elderly gentlemen in suits, the long-faced, white-haired Fairbairn, and the bespectacled Sykes. But as soon as they started giving orders, their manner dispelled any doubts. Precise, no-nonsense, with the kind of authority you just daren't question. Even the men knew by instinct that Fairbairn and Sykes were not to be messed with.

The recruits' initial task was to pull a man to the ground. The tackler was always smaller than the supposed 'enemy', and Nancy was teamed with another Dutchman known as Klaas. One look at him was enough. He was a huge boulder of a man who must have weighed about sixteen stone.

She just couldn't budge him. He never even flinched as she flapped around him like a fly, tugging and yanking, feeling more and more frustrated and incompetent.

A cry of outrage and pain from the couple fighting next to her, and the man toppled and thudded to the ground, groaning and clutching his groin. Iris stood over him with a wicked grin.

Fairbairn clapped. 'Good work, Iris. Always go for the weakest point.' He exchanged a glance with Sykes and the two instructors charged in like a whirlwind. Within seconds, all the standing men were down.

Nancy was open-mouthed. Even Iris paled.

It transpired both men were former members of the Shanghai Police, trained in martial arts and undercover assault. Underneath their tidy suits lurked experienced commandos, wiry, tough and full of surprises.

Sykes fixed his eyes on Nancy. 'Nothing you will be taught here will depend on size and strength,' he said. 'The Germans will almost certainly be bigger and heavier and better-armed than you.'

A sobering but realistic assessment. Nancy began to appreciate the fact that Fairbairn and Sykes' techniques were unorthodox but deadly.

By the end of the first morning, Nancy could fold a newspaper into a sharp point and knew exactly where in the throat to jab to cause an opponent to black out. She'd learnt how to leap in first, to tackle an opponent with a headlock, armlock, or more gruesomely, fingernails to the eyes.

She was still wary of the men though, who were far more proficient, many of them having come straight from army training, but she was determined to keep up with Iris, who, despite her slim figure, was quick, sharp and vicious as a cornered rat.

Before they could break for lunch, all the trainees, including Iris and Nancy, who had taken the cover name Jean, were ordered to line up. The exercise was to garrotte 'Germans' from behind with a belt or scarf. Women had to always have a scarf about their person when passing as a Dutch person in Holland, or a French person in France.

'Go!' yelled Sykes.

Nancy slung her scarf around the enemy's neck. The 'Germans' – hessian sacks which had been sewn together and stuffed with straw – were now dangling from a tree.

'Tighter!' yelled Fairbairn as Nancy tugged on the tourniquet. 'The bastard's still alive. Finish him off!'

Nancy's muscles were still screaming from trying to upend heavier men with judo techniques. She looked to her left to see Iris pulling with a vengeance. Damned if she'd let her win again.

'Good!' Fairbairn yelled. 'Squeeze the breath out of him.'

Nancy gritted her teeth and strained until Sykes called, 'Enough. Good work!'

It was the first time anyone had ever praised her. Her spirits raised. Maybe she could do this after all. Then a notice went up on the training blackboard. Tomorrow they were to start 'armed combat'.

More learning. Before Cranleigh she'd only ever handled a gun once. On a shoot with Andrew. He'd squeezed his hand over hers on the trigger, missed, then cursed her that he hadn't got venison for supper. Later he'd shot a duck and its limp lifeless body had made her nauseous. Now there was to be shooting tomorrow. Ugh.

Nancy dragged herself up to the room she shared with Iris.

Iris was sitting on the edge of her bed, painting her nails.

'I don't know how you've got the energy to do that,' Nancy said. 'What wouldn't I do for a hot bath. I've got aches on my aches.' Nancy eased her throbbing legs up onto the bed.

'*C'est important*. I don't want to turn into a man. Being a woman is a weapon, no? In training, it reminds the men what we are.'

Nancy frowned. 'It's "armed combat" tomorrow. I can't imagine firing a gun with red fingernails.'

'Neither can the Boche. Want some? Or don't they wear it in Holland?'

'I don't know. We might get into trouble with Fairbairn or Sykes.'

Iris threw back her head and laughed. 'Trouble? Already we are in trouble! And we volunteer for it! In France, thank God, French women won't stop being French women, even with the Germans. Nothing a man likes more than to see a woman's red nails against his naked flesh.'

Nancy tried not to look shocked.

Iris screwed the top on the bottle and wafted her fingers back and forth. 'You don't want a man? Have you someone waiting for you at home?'

A hesitation. 'No. Not exactly. There was someone . . . but we agreed to go separate ways.'

'He cheat on you?'

'It wasn't like that. It was my fault.'

Iris raised her eyebrows. 'Ah. The way you talk of him, I can see he means something. I'm right, no?'

'I treated him badly. I should have apologised.'

'Ha, men! No use crying over it now. Besides, you'll have the pick of a thousand German troops soon.' She grinned.

'You wouldn't date a German!'

'If it meant I could kill him, *mais oui*.' A pause. 'My house, it was destroyed when they bomb Paris in 1940. Maman was inside

147

peeling potatoes. Now I have no home, no family to go back to. My brother, Léo, he lives with my uncle now. I do this for him. He will never forgive that they destroy our lives. She was dead when they dug her out.' Iris looked up. 'The Boche have made Paris a graveyard.'

'Don't hold your rifle like that . . . you look like you're holding a doll,' Sykes shouted. 'Take charge of the bloody thing!'

'What the blazes does it matter to you how I hold it as long as it kills the enemy?' With that, Nancy fired off a round of shots into the straw-stuffed dummy.

'Better!' called Sykes. 'That's the spirit.'

At which point, Iris, determined not to be outdone, spattered her dummy into flying strands of straw.

Before the dummies could be cut down, Sykes handed Nancy a smatchet – a dull black-bladed knife. The smatchet, he told her, was designed not to reflect light, and it was for clandestine, nighttime killing. It would be stored at the front of her pack.

Nancy took it gingerly, weighing the solid heaviness of it, squeamish at the glint of its honed edge. Was she really supposed to use such a medieval-looking thing? But Iris was already hacking at her target, so Nancy copied her and leapt in to swipe the smatchet across the dummy's chest. As the hessian split and the straw heart was exposed, she suddenly realised what it was all for. These were not dummies. These were men. The thought wouldn't let go.

Sweating, and aching all over, Nancy flopped down into the muddy grass. She'd had enough.

Fairbairn came over and squatted beside her. She heard the creak of his knees. 'You need to get up,' Fairbairn said, quietly. 'Look, we're talking life and death here. If your cover is ever compromised by a German, you mustn't think. It must be automatic. You must, I repeat must, attack first. Got it?'

She dipped her head in assent, too tired to object. His wrinkled blue eyes were penetrating hers with a peculiar intensity.

148

'Then, whatever happens, don't wait. Persist till the enemy is neutralised – never stop at just an injury, or they might find a way to fight back and disable you. Always go for the kill.' He eased himself back to standing. 'Get up, Jean.'

'I can't.'

'You can.' His voice was like steel.

Nancy blundered to her feet and stabbed and slashed the dummy multiple times until Fairbairn called, 'Okay, Jean, okay – you got him. Well done.'

At night she came out in a cold sweat as she contemplated having to actually use a knife on someone's soft flesh. Later, she woke in a panic with Iris pressing a hand over her mouth. 'You talk in English. Fool. If you do that it will blow your cover.'

Disorientated, but ashamed of her lack of control, she cursed Iris, Fairbairn, Sykes and the whole of the SOE.

By day three, none of the trainees could move. Reduced to going down stairs crabwise because of her aching muscles, Nancy slid into a seat for breakfast to see that even the enormous Klaas was limping in, looking the worse for wear.

At their table they were joined by Fairbairn and Sykes. 'Good job, ladies,' Sykes said, today looking every inch the benign grandfather. 'First few days are the worst, and you've stuck at it. And survival is much more about wit and will than you might think.'

Survival. The word meant so much more to her now. These men, Fairbairn and Sykes, made her think of her father, of his intense loyalty to Britain. Gas attacks and trenches in the Great War had made Father hate the Germans, despite her mother's attempts to build bridges between him and her European friends in Holland.

Father would so be proud she was doing this. Though the irony was, he'd probably wish it was Neil not her, and that she was safe in some secretarial job. She sighed. Neil's old injury had put paid to any sort of combat.

She took a bite of toast and margarine and thought of Neil blithely running this whole show with Beauclerk and Blunt from the dusty corridors of stiff-upper-lip Baker Street. He'd have no actual idea what it meant to be an agent, the fear of having to kill.

And for a moment she wished Tom Lockwood was here to see how well she was doing. She felt different: harder, more alert. She remembered Tom saying that agents in occupied zones lasted about six weeks. The thought haunted her. Six Tuesdays. Six Sundays.

She wanted to last longer than that. Besides, like a train running on rails to its destination, there was no possible way now of turning back.

'What job are you going for?' Nancy asked Iris. From initial hostility, the two had become firm friends. By the end of the course, they were to be assigned roles so they could do further training.

'Courier,' Iris replied. 'They won't let women be *saboteurs* in France. *Et tu?*'

'Wireless op. Though I daren't wear a short-sleeved frock anymore, my muscles look like Popeye! They're sending me for two weeks acclimatisation training – you know, map work, living off the land, Dutch etiquette.'

'Then we wait, eh?' Iris was rueful. 'I can't wait to kill my first German.'

'I'll be stuck behind a radio. Probably won't get the chance.'

Iris shrugged. 'Then make one. I will.'

Chapter 19

Neil picked up the mail from the doormat and sifted through it. Mail was notoriously late now – a shortage of postmen and drivers, plus the fact that the London post offices kept being bombed.

Bills, bills, bills. Then a postcard. A picture of Birmingham Royal Hospital. It looked to be an imposing Victorian building. He turned it over to read it.

Enjoying the training and the work. Birmingham much bigger than I thought. Lots of patients, and am learning to drive an ambulance. Hope you are well and enjoying having the flat to yourself!

Nancy x

She hadn't dated it, so he glanced at the postmark. Only posted a couple of weeks ago, not bad. He shoved the postcard in his briefcase along with the rest of the mail. It would cheer up his desk at work, and it was nice to imagine Nancy doing work with the FANYs. He imagined her in her neat khaki uniform and cap. Much better she was away from here, somewhere safe, where Otto and his fascist friends could never get their hands on her.

Neil packed his briefcase with a round of sandwiches wrapped in greaseproof paper. Carefully, he folded some tissue and another piece of greaseproof paper around his camera, sealed it with an elastic band, and tucked it into his lunch tin. It reminded him of the *Appeltaart* his mother used to make and pack up for him at boarding school.

He closed the lid. No one would examine his lunch. He'd taken the same tartan tin to work every day since he started more than three years ago and he always went out of the office to eat it. The first few times it had been searched, but now Jimmy never bothered. Some days if the film in the camera was used up, he'd drop it to the London Library so Otto could get it developed and send it on to Jack King.

In the office today, Neil took his time to photograph some pamphlets from the Italian Section – due to be dropped over the Italian mainland with the message *Die for Mussolini and Hitler, or live for Italy and for civilization*, a message which was also to go out on all Allied radio broadcasts. This laughable English attempt at anti-fascist propaganda was supposed to undermine Mussolini, who was under pressure from the Fascist Party to respond to the invasion of Italy. Rattled, Mussolini was about to convene the Fascist Grand Council for the first time since 1939.

Neil gave a dry hack of a laugh. Mussolini and Hitler – the most powerful men on the globe! What good would these pathetic pieces of paper do?

He also photographed a memo from the Air Ministry which gave approval for the use of what they were calling *Window* – the aluminium strips manufactured by one of Otto's friends in London, an Austrian named Kohout. Supposedly *Window* would act as a countermeasure against the German anti-aircraft trackers.

But recently he'd had a feeling he was being watched. It was nothing he could pinpoint, but just a feeling. He'd have to be careful, persuade Otto he'd have to wait a little longer for the documents he wanted.

Tom stood outside the bus stop at the end of Princess Road where he could monitor Neil Callaghan as he entered or left the house. He'd done this for weeks, varying his watching posts so

Neil wouldn't spot him. He'd even bought a tweed flat cap from a market stall and taken off his glasses, hoping it would be enough of a disguise; he was under no illusion that Callaghan would certainly know who he was if he got close enough.

Tom shifted his weight and leant on the corner post by the timetable. He was distracting himself, he knew. It was all a waste; Callaghan had done nothing suspicious, unless you could count going to the London Library in his lunch hour and coming out with a pile of books. Callaghan had gone home every night from Baker Street and never ventured out once. Probably reading all those books. Even when the siren went, he stayed put.

Tom had begun to question his own sanity, standing out here night after night. It was Nancy, he supposed, and his urge to still have some connection with her. He wondered if Callaghan had heard how she was, whether she'd ever visit him on leave, yet he baulked at asking him outright. It would be showing too much of his hand. He wished he could just have a chance to sit with her again at the Corner House and iron it all out.

Tom squinted at the blur of his watch. Eight o'clock. He was long-sighted, which meant he needed glasses for coding or close work, but could see distances perfectly clearly. Princess Road was empty, apart from a skinny cat streaking across from one side to the other. Should he go home? If he did, he'd have to give up the idea that it was Callaghan who'd told Beauclerk that Tom was a security risk.

Suddenly, movement. The door opened and Neil hurried down his front steps, striding briskly up the road in his uneven lurching walk, heading, Tom presumed, for Kilburn Park Underground station. He wore a fawn mackintosh and homburg hat pulled low despite the summer warmth. Tom lowered his head and turned away, concealing himself behind the other bus passengers as Neil hurried past, then he began to follow him, walking a good way behind.

He almost lost sight of him at the turnstiles and had to run to keep up. There were quite a few shift workers about, now the evenings were longer. People were anxious to get home before the blackout.

Neil got on the train and Tom made a leap for the neighbouring carriage. As the stations passed, he kept an eye on the platform, but when Neil got off at Piccadilly Circus, he almost missed him and had to lean out of the window to grab the carriage door and haul it open. On the way up the stairs, he lowered his head and kept behind an old woman pushing a bogie weighed down with a roll of singed carpet and what looked like most of her possessions. He fixed his attention firmly on Neil's homburg hat.

As if he could feel Tom's eyes on him, Neil suddenly turned and looked over his shoulder. Instantly, Tom turned away pretending to light a cigarette and let the other passengers rush past him.

Tom ran frantically to catch up, out from the underground tunnel and into the air, scanning the streets. Ah. Just there, turning the corner. Neil glanced behind once, then he was swallowed up by the doors of The Cavendish Hotel. Surprisingly, despite bomb damage, the hotel was still standing and operating. Tom peered gingerly inside, glad to see the lobby bristling with servicemen in uniform. He went in under the illuminated sign, now dark and cracked, but stayed by the taproom door looking into the lounge, which was furnished in burgundy plush upholstery and brass.

He caught a glimpse of Callaghan at a small table in an alcove. He was engaged in a terse conversation with an angular individual with slicked-back fair hair and a prominent Adam's apple. Callaghan looked pale and fearful, whereas the other man, in tortoiseshell spectacles, gave the impression of being a typical aristocrat. Within a few moments though, the aristocrat downed his beer and the two men left, Callaghan limping behind the other man like a dog.

Tom approached the bar, where an elderly barman was wiping glasses. 'I think I saw a friend of mine in here a moment ago – Mr Callaghan.'

'Oh yes, you just missed him.'

'Shame. I thought it was him! Who was that he was with? I don't think I know him.'

'You mean Mr Johnson? He works for the London Library. Researcher. Often stays here when he's in town.'

The library. The place Callaghan went to so often in his lunch hour. 'Is he a particular friend of Callaghan's then?'

The barman stopped polishing his glass and frowned. 'You're asking a lot of questions. Do you want a drink or not?'

'Sorry, yes. Always been nosy.' He tried to extricate himself from the situation. 'I'll take a pint of Charrington's, please.'

The barman pulled the pint, watching him with suspicion as he felt obliged to take a seat at one of the copper-topped tables and sup his pint. He took out a notebook from his pocket and wrote down *Johnson, London Library*.

The next day, feeling like a sleuth, Tom gave up his lunch hour to go to the London Library. It struck him he was becoming obsessed with the idea of pinning something on Callaghan, of getting revenge on whoever had labelled him a security risk. These people were like a tangled knot around Nancy too, a knot he was desperate to unravel.

'I'd like to speak to Mr Johnson, please.' Tom had planned a cover story if Johnson was in there, or turned up – he'd pretend to be a journalist interested in the evacuation of books at the library and try to get a measure of him.

The young red-haired woman behind the desk frowned. 'I don't think we . . . hang on a minute.' She hurried away to speak with another older woman in glasses, who came over to help.

'I'm afraid we have no Mr Johnson. Are you sure you have the name right?'

'Yes. I was told he works here.'

'D'you mean Mr Johnstone?' asked the older librarian. 'But he retired a few years ago when the hostilities started. Could that be him?'

155

'Doubt it, if he's retired. Too old. Mine's a tall chap, glasses, blond hair, late twenties?'

'Oh!' The younger woman smiled, patted her rolled-up hair. 'I know who you mean. Ollie Johnson, right?' She blushed. 'He doesn't actually work here, but he comes in often to read the papers. Reads them all, cover to cover most days, and sometimes he reads all day in the reading room. Books on engineering, mostly. I haven't seen him today though.'

So, he lied to that barman about working at the London Library.

'It's urgent,' Tom improvised. 'I need his address. His father's house was struck by a bomb last night, and I need to contact him. Has he got a library card?'

The young librarian's eyes widened. 'No! How terrible.'

'Let me take a look.' The middle-aged one clipped over on high heels to the filing cabinet and opened the drawer marked G–H. A few moments later she was back with a card. 'Yes, here's his address.' She put it down on the counter.

The Cavendish Hotel. Of course. He lived there, not at a proper London address at all. 'I'm really most grateful,' Tom said. 'I'll go straight there.'

The younger woman picked up the card to put it back. 'I hope you find him. Sad news about his father. If you should miss each other and he comes in here, who shall I tell him was asking for him?'

Tom hadn't thought that far ahead. He glanced at a pile of books under the shelf and picked a name. 'Frank O'Connor,' he said. 'Mr Johnson knows my address.'

As he went out, he could hear the women's buzz of conversation behind him, but time was ticking by, and he needed to get back to work. He walked back to Baker Street with a spring in his step.

Maybe Oliver Johnson was another of their SOE men from another section. Or maybe not; he thought he knew most people by sight. He'd tail him for a few days, couldn't do any harm. He had an instinct something about Callaghan was off-kilter and

Oliver Johnson was involved. He couldn't stop thinking about Callaghan's peaky face when he was talking to Johnson. They hadn't looked like friends or colleagues. In fact, Callaghan had looked scared.

Chapter 20

Nancy gripped the handrail tight as she stepped out onto the platform and took in the dizzying view of the lawns below. Fulshaw Hall must have been a grand house once, because the gardens were laid out in parterres with ornamental topiary at the borders. A peacock was strutting past, the blue-green iridescent sweep of its long tail behind.

Nancy dragged her attention back to the parachute harness and took hold of the straps.

'Ready?' called a man's voice from the room below.

'Ready,' she replied, though she wasn't and thought she might be sick. A window in the left-hand gable of the hall had been removed, and a high stage erected with a hole cut in it, to look like the hole in the floor of a Whitley bomber. Nancy peered through the hole and swallowed. The coconut mat was an awful long way down.

'Remember, legs together,' came the shout. 'Go!'

A whirring noise as someone switched on the fan in the window below. A powerful draught sucked at her knees, mimicking a plane's slipstream.

'Go on, Nancy!' Iris yelled. Iris had done the jump only a few minutes ago, and it had barely ruffled her carefully coiffed hair.

Nancy took a deep breath and stepped out. The cord on her harness was attached to a drum to simulate the pull of an aircraft, and it yanked her sideways at the same time as the fan blew her away from the building.

At the last minute she tucked in her legs and remembered to roll.

For a moment the breath was knocked out of her, but then she stood up, wobbly, a huge grin on her face.

'Slice of cake!' Iris yelled.

Nancy laughed. '*Piece* of cake,' she yelled back.

They were to do five live jumps – two from balloons, two from planes, and one night jump – before being dropped into an occupied country. It didn't seem many. Iris was fearless, but Nancy worried over the jumps all night, terrified of the fact she might flunk them and all her training would be wasted. Somehow she still felt like a fraud, that she should still be knitting socks in the village hall in Glenkyle. Andrew's words kept coming back, that all she was good for was looking at furniture catalogues.

Just after dawn the next day, Nancy and Iris were driven to the airfield at Ringway, to jump from a barrage balloon. The airport buildings huddled invisibly beneath gloom and fog, hemmed in by a pall of smoke belched from the factory chimneys of Manchester and Liverpool. Across a bumpy field, away from the main runway, shivered a silver-skinned monster of a balloon, tethered to the ground, and next to it sat a tiny cage-like contraption with a canvas tented roof. Four men were going to make the jump with them, so it would be a squash.

The assistant flying officer motioned to Nancy to climb in, and the others followed before he tied their lines off for the ascent. She was cheered to see one of the men was Klaas, the Dutchman she'd met at Arisaig.

'Jean!' he said. 'Let's hope no one has a pin.'

'I'm not looking forward to this,' Nancy said to him, steadying herself as the balloon swayed up towards the murk of cloud above, then she took a sharp intake of breath as the cage swung in a crazy arc.

'Nor are we,' joked Klaas, as he steadied himself on the ropes. 'But you know what they say, "ladies first".'

Iris shot him a supercilious glare. 'Cowards. I don't mind going first.'

Nancy looked down and wished she hadn't. The ground was barely visible through a soup of swirling mist.

When the signal came, true to her word, Iris jumped first. Her dark shape whirled downwards. Heart pounding, Nancy followed her out.

Nobody'd bothered to tell them that the parachute takes twice as long to open from a balloon as it does from a plane because there's no slipstream.

Nancy saw Iris frantically tug on her reserve chute and it flew out at about the same moment her proper chute did, but it made Iris spin and veer wildly off course.

She was out of view by the time Nancy landed with a bone-cracking thump that knocked the air out of her. Blearily, she brought herself to a sitting position and began to fold her parachute. She saw a group of senior officers haring off across the field.

'What is it?' she asked the army truck driver who was running back towards the truck.

'Your friend made a bad landing. She hasn't stood up yet.'

'What? Here . . .' She thrust the chute into his hands and set off at a run across the tussocked field. Her legs were weak as water from the adrenaline of jumping, but she could see a knot of men surrounding a still figure in the grass. By the time she got there, men were shouting for someone to fetch a stretcher.

Iris was white-faced, her lips blue. She was crumpled, surrounded by billowing parachute. 'I think I broke something. I can't move my legs.'

'Lie still, they're bringing a stretcher.' She took hold of Iris's hand and kneaded it. 'They'll soon fix you up.'

'If I can't jump, kill one of the Boche for Léo, will you?'

'Don't be a fool. You'll be back in action in no time.'

But her legs dangled like those of a lifeless doll as they eased her onto the stretcher, and two of the men were whispering ominously, 'There'll have to be a report.'

No news all day, and by evening Nancy was subdued. She suddenly realised how much she'd relied on Iris, on her pugnacious strength. When the CO arrived, the sandy-haired Hoyle, she was desperate for news.

'Not good,' Hoyle said, rubbing his chin. 'Fractured spine. Touch and go if she'll walk again.'

'No.' The thought wouldn't sink in. 'She won't be flying then?'

'No. Not for a good while. If ever. She's in Withington Hospital for now until they can transfer her to a spinal unit.'

Nancy slumped into a seat. She began to shake, and her teeth chattered.

'Shock,' said CO Hoyle. 'I'll bring you a brandy.'

He was back in a few moments with a half-full tumbler. She took a gulp and it set her off coughing. Hoyle slapped her on the back. 'Better?'

She nodded through watering eyes, half tears, half the effects of the brandy.

CO Hoyle sat down in front of her and leant his elbows on his knees. 'There's another balloon jump tomorrow. You still want to go ahead?'

She braced herself. 'Iris would be mad at me if I didn't.'

'Good girl. See you at five-thirty. Get a good night's sleep.'

Chapter 21

Tom was watching out for Oliver Johnson from inside the lobby of The Cavendish. He'd switched his attention from Neil Callaghan to his mysterious friend, Johnson. So as Johnson passed through the lobby, Tom followed him, pausing when he hailed a cab, and Tom heard Johnson call the instruction, 'The Ritz.'

Very swanky. The impression Tom got was that the Ritz was more like a millionaire's club than a hotel, and he was surprised that any friend of Callaghan's moved in such upper-crust circles.

Fearing he'd be underdressed, Tom hurried into the gents and parted his hair down the middle with water, fastened up his jacket and made his handkerchief show above his top pocket. He weighed up whether to wear his glasses, but in the end, he kept them in his pocket. They would be too much of an identifier.

Then he walked to the Ritz. He'd have to have another name, but not Frank O'Connor. Frank O'Connor had better disappear pretty quickly. He caught sight of a restaurant called Ralph's near Fortnum and Mason, so decided on Ralph Mason. He'd be Ralph Mason, a journalist, and try to get into conversation.

Taking a deep breath, he breezed into the lobby as if it were second nature, and the elderly doorman, complete with top hat, white moustache and brassy uniform, gave him a cursory nod as if he knew him. The circular vestibule was thronged with well-dressed men and women in cocktail dresses, and Tom straightened his tie. He was a fish out of water here, where wartime rationing didn't seem to apply. At least not to these people. Determined to brave it out, he moved through the throng and into something labelled the 'Grand Gallery', searching for the blond head of Johnson. Tom hoped to God he'd spot him; after all, he'd only had a few glimpses. But the man had a certain arrogant bearing it would be hard to disguise.

Tom lit a cigarette and tried to move subtly from ashtray to ashtray. Everyone seemed to know everyone else, but he met each curious glance with a nod, as if, like the doorman, he dimly recognised them. In one of the lounges labelled the Marie Antoinette Suite, a private function was in full swing, with some sort of delegation of dignitaries. A quick peek inside told him Johnson wasn't in there. So where was he?

Had he moved on already?

Tom's attention was caught by a rather bull-necked woman in salmon pink who was holding court to her friend. 'They're Albanian royals,' she said, waving at the door. 'They've apparently taken over the whole floor, and it's so expensive they're paying for it with their country's gold reserves.'

'Bags I the Albanian prince, then,' said her darker, sharp-faced companion, giving her a nudge.

'Given the choice, I'd rather live in Hitler's Germany than Albania,' the woman in pink whispered.

'Keep your voice down, Marita,' the other said, 'You'll get us arrested.'

Tom smiled at the darker one and she smiled back. He put on what he hoped was a Home Counties accent. 'I say, you don't know a chap called Oliver Johnson, do you?' he asked. 'He said he'd meet me here but I must have missed him.'

'Ollie?' The bullish Marita answered for her friend. 'Yes, he'll be downstairs. In La Popote. Used to be the Grill Room.' She pointed to the lift.

'Thank you,' he said.

Now he was getting somewhere. The lift took him down and clanged open. The door opposite had a sign above with 'La Popote'. Inside, he was plunged into the gloom of a sweaty nightclub. It couldn't have been more different from the genteel atmosphere upstairs. Utility tables were crowded around the dance floor, where a live band was in full swing, and a heaving knot of people gyrated to a wailing saxophone. Candles wedged in bottles gave a smoky, flickering light. Tom scrutinised the couples dancing, but none of them was Oliver Johnson.

What a dive. At least down here in the cellar, if a bomb dropped, they'd be reasonably safe. Perhaps that was the attraction.

Tom moved around the edge looking for a free table, stepping gingerly in semi-darkness over heaped-up sandbags and wooden props. Only now did it click that it was deliberately decorated like a Great War dugout.

A hand on his shoulder. A man pushed past him to get to a table, and as he stepped aside, he saw it was him, Johnson. Johnson was obviously familiar with the place and was returning to a table in the corner where another two men were already seated, deep in conversation.

One of the seats at their table was vacant, and no other seats seemed to be free. Tom hesitated. Should he take a gamble?

He walked purposefully over and said, 'Hello, Ollie, can I join you?'

Johnson looked disconcerted and was obviously trying to remember how he knew him. 'It's Ralph Mason, you remember,' prompted Tom. 'Friend of Marita?'

'Oh yes, of course,' Johnson said, though of course he could have had no idea who Tom was. 'Drink?' Johnson gestured to the bottle of wine on the table and turned up a glass.

'Thank you,' Tom said, taking a seat.

'Oh, we haven't met,' the man opposite shouted above the noise, and held out a hand. 'Though of course I know Marita. Everyone does. Hans Kohout.'

A German. There was an unmistakable trace of an accent. A shiver went up the back of Tom's neck. He tried not to let his surprise show. He thought most Germans had been locked away at the beginning of the war. But this Hans was a friendly looking man with thick brown hair and a ready smile. Tom shook his hand.

'Jack King.' The third man was older, already balding, and looked like a typical pen-pusher. He was studying Tom with an intense stare that made Tom fidget with his pocket flaps.

Tom's heart was racing. He poured himself a glass of wine and took a swig. The wine was smooth and full-bodied and its welcome warmth spread through his face and neck.

'How do you know Marita?' Jack asked.

'I met her here, I think,' Tom said, praying he wouldn't query it, or that, even worse, Marita herself should decide to come downstairs. She looked like a woman who would make a fuss.

'What do you do?' Jack asked.

'I'm in advertising. Sell space in *The Times* for births, marriages, deaths, that kind of thing.' He hoped nobody would check up.

Jack gave a small smile. 'You'll be busy with the obituaries then, I daresay.'

'It'll soon be over,' Oliver Johnson said. 'Though I expect it'll put you out of a job.' He let the others laugh before he turned to look directly at Tom. 'Are you in the club?'

Tom nodded. He'd no idea which club they were talking about, but he wanted to get a handle on Oliver Johnson and find out how he knew Neil Callaghan.

'Good man,' Jack said. 'We're going back to my flat in Edgware soon, for a few more drinks and putting the world to rights. Want to join us?'

'Thank you. I'd love to.' As long as he could keep up his cover, he'd be all right.

'Good. I expect Marita and Eileen will come too.'

A frisson of fear. He hadn't bargained for that. He decided to make excuses, but too late. Marita and Eileen were already weaving their way through the crowded dance floor towards them.

He tensed, looked for the exits.

'Oh, you found each other!' Marita said, glancing delightedly from Johnson to Tom. 'We're ready now. Shall we go?'

The men stood up, Tom with them. This whole evening was becoming more nightmarish by the moment. So far he'd escaped by the skin of his teeth, but any moment they might discover he was an interloper. Should he make his excuses and leave? Or bluff it out?

No, Kohout was definitely a German, and there was something odd about Johnson, who pretended to work at the library but didn't. At least there was no sign of Callaghan.

Jack was shepherding them all outside. They made their way to the door and the doorman shut the door behind them to keep the light in, before calling a bellboy to fetch the men's cars. The two women were about to get in Jack's car with Oliver Johnson, but Tom squeezed his way past Oliver, took hold of Marita's arm, opened the door of the car and said, 'Let me help you in.'

She shook him off with a gesture of impatience, but once she was in, Tom let Eileen get in and climbed in the front seat. He didn't want Johnson to get a chance to talk to Marita alone, and it would give him time to get some background on her.

Jack accelerated away. Tom glanced behind to see the other car was following. In the dim light of the split headlights he could make out the silhouette of Kohout driving and the taller Oliver Johnson in the passenger seat.

'I'm Ralph, by the way,' Tom said, swivelling round to catch Marita's eye. 'How do you know Ollie?'

'Oh, I've known him ages,' Marita said. 'Before the Right Club he was in the BUF – when we started plans for Tavistock to be PM. Of course, all that went belly-up. But we do what we can.'

The BUF. British Union of Fascists. Shit. Johnson was a paid-up member of the fascists. And by the way Marita was talking, it seemed he'd found himself a whole nest of them. Jack King in the front made no comment, so presumably he was one of them.

He prayed Callaghan wouldn't turn up. He'd recognise Tom straight away.

The car grew uncomfortably hot, and Tom wound down a window, glancing out at the jagged shapes of the houses as they passed. He hadn't seriously thought he'd find deliberate treason; he thought he'd find the usual SOE incompetence. But now he could instantly see that Neil Callaghan was connected somehow to this 'Right Club' and these people, and that he, Tom, was in slightly deeper than was comfortable.

'Glad Ollie's found another man for our cause,' Eileen said. She leant forward to talk to him. 'What made you want to join us?'

'Oh ... you know, the state of the country ...' Tom let his words tail off, hoped it was suitably vague.

'Bloody incompetence, you mean,' Marita said from the back seat. 'They're so wishy-washy, the *Wehrmacht* will walk all over them once they get here. And then we can get rid of the people holding the nation back and knock some sense into this place.'

Her words held a kind of finality that brooked no argument, so he stayed silent the rest of the journey and tried to quiet his churning stomach.

The Edgware flat was in a modern art deco block, all smooth curves and impossibly large windows. These had all been sealed in with brown tape and blackout paper. Must have been a big job. Jack King must have money then, to be able to live like this.

Inside though, it was hardly a magazine advertisement. The table was piled with papers, most of which had a thin layer of dust or rings from coffee cups. Obviously many people met here, for there were ten chairs around it, and everyone took a seat, pushing away papers to make room for their elbows. Tom got the impression this was a routine they were used to, and indeed the doorbell rang and two more men were ushered in. Not Callaghan, thank God. One, a man called Higson, and the other a younger man, Faulkner, who looked like a playboy, dark oiled hair and gleaming teeth.

As these men came in, Tom tried to read the papers lying about without looking too obvious. A glimpse showed what looked to be typed technical documents from 'Rolls-Royce' manufacturing.

'So Hans, what news on this new aluminium foil trick that the RAF are planning? Anything from the SOE, Ollie?' asked Jack King, taking a seat at the head of the table. Tom noted how this mild-looking individual had effortlessly taken charge.

Johnson shifted in his seat. 'I'm waiting to hear from Callaghan, but he suspects he's being watched and wants to lay low a week or two.'

Tom felt sweat prickle under his armpits.

'An Air Ministry man came to my factory,' Kohout said. His English was barely accented. 'He's wanting me to up production. He tells me they've made a great success against our *Luftwaffe* with the new "radar".'

'I've never heard of that,' Tom said. 'What is it?'

'A nuisance. Something like a searchlight – a scanner to find aircraft even in the dark,' Marita said impatiently. 'And Hans unfortunately has a factory that makes aluminium foil.'

Kohout turned to Tom. 'The scanner only works if the beam touches metal,' he said. 'So – my aluminium strips. If the strips are thrown out of the aircraft, the metal disrupts this "radar", gives false readings.'

'Let me get this straight,' Tom said. 'Your factory's making aluminium strips that give false readings to German planes?'

'Unfortunately, yes.' Kohout shrugged an apology. 'I found out from the Air Ministry man that in a bomb raid on Hamburg, the *Luftwaffe* were firing at bombers that weren't there. Only twelve of the British planes were shot down out of nearly eight hundred.'

'But Jack, I thought you'd already sent this information to Berlin,' exploded Marita, staring at King.

'I did.' King was unruffled. 'The British have only a tempo-rary advantage. I have no doubt the *Abwehr* will shortly be deploying the technology in exactly the same way. I expect to hear similar success from German intelligence within the next few days.'

'I should hope so,' Higson said, and Eileen gave him a broad smile.

Throughout this conversation Tom felt his belly tighten. Not only were these people fascist sympathisers, but active saboteurs, and Jack King seemed to be the link between England and the Nazis.

'We can't let the Allies have another taste of success,' Eileen said. 'Since Stalingrad, the news from the Russian front has been dreadful. The papers are saying that Hitler's troops are falling back, and that this will mean defeat for our National Socialist nation. Only the other day, a cleaner at my office told me point-blank she thought the Germans were losing.'

'British propaganda,' Marita snapped. 'It's nonsense of course.' But the silence in the room told another story. There was a sense of shifting unease around the table.

'Anyone got good news?' Higson tried to lighten the mood.

Marita smiled. 'You know the reports I gave Jack on mili-tary camps and gun emplacements at Watford? Well, the camps became a target. Shame the bombers missed the camp, but they did destroy several houses and shops nearby. Quite a few killed, I believe. And next time, I'm sure it will be a direct hit, and the British anti-aircraft guns will be taken out.'

'And I'm making progress with the English codes,' Oliver said. 'The SOE pride themselves on being one step ahead of MI6, but quite frankly, they're a bunch of incompetent fools. Callaghan tells me some Bletchley Park expert has introduced new poem codes to try to make the skeds more secure.' He laughed. 'Naturally, he's going to get copies to me as soon as possible.'

Poem codes. The words were like detonators in Tom's head. He felt his face grow red-hot. It would be obvious something was the matter. 'Excuse me a moment,' he said. 'Can you point me to the toilet?'

Eileen pointed. 'Through that door, second on the left.'

Gratefully, Tom headed for the doors in the hall.

My God, he was glad to get out of there. He shut himself in the WC and splashed cold water over his face. He should never have come here. But now he knew for certain Callaghan was supplying Johnson with sensitive information, and that this was somehow linked to this fascist group that was doing everything possible to undermine the Allied war effort. That woman Marita even talked of supplying the *Luftwaffe* with targets. Her bland face when she talked about people being killed! As if the victims were of no worth whatsoever.

Tom tried to corral his thoughts into order. No two ways about it, he'd have to tell someone. Neil Callaghan was a traitor, yes, but this was a much bigger operation. It made his heart pound to even think of it. He'd have to make his excuses and leave. Perhaps he could pretend to have a headache.

He came out of the toilet with his prepared apology in mind.

The atmosphere in the room had changed to something harder, more hostile. As he approached to sit down, the others were strangely silent, a sea of eyes all staring in his direction.

'I don't know you, do I?' Oliver Johnson stepped forward.

'And I don't know you either,' Marita said.

A click. Kohout had a gun in his hand and was pointing it right at him.

'So that begs the question,' King said softly, in his 'benign bank manager' voice, 'Just who exactly are you?'

Chapter 22

Tom sprang back through the living-room door and slammed it behind him. He expected to hear shots as he hurtled down the stairs. Behind him he heard more doors slam and shouts of confusion.

'Get him!' Marita shrieked.

Tom pelted down the stairs and careered out of the front door into the dense nothingness of the blackout. Dark shapes of buildings blurred as he lurched away around the corner and down another lightless street into a cobbled alley. He slithered on the uneven surface and, arms flailing, crashed into a metal dustbin. The lid clattered to the ground.

The gun had set his nerves razor-sharp. The very sight of it had a visceral effect.

He dived into the shadows of another bin and an asbestos-topped coal bunker. At the end of the alley, he saw the dark figure of Kohout and then a blinding light.

Thinking to hear a shot at any moment, he ducked, but no, it was a flashlight.

It raked slowly over the narrow walls of the alley and the top of the coal bunker. Tom crouched lower. No fool would risk a conversation with an armed man, especially not with a fascist fanatic.

Kohout ventured further down the alley towards him, swinging the light left and right. Tom found a coal shovel next to the bunker and gently picked it up. The handle was coarse and heavy in his palm.

'Anything?' Oliver Johnson's silhouette appeared at the end of the alley.

Kohout turned, and his flashlight beam swooped away to make Johnson cover his eyes. 'I thought he went down here,' Kohout said.

The flashlight swung back, and Kohout crept nearer, his gun outstretched in his hand ready to shoot. Tom's mouth was dry, his back muscles painfully taut as he squeezed down to keep out of sight.

Kohout came closer. Just a few more steps.

Tom lurched to upright and brought the shovel down with all his weight. It caught Kohout on the side of the head, and he toppled as if the strings on his knees had been cut. At the same time, the gun went off with a crack that would surely bring everyone onto the street.

Tom dropped the shovel and ran, skidding down the alley, skirting a parked car. Behind him, the clatter of more running feet. But he heard nothing except the blood pounding in his head. At the end of the alley, he emerged panting.

Walk calmly, he told himself. *Don't draw attention*. It was all he could do not to run. He was hatless. It made him feel naked and vulnerable. Damn. His hat was still at Jack King's apartment.

Just as he was about to enter the Tube station, the siren went. From nowhere, the road was full of rushing people, all stumbling towards the Underground. He was overtaken by women carrying babies, by men being pushed along by their wives. He followed the throng down into the belly of the tunnel, where hanging electric lights made everyone's features skeletally stark and grim.

There'd be no trains, he realised.

Only then did he begin to process what had just happened. Had he killed someone? The thought made him nauseous. An

172

unearthly tiredness overtook him. He sank down to his knees then slumped against the tiled wall.

Several other people hunkered down next to him with blankets and pillows, obviously ready to spend the night there.

'You okay, mate?' an elderly man asked him.

Obviously, he must look sick. 'Fine, thanks.' Tom attempted a smile. But then over the man's shoulder he caught sight of King, moving slowly down the platform. King was wearing a tidy, buttoned-up overcoat and carrying a briefcase. Tom curled himself into a ball and pillowed his face into his arms.

He daren't look up. Jack King was alone. Presumably this was his local shelter. There was no sign of Oliver Johnson or the women, or of Kohout.

For the next few hours he stayed there, hardly daring to move. When the all-clear went, many chose to simply stay there, and so did Tom. After the all-clear, when the first train came, he shambled onto the nearest carriage, aware his face must be creased, his clothes crumpled.

As the train pulled out, he could see no sign of Jack King. He began to wonder if he'd dreamt the whole thing. But as the train rattled into central London, he changed to the Bakerloo line to go straight to Baker Street. He couldn't waste precious time going home for a shave, not when he had to confront Neil Callaghan about his friend Johnson.

Nancy would be horrified at what her brother was doing. And then he had the thought that made him sick to the stomach. Maybe she was one of them. Maybe she knew.

Chapter 23

Nancy rubbed the tension from her forehead as she was driven to the Thatched Barn. She'd just endured a week's training in wireless operating, which included the theory of cycles and wavelengths, recognising the beat frequency oscillator (whatever that was) and atmospherics. Struggling to get to grips with all this, she then had to learn how to solder so she could repair the damn machine, and how to transmit in Morse. Every noise she heard became 'dit-dah' or 'dit-dit-dah' and she soon found herself so addled she was decoding the drip of the tap, or like now, the 'tip-squeak-tip' of the windscreen wiper.

At first, the sight of the Thatched Barn brought a lump to her throat and the memory of Tom's face. Had he forgotten about her, she wondered?

She was still thinking of him as she climbed onto a chair to have her hem pinned up. She was being fitted for a jacket and skirt by an exiled Jewish matron, Mrs Leibkovitz. Nancy forced herself to stop fidgeting and focus on the task in hand.

Being able to pass for a Dutch woman depended on more than just an ability to speak the native language, Mrs Leibkovitz told her, after taking the pins out of her mouth. It also meant looking the part. 'If you're a suspect, the *Sicherheitsdienst* will know. Ah, they miss nothing, those bastards. They employ textile men to pick through the weave of your clothing,' Mrs Leibkovitz warned. 'British weaves are quite different from continental weaves, and easy to spot. So we make your skirt of Netherlandish cloth.'

Nancy marvelled at the meticulously sewn seams, fashioned in the continental style, and the way her clothes all had Dutch labels sewn into them. Even her shoes were fashionably square-toed, but scuffed to look worn.

'You must look like a provincial Dutch woman,' Mrs Leibkovitz said. 'Nothing flashy to draw attention. At the same time, everything must have concealed pockets for the items you'll need to carry. See? There. A pocket in the side seam of your skirt.'

The fact that everything was so detailed should have reassured her, but instead it only emphasised the risk.

'Don't trust your Dutch compatriots,' Mrs Leibkovitz said, wagging her finger. 'Many are in the pay of the Nazis in Holland. They will betray you if they think it could serve them, so you must give them no possible excuse.'

Nancy shivered. They said she'd be flying on the next full moon, the fifteenth of August. And then she'd be in Holland, a place she hadn't visited since she was twelve years old. They still hadn't briefed her or told her exactly what her mission was, and the not knowing was eating away at her.

Nancy ran a finger around the serge collar of her FANY uniform, wishing it was cooler. All the female agents had these uniforms while in training, it stopped people asking questions about what they did, but the briefing room's blind was open, and the hot sun was pouring in. Her commanding officer, Sergeant Caxton, was giving her final instructions.

'The aim of the SOE is to build a disciplined force in Holland. As a wireless operator you will be expected to arrange and coordinate the air drops that will supply arms and cash for the Allied war effort, and to help to develop ways to hide these resources as quietly as possible under Nazi noses. You will link up with soldiers of the resistance engaged in sabotage activities, and with those Dutchmen prepared to fight from within. We want everything in place so our army will be fully armed and able to function when the balloon goes up and the Allied offensive happens. You will message for us under the agent code name Ludo,' Caxton said. 'All the agents operate under the names of sports or pastimes. Here are your completed papers with the photographs attached. I assume you've learned your cover story and are happy with it?' He pushed the documents across the table.

'Yes, sir. I'm to be a widowed milliner and seamstress from The Hague.' On the pass, a photo of her own face looked up at her, under the typed name: Gusta Hendriks. Gosh, she looked grim. She wished she'd ventured a smile for the picture.

'You and agent Hurling will be dropped together. On the ground you will meet up with agents Hockey and Tennis, who are part of the network you are both to join. Hockey and Tennis will supply you with all the contacts and safe houses you will need to travel to Amsterdam.'

'Amsterdam?'

'Yes. Part of your remit is to organise thirty thousand guilders for the Resistance with Herr Verhaegen at the *Berg en Leiden* Textile Factory. The Resistance there is desperate for funds. Your job will be to arrange the rendezvous by radio, whilst Hurling will make the actual transfer. Agent Hurling is still in sabotage training, but he'll join you at the aerodrome as soon as he can.'

Nancy hoped agent Hurling would be good to work with, and not one of those arrogant types who want to boss you about.

Caxton interrupted her thoughts. 'The money's here.' He opened a small suitcase with stacks of brown fifty-guilder notes. She'd never seen so much cash in her life.

'There's room for some clothes on top,' Caxton said, as he shut it with a bang and closed the clasps. 'You won't be carrying it when you jump, or your transmitter. They will be stowed in one of the containers that will drop at the same time. One of the other agents will help you retrieve it. Here's your small change – you can have this in your pocket when you jump, along with your papers.' He handed her a leather purse of coins and notes.

'Agent Hockey, our most reliable man underground, tells us Verhaegen's a Dutch businessman sympathetic to our cause, and the money's been requested by the biggest Resistance network in Amsterdam. We radioed ahead so he'll be expecting you to call. Maps are printed on the silk in the cuff of your coat, and so is the WOK code, which you must keep separate, somewhere else on your person. Once Hurling has delivered the cash to Verhaegen and the Resistance, find a safe place to transmit so you can contact us to tell us you're done.'

'What then, sir?'

Caxton blinked. It was as if he had never considered the question. 'One thing at a time. More instructions will be radioed to you. After three months you can ask for a replacement, and I suppose you must arrange to travel back to England through the Dutch–Belgian border. There's a safe house at Rue Peclet in Paris, and then out via the "Vic" line over the Pyrenees.'

He made it sound like a walk in Regent's Park. But then she realised. It wasn't carelessness at all. Just that he wasn't really expecting her to return.

Nancy picked up the telephone in the public telephone box, pressed 'A' and got the operator to put her through, even though it was something the training officers had expressly advised against. But she couldn't leave for the Netherlands without speaking to her mother.

'It's so lovely to hear your voice,' her mother said.

The slight Scottish burr over her Dutch accent brought tears to Nancy's eyes. It reminded her so much of home, and suddenly she was terribly homesick. She clutched the cold receiver to her ear. 'Did you get my postcards?'

'Yes, your father has them all propped up on the mantelpiece so he can tell people from church how well you're doing. Tell me about nursing, what are your colleagues like?'

This was exactly what she'd been warned about – that she'd be asked too many questions and might trip up. It was hard enough to remember her cover story and her new Dutch background, without having to invent a whole new previous career as a nurse.

She tried to deflect her mother by asking after news from the village. 'Have you seen anything of Mrs Fraser?'

'We don't speak now. Just nod if we pass. But I know Andrew Fraser's engaged to Audrey Hamilton. She's joined the WAAFs though, so the wedding won't be until next year. Honestly, you'd think he was royalty the way everyone's fawning over them. But when I met Mrs Falkirk in the post office she told me that since Audrey went away, Andrew's been having a secret fling with one of his patients. A married woman! You did well to escape him, darling, he's a proper Lothario. Have you met any nice young men in Birmingham?'

Tom Lockwood immediately sprang to mind, but she pushed the thought away. 'No time, Mother. I'm too busy for romance. I've got bigger things to think about.' *Like how she was about to be dropped into occupied Holland.*

They chatted some more about the Women's League and her mother's efforts at collecting bilberries for jam, before the phone started to beep and her money had almost run out.

'Have you written to Neil?' her mother asked.

'I've got to go,' Nancy choked out, 'but I'll send Dad more postcards for his collection.' She imagined him in his familiar armchair before the fire, the pipe dangling from his mouth. 'Tell him I love him.'

'All right, darling. Do try to ring again soon. I'll—' But her mother's words were cut off by the pips, and though Nancy raked through her pockets she had no more pennies.

She wished she could have told her what she was doing. She

178

wrapped her arms tight around herself in a pretend hug before heaving open the heavy iron door of the telephone box and stepping outside.

She looked up at the night sky. A few stars showed beneath passing wisps of cloud. In a few days' time she'd be flying up there, and then after that she would no longer be Nancy Callaghan, but Gusta Hendriks, a woman with a mission in an enemy land.

She kept running away, she realised. First from Andrew, then from Tom. Most of all from Tom. And look where it had led her. Instead of running away from danger, she was running headlong into it. But at least Andrew Fraser couldn't accuse her of doing nothing but roll bandages.

Chapter 24

Neil was always last to leave the breakfast meetings with Beauclerk and Blunt, helpfully offering to tidy up, empty ashtrays and dispose of memos to the incinerator. In practice, these post meeting minutes were spent furtively photographing anything that might keep Otto happy. Today was no exception. He shut the door after Beauclerk left and scooped up a memo giving details of fledgling plans for a forthcoming Allied raid. American B-24 Liberators were about to carry out their first bombing of a Messerschmitt arms plant at Wiener Neustadt, close to Vienna. Otto would salivate over this information.

Click. Click. A couple of shots. Neil had got quick at using the camera now, though his efforts were often hampered by his shaking hands. *Too much nicotine*, he thought to himself.

He had just put the camera into his pocket and was heading out of the meeting room with the sheaf of papers under his arm, when his path was blocked by Lockwood. Neil avoided his eyes and made to go past him, but Lockwood stopped him by putting his long arm across the corridor. Lockwood looked terrible; his face was haggard with a growth of stubble, and he looked like he hadn't slept in a month. What did he want?

'Where are you going with those papers?' Lockwood asked.

'To the incinerator,' Neil said, frowning at Lockwood's belligerent tone.

'Not to Oliver Johnson, and your Nazi friends?'

Neil winced. He stood there, even though everything inside him was inwardly collapsing like a tower of cards. He swallowed, stood up taller. 'You do talk a load of nonsense, Lockwood.' His best hope was to brazen it out. 'What are you accusing me of? Tidying up?' He took a step forward but Lockwood still didn't move.

'We need a private chat,' Lockwood said. 'Your office is the nearest.' Lockwood pushed open Neil's office door, which was next to the meeting room.

As Tom was blocking his path, Neil had no option but to go inside. Lockwood followed him in and shut the door. It felt strangely final.

'I don't know what all this is about,' Neil blustered. 'What do you want?'

'One of your friends tried to kill me last night. A man called Hans Kohout, an Austrian, and a friend of Oliver Johnson. Don't deny you know him, because I saw you meet with Johnson at The Cavendish, and the barman said you met there often.'

'So what? Johnson's a friend.'

'The game's up. He told me you were spying for the British Union of Fascists. Oh yes, I met them all. King, Higson, Faulkner. Those two awful women. Eileen and Marita. Fascism seems to be alive and kicking, even in our offices.' Tom advanced and Neil retreated, putting his desk between them. 'But there's one thing I need to know. Was Nancy working with you and these fascists? Is that why you had her spy on me?'

'Nancy?' Neil shook his head. He was confused. What had she got to do with anything? 'Nancy's in Birmingham.' He was desperate to deflect Lockwood from the BUF. 'Look, I got a postcard from her only last week.' He snatched the postcard from his desk and waved it at him. 'Have you not heard from her?'

Lockwood made a grab for the postcard, but then held it as if it burned him. He turned it over and read the back, his forehead creasing. The look on his face darkened. 'Where did you get this?'

What a daft question. Neil sighed. 'In the post, like all the others.'

'Others? Do you have the others?'

Something had shifted in the room, but Neil didn't know what. Tom looked like he'd been struck. 'What is all this?' Neil bluffed. 'Stop hounding us. Leave my sister alone.'

'The other postcards. I have to see them.'

'Why? If she'd wanted to write to you, she would have.'

'Because she's not in Birmingham, you oaf!' Lockwood said. 'This is the postcard agents send as a sap, to keep their families happy. Now show me the rest.'

Neil backed away. 'But it's Nancy's writing, not an agent's.'

'Are you stupid? Do you know where Nancy is now? No. Only by these postcards, which tell you nothing at all. Has she telephoned you? Written any other sort of letter?'

Neil couldn't answer. He'd only had the postcards. He opened his desk drawer and took out two more, turned them over and read them. As Lockwood said, they told him nothing. Just a bunch of platitudes. The truth began to dawn.

Lockwood was still talking. 'I saw postcards just like these at the Thatched Barn. They were for agents going out into occupied zones and were written before they went. Are the others all written in the same pen?'

Neil turned cold. Was Lockwood suggesting Nancy was an agent? He stared down at the postcards. All in the same pen. All nearly identical. Could have been written on the same day.

He put them down on the desk as if they burned.

Lockwood snatched them up. A glance and he held them out again for Neil to take. 'Where is she? France? Holland?'

Neil crumbled. 'I don't know.' It was all too much to take in. He couldn't keep up. 'She said she was joining the FANYs.' The full horror of Lockwood's words finally caught up with him. Holland.

They might send her to Holland. And Neil knew what that would mean. 'She can't be an agent. She'd have told me.'

'And break the Official Secrets Act?'

Neil wavered. He knew she wouldn't. 'Shit. The N Section networks are all under German control.'

'D'you think I don't bloody know?' Lockwood was leaning both hands on the desk. His voice grew oninously quiet. 'I've been telling Beauclerk for months! You're in with Blunt. You'd better damn well find out if she's with F Section or N Section, and where they're sending her.'

'How can I?' Neil protested. 'It's all classified information.'

Lockwood stabbed the air. 'Classified information? Oh yes. You can find classified information quick enough for the Germans! You'll bloody find out, or else I'll tell Beauclerk about Oliver Johnson and your friends in the BUF. Because if she's training for N Section, and anything happens to her, I'll personally see you hang.'

Tom had to go for a walk outside to clear his head. He strode down the street letting the fresh air revive him, though the air was sultry, the clouds massing like dark smoke. He felt like death. He could barely credit it – all the time, it was Callaghan – he was the one talking to the BUF. Just when things couldn't get any worse, now he was almost certain Nancy was training to be an agent.

Of course, now he'd seen it, it was blindingly obvious they'd use her. She already had the coding and language skills, not to mention the intelligence for it. She'd even managed to fool her own brother.

The tightness in his belly increased. He walked down Marylebone High Street and by habit turned into Francis Edwards' Antiquarian Bookshop, hoping they'd restocked. He needed something to stabilise him, something gentle. Something sane. Maybe a book about cricket he hadn't already got – there was something about the gentle thwack of a ball against willow that was quintessentially English.

The shop was gloomy, and he wound his way down the twisting stairs to the basement, where the books on sport were kept. On the way he kept looking over his shoulder; he was still jittery from his encounter with Kohout, could feel the judder up his arm and the terrible noise of that coal shovel hitting a man's skull. He hoped Kohout wasn't dead.

Or should he be hoping he'd killed him? War had made all boundaries uncertain. Tom pulled out a book on cricket. He opened it randomly at a chapter called 'Fair Play'.

He hadn't left any clues with Jack King as to his identity, had he? Only his hat. But they couldn't trace him from a hat, could they?

He stared at the book, barely seeing it. In the distance, a rumble of thunder. He'd have to tell Beauclerk about the meeting in Edgware, about Jack King, about Kohout and Johnson and those nightmarish women. And in doing it, he'd have to tell them Neil Callaghan was involved. Callaghan was passing secrets to Johnson. Johnson had said so.

At the same time, the Right Club now knew someone was on to them. He'd passed himself off as Frank O'Connor and Ralph Mason, but nothing could link those aliases to him, Tom Lockwood. At least he was fairly sure they couldn't, unless Callaghan gave him away.

He pushed the book back on the shelf and picked out another, flipped through its thick foxed pages. He daren't do anything about the Right Club until Callaghan had got some information about Nancy.

If he turned Callaghan in now, Callaghan would be arrested. Without Callaghan he'd never get the information from Blunt that he needed to find out where Nancy was going.

Not N Section. Thoughts of agent Fenna's 'accident' revolved in his mind.

Threats didn't make him feel good, but if it was the only way he could persuade Callaghan to play ball, then he'd do it.

And Blunt would be much more likely to tell a brother about Nancy's whereabouts.

Acts of treason carried the death penalty. He didn't like Neil, but could he really tell on him, knowing he'd be condemning him to that? What would Nancy think if he turned in her brother?

The answer was already needling him in his heart. There'd never be a way back for them from that betrayal. He shoved the book back on the shelf and sat down on the stairs.

Nancy Callaghan. He remembered her smile, and the way her eyes lit up when she saw him. He still carried a torch for her, one that ate up his nighttime thoughts. Where was she? He knew agent training was on average about six weeks.

He counted the weeks since she'd left. She'd been gone five weeks. And she wouldn't need coding training.

And it was his fault she'd gone. If they hadn't argued like that . . .

They'd have to move fast if they were to stop her walking into a Nazi trap. Neil had to help him, had to get word to her. He bounded up the stairs. Outside the summer storm had broken and the rain was sheeting down, the streets already swimming. He put up his collar and ran.

Tom dodged through the rain and hurrying pedestrians back to Baker Street, and took a quick look into the cipher room. The girls were working on indecipherables just the same as always. With a pang, he saw Nancy's empty chair had been filled by a blonde with too red lips.

He shut the door on it all and went to his office, where shoulders steaming from the wet, he picked up the phone, dialled the operator and asked for Callaghan. The line was engaged. Curses. He tried Marks, but was told he was off sick. He grabbed the receiver again and a frantic morning of phone calls to FANY head office got him through to Commanding Officer Marian Gamwell at Ketteringham Park, Norfolk, where the First Aid Nursing Yeomanry recruits were trained. He soon established that no Agnes or Nancy Callaghan had enrolled for training in the last two months, and that they had nobody of that name anywhere in the service.

So where was Nancy? He flipped through his desk diary to find the next full moon when a flying operation could happen. No. The full moon was tomorrow . . .

He hurried down to Beauclerk's office and braved Beryl's lair. 'I have to see him,' he said stubbornly.

'Do you never think to book an appointment?' she said dryly.

'It's urgent,' he said.

'With you, it always is.' A sigh. She picked up the phone and dialled. 'Lockwood's in the outer office again, sir. Says it's urgent. Will you see him now?'

She held the phone away from her ear, and he could hear cursing from the other end. She put the phone down. 'Be my guest. And Mr Lockwood, he's not in a good mood.'

Without preamble, Tom asked Beauclerk if Nancy was training to be an agent.

Beauclerk sucked in his lips. 'She left here and moved on to the FANYs, I believe.'

'Don't try that with me. You know as well as I do, they have no record of her.' Tom explained about his call to the FANY centre and the postcards.

'Damn it, man! Even if I knew anything, you know I can't tell you. We've all signed the forms. All agents operate under strict secrecy, and even if Miss Callaghan were to be taken on, we couldn't give out any information. Especially to someone who has let personal considerations override his judgement.'

'Personal considerations? When I have evidence of the infiltration of the Dutch lines and—'

'Please, spare me. We've been here before.' Beauclerk tapped his pen on the desk. 'I'm tired of you, Lockwood. Have you any idea what it takes to keep this damned ship on an even keel? I can't function amid all this baseless scaremongering. I'm tired of it all.'

'But I know for a fact that N Section is compromised. I've proof that Callaghan is working for the Germans—'

'For God's sake, man! Don't you ever listen? I refuse to hear any more of your wild talk. Go home. We don't require your services right now. We'll find a place to redeploy you – somewhere out of my hair. That's all.'

Tom was struck dumb. When his voice returned, it was faint. He said, 'You're sacking me?'

A sigh. 'No. You're overreacting again. I believe that this department is not the most suitable place for you, but we don't want to lose you, so we will consider carefully where best to use your particular skills. Bletchley again, or Radio Signals. In the meantime, clear your desk and go home. We will contact you by letter to offer you a transfer.'

'It's a sacking. You know it is. Because you don't want to hear the truth.'

A flash of lightning outside the window.

'Enough!' Beauclerk jumped up and wrenched open the door. His face was white. 'Out. The doormen will be told you are not to be admitted into Baker Street after today. And by the way, don't be thinking to take anything with you. Jimmy will be asked to search you on your way out of the building.'

The humiliation was more than Tom could bear. 'Damn you all to hell. If we lose the war, it will be because of people like you. People who prefer to sit in their comfortable ivory towers rather than listen to uncomfortable truths.'

'At least we behave like gentlemen. We don't make rash accusations about our colleagues with no evidence.'

'But I'm telling you, I've been there! There's a flat in Edgware where we went after the Ritz, and a man called Oliver Johnson told me Callaghan's a paid-up member of the Right Club and—'

'"A man told me". Drinking at the Ritz? All loose talk and rumours. Where's your hard evidence?'

None. He was banging his head against a brick wall.

'But I was there!' Tom shouted. 'Are you just going to stick your head in the sand like a bloody ostrich? People will die unless you do something.'

'Moderate your language or I'll call security.' Beauclerk grabbed hold of his arm and almost frogmarched him out. Tom turned back and slammed the door into its housing as hard as he could. Beryl cringed as he shot past.

Unbelievable. The man was an idiot. Well, if he was going, he'd have to grab as much information as he could today. Especially about skeds featuring agent drops. If Nancy was going to France, then he knew her chances of return were slim. But if she was going to Holland, they'd be non-existent.

Tom hurried across the road to the telex office, getting soaked again, and asked to see the files of messages that had gone out in the last week. This was not unusual, as he often double-checked the messages that had been sent by the telex system against new incoming ones. He took the files from F Section back to his office and trawled laboriously through them, hair dripping, trying to find out if there were any agents he had not seen, any agents at all whose code names he didn't know.

In the middle of the day, a clerk arrived with a stack of card-board boxes. 'Beauclerk's orders: you've to put everything in here,' he said. 'Just leave them by the door.'

Tom felt his heart lurch. It was really happening. He was really expected to leave Baker Street.

Chapter 25

Meanwhile, Neil was on his sixth cigarette and was light-headed from the sting of too much nicotine. He'd been unable to contact Blunt, who was in a meeting with MI6 over at Broadway. Neil had left Blunt a message and was willing the telephone to ring. He'd asked a clerk to bring him anything he could about agents in training for N Section.

When it arrived, the list was a short one. He ran his yellowed index finger down the details. There was only one woman on the list since May. He stared at the entry, which was by now sprinkled with his ash.

Jean Avison: Nationality – British (Scottish)
Languages: Bilingual Dutch, fluent French, good German
Code name: Ludo

It had to be his sister. Scottish. Bilingual Dutch. Too many coincidences to ignore. And so typical of Nancy. He should have known she'd never be satisfied with a desk job. Why in heaven's name didn't she talk to him? But then he realised he'd not exactly made it easy. And that smooth-talking Tom Lockwood hadn't helped. Lockwood was right, of course, about the Dutch lines – Giskes had had total control of them since Lauwers was first dropped.

In a cold sweat, he called the Air Liaison Office from the internal Baker Street switchboard. Was there a drop planned with an agent, code name Ludo?

'Yes,' came the crackly reply. 'For tomorrow. The fifteenth. Can't give you the drop zone though, classified.'

'You'll need to abort the operation.'

'By whose authority?'

'Major Blunt.' Neil crossed his fingers. The line was terrible. Must be the storm. 'Major Blunt,' he shouted again.

'And who did you say you were?'

He hadn't. He hesitated. 'An aide.' He didn't want to give his name. 'Who is this?'

Neil gripped the receiver tighter. He could almost hear the suspicion through the line. He needed to find out about Nancy, but it was all too difficult to explain without giving himself away. A crack of thunder made him startle.

'Whoever you are,' the voice crackled, 'I'll need that in writing from Blunt himself and he'll need to call up my superior to okay it with him.' The man on the other end was definite.

Neil put the phone down. He'd got the information he needed. But there wasn't much time.

He'd have to call Beauclerk.

Beauclerk had left the office, Beryl told him. He'd had an argument with Lockwood who'd behaved like a madman, and he was suffering from a migraine.

Neil groaned aloud and slammed down the receiver. There was only one option left. He'd have to beg Otto to help him. Would he do them a favour? It was Nancy after all. They'd all been good friends once. Like family. He remembered Otto and Nancy giggling as they pelted each other with snowballs. But Otto had not been that boy for years. Now the boy in him had been pressed down by Nazism and buried and hardened like coal. And Otto had never compromised for Neil. Would he be any more inclined to do it for Nancy?

190

He thought of the guns in the locked cupboard. He might have to threaten Otto to get what he wanted.

With a sense of unreality, Neil picked up his briefcase and went to open the key cupboard next to Jimmy's desk. 'I need some more carbon paper,' Neil said. 'I'll just take the key to the stationery store.'

'All right, Mr Callaghan.' Jimmy barely looked up from the crossword he was doing.

Neil opened the cupboard and took out two sets of keys and scrambled down the stairs to the basement storerooms. Fumbling, he unlocked the metal gun cabinet and chose a small pistol. He knew little about modern guns, but this one was a good size and was resting on top of a box of ammunition, so he emptied some into his tartan lunch box and put the camera in the empty box in its place. With a bit of juggling, he managed to wrap the gun and ammunition in greaseproof paper and put it back in his lunch box.

Footsteps were coming down the stairs.

Heart thumping, he shoved the lunch box back in the briefcase and Beryl appeared just as he'd locked the gun cabinet. 'Raiding the stationery store again, Mr Callaghan?' she said, smiling. 'Jimmy says you've got the key.'

'Carbon paper. We don't half go through a lot of it.'

He took the second set of keys and opened the stationery store, which was actually a small windowless room. Beryl took a stack of envelopes from the shelf, and he was about to lock the door when she turned. 'You forgot your carbon paper.'

'Oh. Yes.' He took a box and followed her up.

A few moments later the keys were both back in the cupboard. Jimmy made him open his briefcase as usual and gave it a cursory look. Good job Jimmy never searched his lunch box. Now to go to the London Library. Find Otto. He hesitated on the threshold at the sight of rain bouncing up waist high from the pavement.

* * *

Poring over the files was long and tiring work, and Tom still hadn't found anything or got through to Callaghan. The clock from St Marylebone's struck five. He stood up in a panic. Soon the cleaners and security guards would be round and he'd have to clear his office. He'd be turfed out of Baker Street for good, and he was no further forward in finding out about Nancy.

Tom hot-footed it over to Neil Callaghan's office to find out if he'd gleaned any more information from Blunt about agents in N Section.

'Mr Callaghan's not here,' said one of the junior clerks. 'He went out, said he wouldn't be back until tomorrow.'

Tom let out a sigh of frustration. What the heck was Callaghan playing at? Now he'd have to go and see him at home. And who else might be there? He didn't fancy another run-in with Neil Callaghan's Nazi friends.

Back in his office, Tom cleared the shelves of books and papers and files until frustrated, he snapped open his briefcase and emptied the contents of his drawer into it. Hurriedly he scraped all his pencils and pens off the desk. He ran a hand over his trusty typewriter and glanced around the bare shelves. It physically hurt. But he fastened up his briefcase, put on his mackintosh and crashed down the stairs.

At the door he let Jimmy search his briefcase and pockets, tight-lipped. If the good-natured Jimmy knew it was the last time he'd see him, he said nothing. Just a cheery, 'Goodnight, sir,' though Tom thought he saw a shade of regret in his eyes.

He got on the bus to Kilburn and watched the wet grey streets go by. Rain was still falling steadily, and the world was washed out, as if it too was tired to even have a summer and wanted to give up the fight. But Tom wasn't for giving in; he was going to Neil Callaghan's to see if he had any news about Nancy.

* * *

The London Library was still open to members until eight o'clock through the summer months, though today the streets were slashed with rain. Neil's shoulders were already drenched, and his shoes made a squelching sound as he squeaked along the tiled floors. He went into the public toilets by the entrance, and with damp and shaking fingers, he loaded the gun and wrapped it in a handkerchief in his raincoat pocket.

He knew where he'd find Otto because they'd met there often before, but his hand was sweaty on the brass handrail as he climbed the front stairs and went into the lift. It clanked upwards in slow motion and Neil's wet mac dripped into a pool on the floor. Once he'd pulled open the doors, he wound his way past the ranks of book stacks to the first-floor reading room.

The room was empty, but Otto was there, his bowler hat placed precisely on the table next to the book he was reading. He didn't look up until Neil spoke.

'What are you reading?' Neil's voice came out as a croak.

Otto startled. Then he frowned, relaxed. Neil saw him take in his damp and dishevelled appearance and knew it did him no favours.

'You. What?' Otto said.

'Can we walk?'

Otto glanced out of the window. 'Now? It's pouring. Can't it wait?'

'No. It's urgent.' Something in Neil's manner must have persuaded him because Otto sighed, put on his bowler and his raincoat and set off downstairs, his umbrella hooked neatly over his arm. Neil knew to give him a few more minutes before their rendezvous outside the tobacconist kiosk on the corner of St James's Square.

When he got there, Otto was just coming out of the public phone box. 'I'll give you ten minutes,' Otto said. 'I'm supposed to be meeting Faulkner and King in Edgware at six-thirty. I've told them we're meeting and I'll be late, but the next bus is in fifteen minutes and I need to be on it.'

He set off round the square and Neil fell into stride beside him as they entered the gate to St James's Park, past the bronze of William III on his plinth.

Otto put up his umbrella and squinted through the needles of rain. 'Well?'

'Nancy's done something stupid.'

'What?'

He swallowed the lump in his throat. 'She's volunteered as an agent for N Section. I want you to leave her alone.'

Now Otto paused, and then threw back his head in a laugh, before he headed for the shelter of a dripping horse-chestnut tree. The square was empty; the downpour had cleared the streets. 'Tell me.'

Neil lowered his voice and told him what he knew. 'So I believe she'll be dropped tomorrow. I know agents can be treated roughly and I just want you to make sure she's safe.'

'Me? What can I do? Call Giskes and tell him to "be nice to my friend"?' he lisped. 'It's war, Neil. Not a game of tag.'

'Think of Nancy, Otto. She doesn't know what she's going into. You must be able to do something.'

'You mean leave her like a loose cannon, swanning about Holland to plot against the Reich? You know I can't do that. It's not my fault your foolish sister's got herself in this fix. You should have stopped her.'

It was close to the bone and it made his shoulders sag. Neil could see his words were failing. 'What do they do to them?'

'Depends on her,' Otto said. 'If she gives up her contacts easily, probably nothing.'

'You know Nancy. She's stubborn. She'd never betray anyone else.'

Otto gave him a long hard look. 'They all say that in the beginning.'

The air-raid siren let out its piercing wail. Instinctively they both glanced up at the sky. Rain stung Neil's eyes. Close by, something exploded with an enormous 'crump'. People were scurrying for the shelter, too many people. And the screech of the siren hurt his ears. He could never bear that much noise.

Make it stop, he willed. It was like the sound of his own internal screaming.

Otto shrugged. 'I can't do anything, Neil, you know I can't.'

'You bastard.' Neil pulled himself more upright and lurched towards Otto. His hand snaked into his pocket, he withdrew the pistol and pressed it to Otto's chest.

'You'll help her or it'll be the last thing you do.'

Otto gave a smug little laugh. 'You'd never dare.'

Neil was filled with sudden fury. The noise of the air-raid siren was tearing him in two. Did he imagine the heartbeat, or was it his own? A split second, and his finger curled around the cold metal of the trigger and pulled. He felt the click before he knew it. And then the recoil snapped and reverberated up his arm making him step back.

Otto's face was puzzled, but then a recognition flashed in his eyes before he registered the shock. It was a sliver of a second before he glanced down to see a bubble of blood, and as if the sight deflated him, his knees buckled.

Neil slid the gun back in his pocket. The barrel was still hot as he limped quickly away. When he glanced back Otto was heaped on the ground, and summoned like ghosts, a knot of people had gathered around him. Neil turned off St James's Square and threw up into the grating of an overflowing gutter. The siren continued to wail, followed by another explosion and the seesaw sound of an ambulance.

Chapter 26

Tom was sheltering in the bus shelter outside Neil and Nancy's flat when Neil Callaghan limped down the road towards him. Though the rain had eased off, Neil's head was bowed and he looked like an old man. Tom hurried towards him, too impatient to wait for him to arrive.

Callaghan saw him coming and his face fell. He stopped and wearily leant up against a lamppost. When Tom got to him, he saw he was soaked, his shirt sodden under his dark-stained raincoat, his hair plastered to his scalp. His white face was haggard.

'Where's Nancy? What did you find out?' Tom asked.

Callaghan shook his head. 'You'll have to come in,' he said. 'I need a drink.'

Tom wanted to shake him, but he followed him inside. Since the last time he'd been there, the flat had become a hovel, a stash of unwashed plates shoved under the sofa, piles of old newspapers and discarded clothes on every surface.

Callaghan opened a cupboard and got out a half-empty Dimple bottle of whisky. He divided the contents between two smeary glasses and handed one to Tom. 'Trust me,' he said, 'you'll need it.' He glugged a great gulp. 'I just shot someone.'

'What?' Tom, who was sitting gingerly on the sofa, waited.

Callaghan took another great swig but nearly heaved it up.

'Take it easy,' Tom said, as Callaghan coughed.

'Oliver Johnson. Or should I say Otto Hefner.' He took a pistol out of his raincoat pocket and laid it down on the floor as if it might bite him. 'With this.'

'Where the hell did you get that?' Tom asked.

'SOE gun cabinet. Didn't know if it even really worked.' Callaghan stared down at it. 'Makes a hell of a bang.'

'Neil,' Tom said urgently, 'did you find out anything about Nancy?'

'You were right. It's N Section. She's to go on tomorrow's full moon. RAF Tempsford. I rang the Air Liaison Office but couldn't get them to cancel it or change it without Blunt's say-so. Blunt's not in his office. Beauclerk's off ill. And I tried to get Otto to help, to get them to go easy on her at the other end, but he just laughed at me. That's when I shot him.'

'Jesus. Is he dead?'

A nod. 'I think so. Point-blank range in the chest.' Colour was coming back to Neil's face and his cheeks were blotched and red. 'I'm ready to go to Beauclerk now and tell them the Dutch lines are all manned by the Gestapo.'

Tom was silent a moment. To confess to that was inviting a death sentence. He had to remind himself this wasn't just anyone – but Nancy's brother, Neil. Eventually, he said, 'You sure?'

'I killed a man,' Neil said. 'It was too easy. Just a crook of a finger.' He demonstrated. His face crumpled. 'Otto was my friend. My best friend, before . . .' Tears began to leak and trickle down his cheeks. 'He stopped liking me at university because I couldn't play sport or get a girl. I could tell. He despised me, and I couldn't bear it anymore.'

Tom shuffled in his seat and took another drink. The whisky burned his throat. Neil was sobbing now, and all Tom could do was offer him a handkerchief.

'Otto's mother. What can I tell her? How will I look her in the eye? She was a lovely woman, always smiling. How will I tell my father?' Neil tried to control his heaving shoulders. Finally, he blew his nose, hard. 'Sorry,' he said. 'It's been a bastard of a day. I'll come with you to Beauclerk in the morning. Explain what I know about what the Germans call *Englandspiel*.'

'What's that?'

'The English Game. They call it a game.'

Tom took a deep breath. 'You'll have to go alone. They won't let me in. They took my pass. I've been sacked.' He told Neil what had happened.

'But we have to find Nancy.' Neil shot to his feet. 'The Germans will kill her. Torture first then execution. None of them come back, you know they don't. But I need you to back me up. I'm going to call Blunt now, tell him to stop the operation.'

As if someone had read their minds, the phone began to shrill. Neil looked at Tom.

'Answer it,' Tom said.

Neil picked up the receiver. 'Hello?' A moment later, even from this distance, Tom could hear a click and the dialling tone. Neil put the receiver down again. 'Strange. Nobody there.'

It made Tom uneasy, but Neil flipped through his telephone book to find Blunt's number and dialled again. The phone was a long time ringing, and Neil had to put the receiver down and start again. A momentary pause once it was answered, and Neil asked for Blunt. 'He's at his club . . .? Sorry to disturb you, Mrs Blunt. Okay. I need to see him urgently. Tell him I'll be waiting outside his office . . . Oh.'

Obviously, by Neil's tone of voice, that was a problem.

'Neil Callaghan.' Neil dictated his number to Mrs Blunt. 'Got it? Tell him to ring me back as soon as he can. It's urgent.' He put the phone down.

'What if he doesn't ring back?' Tom said.

'I don't know. Mrs Blunt was pretty offhand with me about being disturbed. She obviously doesn't believe Blunt's at his club, or that he'll be in the office before midday. Her exact words were,

"If you can prise him out of bed with that bloody woman, you're doing better than I can.'"

Damn, Tom thought. They needed to get some action quicker than that. 'Can we send a telegram?'

'No. All telegrams to air traffic control are censored and monitored, and Tempsford is so secret half the RAF don't know it even exists. And there's no time to—'

The buzz of the doorbell. Tom strode to the window and peered out through the blackout blind. A car was at the kerb. A car he recognised. King's car. He repeated the registration plate number to himself. There was no mistake. He let the blind drop. 'Don't answer the door.'

Neil stopped, mid-step.

'We've got company,' Tom said. 'Jack King's car. Looks like Higson and Faulkner.'

'Otto was supposed to be meeting King and Faulkner after he met me,' Neil said. 'He won't have turned up. And he told them he was meeting me first.'

'If they've found out he's dead, they'll be armed.' He thought of Kohout and his gun.

'What should we do?'

'Is there a back way out?'

'Fire escape at the back, bathroom window.'

Tom went to the bathroom and, still in the dark, lifted the blackout blind.

A man was standing at the bottom of the fire escape. Faulkner, still looking like a leading man.

'No go,' Tom said.

'There's only the one set of stairs.' Neil was panicked.

'Who lives underneath?'

'Mrs Hartley. But she's an old lady.'

'She might be our only chance.' Tom scooped up the gun and gave it to Neil. 'Load it,' he said.

Neil fumbled to slot more bullets into the gun.

The bell went again, more insistent now. 'They know you're in,' Tom said. 'That's why they rang you up.' He shepherded Neil to the door and down the stairs. 'Cover me,' he said.

'I don't know how.'

'Just point the bloody thing. Like you shot Otto.'

Neil pointed the pistol nervously at the front door. Tom knocked hard at Mrs Hartley's apartment. The door opened on a chain, and Mrs Hartley's voice asked, 'Who is it?'

Tom signalled frantically to Neil.

Neil understood. 'Just me, Mrs Hartley. Neil from upstairs. I wondered if you could spare some milk?'

A rattle as Mrs Hartley unhooked the chain. She let out a cry as both men pushed their way inside.

'Lock your door,' Neil said. 'There are looters outside.'

Mrs Hartley backed away, pulling her housecoat closer over her chest. Her worried eyes looked out from a face slathered white with face cream, her hair in rollers.

'Sorry, Mrs Hartley,' Neil said.

She saw the gun then and began to scream. At the same time there was a thumping on the front door as if to break it down.

'The back window,' Tom said. He dived for the sash window and, fighting through Mrs Hartley's bedroom blackout blind, thrust it upwards.

In the hall, the echoing sound of voices and men's feet on the stairs.

Tom was out first, dropping down with a squelch into what felt like a flower bed, and Neil tumbled out with a grunt after him. At the bottom of the garden was a high wall with a gate, but thank God it was open. Tom plunged through, only to retreat back as he made out Faulkner still looking up at the fire escape. Neil cannoned into Tom's back.

'Into the next garden,' Neil whispered. 'It leads to the back of the public wash houses.'

They scrambled over the neighbour's wall and ducked down,

just as a sliver of light from a torn blind showed that the lights had gone on in Neil's flat.

'They're in there,' Neil said, his voice incredulous.

Never mind them,' whispered Tom. 'Watch out for Faulkner.'

They sneaked out of the neighbour's vegetable plot and around the edge of the wash houses and crossed Percy Road. A quick glance behind.

Damn, Faulkner must have seen them go and was after them at a run.

The doors of the Salvation Army Hall were open and Tom and Neil rushed in. The hall was in chaos, seething with damp wartime bomb evacuees who had escaped with their lives. Men, women and children in various stages of sleep littered the floor, huddled in blankets or quilts. Tom and Neil picked their way across the bodies and into a kitchen where a group of Salvation Army women in uniform were cooking up soup.

Tom muttered an apology as they rushed through, out of the back door and into some mews which housed the yard of Wills' tobacco factory. A fleet of lorries were parked there and they dived for their shadows, breathing hard.

Women's indignant shouts from inside filtered into the court-yard. Then Faulkner stuck his head around the door into the darkness. He peered slowly around the yard.

Tom tried not to breathe, his hand gripping Neil's arm tight to keep him still.

Faulkner disappeared back inside. All was quiet. The smell of broth drifted across the yard.

'What now?' whispered Neil.

'Sssh. I don't know. Wait a bit, until Faulkner's gone.'

'Wouldn't mind some of that soup,' Neil said. 'If I can't go back home for Blunt's call, how will we stop Nancy from being on that plane?'

'I'll think of something,' Tom whispered. But in truth he had no idea what to do. Could he rely on Neil to get a message to

Blunt and trust it would get through? From what he knew of Neil, he was doubtful.

What if Faulkner ambushed Neil at his flat and no message got to Blunt at all? He couldn't risk that they'd be too late. The only thing he could think of was that he would have to put Neil up for the night, and that if he had to get to RAF Tempsford, he needed a car.

Chapter 27

Tom smuggled Neil into his house by creeping silently past the landlady's door and into his bedsitting room. Neil looked terrible; already thin, now he had a face full of shadows. Tom suspected he never ate, and fed him his small ration of cheese on a slice of bread. As there was only a single bed, he gave that to Neil and installed himself in an armchair, his feet on an old ottoman.

'Get some sleep,' he said.

A vain hope. He heard Neil fidgeting for a few more hours before his breathing settled. Tom didn't sleep much either. He was worried about Nancy, and he woke Neil as soon as his alarm clock said 5 a.m.

'Here's the plan,' he said. 'You go to Baker Street first thing, and before you do anything else, you get the keys to one of the cars.'

'But—'

'I don't care how you do it, just get them. I'll wait near the newsagents on the corner of the street, and you hand the keys over to me. I'll drive to the airfield and try to bluster my way in with some sort of story, and try to persuade them to let me see Nancy.'

Neil's expression was sceptical. 'What if you can't get in? There'll be guards on the gates, won't there?'

'I'll just have to risk it. I can't think what else to do. You'll be doing plan B, like you said yesterday. Which is – soon as Blunt arrives at the office, you go to him and tell him everything you know and get him to close down the agent drops to the Netherlands.'

'I'll try. But I don't know if they'll do it for one woman. Or whether they'll trust me once I . . . well, once I confess to what I've done.'

Tom wanted to grab him by the shoulders and shake him till his teeth rattled. Trying wouldn't be enough. Neil was like a piece of wet string; he didn't look like he was going to have the guts to go through with it, and he just had to, for Nancy's sake.

'Get to Blunt early,' Tom said in a brisk voice. 'The more time he has to sort it out, the better.'

Neil bit his lip. 'He never gets in before ten. We all know about his affair; everyone does. I don't know what he'll do when I tell him I shot Oliver Johnson. Whether he'll arrest me. I know Otto was the enemy and all that, but it's murder.' His eyes filled with tears again. 'And it will be impossible to explain how I know him unless—'

'Don't think of all that,' Tom said desperately. 'Think of Nancy.'

Neil's mouth was dry as he greeted a dozing Jimmy at the door to the offices on Baker Street. He hadn't slept much and his hands were shaking more than ever. At Tom's flat, he had managed to borrow a razor and he'd washed and shaved and Brylcreemed his hair, though he had a hollow at the pit of his stomach. He knew this was one of the biggest days of his life and it probably wouldn't end well. It was a mess, and he hated mess, hated being out of control. And they'd all be disappointed in him. Though with Otto gone, it was as if a tiger had stopped terrorising a village; he hadn't realised how afraid he'd been until the fear of him was gone.

Neil blew his nose. Tom would be waiting. He yanked a set of car keys from the wall-cupboard in the main-line office. The book

204

for signing out transport was on a shelf underneath, and after a moment's thought, he signed it with an illegible scrawl.

As he hurried to the car park at the back of the building, an air-raid siren went off. He took no notice, because yesterday's raid was a false alarm. The blitz seemed to have ended and there'd been a respite in the German bombing, apart from a few concentrated incendiary attacks.

He ignored the ear-splitting din and jumped into the car. There was plenty of fuel, he was glad to see, and the traffic was still light before eight o'clock. Another bang shook the road and made him swerve without thinking. Neil drove the few hundred yards around the corner to see Tom waiting anxiously by the newsstand, facing the wrong way up the street, watching a huge plume of smoke unroll into the sky. The street had emptied, just a few businessmen running for cover. Neil parked nearby, and after checking nobody was watching, he got out of the car and walked over to tap Tom on the shoulder.

Tom startled and turned. 'There's an air raid. Something's been hit. An ominous drone of aircraft made him look up.

'Here,' Neil said, handing him the keys. 'The car's round the corner.' He pointed. 'The grey Rover.'

Tom took the keys and shook his hand. 'Good luck with Blunt,' he said. 'Best get to a shelter, looks like the Jerries mean business.'

Neil stood a moment to watch Tom go. How far was it to Tempsford? He hoped Tom could get—

The thought was cut off as a huge flash lifted Neil off his feet and flung him down like dough onto a table. The deep boom of the explosion was fractionally after. Choking dust. Around him, masonry crumbled and rained into shrapnel, and glass exploded into fragments of silver. Neil opened his mouth to call but then a sudden feeling of weight pinned him down, and the breath shot out of his lungs.

* * *

Tom gripped the car keys at the whine of a bomb. A massive blast shook the ground. Instinctively, Tom ducked and covered his head with his hands. A chunk of flying debris landed right in front of him and shattered into shrapnel. Something sharp spattered the back of his hands. The air was thick with dust and the smell of gas. In the distance, there was another storm of explosions and shouts.

He compressed himself into a crouch until the noise of falling bricks and scattering mortar stopped. When he looked up, he was in a fog of dust. His eyes streamed. He rubbed the grit from them as he turned. The pavement where he and Neil had been standing was a sea of shifting rubble.

Where was Neil? He couldn't see him. A man staggered out of the chaos, half his arm missing, streaming blood. Not Neil. A man from a passing car grabbed the injured man to stop him wandering and made him lie down, right there in the traffic.

Tom ran across the road calling, 'Neil?' but his voice was a croak from all the dust.

The newsagent's papers were blowing, some alight, like fiery birds caught up in the wind. His feet crunched on broken glass.

A woman clutching a bloodied head limped out of the wreckage.

'Have you seen a man in a brown suit, fair hair?' Tom asked, grabbing her by the shoulders.

She shook her head, eyes blank and dazed. He scrambled over the rubble covering the pavement. Close to where the shop had stood, two beams from the shop window had fallen outwards, pulling the torn awning with them.

'Neil?' Tom shoved the car keys in his pocket, but he couldn't move the beams or the awning on his own and he worried it would collapse if he tried. 'Neil, is that you?'

'Tom?' the voice was barely audible. 'Can't move.'

'Neil. Just stay still. Hang on there. We'll get you out.'

In the distance, two ARP wardens in blue boiler suits and tin helmets were assisting the injured man, tying a tourniquet to his arm, while another two were pumping a stirrup pump to tackle a burning car.

'Help!' Tom yelled. 'There's somebody under here!'

Two more ARP men shifting rubble left it and ran over. 'Where's the casualty?'

Tom showed them the collapsed shop window. 'Under here, but I daren't move anything on my own.'

The wardens had ceiling pikes – long poles with hooks on – and began to rip at the canvas awning. Beneath, it was worse than he feared. Neil's face and one shoulder were visible, but he was lying at an awkward twisted angle and the rest of his body was pinioned by brick and cement. A long wooden beam lay across his chest. His face was whiter than the dust, his eyes closed.

'Neil. Don't worry, we'll soon have you out. Talk to me, Neil.'

No response.

One of the wardens clambered gingerly over the wreckage and put a hand to Neil's neck. 'He's alive.' He turned to Tom. 'Best thing you can do is stay here, keep talking to him. I'm going to fetch more men.'

Tom kept talking. He talked nonsense about films that he had seen, about music he liked, about books he'd read. About Nancy and the Corner House. All the time there was no response.

Finally, more men arrived and began the painstaking process of lifting the debris brick by brick. Neil was still unconscious. Tom couldn't leave, not until he knew if Neil was going to be okay. Finally, inch by inch, they dragged Neil out, and for the first time, Neil groaned in pain and his eyes flickered open.

Two medics appeared with a stretcher to take him to the ambulance. One of the men who'd dug Neil out came to speak to Tom. 'He's in a bad way. Broken ribs, both legs smashed and maybe internal injuries. His chances aren't great. You a friend?'

'Yes,' he said, suddenly choked.

'Can you get a message to his family?'

'Of course,' he said.

'We'll take him to Marylebone. And you'll need to get those cuts washed.'

He looked down at his hands, where many small lacerations were weeping blood. He hadn't even felt them. His mind was racing. He had to get to Tempsford.

He followed Neil to the ambulance. 'They'll soon fix you up,' he said to Neil.

Neil tried to speak but he was in too much pain, and enough breath wouldn't come. But Tom knew what he was trying to say. One word. Nancy.

Tom's legs trembled like a drunk as he picked his way past broken bricks and glass. *Adrenaline*, he thought. It would subside if he just took some deep breaths. He could taste mortar dust on his tongue as he navigated down the grey ruin of a street.

He was grateful the number plate was written on the key fob, so he found the car immediately. It was shrouded in a thin layer of dust, but otherwise it seemed intact.

Shakily, he climbed in. He blew out, then began to focus on his priorities. Neil was in the best hands, and there should still be plenty of time to get to Tempsford before nightfall. Nancy wouldn't fly until then, and she'd need to know about Neil. There was a map in the glove compartment, so he took a few hasty moments to look at it before he started the car up. The London traffic had come to a standstill as drivers had run for cover, but he had to creep in first gear around potholes and diversions where bomb damage had made some routes impassable.

The familiar act of driving calmed him. He tried to find a phone box. If he could get through to someone at the SOE and tell them Nancy's brother had been in an accident, maybe they'd stop her flying. He tried two phone boxes but both were out of order.

The image of Neil half-buried under the rubble wouldn't leave him. It was as if his whole world had jolted sideways. Everything had become sharply focused, important. Death had pushed his nose into Life.

Once past Hendon, Tom put his foot down, and headed out on the main North Road towards Peterborough. Neil had told him last night St Neots was the nearest town to RAF Tempsford and agents were billeted near to somewhere called Gibraltar Farm. With any luck he'd be able to find Nancy there. Only now he'd be the bearer of bad news. It was only then that he noticed a car behind him. Another car covered in white dust.

The first time he saw it, he paid it no attention, but after half an hour it was still on his tail. A sense of foreboding. He was rattled, and he accelerated away, but so did the other car. It slowly drew alongside and he was able to see the man inside. The profile was unmistakable: the long straight nose, and the thick dark hair springing vertically from his forehead. Faulkner, one of the men from Jack King's Right Club.

Tom pulled back and hoped Faulkner would overtake so he could look for a side road and lose him. He slammed on the brakes and Faulkner swerved and shot past.

Behind him, another motorist blared his horn as Tom skidded to a snail's pace then pulled onto the hard shoulder.

Tom cursed. Faulkner must have been watching for Neil outside Baker Street and then seen Tom get in the car. Tom shoved the car into first and veered back onto the tarmac to find Faulkner had also slowed in the outside lane.

The turn-off to St Albans was ahead if he could fool Faulkner into passing it.

Tom shot into the outside lane and drove his bumper up to the back of Faulkner's car. He had to keep directly behind Faulkner until the junction. When it came, he yanked the wheel to the left and shot off on the side road towards St Albans. A slow-moving tractor pulling its cart of hay loomed up in front of him. Another haul on the wheel caused a squeal of tyres as he sped past.

Pressing his foot to the floor, he accelerated to a hair-raising speed. Had he left Faulkner behind? He daren't look. He shot through the small village of Colney Heath.

A roar of an engine. He glanced in the rear-view mirror. Faulkner was still on his tail. What the hell did he want?

He returned his attention to the road. It curved into an unexpected right-angled bend.

He hauled on the wheel, but the car was going too fast, so he oversteered. A hedge came towards him fast. He yanked the wheel again, but he grazed the hedge and a sudden tilt told him the two nearside wheels had slipped into a ditch. A judder and he was catapulted sideways. The car puttered to a halt.

His immediate thought was that Faulkner could be armed. He leapt out of the driver's door and crouched behind the car. Faulkner's car had turned around and was cruising towards him up the road. There was nobody else in sight. Flat fields of barley stretched to the left and right. A ripple of apprehension shot up Tom's spine. There was nowhere to go.

Faulkner pulled the car to a halt. The rasp and clunk of the handbrake.

Faulkner stepped out in a leisurely way. His clothes were immaculate, his shoes of polished leather. 'Seems like you had a narrow escape, eh, Lockwood? Where are you going in such a hurry?'

'Why are you following me?'

'We don't like spies.'

'I'm not a spy. But it seems you are. You ran me off the road.'

'This is a warning. That's if you haven't already received enough of one from the *Luftwaffe*. Kohout needed fourteen stitches in his head and will be laid up unable to work. We would have pressed charges, but for the fact that a word from me, Lord Faulkner, is infinitely cheaper than the judiciary. I'm quite prepared to say I saw you mug him and try to burgle him, unless you leave us alone.'

'Are you trying to blackmail me?'

'Bargain. I'm bargaining with you. You keep quiet about the existence of our club, and we leave you alone. Simple.'

'I don't bargain with people who are working for the enemy.'

'Enemy? I suggest you consider carefully who is the enemy of this country. Churchill, with his antiquated notions of chivalry, or Hitler, with his desire for a unified and prosperous Europe? Though I suspect you are too stupid to realise it. Maybe this will help you make up your mind.'

Faulkner started to withdraw something from his pocket. Before the barrel of the gun was even visible, Tom dived for cover, muddy water sloshed over his ankles. Crack! Crack! Two shots. Then Faulkner calling, 'Unfortunately, King says I haven't to shoot you, just threaten you with a prison sentence for assault. Shame.'

Tom fought the urge to stand. The car engine started up. There was another bang that sounded like an exhaust, and when he looked up, Faulkner's car was disappearing in a haze of smoke.

Tom checked himself. Nothing. Except for the fact his hands still stung. He clambered up the bank to try to figure out how to get the car out of the ditch. He'd have to flag down another motorist. He glanced up and down the road, but there wasn't a soul in sight.

He walked around to assess what he could do, and then he saw it. Both offside tyres had been shot and were now totally flat. Even if he could get the car out, it would be useless unless he could get new inner tubes. And he had to get to RAF Tempsford before nightfall. He grabbed the map from the car and did a rough calculation by finger and thumb.

Maybe thirty miles as the crow flies. Too far to walk, and if someone came by, he couldn't explain bullet holes in the car tyres. He'd have to hope for a lift, or a bus. Reluctantly, he retrieved the map and a torch from the boot, and set off walking.

Chapter 28

Just as Tom began walking, thirty miles away Nancy was hurrying between the wooden slatted huts at Stoke Mandeville Isolation Hospital, searching for Iris's ward. She was dressed in her FANY uniform, and in her arms she clutched a bunch of roses, bought at enormous expense, for no one dared grow flowers these days. She had to do something to take her mind off tonight. These were her last few hours in England, and she was restless, nervous, and needed to talk to Iris, who would understand.

Visiting hours were two until four, but Nancy hadn't been able to get there until half past three due to a shortage of FANY cars and the fact agents weren't allowed to go out unaccompanied. She had at last persuaded Madge, the driver, to bring her, and wait in the car.

Now, finally, after peering at signs marked 'pathology' and 'plastic surgery', Nancy found the one she was looking for – marked with a sign for 'spinal department'. London hospitals were reserved for bomb casualties, so Iris was here, where the wards had been thrown up in a hurry and were more like army barracks than a hospital

She asked for Madeleine Dubois, and the Irish nurse at the desk inside the door told her to wipe her feet and pointed out

Iris's bed. Nancy couldn't get used to the idea that Iris wasn't really Iris but someone called Madeleine.

Nancy hurried past several other patients with cages keeping the sheets above their legs before she found Iris. She was sleeping, her dark hair fanned out on the pillow. A red rubber tube from a hanging urine bag led under the sheets. One arm lay over the hospital cover, but already it had grown painfully thin, not like the muscular arms of the woman who had shinned up ropes, rowed a boat against a freezing tide, and wrestled grown men to the ground.

Nancy glanced at the chart on the end of the bed labelled 'Madeleine Dubois'. *Turn her regularly*, the chart said.

It made Nancy feel guilty, to be so fit, so ready for her mission, when Iris, who had always been much the stronger of the pair of them, was lying here through no fault of her own – unable to finish the job.

Should she wake her? She placed a hand over hers. Iris opened her eyes, her face fearful, but then she smiled. 'Jean!'

'It's tonight,' Nancy said. 'I had to come. I couldn't go without coming to see you. How are you doing?'

'No change.' A sigh. 'They talk now about wheelchairs, and an *institution*.' She pronounced it in the French way, with a bitter twist of her mouth.

'I'm sorry,' Nancy said. 'It seems so unfair.'

A small shake of the head. '*Non*. I'm glad it's your time.' She dropped her voice to a whisper and Nancy leant in to hear her words. 'You have the training, yes?' Iris said. 'We didn't go through that shit for nothing, hear me?' Her eyes blazed. 'If I am the cost of this training, so what?' Her hand gripped Nancy's wrist so the nails dug in. 'If the Germans win, they will eliminate those of us who cannot work. They only want the strong in their nation. Yet it can happen in an instant. The strong become weak. Do it for the weak.'

Nancy squeezed her hand. 'You are a brave woman, Iris.'

'No. It is you who are the brave one. No one else from the Firm has been to visit me. Not a one. They are all too scared. They are not scared of Nazis, but they are scared of what to say to a woman who can no longer walk.'

They talked a little in low voices, reminiscing about the Scottish landscape but mentioning nothing of Arisaig and the training.

'That man you love—' Iris began.

'What man?' Nancy interrupted.

'Eh, don't pretend there is no one. The man you wouldn't tell me about. Now is the time to write. Mend your bridges.'

'I can't. It's not allowed. You know it's not.'

'Pah. There's always a way. You don't have to say where you are. Tell him you care about him. Just a simple note. It might be your last chance to say it.'

Iris had always been blunt.

Their conversation stopped when the nurse appeared. 'Sorry, but visiting's over for today. Time to say goodbye, but you can come again tomorrow.'

Nancy and Iris exchanged amused looks, knowing tomorrow was not an option.

'What gorgeous roses! Shall I put them in water?' The nurse reached to the bedside cabinet for the water jug and took it to fill it.

'I don't know when I'll get out of here,' Iris said, beckoning her closer. 'But it will please me to think of your green face as your feet hang out of that hole,' she said. 'Come and see me when you get back, won't you?'

'I will, I promise.' She bent to hug her fragile friend.

'*Merde alors*,' whispered Iris. It was what they said to the agents about to drop into France.

The words made Nancy catch her breath.

Madge drove Nancy back to Hazells Hall, a draughty eighteenth-century manor house where she was billeted. Nancy arrived there, sober and silent, and shortly before seven was offered a stew of meat and vegetables – a rare treat. She forced it down, though she had little appetite. Her nerves had begun to kick in, but she reminded herself she'd no idea when she might next eat. She sat alone, as was the custom for those going out on a mission. It was a tense time, and the agent needed to muster all their reserves. Now there was nothing to do but wait for the night transport, and go over her cover story again. *Gusta Hendriks. Milliner from The Hague, husband dead, looking for any kind of sewing work.*

The waiting was the worst. She couldn't be still, kept checking her papers over and over, memorising every detail. There was paper and a pen in her room. She sat down, picked up the pen and wrote a brief note to Tom, surprised at how just the thought of him could move her and make her tearful. *Pull yourself together, idiot,* she thought.

I'll never forget you, Tom. I'm sorry for everything.

I don't know if we'll meet again, but when you next read the encyclopedia, think of me when you get to the N section.

With fondest love, Nancy.

She pushed the note into an envelope and addressed it, and stuck on a stamp. She didn't seal it because it would be censored anyway. Perhaps it wouldn't get past them with that reference to N Section. She took it to the wire out-tray in the hall but then had second thoughts. What was the point? He'd probably forgotten all about her by now.

Slowly she tore it into shreds and put it into the open fire in the hall. It smouldered and smoked then shrivelled to nothing. When it was gone, she steeled herself to take a walk outside. A glance at the sky showed the moon had not yet risen, but the night was fine, just the hint of a breeze. A rumble of an engine and two slit headlights approaching down the drive announced the arrival of the air liaison officer who was to pick her up and take her to the aerodrome.

Here already? Nancy's stomach flipped, and she had the sudden urge to hug her mother goodbye. She thought of her mother, and

Neil, and most of all of Tom. She wished she'd told him the truth, instead of running away. But now it was too late.

Heart thudding like crazy, she scooted upstairs for her things, then hurried across the lawn towards the waiting car.

Tom's legs were so tired it was all he could do to keep going. He'd thought himself pretty fit, until this – this hike across marshland and stubble, following the map towards the RAF station in the middle of blasted nowhere. No buses had passed, and though he'd got a lift for about twelve miles with a milk delivery wagon, he'd had no further luck. So now he was going across country desperately trying to save time. The fact there were no lights and no signposts made it even harder to check his map and his route, and several times he'd had to climb through wire or drag his leaden legs over hedges. When he came to a road, he always tried to flag someone down, but since it got dark, he'd had no luck. And who would want to pick up a stranger in the dark in wartime anyway?

His feet were soaked and his shoes squelched; both hands were covered in scratches. His suit was still dusty from the explosion and at times he wondered what the hell he was doing, staggering around in the dark, but the thought of Neil's white face, and then the thought of Nancy, and what might happen to her, propelled him onwards.

Panicking now that he'd get there too late, he stopped often to wind his watch, scared it would stop going before he got to Tempsford. The moon had just risen and he could see now it was after ten o'clock already. What time did they fly? He'd no idea. All he could do was doggedly keep on walking, mile after mile. After all, he'd got this far. No point now in going back.

One in the morning. The moon had been swallowed by cloud and his feet were blistered in his office shoes. He hadn't seen a telephone box, so with Neil in hospital, there was zero chance the whole thing had been called off by now. A faint grey blur of a road lay ahead curving away into the distance. No earthly chance of a lift at this time.

He ignored it and pressed on through the fields in what he hoped was the right direction.

But about three miles from the airfield, Tom saw the glimmer of car lights. If he remembered the map right, the car was heading down the only road to the airfield. He broke into a ragged run. He'd nothing to lose, he was exhausted. He'd try to flag a lift.

He blundered across the ploughed field towards the road, but he was tiring; his legs were burning and his lungs unable to suck in enough air.

'Stop!' He yelled and waved his arms just as the car flew past. He was sure the driver, a man in the peaked cap of the RAF, had seen him, but he didn't stop. The person in the back was in shadow. He chased after it for about a hundred yards, shouting and waving, before he staggered to a halt.

His hopes crashed. He hung his head, bent double over his knees to try to get his breath back.

The air liaison officer briefed Nancy and took her from Hazell's Hall to Gibraltar Farm in his car. In the mess hall they entered a barn where four pairs of curious eyes raked over the newcomers, but she could see they tried not to stare. It was by now two in the morning, which was really twelve o'clock since the wartime English Double Summer Time had been introduced. And even in summer it was chilly. The mess hall was simply a brick and wood constructed hut, made to look like a barn, pasted on the inside with brown paper to try to keep out the draughts, and it stank of coal dust from the one unlit stove, and smoke from the men's cigarettes. The night was dark because the moon floated high behind the inevitable English cloud.

The men were quiet, sitting on metal and canvas RAF-issue chairs, feet tapping their nerves through their boots. The pilot, co-pilot, and two despatchers. They were all carrying parachute packs, even though it was only she and Hurling who were expected to jump. Outside, as she passed by, a group of other men ferried the huge bullet-shaped metal containers out to the aircraft, a modified Whitley, which was silent, waiting like a beached whale on the makeshift runway.

'Won't be long now,' the air liaison officer said.

She huddled into herself, not for the first time wondering what she was doing, how she'd ended up here. It was like a nightmare. She'd seen a man running after them down the road, a man that looked like Tom, but she knew her mind must be playing tricks. It was the fear. Every jump made her quake. Every jump reminded her of agent Fenna who hadn't come back, and Iris, who was still paralysed from the neck down. Her training for this role suddenly seemed pitifully inadequate. For a start, how was she to go about identifying people who were resisting the Nazis, let alone set up radio networks with them, or carry messages or guns? The prospect of living under Nazi rule suddenly seemed an impossibly dark and terrifying one.

I am Gusta Hendriks, she repeated to herself, drumming her alias into her head.

'Want a dram?' One of the men, Simpson the co-pilot, offered her a flask.

She shook her head. 'No thanks.' She patted her parachute. 'I'll have enough trouble untangling myself from this thing without being drunk and disorderly.' Her smile was met by an understanding look. No one mentioned this might be a last flight for some of them. She remembered that in training they were told that the chaplain didn't say prayers for agents, only for bombers who were going into battle.

When the growl of the engine started, it made her leap to her feet.

'Easy,' said Simpson, gesturing at her to sit. 'It'll be a few minutes yet. Mechanic's got to get her warmed up.'

A few more minutes of anxious waiting. At the last minute, another agent, a huge, bear-like man strapped into a parachute, appeared, and was offered the flask of brandy.

Nancy stared a moment then leapt up to greet him. 'Klaas!' she said. 'I'd no idea!'

'Jean! Well, I'll be darned. You Ludo?' he asked, grinning. 'They told me I was having a female wireless op, but I never thought it would be you.'

'Yep,' she said. 'Not Jean now, though, it's Gusta. Gusta Hendriks.'

'I'm sticking with Klaas, but London calls me Hurling.' His familiar accent reminded her of her mother's. 'Good to see you again, Gusta.'

He sat on one of the chairs, dwarfing it. She guessed he was too tense to talk, because his foot drummed constantly up and down, and he puffed on his pipe until he was surrounded by a fog of smoke.

When the pilot and co-pilot got up and went out into the night, she was suddenly light-headed. She looked to the air liaison officer who got up and silently gestured to Klaas to get ready. She stood up. He shook Klaas by the hand, then turned to her and shook her hand too. There was something solemn in the way he did it, and it left her in no doubt. This was it.

Chapter 29

Neil drifted in and out of a haze of pain. The nurse had given him an injection that made him woozy, and his chest was so tight he couldn't breathe properly; they'd put some sort of mask over his face. The stink of rubber made him want to gag.

It was only an hour since he had made sense of the fact he'd been hit by a bomb. At the same time, what he'd been doing when the blast hit came back to him. Immediately he tried to get out of bed, but his legs were strapped into something rigid.

He fought and yelled until the nurse came back and told him both legs were smashed and he'd be in plaster for a long time. The feeling that he could do nothing for Nancy enraged him.

Otto's words about the Germans' killing efficiency came back to him in startling clarity. *'The best agents die quickly. They accept that death is coming . . . 'The weak ones are the ones that will suffer. The ones that fail to see that their time has come and try to cheat death. They are the ones that are tortured and have to dig their own graves.'*

Tom. He had to put his faith in Tom. He had never prayed so hard in his life. Even his father would be proud.

* * *

Tom kept on jogging down the road, under the moonlight, his feet in agony in his unsuitable town shoes. After about another fifteen minutes, dim red lights ahead indicated some sort of checkpoint. Thank God. He must be at the perimeter.

Elation gave him fresh energy. He crouched behind a tree while he wondered what to do.

'Who's there?' A young army cadet flashed a torch towards him,

'There's nobody there, you daft bugger,' the other man on duty replied, puffing on a cigarette. And put your torch away, the lights'll attract the Jerries.'

'Well, you put that fag out. They can spot cigs an' all, from the sky.'

'No they can't, that's rubbish.'

Tom left them arguing. He wasn't going to risk getting held up. He'd have to avoid the road and go across the fields again. His legs protested, but he forced them onwards.

As he crossed the fields the moon drifted out of the clouds and the airfield came into view: a short tarmac runway, grey in the moonlight, flanked by a group of buildings that could be stables or barns. A windsock hung limply from a pole. This must be the place. Two more soldiers were leaning on the metal gate to the farmyard, thin spirals of smoke curling up from their cigarettes. He slowed and walked on tiptoe in the lee of a hedge. He didn't want them to see him before he had a chance to find Nancy.

Despite his blistered feet, once out of their view, he was fired with the thought he was so close, and broke into a crouched run, heading for the buildings, which loomed up like the hulks of ships at sea.

A Whitley aircraft was standing on the tarmac about fifty yards off, facing down the runway. Thank God. They hadn't gone yet. Tom skirted the edges of the buildings, looking for signs that anyone was there. A crack of light shone from one of the barn doors like a needle. He took a deep breath. It was all going to take some explaining. He made a dash for the doors.

221

'Whoa!' a man emerged from behind the barn, another army man, pointing a rifle at him. 'Get away from that door.'

Tom put up his hands. 'It's all right,' he said, 'I'm English. This is RAF Tempsford, right?'

'It's a restricted zone,' the soldier said. He looked like a young cadet, agitated, full of nerves.

'I know that, I've come to speak to someone here. A woman. She's to fly tonight.' He stepped forward.

'Stay back.' The cadet jabbed the gun towards him.

'Trouble?' An older officer, also armed, appeared.

'He's looking for a woman, he says.'

A snigger. 'Hey mister, the town's thataway!'

'I need to speak to someone in charge,' he said, gambling. 'I've got instructions from Major Blunt.' Maybe the name would do the trick.

'Never heard of him.'

'It's urgent. I need to speak to a pilot then.'

They remained unmoved. 'I've important information they need to know. Information that could mean life or death for them.'

The young one turned to his friend. 'What d'you reckon, Sarge?'

'No. We have our orders. And orders are, no one gets past the perimeter. Let's search him, then take him to the lock-up until we can get him checked out.'

Just then the door to the barn opened and two RAF pilots appeared. 'What the hell's going on? What's all the noise?'

Tom kept his hands up. 'My name's Tom Lockwood. I'm from the SOE. I need to speak with agent Ludo.'

Nancy and Klaas were having last-minute checks of their pockets by the air liaison officer in case they had anything that looked English. Nancy could hear the pilots' voices arguing outside. Klaas frowned, and when nobody appeared, they glanced at each other and the air liaison officer stuck his head out into the dark to see what was going on. More raised voices.

Moments later he was outside, and his voice drifted in to them through the door. 'You can't see her,' he insisted.

Nancy peered around the edge of the barn door to see what was going on. A figure burst towards her.

She took a step back, shocked. 'Tom?'

He looked like a tramp, his eyes glinting wildly in the moonlight. 'You've got to listen, the German lines are all compromised. You mustn't make that drop.'

'No. What are you talking about?' She didn't want to hear it. Not now.

'The *Abwehr* have nailed all our agents. The Gestapo'll be expecting you. You must abort the operation.'

Klaas stepped up. 'Who the hell is this guy? Where's he come from?'

'Tom Lockwood,' Nancy said. 'We used to work together.'

'How the blazes did he know we were here? He can't just walk in from nowhere and throw a spanner in the works like this.' He squared up to Tom. 'Where's your authorisation?'

'There wasn't time, you've got to believe—'

'We only take orders through the proper channels.' The air liaison officer was definite. 'Escort him off the premises and put him somewhere secure.'

'No!' shouted Tom. 'You mustn't fly. It's a death sentence!'

Nancy stood in horror. What must Klaas think? She couldn't stop now; she'd spent so many sleepless nights gearing up for this moment.

Klaas saw her indecision. 'It's always risky. But I'm not chicken. How about you, Gusta?'

Nancy swallowed. Tom was looking at her in a beseeching way, and she longed to have time to find out what all this was about, but she couldn't let them all down. Klaas needed his radio op, and she couldn't back out now. 'Tom, I can't . . .'

The pilot stuck his head out and tapped his watch. 'We need to go in less than thirty seconds or we'll have no chance of meeting our rendezvous.'

Tom tried to take her hand, but she stepped back. 'It's Neil,' Tom said. 'He's in hospital. He got caught by a German bomb blast. He needs you.'

She felt her legs sway. 'Neil?' She tried to take it in. 'Is he all right?'

'He's badly injured. They don't know if—'

'Don't listen to him. He's just saying that to make you stay,' Klaas said.

Nancy glanced from Klaas to Tom. Tom wouldn't do that to her, would he?

'Agent Ludo?' The pilot tapped her on the shoulder. 'We need to go.'

Nancy was still a moment. She took in all their faces staring at her. Suddenly, she just wanted out of there. 'Okay, let's go.'

She turned and walked shakily towards the plane. Behind her she heard Tom shouting, 'Nancy!' Shouts and scuffling feet. But she didn't answer. A car revved up and then drove away. All noise dropped; a blanket of silence.

She hesitated again, torn.

How could Tom think she could stop now? Let them down after all that training?

The pilot and co-pilot were already on board, and the plane's engine suddenly roared above the ratcheting whirr of a propeller.

Klaas grabbed her arm. He was solid and reassuring despite the fact that the walk to the plane felt unreal, as if someone else was walking out there, about to leave all she loved behind. She climbed in like a robot. Her hands fumbled as she tightened the webbing straps on her parachute pack. Klaas was tight-lipped as he did the same. Curse Tom. What did he think he was doing putting the fear of God into them all?

224

At the same time, she knew in her heart he wouldn't have come unless there was some truth in it. Was that story about Neil really just to stop her going? If so, he hadn't succeeded. The plane began to move.

A visceral terror gripped her now, and in a panic, she went through her briefing in her mind again, imagining the layout of the countryside she'd seen on the map.

Klaas didn't speak. She guessed Tom's words had got to him too.

She felt through the slits in her flying suit to her skirt pocket for the two tablets the air liaison officer had given her: Benzedrine to keep her awake, and something called an 'L' tablet, a rubber-coated pill in case you were captured. If you bit down on that, it would be the end. She hoped Klaas had his within reach.

Tom had fought to go and speak to Nancy again, until one of the soldiers pointed a pistol to his head as the other heavier man manhandled him towards an army-type vehicle.

'Don't try anything funny,' the soldier said.

Just at that moment, Tom heard an engine begin to thrum. He glanced back towards the airfield. A Whitley aircraft was taxi-ing away down the runway. Within seconds it had disappeared into the black cowl of the sky.

They thrust him into the back seat of the vehicle, but he didn't resist. His heart was crushed. He knew in that instant it had all been for nothing, because he hadn't been able to make her understand. Or perhaps she'd understood, but her loyalty to the SOE was such that she'd chosen to ignore him. And the thought of it filled him with both admiration and terror.

PART THREE

Chapter 30

Nancy gripped tight to the parachute line that attached her to the inside of the aircraft as if she was clinging on to sanity. Klaas cracked his knuckles over and over and she longed to snap at him to stop. About a half-hour into the journey, she heard the rattle of gunfire. Tyler and Butler, the despatchers in the belly of the plane with her, exchanged wary glances. They were the men who were there to ensure the consignments, which included a five-foot-three woman in an SOE flak suit, code name Ludo, did actually get out of the plane. And they looked worried. Someone must have told them about the scene at Tempsford. Klaas said nothing; he looked even greener than she did.

Another burst of fire. Nancy let out a cry as the plane juddered and dropped, leaving Nancy's stomach somewhere in mid-air. A hole like torn paper appeared in the fuselage near a boarded-over hole. *It's a flying tin can* was Nancy's only coherent thought.

'Just German ground-air defences over the coast,' Tyler said. 'Through it now.'

'Christ, I hope that still opens,' Klaas said, looking at the gaping hole by the trapdoor.

More gunfire that seemed to be one long scream. Nancy closed her eyes, willing it to stop, gripping tight to the straps of her parachute. After that, the journey was quieter except for their chattering teeth. The metal fuselage was freezing, and every muscle became rigid with the effort of keeping the cold and fear at bay.

Finally, the plane began to climb again before dropping low, and the noise of the engine shifted to a lower churning noise. Tyler and Butler wrestled with the damaged trapdoor, as Simpson, the navigator and co-pilot, appeared to check for landmarks below through a thick blanket of cloud.

'Can't see a damn thing,' he shouted. 'But I think that's the Lek River below us. I'm looking out for their lights.'

The plane heaved and turned a circle to come in lower. Now Tyler offered Nancy a flask and she took a large swig. Rum. The fumes made her eyes water.

A clunk, and the gaping hole in the underbelly yawned open. An icy draught plastered her suit to her body. Below – black shapes, grey outlines of fields, dots that could be cows. The thought of jumping into that void transfixed her.

Behind her she could hear the scrape of metal and the jangle of lines and clips as the canisters were hitched to the line ready for their descent. The supplies would go first to avoid the agents getting entangled in their lines. All of a sudden the engine noise died. The silence was deafening.

Watching the canisters plummet one by one only increased her fear.

'D'you think your friend was right?' Klaas suddenly asked.

She shook her head. She didn't know what to think.

Klaas grabbed her hand and squeezed it. He hovered on the edge a moment until Tyler the despatcher gave him a shove. He was out before she knew it.

Her turn. *No turning back now*. The red light in front of her glowed as she shuffled to the edge, feet dangling over the void. No time to think; the light flashed green.

'Go!' Tyler yelled.

And then she was out, falling, a twisting fall. A blast of freezing air to the face as she hit the slipstream and saw the plane under-carriage veer away.

She hurtled downwards, too fast to take a breath. A jerk, and the automatic line hauled her skywards again. Above her the parachute opened in a glorious billow of silk, and she gasped and almost cried with relief. Below, the landscape looked benign, far away like a picture of a child's farmhouse toy. She was floating . . . floating. The thought fled in a panic. The ground was shooting towards her far too fast.

She tucked in her feet and tried to roll sideways just as she had been taught at Ringway in Manchester.

Crack. Thud. She fell awkwardly and her knee smashed into her jaw. For a moment she blacked out. When she came to, blood had filled her mouth, but she spat it out. She must only have been out a few seconds, for in the next field she saw three or four of the ghostly pale canisters and the silhouette of Klaas still floating down on their chutes into the next field, where flares were lit, about two hundred yards away.

She'd bitten her tongue but her legs seemed to be working. She had the mad desire to shout to Iris that she'd made it, but then she scrambled to her feet to drag her parachute in. Automatically, she unshackled the spade strapped to her leg and thrust it into the ground. It rebounded with a judder. Damn. The earth was parched and as hard as a rock. She'd never be able to bury the chute here. She dragged the silk towards a hedge and dyke and began to stuff it down.

A roar of car engines, and then voices. Her contacts. Thank God.

Nancy stood up, still shaky from the rough landing. She glanced over the hedge. The next field was surrounded by armoured cars. Not Dutch *wagens,* but German armoured cars. Though Tom had warned her of this, the actual reality of it was still a slap to the face.

Instantly she dropped out of sight. Heart hammering, she crouched into a ball, trying to cram the bright white silk into the ditch. Through the undergrowth she caught glimpses as the Germans got out of the trucks and headed towards the canisters, their helmets and tips of their rifles a dull glimmer in the watery moonlight. '*Hände hoch!*'

Klaas was a lone boulder surrounded by *Wehrmacht* guns.

She was so engrossed in watching that she didn't hear the man approach behind her until he was almost on top of her. 'Good evening, miss,' he said quietly in Dutch. She spun round. A painfully thin-looking fellow in the soft jacket and canvas trousers of a farmer. Not a German soldier, thank goodness.

'British?' he asked.

'*Ja,*' she said in Dutch, smiling with relief. This must be their contact.

He grabbed hold of her arm to help her up. She let him pull her to her feet, hoping the Germans would not look this way.

'Hey!' he yelled, gripping her tightly with both hands. '*Hier drüben!*'

Despite his skeletal appearance he was strong. A moment of shock before it clicked. This was not someone here to save her, but someone to turn her in. She hesitated only an instant before she began to fight back. Everything she'd learned in training school ran round in her head.

No time. He had to be silenced. A sharp knee to his groin and she whipped away as his grip loosened. She scrabbled for a handful of dust, and with a grunt, she threw it in his face. When he doubled over, she aimed a sharp edge-of-the-hand blow to the back of the neck.

He dropped forward like a sack of potatoes. Her hand throbbed.

A glance to her right. The Germans hadn't heard him, thank God. They were too intent on Klaas and the canisters.

Had it worked? She was shaking. She crawled frantically away from him, fearing that at any moment he'd sit up and move.

No sound from him at all. Warily, she crept back and crouched next to him. No sign of a breath. Could she really have killed him?

It didn't seem possible. What had Fairbairn taught them? Always two shots. Always make sure. But she had no weapon. The smatchet. Where was it?

In the front of her reserve chute. She pulled it out, took a deep breath and hacked hard into his kidneys as she'd been taught. Once, twice. A dark stain oozed like oil onto the ground. She didn't dare turn him over to see if he was alive.

He couldn't be.

She threw the smatchet into the hedge, overcome with revulsion. Only then did she think to run. Head down, close to the hedge, the horror of killing a man trailing after her like a ghost.

She had to find help. A woman alone at night was always suspicious, and when daylight came, someone would soon find her Dutch farmer friend who had been so keen to give her away. She'd landed off target, but only now did she realise how lucky that had been. She crept along the edge of the field, reluctant to go out onto the unmade road in case the Germans came the same way. The moon shone onto the road, lighting it up silver.

Across the road lay a huddle of farm buildings. She squinted through the hedge at the dull grey edges of two silos and a group of barns. Though it offered cover, it was too close to the landing site. They'd be looking for her and every person would be a risk. If the Resistance wireless ops here were already blown, then she couldn't even get a message home.

Just at that moment, the moon dipped behind a cloud and the road plunged into darkness. She burst out of hiding before she could think and ran across the road towards the farm, frantic to find somewhere to hide.

But next to the gate, a bicycle. She grabbed hold of it and pulled.

Chained to the gate.

She had wire cutters in her front pack, designed to cut her parachute loose from overhead telephone cables. Hands trembling, she wrenched them out. The chain was tough and the cutters too blunt.

Quickly, quickly! Frantically she champed at the metal until a volley of barking and snarling broke the silence.

A dog had heard her and now strained on its chain. Another crescendo of barks. She could just make out the glinting of its eyes.

Hands fumbling, she squeezed as hard as she could on the cutters.

Men's feet running. The dog still barking.

A twist and a tug and the chain clanked free and she leapt on the bicycle. She wobbled over the crossbar, straining to reach the pedals. A shot whistled past her and struck up sparks in the road.

They'd seen her. She stood up and pedalled furiously. Thudding footsteps were gaining on her, and another shot whizzed by to hit a tree, but then as she pumped her legs faster, the slap of boots grew fainter, and she heard men calling to each other in German.

Yes! She'd outrun them. She felt a moment of euphoric triumph before she heard the roar of the *Wehrmacht* engine start up behind her.

Immediately she dumped the bike and set off across fields, stumbling into ditches in the dark, anything to be out of sight of the road. From about four hundred yards she could see the squinted headlights of the German trucks as they stopped to look at her cycle. Torches flashed towards her, but she stayed flat to the ground, heart thumping hard against the earth.

A low rumble made her look up, and then she saw a formation of what she assumed were Allied planes go by. They strafed the German truck with a blitz of flashing machine-gun fire. It gave her the time she needed to put more space between herself and the Germans.

Some Germans must have been injured, as the vehicles turned around and the lights slowly disappeared down the road and out of sight. Nancy rolled over and looked up at the night sky. The moon was bright, a still presence set like a pearly eye in a halo of light. Its milky glow seemed to come from another world, one where killing had no place, and she squirmed under its unblinking gaze.

She was in deep trouble. Her suitcase of clothes was in Nazi hands. The money she was supposed to deliver to Verhaegen was gone, and she'd killed a man in cold blood. These things would all make the Nazis determined to find her, and she had nowhere safe to go.

She stood up and struggled out of her front pack and flying suit, down to her skirt and jersey, but her boots would look strange on a woman who wasn't supposed to be in the military. Thank God her papers and purse were in her front pack, so at least she could *be* someone. Also, there was a torch and the map, and the vital silk code square was sewn into the lining of her brassiere. Mrs Leibkovitz had thought it would be safer there than in her cuff.

She squatted down to shield the light over the map and get her bearings. She must find a transmitter and contact England somehow. The map showed a railway line and she knew this was her best chance to get out of this area altogether and forge links somewhere new. She stuffed everything into her skirt pockets and vowed that the first thing she would do would be to buy a bag. Leaving the remnants of her clothes and pack behind, she felt like a newly shorn sheep, cold and vulnerable.

She thought of Iris, safe in her clean white hospital bed, and was almost envious, but she knew she had to do what she came here to do. Granted, she'd lost the money. Agents Tennis and Hockey would never come to meet her. But she could still try to find Verhaegen, offer her help. He'd be in touch with other Resistance members, she was sure, and she had to get a message back to England somehow.

Tom had been right. She should have listened to him. If she had, maybe Klaas wouldn't be . . . No. Don't think of it. She must tell Baker Street to believe Tom. And tell them not to send anyone else. If Tom had been right about that, had he been telling the truth about Neil? The thought wormed its way into her mind and wouldn't leave her be.

A train whistle in the distance. She could do nothing for Neil here.

Please, let him be all right.

She set off, doggedly putting one foot in front of the other.

The trains didn't slow unless there was a station, so she was forced to keep stumbling through the night, over stiles and ditches, keeping the tracks in her sights. Few trains passed her out here in the countryside, and those that did were moving far too fast for her to get aboard. Eventually she came to a cluster of houses at the edge of a village, and a station. It was almost dawn, and she knew people would be stirring soon.

One of the houses had a washing line with clothes that had been forgotten and not taken inside. This was a trick she'd learned at Arisaig, to steal washing from a line. A flowered blouse and a navy skirt, both too big, but she grabbed them anyway; perhaps she could bargain with someone for them. Shame no one hung shoes out to dry. She folded the clothes and stuffed them inside her jumper. She dare not wait on the platform, but instead hunkered down beside the fence until she heard a vibration and the distant rattle of a train.

Voices. Speaking German.

Two men emerged from the waiting room, both in *Wehrmacht* uniform and armed. She sank lower, her eyes glued to them, as the train chugged into the platform.

It looked like a milk train, only open wagons, no carriages. The soldiers approached the engine and began a conversation with the driver. Some sort of inspection. They patrolled the wagons, peering over the edges to see what was there. She didn't dare move. Not yet.

One of the *Wehrmacht* lifted a hand as if to wave the driver on, and the train began to creak into motion. The Germans still had their backs to her. Could she? She summoned up a picture of the assault course at Arisaig, thought of Iris.

Now!

She forced her legs into motion and ran for the back of the train as it passed. She leapt and clung to the open wagon, her fingernails gripping the rusty iron. A heave, a scramble, and she was aboard.

The Germans had seen her. 'Hey!' One of them lifted a rifle, but he didn't fire.

She ducked out of view, panting, feeling the sway and rhythm of the train as it clanked along picking up speed. It felt good to be moving, leaving the drop site behind. The wagon was empty except for a pile of empty crates.

After a mile or two, she peered out, but there were no Germans in sight. She scanned the map again, looking for a small station near a big town, where she'd be less conspicuous and there'd be shops. She had to get civilian shoes. And thank goodness she had her watch and a ration card, even if nowhere to stay. She hoped her forged papers were good ones.

She passed through three more small stations but kept low and out of sight. Nobody came near her wagon, but she heard the clank of bottles and crates from the wagons ahead of her.

She followed the starts and stops on the map, and then, as the engine slowed for a bend, she balanced on the edge of the wagon and jumped away, using her parachute fall technique to buffer the landing. This time she landed cleanly – though her jaw still ached from the last drop.

From there she took two more trains, getting off before major towns and walking betweentimes, sleeping rough. She kept to small roads and the towpath of the canal to walk towards the city of Amsterdam. She desperately needed to find someone with radio contact. By now the Germans would have her transmitter. With luck, Klaas would pretend he knew nothing about her. That was a slim chance though; she'd been told what they did to those who didn't cooperate.

She wished he was there for her to talk to. They hadn't mention-ed this in the training, the intense feeling of loneliness, of the longing for someone to share it with, to help in all the decisions she must make.

Perhaps Verhaegen, the man Blunt said was a sympathiser, would be a kindred spirit. If she could only make contact with him. But she was wary now; he could be in the pay of the Germans too, so she'd need to recce the place first.

She kept her head down and her eyes open. She passed a few other people on the canal side, all scavenging. Most were desper-ately thin. She stood out simply because she was of normal weight. When nobody was about, she hid behind an abandoned house and put on the shapeless blouse and skirt that hid her figure and made her look thinner.

Abandoned houses along the route had their shutters torn off and windows smashed. In one of them, with the doors hanging askew from their broken hinges, she found a canvas shoulder-bag with a hole in it, but she took it and stuffed in her other clothes and her papers. The larder of the house was bare and the shelves peppered with musty mouse droppings. She was already weak from hunger, but everything she'd seen so far told her that food would be scarce.

Nearer the city, the canal gave off a glutinous stench that made bile rise in her throat. She passed two human corpses, bloated and unrecognisable, except one had a submerged yellow star on the sleeve. If she'd been in any doubt what life was like under Nazi occupation, she saw the reality now.

As the city of Amsterdam came into view, its stillness and silence was eerie. Tall houses, but dark and eyeless, no smoke from any chimneys, and around the city every tree was a hacked-off stump. Shortage of fuel, she guessed. No hum of traffic either, but many bicycles passed her on the towpath, most in a decrepit state of repair, held together by string and a wish.

She slung the bag crosswise over her chest and glanced over into a field where movement caught her attention. There were knots of people bending over, digging up what looked like onions. She wondered if she could find someone sympathetic there. But she'd have to be careful.

With practised ease, she climbed over a gate and joined the people digging, using her fingers. She unearthed a few hard lumps and sniffed them. Bulbs. She called to the woman next to her in Dutch. 'You can eat these?'

'If you're hungry enough,' the woman replied. The woman had a deeper voice than Nancy was expecting. She was bundled up in a print dress with a moth-eaten astrakhan fur coat over it and a headscarf tied under her chin. When she saw Nancy staring, she turned away to continue to dig.

Nancy approached her. 'How do you cook them?'

The woman stood up again. 'You've got fuel? Then you're lucky.'

Nancy stared at the woman's feet. Encased in too-small sandals, they were big and bony, and black with filth. Her hands were sinewy and strong. Nancy was certain this was not a woman but a young man. She bit her lip, wondering what to do; how to broach it. If he was in disguise, it could be that he was someone she could trust, yet the fear of the reprisals if she was wrong kept her hovering there.

'What are you staring at?' he asked. 'Go away. Find your own food.'

'I'm looking for somewhere to stay,' she said, aiming for a half-truth.

No answer.

'With sympathetic people.'

He stood now and looked her over. 'Can't help you.'

'But you're hiding from someone. I can see that.' She met his gaze steadily. 'I'm the same. I need a place to hide.'

'Are you a Jew?'

She shook her head. 'I just arrived in Amsterdam, and I need to hide from the authorities.'

'You done something wrong?'

239

Another shake.

He assessed her, glanced at her bag. 'If you can pay, then maybe my mother can help you.'

'I can't pay. My money was stolen.'

He returned to his digging, but then looked up, frowned. 'Who stole it?'

'The Germans.'

She saw his eyes flicker with a common sympathy. 'Then dig,' he said.

'All right.' She gathered a few more bulbs in the corner of her baggy blouse. 'What shall I call you?'

'Mika,' he said.

'Gusta,' she replied. 'What are these bulbs we're digging?'

'Tulips. Where did you say you were from?'

'I didn't,' she said. She'd been foolish to ask about the bulbs. Most locals would know what they were. There was too much to learn, too much to take in. But Mika said nothing more, just continued to prise up lumps out of the black claggy soil with his bare hands.

After about another half an hour, he said, 'Show me.'

She held out her bag, now heavy with bulbs.

'Come on then,' he said. 'We need extra help around the house.'

Chapter 31

Dordrecht, Holland

Two guards pushed Klaas in through the door of what had been the local mayor's office. Klaas glanced with envy at the jug of clean water on the German's desk. He'd had nothing to eat or drink for twenty-four hours and his mouth was parched and stiff with dried blood.

'You are the agent known as Ludo?' the German asked. He had a slim pointed nose and a small moustache, and his English was good – barely a trace of an accent.

Klaas remained sullenly silent. He'd already lost two teeth to the bastards, and his face was so swollen he could hardly speak. He was furious at Baker Street. What was the point of putting him through all that training, only to deliver him to the Nazis like a pig on a plate? They knew – they bloody knew – or how else had that crackpot come to warn them?

'We were expecting you.' The plain-clothes Gestapo man didn't even rise from the desk, but looked him over with cool detachment. 'Your friends in England told us where and when you would be dropped, and we have your transmitter. So now you will transmit a message to London to say you have arrived safely.'

'Can't, can't remember the codes.'

This last statement gained Klaas another smack across the back of the head with a rifle.

'It's no use withholding information, for we have it already. Your friends with the foolish sporting names – Hockey, Football and Tennis – have already told us what we need to know. You are on your own now, yes? No one will come to rescue you. We run the whole network. Of course, you could have met with an accident on the way down,' he said. 'That sometimes happens to careless parachutists. Their chutes fail.' His grey-green eyes were hard as slate.

It was a threat and it rippled through Klaas like cold water. Klaas looked down through blurred vision at his trembling hands and willed them to lie quiet.

'You will transmit to England. Our officer will set up your transmitter along with the others.'

Klaas swallowed again. What was the point of objecting? If they knew everything and were running the whole show? He was stuck here on his own. It was all right in training, thinking you'd be brave and never give anything away. But that was before you were handcuffed in a cell, with two Nazi guards breathing down your neck and a Gestapo officer staring you down. What had seemed like a great adventure, like being part of a crack team from a *Boy's Own* comic, had turned out to be just this – a choice between a lonely death or to do as they said. They'd frisked him and taken his 'L' capsule straightaway, along with his belt and shoelaces and all the kit in his pockets. The Geneva Convention might save him – if he lasted long enough and made it to the end of the war. He might even meet up with other British agents who'd been caught. And it wasn't as if anyone in England would ever know, was it?

A knock behind him. 'Major Giskes, we searched the drop zone as you asked, and there's a body. Herr Helk is dead. Stabbed.' Klaas's German was enough to make out the gist.

242

'That's odd. We intercepted straightaway.'

'We saw a woman running away. She went across country, but we couldn't catch her because of an English raid. We also found a suitcase. It contains women's clothes.'

Frauenkleider, Klaas thought, translating the word. Women's clothes? So they hadn't found Jean yet.

'Bring me the case.' He turned to Klaas and spoke in English. 'You have some questions to answer, Ludo,' Giskes said. 'Take him away. I'll send someone to interrogate him once I've looked at this suitcase.'

Klaas was taken back to his cell, a six-foot-square brick-built box. So the Jerries thought he was Ludo the wireless op, did they? And not agent Hurling. Well, he'd keep that up as long as he could. Ludo, who he knew as Jean, the girl who'd jumped with him, had always impressed him right from training camp. She was a brave woman. She hadn't let that crazy man at the airfield get to her. She'd jumped, despite his warnings.

Maybe the man hadn't been so crazy after all.

Klaas sat on the wooden bench and nursed his sore head. So far, the Nazis didn't seem to know an agent called Hurling existed. Probably because he'd only just finished his sabotage training, and Churchill was keen on getting as many men out there as he could, before the big push.

A few days later, Giskes took him to a room stinking of disinfectant. A table with a washed oilcloth bore pliers, hammers and an iron crowbar. He guessed this was the room where men were given beatings. Klaas was a big man, but still, he tried to breathe deeply and hold his nerve as two men followed him in. They couldn't know anything about Gusta Hendriks if they thought he was Ludo.

He couldn't think of anything once they started, except praying for it to stop. Gortner, a thick-lipped blond officer who could speak English, led the interrogation. It gave him pleasure, after his ribs were cracked by the swing of an iron bar, to tell them point-blank he knew nothing about any female agent, or why she was dropped, and that he hadn't been told her name.

'She must be trained. She killed one of our contacts,' Gortner said in his grating accent, weighing the bar in his hands.

'Perhaps it wasn't her who killed him. Perhaps people didn't like "your contact" being a collaborator,' Klaas said, shooting Giskes a barbed look, through swollen eyes.

Giskes looked sceptical. But he raised his hand for the beating to stop.

Klaas stood like an ox. He knew they had to let it go, or kill him.

The next day Klaas was dragged to the wireless room, even though he could hardly stand for the pain. He expected to see some English agents there, but to his horror the men at the long counter were all uniformed German officers. A cold feeling of dread snaked in his belly. So that was why they'd left his hands alone. They thought he was Ludo and needed him to be able to tap out Morse.

Gortner was there again, strutting around like a lord. He pushed Klaas towards a crystal set and headphones, and sat him down at gunpoint. 'You will tell England you have arrived, and you will transmit at your scheduled times. Tell them you will deliver to Verhaegen as Hockey arranged.'

So they knew all about Verhaegen. Where did it end? The Nazi tentacles were all over their networks.

'Begin,' Gortner said.

Klaas wished he'd paid more attention to coding in training. He didn't know Ludo's poem, or even if she had one. How could he? 'Can't remember, my head aches like the devil,' he said. 'If you beat the shit out of me, what do you expect?'

Gortner lashed out with a punch to the nose that left him reeling. Now he really couldn't think.

A whispered conversation between Giskes and Gortner. Finally, Giskes instructed one of the men who was transmitting as Hockey to send for Ludo's new codes from London, claiming Ludo had forgotten. Klaas feared that as they thought he was Ludo, they were only keeping him alive to watch him transmit so one of their men could replicate Ludo's transmitting style, see if he remembered her send code, which of course he would not, and check which bandwidth she was on. At the same time, he was blearily aware that confessing he was Hurling now would give them no reason to keep him alive.

What would London do, when he failed to make contact?

The sight of all those Germans at wireless stations had made him certain he wouldn't be staying there. Would it be a camp, or a bullet through the head? All he could do is play for time, and hope God was on his side.

To Klaas's despair and disgust, Baker Street saw nothing suspicious in Hockey's request, and less than a week later, the new poem code for wireless operator Ludo arrived from London via a sked to Hockey, who was of course one of Giskes' men. Giskes had Klaas brought to his office but made him wait just outside the door, probably because after a week without washing and his wounds festering, he stank.

Klaas gathered from Giskes that he would be expected to use the new code and show Gortner how to encode it the way he'd been taught. He supposed this was so they could keep up with any new changes to English coding methods. So for the next transmission, Gortner was breathing down his neck again, acting like his dog handler, shouting out orders and hitting him when he didn't understand. Klaas followed the written instructions London had sent with the poem, an extract from 'The Owl and the Pussycat'. It seemed ironic; was he the owl or the pussycat? Finally, the encoded message was there in front of him and he began the laborious business of 'dit-dit-dah'.

All this time he was closely watched by Gortner, who was making notes on a small pad.

His fear was thick as tar. He was the only Englishman in the row of uniformed Germans. When the Morse was done, he finally signed off with MS/G ENDS.

He took off the headset to find Giskes had arrived again with two more guards armed with rifles.

'*Alles gut?*' Giskes asked Gortner.

'*Ja, ich kann das tun,*' Gortner said.

He could do it. Did that mean blubber-lipped Gortner was to take over Ludo's skeds?

Giskes nodded and Gortner led the way down the corridor. Klaas was reluctant to follow him, but the soldiers crowded him and pushed him forward.

Klaas began to pray as soon as he realised they weren't going back to the cells. Instead, at gunpoint they bullied him down a narrow corridor towards a grey-painted door. As Klaas followed Gortner's rigid back, he heard ominous clicks as the rifles behind him were loaded and cocked, and his eyes silted with hopelessness. Not a single English or Dutch agent had he seen.

Gortner yanked open the grey door to let Klaas pass through. A high-walled yard. The walls splashed with flowers of dried blood. Klaas turned to run, but one of the soldiers already had his gun raised. The first shot caught Klaas in the shoulder, and he staggered to the other wall looking for any chink, but the walls were solid stone and mortar. He looked up, astonished to feel the sun, warm on his face. He turned from the light, in time to see a muzzle pointed at his chest. The last thing he saw was the blink of the soldier's eye as he fired.

Chapter 32

In the last remaining light of the day, Tom sat by the window of his cramped bedsitting room, determined to write to Neil. Frustratingly, although he'd telephoned the hospital several times last week, they wouldn't tell him anything except it was 'family visitors only', and Neil was 'comfortable'. What did that mean?

So now he had no alternative but to write. Tom paused to refill his fountain pen, wondering what to tell Neil about Nancy. It still hurt like hell that he hadn't been able to stop her. And he kept reseeing her face in his mind's eye. That closed look in her eyes that shut him out and meant she had chosen her SOE orders over his pleading. And, of course, he'd no way of knowing where she was now.

The army sergeant at Tempsford, on checking Tom's identity, had contacted Beauclerk. Of course he had. The Tempsford sergeant was keen to play down the fact he'd failed to stop an intruder, especially a member of the Special Operations Executive – and, after some string-pulling by Beauclerk, the authorities had labelled it as a test mission, saying they'd sent Tom deliberately in order to tighten up security. Supposedly that would quash any rumours about what the devil he was doing at a remote airfield in the middle of the night.

Of course, he couldn't tell Neil any of this in the letter. The censors would have a field day. Nor could he tell him about his thorny meeting with Beauclerk. After they'd let him out of the cell at Tempsford, Beauclerk had been to see him for debriefing and been aghast at what Tom had attempted to do. 'Bloody idiot,' he'd said. 'I thought you'd more brains than that.'

Though Beauclerk had expressed sympathy for Neil, he'd given nothing away about Nancy. Tom could no longer, in all good conscience, expose Neil, when Neil himself had volunteered to confess. And besides, it was clear Neil had been acting under threat from the thugs of the BUF. More worryingly, the Baker Street secrecy, instead of it being its usual loose knitting, all holes and dangling threads, was suddenly impregnable. No matter how he begged, Beauclerk wouldn't budge on giving him information about agents in Holland.

Tom gazed at the writing pad and wished he had better news for Neil. In the end, he opted for something as succinct as he could make it.

Dear Neil,
I did get there in time. But Nancy decided not to take my advice. I couldn't stop her, though I tried. Soon as they let me visit, I will. I hope you are feeling better. Such rotten luck.
Tom

He put the letter to Neil in an envelope, and addressed it.

He must get ready for work. In some sort of petty vengeance, after the Tempsford fiasco, Beauclerk had transferred him to Arkley View, a Y-station unit in Barnet, north London – part of the Signals operation network. It acted as a data collection centre, where coded traffic was collated and passed on to Bletchley Park. *Where the real work was done*, he thought bitterly.

Arkley View was a definite demotion, and even though Tom knew he deserved it, it made his blood boil just thinking of it. It was dull, routine work; work that any pen-pusher could do. He wondered what Beauclerk had told his boss, Mr Marks, about his sudden departure. He felt bad about it, leaving with no notice.

Since then, Tom had tried to wear Beauclerk down, hoping to get news of the drop in Holland. He called him frequently at the office, but his calls to Beryl were met with, 'Mr Beauclerk is not available'. After a number of calls to Blunt and N Section, all fobbing him off with 'try later', the switchboard blocked his incoming number.

If he hadn't been so pig-headed, Nancy would never have volunteered. She'd still be in London, safe in the cipher room. He cursed himself. He knew the risks; knew agents' life expectancy.

There must be something he could do. He couldn't just sit and wait. At least at Arkley View he'd access to a receiver. And he wouldn't give up trying to find out what had happened to her.

'Do me a favour, would you?' Tom asked Bennett, his deskmate in the cramped and seedy suburban house that was Arkley View. 'Let me know if you hear anything at all about the Netherlands.'

'Why?'

'Just interested. I know someone who lives there.'

Bennett nodded, but Tom could tell he hadn't really taken much notice.

Tom sighed and turned back to his desk. His new job was to sift through any suspicious enemy broadcasts that had been picked up by the volunteer radio hams, log them and send them to the Barnet post office, from where they'd be telegraphed on to Bletchley. Several of these reports came in by motorcycle courier every day, leading Tom to feel more and more that the Germans were pushing hard and the English were staggering on the back foot.

He'd spent the last few days trying to discover any reference at all to agents in Holland. It was like picking at a scab, painful but irresistible, because he had to know whether any agents from N

249

Section were still alive. Now he held the headphones tight to his ears and was wading through static. The frequencies he was tuning into were not officially part of his remit, and besides intercepting foreign radio signals, ironically, he was supposed to monitor local messages to detect possible spy infiltration. He dreaded one of his own team flagging him up as a rogue operator.

Through the blur of static, he kept thinking of Kohout and King and their fascist cabal, but he didn't dare do anything. To report it now would put Neil back under the microscope, and wasn't Neil in enough trouble already, from those fascist bastards? Through caring for Nancy, they'd become staunch allies if not exactly friends.

A tap on the shoulder made Tom startle. Bennett, his desk companion, mouthed the words, 'Lunch, mate?'

Tom gave him the thumbs-up, but ignored his lunch break again and kept listening, tuning into any frequency he could remember from N Section until he thought his head might burst, hoping against hope that he'd hear something – anything – that would convince him Nancy was still alive. That he'd been mistaken and N Section was safe as houses.

Every night he went home with a throbbing head, dreading he'd hear about agents captured by the Nazis with the feeling that he was wandering Minotaur-like in some labyrinth of wires and white noise. Today he glanced at the hallstand in case there was mail.

A letter from Neil. Damn, their letters must have crossed.

Tom,
I'm sorry I failed to shut down the line, but I trust you got there.

A twist of guilt. He carried on reading.

I can't have any visitors except family, so please, if she's in London, ask Nancy to come. I'm in a pretty bad way and I need her to break the news to my father and concoct something plausible

250

about the real job I do, and why I can't go back. Tell her I cocked up, and I'm sorry.

   Neil

Tom sat down on the cold stairs and weighed it in his hands. What to do? Infernal post office. His letter must be lost in some sorting office somewhere. He imagined Neil waiting in his hospital bed for Nancy's visit that would never come. The thought of it made him screw up the envelope into a tight ball.

Neil shifted in his hospital bed, grateful for the clean white sheets and quiet orderliness of the routine. Morphine had helped ease the pain, and now his legs were set in splints he was able to move a little without too much discomfort. Enough at least to drink a cup of tea, though that still hurt as if knives were pressing in his chest. Broken ribs they'd said.

For the last week, he had slept most of the time. Exhaustion had dragged him under like drowning. He still had vivid flashes of what had happened, of the flare and rip of the bomb.

The thought of it still made him tremble. The way he was thrown so suddenly against a wall and the way the ground shook. He remembered Tom's face through the dust and knew he'd helped get him out.

Better not to think of it. Better not to think of so many things.

He'd been supposed to talk to Blunt, but after the blast nobody would let Neil call him. When he protested, they just filled him with morphine again.

Neil bit his fingernails; the griping fear at the bottom of his belly never eased. If Father found out he was a coward and a traitor, or worse, that he'd killed someone against all the Christian commandments, Neil would never be able to look him in the eye again. Now though, the thoughts wouldn't stop. When he wasn't worrying about Nancy or about his father's opinion of him, he was worrying over the sentence he'd get

251

for Otto's murder, and if he wasn't worrying about that, he was terrified of the British Union of Fascists, that they'd all be bombed again in their beds, or that the Germans might invade and put all of them to death.

The ward door clanged open and his heart gave an unpleasant jolt.

'Visitor,' the sister in charge said. 'We'll just get you respectable.'

She bustled away with the bedpan. Neil was disconcerted; it took him a few moments to realise something different was happening, and he was in a daze as she returned to haul him upright.

A sudden hope lit him up. Maybe Tom had got word to Nancy after all. *Pull yourself together.* He put on a smile for her, prepared to pretend everything was all right.

But when the door opened, he could see the shape of a man bundled in an overcoat. Sister led the man towards him.

Neil's head began to swim. His father stared back at him.

'Father.' He could barely get out the word. He'd be disappointed in him, again.

'What's all this, son?' His father looked older, his grey hair thinning, his face no longer taut and forbidding, but heavy-jowled and blotchy under his greying moustache.

'How did you know? Who told you I was here? Was it Nancy?'

'No.' His father shook his head wearily, but his eyes were their usual penetrating blue. 'Why in God's name didn't you telephone us when you were in trouble? We didn't even know you were in hospital—'

'There wasn't time, and I didn't want to worry you—'

'You mother's frantic. If it hadn't been for Tom Lockwood, we'd never have known. He telephoned the post office at Glenkyle and they fetched me to the phone. Your mother and I rang the hospital straightaway, but they wouldn't let you have visitors. As soon as they'd let us come, we got the early train. Mother's back at the hotel; she's waiting for me to go back and tell her what's what.'

'Tom told you? Did he tell you about Nancy?'

'Nancy doesn't know. We didn't want to worry her. Thought it was better to wait until you're a bit better.'

'So you've not heard from her?' He wanted to get it straight.

'How are you feeling?' his father asked.

'Lucky to be alive. But sore.'

Neil told him what was broken, and his father nodded. 'Tom says there was some sort of trouble at work too, and he thought you might need some sort of heavyweight help from someone who knows the army and the law.'

'Tom doesn't know what he's talking about. I don't need any help.'

His father's eyes grew glassy. 'You don't get it, do you? We have to help. You're our son. We love you. If you're in trouble we can't just sit and do nothing. It would kill us.' He sat down and reached his hand to place it on Neil's arm. His father's hand was old and veined, and the sight of it crumbled something in Neil's chest.

'Tell us what's happening, please.' His father had a begging expression. 'Tom wouldn't tell us anything, just told us to come.'

Neil looked down at the grey hospital blanket. They didn't know about Nancy, and Tom hadn't sent her, which must mean Tom too had failed and Nancy was in Holland. The weight of it, that he should have told Blunt about Johnson, should have insisted right at the beginning that N Section was compromised, was suffocating.

'Neil?'

He looked up, his eyes blurred. 'That's just it, Father. I can't tell you anything. I swore not to.'

'Who did you swear to? Who's leaning on you?'

A whisper. 'The country.'

His father's eyebrows shot up, then he closed his eyes for a long moment. When he opened them, they were soft. 'I never knew. I thought you were just some office clerk.'

253

'Don't. I'm no hero.'

His father's mouth set in a hard line. 'You are to me.'

'I made a mess of everything. I deserve everything that's coming to me.'

'Whatever it is, we'll get the best lawyer. The best advice. Once you get out of hospital.'

Neil's stomach knotted. 'I just want to tell the truth. I'm tired of hiding everything. It eats me away from the inside. I just want to come clean.'

'Don't admit to anything, though, hear me?'

Neil felt panic rising again. 'You want me to lie again, don't you, so I'll get off being punished? But I can't, I killed—'

His father hit the bed with his fist. 'Shut up!'

Sister hurried over. 'What's going on?'

'Sorry.' His father wiped his forehead. 'Sorry.' His mouth worked, and his shoulders slumped like a deflated balloon.

'No, Dad, I'm sorry.' He hadn't called him Dad for years. He put a hand out towards him and his father reached it and clasped it so tight it hurt.

'Neil. For the love of God, just don't say anything out loud you'll later regret. We'll sort it out. Whatever it is, we can deal with it, okay?'

Neil wanted to tell him about his fears for Nancy but couldn't bear to. His father looked small and old and bowed down. They looked at each other for a long time, gripping hands, before the bell rang for the end of visiting.

Chapter 33

In the pre-dawn gloom, Nancy put on the threadbare tweed coat and the shoes that pinched because they belonged to Mika's mother. The diminutive Mama van Hegel had taken her in without question, and in return Nancy had been helping her with the household chores. It had been good to have something practical to do for the first week while she got used to the Dutch idiom and got her bearings in Amsterdam. But now it was time to do what she had come here to do. This morning she must brave Verhaegen's factory, *Berg en Leiden*, or at least take a look at it, and it was away across the other side of the city.

'There,' Mika's mother said. 'Now you look poor, just like us.' She did up the top button of Nancy's coat in a fussy, motherly kind of way that made Nancy's heart ache for home. Mama van Hegel was a small, wizened woman, with a face lined before its time. The war had certainly taken a toll on her; she was grey from her head to her feet.

Nancy brushed down the coat, which at least had a fur collar – though moth-eaten. 'Thank you for letting me borrow them.' Nancy hugged her, for she knew this was a precious piece of warmth Mama van Hegel could ill afford. Though it was summer, there was a chill this early in the morning, and besides, it felt like extra protection.

As soon as the siren signalled the end of night curfew, Nancy kissed Mama on both cheeks and set off. She glanced back briefly at the tall, red-brick terraced house that leant towards the street before walking briskly through the growing dawn. She had been lucky, she thought, to meet Mika. From Mama van Hegel she'd learnt that Mika was just sixteen and eligible for transportation to work as forced labour in Germany.

'All the men must have employment certificates,' Mama van Hegel had said. 'If you can't prove you're working, you just get taken. You're lucky to be a girl, but best to be a poor ugly one, you understand? That's why I tell Mika, better to be a girl.'

Two of Mika's elder brothers had been rounded up at gunpoint, but now they'd changed the rules and Mika was eligible too. Mama dreaded him leaving because her daughter, Lotte, who was only eight, had caught polio and had a withered leg. The Germans were taking these sorts of children away from their parents, and Mama needed Mika to scavenge food while she schooled Lotte and kept her away from nosy German eyes.

And as Nancy hurried down the streets, it was noticeable there were no men. The city of London, and especially Baker Street, had been full of men in their suits and bowler hats. Now Amsterdam was a city of women. Women trudging drearily to their work. Great queues of them lining up to buy what they could, or hurrying in droves to the factories.

After forty minutes walking, she began looking for the address on the outskirts of the Northern Quarter. You couldn't miss the factory – a long, low brick-built shed of a place at the end of a cul-de-sac. A billboard outside shouted the Dutch equivalent of 'Make Do and Mend'. Nancy walked around the walled perimeter and noticed that the paintwork was peeling around the windows and anti-Jewish graffiti had been scrawled on the doors. It was obviously under *Wehrmacht* control, with armed guards patrolling the gates, so she'd need some valid excuse to get past them.

A klaxon sounded and the doors all round opened. A coughing group of night-shift workers straggled out from the low brick buildings into the humid air – mostly women, and a few old men, their heads bowed, wooden clogs a-clatter on the road. At the same time, another horde of women jostled up the road and funnelled into a queue to have their papers examined at the gates.

So that was the routine. Nancy didn't want to show her papers. If they were recognised as false, she'd be no use to England. Not in a German prison cell.

In Dutch, she asked a grey-haired woman who was on her way in what they made in the factory.

'Nothing,' the woman said, bitterly. 'We can't get the cloth. We just mend things now. Most of the workers were Jews, and they've scarpered. After their houses are cleared, we get their stuff here to mend and sell on. Of course, the Germans get the best stuff, we just get the chaff. But they'll take you on if you've sewing experience.'

Nancy thanked her. She'd limited sewing experience, though her cover story was that she was a milliner – they'd thought carrying a hatbox might be useful. Where was she supposed to get one of those in occupied Amsterdam? It made her smile, that they had prepared her so meticulously but also had no idea at all what the place was really like.

Robbing Jewish households seemed an odd business for a Resistance worker like Verhaegen, but it was probably one that wouldn't rouse suspicion.

To be on the safe side, she headed for Centraal Station, where she knew there must be telephones, and queued for a kiosk so she could arrange to see Verhaegen. She'd memorised his office number back in England, so she dialled, and while she was waiting, through the glass window she saw two German soldiers dragging a skinny man along the platform by his arms.

The phone clicked, and a crisp, no-nonsense woman's voice answered, 'Yes?'

Nancy dragged her attention from the man and asked for Verhaegen. After a couple of moments, he came on the line.

She enunciated the code words carefully in Dutch. 'Can you spin flax into gold?'

A silence on the other end, before he replied, '*Repelsteeltje.*' Rumpelstiltskin, the correct answer.

'Gusta Hendriks,' she said. 'Can we set up a meeting?'

'Who?' A hesitation. Then, 'Ah. I was expecting to hear from you,' came the wary answer. His voice was like gravel.

'Any news of my colleague?' she asked. Klaas had been preying on her mind.

'Your colleague?' Again that odd pause. 'No news yet. It can take some time to . . . to get information. Where are you staying?'

She held back. She didn't want to mention Mika's family. 'Close to the Centraal Station,' she said. 'Can you see me now?'

A pause. 'I need some time to make sure we are secure. You must wait until noon tomorrow.'

'Not today?'

'No. Noon tomorrow is the earliest I can do it.'

She swallowed her disappointment. 'All right. I'll be alone,' she said. A silence. She got the impression he was distracted by something. 'Herr Verhaegen?'

'Yes, when you arrive, go around the back to the gate with a single sentry. Tell him your name and that you have an appointment, and he won't ask for your papers. Tell him you have some samples of fabric stiffener for me. You have the suitcase with the delivery I asked for?'

'Agreed. I'll be there.' She skirted past the issue of the suitcase and all that money lost to Nazi hands. She couldn't risk that he wouldn't want to meet her. How else could she get word to the SOE in England without his help?

She came out of the telephone box to see a Nazi soldier watching.

258

The station was teeming with them, like maggots round a wound. She had to remind herself that from the outside she wasn't an English agent, just Gusta Hendriks telephoning her mother for news. She put a smile on her face even though as she turned, she felt the soldier's gaze prickling on the back of her neck, and a cold shiver made her pull her coat tighter across her chest as she walked quickly away.

Her terror of these big armed men was reflected back by the whole population. She could blend in because they all feared the same enemy. Everyone had their heads down and avoided eye contact with anyone else.

She took a deep breath as she crossed Dam Square, feeling an easing of tension for the first time. Thank God she'd made contact with Verhaegen. She just had to hope he'd have a transmitter and could get word to London. The quicker the better, before more men followed Klaas. She hurried faster so she didn't have to think about Klaas and whether he was dead or alive.

'You met the man about work in the factory?' Little Lotte came up to her as soon a she got through the door, excited, a sparkle in her eyes.

Nancy smiled at her. 'I've an appointment for tomorrow,' she said.

'Will you get lots of money?'

'Maybe. We'll see.'

She shooed Lotte back towards the tub in the kitchen sink and picked up a blouse to help wring it out. Lotte flicked her plaits out of the way, took the other end and twisted until the water dripped out. Despite her leg, which was locked into a calliper, Lotte always helped her mother in the house.

Mama turned and gave them an affectionate smile.

'Here, Mika.' Lotte handed Mika the basket of wrung-out washing.

How had the boy Mika managed all this time under German scrutiny? The Nazi occupiers were everywhere, looking for a fight all the time, as if the minute they put on a uniform they had to become a 'force' and not human beings.

Mika was about to go past Nancy to hang the laundry out to dry in the back yard when she stopped him. 'I'll do that,' Nancy said. There was a shadow on his chin. Soon Mika would have too much of a beard, and he'd be unable to pass as a woman. What would happen to Mama van Hegel and Lotte then?

When Mamma came out to put the last of the washing on the line, Nancy heard the neighbour call from over the wall, 'You and your girls got a visitor, Mrs Van Hegel?'

It was an innocent enough question before the war. Now it was like dynamite. 'My sister's girl,' Mamma insisted, 'come to look for work.'

When Mamma carried the empty laundry basket back in, her face was even more worried than before, though she gave Nancy a tight smile.

Nancy returned the smile but knew she must find somewhere else soon. It was all right for her; she had assessed all the risks and been trained for them. She'd learnt a few tricks. But Mamma van Hegel and her children, Mika and Lotte, had no killing skills, no safe houses, and they were risking their lives for her just as much, out of sheer goodness. It humbled her.

In the morning, Nancy left a note propped on the washstand in her room; it said simply, *'Thank you. Gusta.'* No use to make a fuss over goodbyes. She must move on from the Van Hegel's house; she was a risk to them. In the square next to the canal, she spent the last of her coins at the flea market bargaining for a suitcase. Good suitcases were scarce because so many folk were on the move, and the black market made everything expensive. She bargained with a toothless old man for a battered case with a handle attached by string, and a pair of shoes that were her size. So what if the soles were holed? At least she could walk better than in the ones she'd borrowed from Mama. She slipped them on and put Mama's in the case to give it some weight.

The sentry at the back of *Berg en Leiden* looked bored. She told him she had an appointment, and he waved her through. She supposed she looked like every other worker, and the thought gave her confidence. She marched in through the door and smiled at the girl behind the reception desk who was typing a letter.

'Gusta Hendriks,' she said over the clatter of the typewriter. 'I've some samples to show Herr Verhaegen.'

'Yes. He knows you're coming. Second door on the left.' She didn't even look up.

In the distance, the midday church bells began to chime the hour.

Her first impression of Verhaegen was that he was older than she'd imagined. She'd somehow thought all Resistance men would be young people like herself, but he was well into his forties, paunchy and balding, with a small grey wisp of a moustache. His office was cramped and piled with what looked like old files. She squeezed past them to get to his desk.

'Ah, Miss Hendriks, good to meet you.' His eyes searched out her suitcase.

The telephone rang, and he held up his hand to her a moment while he answered. 'Yes.' A pause, as he listened. 'Yes. Now.' He put the receiver down and gave her his attention.

'I need to get word to London,' she said. 'The line is blown. They were waiting for us and, as I assume you know, agent Hurling got caught. I was lucky, I landed out of sight.'

Verhaegen shook his head. 'It happens,' he said. 'It's not the first time.'

'And I'm so sorry, but the suitcase is empty,' she said. 'They got that too.'

'What?' His eyes sparked. 'My contact never mentioned that.' A frown. 'You're sure?'

261

In response, she flipped the case open on his desk to reveal Mama's old shoes.

He pursed his lips. 'Did you see the Germans pick it up?'

Didn't he trust her? Something about his attitude, and the lack of niceties, bothered her.

'No . . . I mean I can't be certain. It was hardly wise for me to hang about. If we don't want it to happen again we'll need to tell London as a matter of urgency,' she said. 'Do you have access to a transmitter? I was hoping . . .' She turned as she heard someone open the door behind her.

Helmet, gun. The shock made blood rush to her head. A German in uniform, armed with a revolver. What was going on? She swivelled back, took in the bland lack of reaction on Verhaegen's face.

With a jolt, she turned again to see another grey-green hulk brace to block her exit.

A trap. No time to think.

She thrust the suitcase across the table and upwards towards Verhaegen's jaw. It hit him full in the chin with a crack. He toppled backwards in his chair.

It was enough. A burst of adrenaline made her lightning fast.

In one fluid movement she stepped back to elbow the nearest German in the pit of the stomach. It was like hitting a wall, but he buckled and made a grab for her. Quick as an eel she slipped past him, knocking files and papers into a scatter on the floor. The other man lurched after her, skidding on the debris, but she banged the door in his face with all her strength. She heard the metallic clang as it hit his helmet.

Not past the guards at the gates. Another way.

Two routes. She chose the one into the factory.

Avoid open ground. Find cover. That's what Fairbairn, her trainer, had said. His words echoed in her head.

She shot down a corridor to where she could hear the whirr of machines behind a grey door with a ground-glass window.

Breathing hard, she thrust open the door to see a sea of women all at sewing machines.

Calm. Stay calm. Ignoring the thump of her heart, she walked purposefully to an empty machine, took off her coat and turned it inside out to its tawny silk lining. She lifted the lever and slid the coat under the foot of the machine. Her foot on the treadle made the cloth shoot towards her too fast, but she took it out and started again hoping no one would see she'd just sewn up a sleeve.

A couple of the girls who were chatting as they worked stared curiously at her, but nobody said anything. She assumed they'd think she was another worker. She found a square of cotton in a basket next to her and tied it over her hair as a headscarf. Then she lowered her head and kept sewing.

Stupid, stupid. She should have guessed. If the lines were blown, Verhaegen would be in the German's pay too.

Male voices in the corridor. From the corner of her eyes, she made out the blurred outline of *Wehrmacht* uniforms outside the door. The door opened and the atmosphere in the room sharpened. The women bowed their heads and worked the machines harder.

Nancy did the same. Without the coat, and wearing a scarf, she'd be much less recognisable. Desperately she kept her foot on the treadle, hoping the officer hadn't caught enough of a look at her to remember her face. The door shut again.

She exhaled but carried on sewing the same patch over and over. All she could think was that Mama's coat would be ruined. After ten more minutes, when there was no sign of anyone else in the corridor, she eased her foot off the treadle, slid the coat out from under the needle and cut the threads. Strolling as if in no hurry, but with her heart pounding, she walked out of the sewing room with the coat over her arm, and down the corridor, scanning for an exit.

She pushed open a door into a smaller room. Again full of women, this time winding the handles on heavier, noisier machines.

They were mending leather goods – bags, shoes, belts. There were piles of these.

With a sharp intake of breath, she understood these must be the belongings the Jews had left behind in their houses. They were being recycled and sold on. She shut the door quickly and ran on until she came to a set of double doors where two men were loading boxes heaped with leather goods into a car boot.

Should she run for it?

German voices from behind her.

She froze. Running would draw attention, and there were guards at the gate. On the floor by the doors were a few butt ends of cigarettes.

A thin-faced girl was standing there in the cold, smoking. Nancy bent to pick up a butt and joined her, trying to appear nonchalant, asking her for a light. The girl handed over her cigarette and Nancy lit the butt from it.

By the gate the two guards gave her a cursory glance.

'Not seen you here before,' the girl said. 'You work in the office, do you?'

'Yes. Clerk,' Nancy said.

'I'm Ada. Don't stand there in front of the door, the sewing girls will be out for their lunch break soon.' No sooner had Ada said this than there was a klaxon and a clatter of shoes. Women pushed past her and out of the double doors, thronging towards the gates.

Nancy saw her chance and took it, hurrying behind a group of about five women. The guards stood back to let them pass, and just as she weaselled through, a pistol shot echoed in the air and a voice yelled, 'Close the gates.'

She didn't dare look back.

Nowhere was safe. No Resistance members could be trusted, she realised with a cold certainty. She was stranded in enemy territory, and she was alone.

Chapter 34

Nancy had no option but to return to Mika's house and hope they'd let her stay a little longer. As she approached, she saw that the door and downstairs windows had been roughly boarded up, but already there were looters ripping it down.

She stood outside, at a loss.

On the pavement was a sticky red-brown patch. Blood. She was sure of it.

The nosy neighbour appeared, dressed in a ragged housecoat, her eyes bright and furtive. She jabbed a finger at Nancy. 'You're not a relation of Mrs Van Hegel. I could smell it.'

Nancy didn't answer. She was still staring at the house.

'I thought not. They've gone,' the woman said with a cat-like grin. 'The *Wehrmacht* came. They took the girl who turned out to be a boy. And the younger one with the withered leg. Mrs Van Hegel tried to stop them.'

'They took Lotte? Where's Mrs Van Hegel?'

'They shot her, then loaded her on a cart.' The woman licked her lips, staring.

Nancy sank to her haunches. It couldn't be true. She'd only been gone a few hours. But a glance at the neighbour with her hard expression told her the stark truth.

'You informed on them.' Nancy stood up. 'You disgust me.' She couldn't bear to look at her. She turned away and walked unsteadily back down the street.

'She deserved it,' the woman shouted, her voice shrill. 'It wasn't fair! She should have sent her son to Germany like the rest of us!'

Nancy trudged away from the house. Caution told her not to go back in case the Nazis returned. It was still urgent she get a message to England, but she had no idea what to do. She sat on a low wall outside a house a little further down the street, while she tried to formulate some sort of plan. She was empty-handed, apart from her papers and the silk code still pressed against her heart. It seemed so long ago that she was in the cipher room, smiling with Tom Lockwood when it had been just an idea. She had never thought she would be the one who would have to use it. That's if she could ever find a transmitter.

'Hey.' A low female voice from a window. 'Quick! Go around the back.'

Nancy glanced back up the street. The collaborator, Mama's neighbour, had gone back inside her house.

Shaken, and uncertain whether to obey the instruction, Nancy hesitated. At the small window, a figure behind the glass was frantically beckoning. Nancy stood up. Maybe it would be third time lucky. She had to trust it would be all right; after all, she could defend herself if necessary.

Warily, she peered around the back of the house to where a door stood open into a narrow, tiled kitchen. An old woman poked her head out. She had lively black eyes behind her spectacles. 'It's all right. I saw what happened to the Van Hegels. I want to help. Come in.'

Nancy entered the tall terraced house with all her senses on red alert, but there was nobody else there. No men. No Nazis. Just this little old woman with a halo of white candy floss hair over brown skin creased into a hundred wrinkles.

'I saw you go past a few times, and word spreads quickly,' she said. 'You're the sister's daughter, right?'

266

Nancy swayed. Exhaustion hit her like a wall. She was tired of pretending. 'No. That was just a story. The Van Hegels took me in when I needed somewhere to stay. They were so kind. Do you know how the Gestapo found out about Mika?'

'The boy? Probably the neighbour.' The old woman shook her head sadly. 'Mrs Visser. She had three boys taken by the Germans too, but she's gone feral with grief over it. I knew nothing about the Van Hegels until I heard a shot and went to the window to look. Wish I hadn't.' She gestured to a chair.

A wave of fatigue made Nancy glad to sit down.

'By the time I had the stomach to look,' the woman went on, 'Mrs Van Hegel was already dead, shot through the head. And they'd stripped the boy at gunpoint in front of the whole street. He was terrified. I've never seen anyone so shockingly white. He was too scared to move – he was surrounded by guns. Can you imagine that? His mother must have tried to protect him but they'd put a bullet through her by the time I looked out.' Her face grew grim with anger. 'Bastards. They were laughing like it was sport. The girl was at the window. I saw her hands pressing against the glass. She must have seen it all.'

'Where are they now?'

They dragged the girl out, put her in the car and drove them both away. They were both too shocked to even cry by then. An hour later they sent a *Wehrmacht* truck for Mrs Van Hegel's body. Then they boarded up the place to stop looters, so they can loot it themselves later.' A hard laugh. 'They'll be too late of course as they haven't set a guard. Where will you stay?'

Nancy shrugged. 'Don't know.' She examined the woman in front of her. She was so frail, with hands that were now clenching the edges of her darned cardigan. Could she trust her? She took a gamble. 'I was hoping to find . . . to find someone who had contacts that could put me in touch with the people fighting for Holland.'

The old woman stared a moment. 'You? But you're so young.' Then she smiled and her face lost its creased look. 'Then you're in the right place. You're not from here, are you? Your Dutch – it sounds a little antiquated, even to me. Not something a German would notice, but something we Dutch certainly would.'

'Really?' Nancy was disappointed. She'd thought herself fluent.

'You're English?'

A nod. 'Is it that obvious? I desperately need to get in touch with home.'

'Not so easy. But I know someone in the city who can help. We can't go there now, though. We have to wait until after four o'clock; the Germans change watch at four-thirty. I don't want them to see me going in and out too often. Though they don't look twice at an old lady like me, I still don't want to take chances. I'm Mrs Timmerman, but best you call me Anna.'

'Gusta.'

'Good choice. Quite common these days. And I will make tea.' She smiled. 'I have a little put by for people like you. You will be missing your English tea, no?'

At four o'clock the little cuckoo clock on the mantel made its piping call and the bird popped out. It set off the butterflies in Nancy's stomach, but wordlessly Anna put on her battered felt hat and coat, and took a large handbag from the hook on the back of the door.

'Put your arm in mine,' Anna said, 'like we're grandmother and granddaughter out to buy goods on the black market. And keep talking to me, like you're helping me and telling me something about the price of potatoes. That way we don't have to look at anyone.'

Anna locked the door securely behind them and they walked slowly down the road keeping up the pretence of chatting. It was slow progress as Anna's knees were bad.

'Just age,' Anna said. 'Never get old, hear me? Everything creaks.'

Nancy squeezed Anna's arm as they approached the city centre, now hung with Nazi red and black. There were Nazis at every intersection, and just the sight of them gave Nancy a shudder.

So many men with guns, bringing the spectre of death to every street corner.

Finally, Anna escorted her into a department store in the centre of Dam Square – the *Bijenkorf*, the Beehive.

'See, no Germans on the doors,' Anna whispered, 'but there will be when we come out, so keep your head down.'

The shop was busy, though the goods were few and shabby; many of the areas of the shop were cordoned off, or had empty shelves. At the small booth that held the shoeshine and shoe repair counter, a young man with dark springy hair and an intense expression was buffing a pair of black German boots to a high shine.

'I'd like these repaired, young man,' Anna said, taking out a pair of scuffed, brown lace-up shoes from her large handbag. One of the shoes had a worn-through sole.

The young man stopped brushing. His long bony fingers and sharp cheekbones spoke of not enough food or too much stress. With a furtive glance around, he urged, 'The man who owns these boots will be back for them in half an hour, so you'd better be quick.'

'Danny, this is Gusta. She needs to contact England.' Anna spoke in a low but firm voice.

Danny showed no surprise at Anna's appearance or request.

She's done this before, thought Nancy.

Danny turned his dark eyes to Gusta. 'Meet me near the third bridge on the Brouwersgracht canal at seven o'clock. I'll ride past on a bicycle. After that, just follow my lead. If you lose me, don't worry, just keep walking, and I'll come back for you.'

Just as he was finishing these words, Anna, who'd been watching her back, suddenly said loudly, 'I'll leave these with you then, and collect them in a couple of days.'

'Very good, madam,' Danny said. He re-parcelled up the shoes and took them into a back storeroom just as a German officer arrived. Nancy and Anna walked away arm in arm, not looking at him.

'Hey, you two.'

Anna stopped. Her grip on Nancy's arm was tight.

'Show some respect for an officer, hey?' He was a solidly built man in a stiff greatcoat and cap. His very bulk made Nancy feel flimsy and insubstantial.

'Oh, I do beg your pardon,' Anna said, her voice suddenly more wavering. 'Forgive an old woman. My eyesight is not what it was.'

'Heil Hitler,' he said. His sunken eyes narrowed as he waited for a response.

'Heil Hitler,' repeated Anna obediently, with Nancy echoing it just after.

'Come on, grandmother, don't dawdle,' Nancy said, as the officer gave a nod of dismissal, and they walked as calmly as they could to the stairs.

Once they were out in the square, Nancy blew out through her mouth. 'I thought he was going to ask me for my papers.'

'You do have papers, then?' Anna said, no longer weak and quavering.

'Yes,' Nancy replied. 'But I'm not sure how good.'

'Get Ralf to look at them. He'll tell you if they'll pass.'

'Who's Ralf?'

'You'll meet him tonight, I expect.'

Nancy stopped. 'Anna, you don't look like . . . I mean—'

Anna chivvied her back into motion. 'You mean you're surprised there's life in the old dog yet? You young people think you're the only ones who can do something! My shoes have been for repair at least forty times this year. They never get mended because they're more use broken. Some of us are like those shoes. We might be old but we all do what we can. Besides, if my life is cut short by a few years who's to care? My Walter died seven years ago.'

'Do you have children?'

'No. They never came.' She paused and sniffed. 'Now, I think that's a blessing.'

'Why hasn't Danny been sent to Germany like the rest?'

'Because he's only fourteen. And because the Nazis need clean boots,' Anna said.

That evening, cold drizzle fluffed Nancy's hair into frizz as she walked purposefully towards the bridge over the canal. Two Nazi soldiers were on guard above its parapet making spot checks. One pointing upstream and one down. Their presence made her mouth dry. She smoothed her hair and kept her eyes down as she approached the bridge, feeling their gaze on her as she strolled by.

'Papers,' shouted one of them in heavily accented Dutch. He gestured at her to go up onto the bridge.

As calmly as she could she walked up and gave him a smile. Inside, her chest was tight as she drew the papers from her pocket.

'Nice evening,' she said, hoping to distract him.

'Where are you going?' he asked as he opened the papers to the photograph.

She felt herself tense. Where was she going? 'My mother's,' she said. 'She's cooking my dinner.'

The officer folded her pass. 'Have a nice evening,' he said, as he handed the papers back.

She almost fainted with euphoria. God bless the SOE. The papers had passed. It made her almost tearful. Hurriedly she descended back to the towpath, and each time she heard the soft hiss of tyres behind her, her heart leapt. Finally, the skinny figure of Danny rode slowly past her and she walked as quickly as she dared after him, her eyes fixed on his gangly legs as they pedalled ahead of her. Several turnings later she found herself in a long potholed road of small workshops and garages.

The bicycle was parked outside the last block.

'Gusta!' He waved her in through a side door of a ramshackle garage. A car stood over the pit, a Daimler, the sort the Germans favoured. At one end a set of rickety stairs led up to a makeshift office, built out of flaking wood and partitioned on stilts from the rest of the building.

Danny gestured for her to go up. 'I'll keep watch.'

Two men were in the office already as Nancy entered. A ruddy-faced man in overalls, his big hands grimed in oily stains, introduced himself as Ralf. His hair was thick and black, reminding her of a lion's mane. He grinned, showing uneven teeth, and spoke in Dutch. 'Danny tells me you're one of Anna's "lost chicks".'

Lost chick? She almost objected, but then thought better of it. 'I needed somewhere to stay.'

The other man, a tall, well-built man wearing threadbare trousers and a fawn woollen jumper much too small for him, had sharp eyes that scanned over Nancy like a man who'd had training.

Ralf gave him a cursory glance before returning his attention to Nancy. 'And now you need to contact England, right? Like Edward here.'

Edward? She swivelled to look at the other man again. 'You're English?' she asked, reverting to her mother tongue.

He smiled, replied in English. ''Fraid so. Got shot down, and now I need to get out of here, and get back to where I can be some use. Ralf and these good folks are helping me.'

'You too? I can't believe it,' Nancy said. 'I thought I'd never find anyone in the Resistance. I was dropped in more than a week ago, but I couldn't find anyone with any contacts. The cell I was sent to's been blown. What about you?'

'Plane got shot down going home. But I'll get there. Gosh, it's great to hear an English voice. My Dutch is non-existent.'

Nancy turned back to Ralf, said in Dutch: 'Do you have a radio?'

'Of course,' Ralf replied. 'But not here. It never stays in the same place twice.'

'Good,' Nancy said. 'I'm a trained wireless op. How soon can you get me on? I need to broadcast at 22:00 hours, or 11:00 hours, if possible. That's when they'll be listening for me, if they haven't already given up.'

Ralf gave a meaningful look to Edward. In broken English, he said, 'What do you think?'

Edward smiled. 'She'll do.'

Aware of some subtext she didn't understand, Nancy asked Ralf, 'What?'

Ralf returned to Dutch. 'We need to get Edward out, and it will be much easier if he can travel with you as a couple. Especially as you speak Dutch and Edward doesn't.'

'What do you mean, "out"?' A sharp stab of disappointment. 'But I've only just got here.'

'I'm a hard person to hide,' Edward said, evidently reading her expression and tone of voice. 'These good people have done enough. I need to get back, get back to the fight. If you'd be my escort back to England, I'd be very grateful.'

'But my work? I was supposed to set up a network here and—'

'You say your line's been blown,' Ralf interjected in Dutch. 'So this is the task where you could be most useful. We all risk our lives while he stays here.'

'But I take my orders from England, I'll have to contact them to see what—'

'I understand your reluctance,' Edward interrupted. 'And if you'd rather not, then we'll just have to find someone else, but I've had a few narrow escapes running from the Nazis. I shot one of their officers when my plane came down, and I get the feeling my time's running out.'

'It's not an easy task,' Ralf spoke in Dutch, his brown eyes persuasive. 'You'll have to cross into Belgium, and the Nazis control every border crossing. But it's Edward's best chance.'

Nancy swallowed. She wanted to finish her mission, and didn't like to give up, but she couldn't think of a single reason why she shouldn't help Edward, apart from her own stubbornness. An image of Mamma van Hegel flashed into her thoughts. The Dutch had been good to her, and how could she live with herself if Edward got picked up by the Gestapo? 'All right. As long as I can contact England first. If I'm going to change my plans, I owe them that much, to let them know what happened to Hurling.'

'Hurling?' Edward asked. 'Who's Hurling?'

'The other agent who was dropped with me. He didn't make it. They took him at gunpoint.'

Chapter 35

That night, Nancy clung on tight to Ralf's solid waist as she was driven to the city centre on the pillion of his motorcycle. They pulled in outside *Ambika's* – a hairdresser's with a plate glass window at the front and the name scrolled above it in pink. Inside, a long counter ran in front of framed mirrors set on a candy-striped wall, and swivel chairs were set at each station. A young woman, presumably Ambika, with auburn hair curled into a rigid quiff in front and rolls at the back, let Nancy in and locked the door after her.

'Permanent wave, madam?' she asked in Dutch, grinning through red lipstick. 'Only joking.' She told Nancy to sit down and draped her with a cotton robe and towel.

A small pink leather case lay open on the counter in front of her. Nancy almost gasped. A crystal radio, openly there for all to see, amongst the brushes, the combs and the bottles of setting lotion. Her eyes followed the long wire aerial where it snaked up the wall and out of the back door.

'Go ahead,' Ambika said. 'The only good thing about German soldiers is they know nothing about hairdressing. They look in and see the back view of me doing something with a client and have no idea if they're looking at a perming machine or some beauty gadget. And they expect wires, and this . . .' she wheeled over a drying hood. 'They won't see your headphones under this.'

In the mirror Nancy glimpsed the shop window behind her and many people passing by. Nobody paid them the slightest attention.

'It's all right,' Ambika said. The front door's locked. Ralf's gone to the back door with his motorcycle in case we need to get you out in a hurry. And I'll just yell that we're closed if anyone comes.'

Nancy slid the coded WOK out of her sleeve. She'd unpicked it from the lining of her brassiere and had spent the afternoon working out what message to send, to make it as compact as possible. The soft square of silk reminded her painfully of Tom Lockwood. Why hadn't Beauclerk listened to him? The thought of Tom still hurt. How he'd tried to warn her and his stricken expression when she'd ignored him. She pushed the memory of him away; she had more important things to do. She tuned in the radio to the correct frequency, searching for a channel.

In training the white noise and static had been just a nuisance. Here it had transformed to a black metallic haze that fogged her brain, and made it impossible to think. Now, when she had something urgent to say, the amount of interference was unbearable. Especially as she was fiercely aware of the dangerous situation she was in. In the mirror she caught sight of a German soldier looking in. She stared at him in the glass as she kept tapping out her call signal in Morse.

Finally, she got through and a reply came. GO AHEAD LUDO. Relief flooded through her. Tears sprang to her eyes. Her contact was actually in England, a place where people were not shot on the street for trying to protect their children.

She tapped out the message leaving out the first two letters as the duress code, just as she'd been taught, to show something had gone wrong. Decoded, it would read: SORRY FOR LATE CONTACT. THE BALL HAS BEEN LOST. HURLING CANT PLAY FOR TEAM. PITCH IS WATERLOGGED. AWAIT REPLY. LUDO.

The message came back that she'd been received loud and clear.

She sagged with relief. The SOE would surely do something now. The message she'd sent was one she'd been told to send if things went wrong. Later, she could send that she was going to accompany Edward back to England, but right now she had no idea what that might entail, or how safe her contacts might be.

She removed her headphones and exhaled, coming back to the world of reality. Ambika packed up the box and rolled the hairdresser's hood away on its castors before beginning to wind the aerial onto a reel.

A sudden insistent bell made her startle.

She swivelled. A German vehicle on the pavement, and two *Wehrmacht* men with rifles. The butt of a rifle broke through the glass with a shattering crash.

'Shit.' Ambika grabbed the radio from the counter, battery wires trailing. 'The detector van's here. Quick. Out the back.'

Ralf's engine was already running. Nancy leapt onto the pinion as Ambika shoved the wireless set into its beauty case and into the motorcycle pannier.

With a roar, Ralf was away, and Nancy had to grab at his thick waist to keep from falling. Flung from side to side, she clawed on to his shirt as he skidded down dark streets, engine screaming. Parked cars and bicycles shot by as they plummeted and twisted through the narrow avenues.

The whine of his engine alerted two Nazi soldiers at a checkpoint and they stepped out to stop him. Ralf spotted them and turned sharp right, the back wheel dragging in a squeal of rubber. Nancy found herself airborne.

The road hit her hard in the shoulder and hip but she leapt back to her feet, dazed with shock. The Nazi soldiers took aim and yelled at her to halt. She ignored them and pelted after Ralf.

Bullets bounced off the side of the building next to her. Terrified, she stumbled on down the street until she saw a gateway into a large yard full of scrap metal. Old cars, bits of iron fence, cisterns, axles and railings, all piled up in rusting heaps. She skidded past a battered bath stacked with old kettles and tin buckets, squeezed past a giant bomb casing, and dodged behind an old tractor with no tyres.

At the back of the yard, two men loading an anvil onto an already stacked cart stopped mid-movement. 'Hey!' one of them shouted. But neither seemed inclined to put down the heavy anvil, and she hared past them out of the back gate.

She was on a different street and had no idea where she was. The Nazi soldiers must have decided not to leave their checkpoint, but she'd lost Ralf. She tried to look nonchalant now as she continued down the street, examining the road for some sign of where Ralf might have gone.

At the end of the road was a T-junction. Which way? She was about to choose the right turn when a Nazi on a motorcycle and sidecar came slowly up from the left. He stopped and said in broken Dutch, 'You want lift somewhere?' He had a broad face and very pink cheeks and was smiling pleasantly at her.

'No. No, thank you,' she said, curbing her breathlessness. 'I'm waiting for my boyfriend. He will pick me up.'

'Have you waited long?'

'No, I've just got here. He'll be here soon, I'm sure.'

'Be careful. A woman alone is not safe on these streets.'

The irony of it almost made her smile, but the man had a serious expression, so she thanked him and he drove away. Only then did her heart began to quieten from its hammering.

She stood a moment, to look as if she was waiting. Another engine. She turned to see Ralf coming back for her. She sagged with relief.

On the way back, they passed the motorcycle patrolman, and Nancy waved at him. He waved back and shrugged.

Back at the garage she almost fell off, her legs shaking. She put a hand to the wall to steady herself.

'That was close,' he said. 'Why were you waving at that soldier?'

She explained. 'I thought I'd have to go with him, but surprisingly, he did take no for an answer.'

'They're not all bad. But they're all the enemy, all the same.' He rubbed his stubbled chin. 'Tomorrow, we go back to check if Ambika's all right.'

'When can I transmit again?' she asked, once they were back inside the garage.

'Don't know. Not for a few days. Thursday. Tomorrow, we have someone else who needs to use it, and anyway, looks like we can't use Ambika's again. Bloody detector vans are getting quicker at finding us.'

'Have you a knife?' she asked him, sitting down at the desk and taking out the WOK silk.

He handed her a penknife. A box of matches lay next to the ashtray. Within a few moments, the code for her first transmission was ash.

'You look sad,' Ralf said.

'It's nothing,' she said, wishing Tom Lockwood would keep out of her thoughts.

Nancy managed two more transmissions via Ralf's contacts. After the second one, a message came back that she could make no sense of. It said they were going to issue instructions about a drop of equipment she'd requested. She hadn't requested a drop. She'd only said she was accompanying a 'Joe' back to England. Joes were what they called all English pilots. She frowned at the coding once she had transposed it. Where had the message come from? Not her, anyway. She was using the correct coding and the correct times. It was disconcerting. The tenuous link between the Netherlands and England had never seemed so fragile or frustrating.

She wondered about Klaas, agent Hurling. Whether he was still alive. It seemed strange to be ferrying a stranger back to England while Klaas was still somewhere in German captivity.

Nancy stayed at Anna's, in her spare box room, as they planned how best to get Edward back to England.

Anna was ever surprising with her knowledge of escape routes. She was an experienced courier, it seemed, and anxious to help. 'I just wish I had younger legs,' she said, regretfully. She had long conversations with Ralf at the garage – and Nancy interpreted so that Edward would understand what he had to do. They were to leave for Antwerp, from there to Brussels, and from there to a pickup point; just as soon as their new travel documents arrived.

When the documents were finally ready, Edward scooped them both up from the table and looked them over. 'Mr and Mrs Meijer. Well, I'm glad Mrs Meijer is so pretty. Though I dare say my wife would not agree.'

'You're married?' Nancy couldn't contain her astonishment.

'Yes, five years. Susan. She lives in Cheltenham.'

This should have made her feel less uncomfortable, but his attempts to charm her only made her step further away. He was too much like Andrew, a man used to getting his own way. She reminded herself she could give as good as she got if Edward tried anything.

Ralf and Danny were used to people on the run and supplied them with guilders and a single pistol for their journey, which Edward took charge of, as if it was his right. Nancy had to mask her resentment, especially knowing that Edward probably didn't have the weapons training that she'd had. She tried not to mind, but still, it bit hard.

For the journey, Edward was dressed in an old suit with his jumper underneath. These clothes were what would suit the average Dutchman but on Edward they looked as if they were on the wrong man. Edward had well-cut hair and an air of a superior Ivor Novello. The peaked cap did little to convince. His cover story was that he was a railway man, a reserved occupation for Dutch men working for the *Nederlandse Spoorwegen*, which transported German goods – and Jews – all over the Netherlands.

280

They'd had limited time to learn their new cover stories, and Nancy was still getting used to the fact that her name had been suddenly changed from Gusta to Mina, and that Edward was now masquerading as her husband Willem. She had to learn his cover story as well as her own, as she would be the one speaking.

Nancy buttoned up the jacket that Anna had managed to alter from one of her old ones. Ralf supplied her with a suitcase of clothes and a handbag for her documents. She wondered if all these items had once belonged to dispossessed Jews. She shuddered, and thought of Verhaegen, wondering how many other agents he'd betrayed.

Setting off with Edward to the train station was a reminder that Holland had turned into a poor country overnight. Her mother would've been horrified at the state of her homeland. *If only I could do more to help*, Nancy thought. It irked her that she'd done all that training, and now she was just to be someone's wife.

As if to read her thoughts, Edward turned to her, 'I don't need nannying,' he said. 'I just need you to translate, that's all. Otherwise, you do as I say.'

'What?'

'I'm in charge here, that's all. I don't need you to tell me what to do.'

Nancy bristled. 'I thought we were working as a team.'

The conversation had to stop as they'd arrived at the station. There were even more soldiers than before. Edward took hold of her arm and steered her onto the concourse. His grip was tight, and perhaps he was more nervous than he was letting on. Ranks of armed men in grey-green, helmets gleaming in the morning sun, manned every platform, looking for Jews trying to escape the city.

'Don't worry,' she whispered in English. 'I'll speak for both of us. Now hold on to my arm and act stupid.'

He frowned but didn't object.

They had tickets but needed to show them and their papers at the turnstile. There were two men at each gate, and Nancy

281

chose the one with the men that looked the most bored, whereas Edward hauled her over to a different turnstile. Cursing him, she gave Edward her papers and pass, and he handed them over with a dazzling smile.

'You go all the way to Antwerp?' the guard asked Edward in bad Dutch.

'Yes,' she said, pushing in front of Edward and acting disgruntled. 'My poor husband has been told to report there. They're short of drivers because the Belgian authorities have convinced their railway men not to cooperate in the deportations. So now we have to go all the way to Antwerp. Have you ever heard of anything so ridiculous? We'll be away for a few days—'

Impatient to be rid of her, the guard gave Edward a wink, folded the passes and passed everything back to him. Relieved, Nancy watched him pocket them and pick up their cases.

'See? Easy,' he said, taking her by the arm again and hurrying through the turnstile.

'*Halt!*'

Edward stopped dead and turned, forcing her to stop too. Behind them, a young man was running across the concourse.

'Don't you know anything?' she hissed, hauling him forward. 'If they shout and you stop, it makes you look guilty. Just keep on walking. Whatever's happening, never admit it's anything to do with you.'

He glared down at her. 'It's not my fault. I can't understand.'

'You understood "*Halt!*", didn't you?'

He looked bullish. 'So what? They gave us a little German in training.'

It was then she realised that getting Edward back to England was not going to be as straightforward as she'd hoped.

Chapter 36

Once in Belgium, Nancy and Edward travelled from Antwerp to Brussels, using the same railway man and wife cover story. Not only did Edward have no Dutch, but he had no French either, only English and a smattering of German, so Nancy had to speak for them both. She could see it annoyed Edward, him having to take the back seat when anyone talked to them, and she was constantly afraid he'd butt in and try to speak, and it would give them away.

In Brussels, they met Ralf's contact, French-speaking Pierre Duval, in a café close to the Parc Duden. Pierre was an archaeologist, whose teacher-ish look belied a sharp intelligence. In the park, Pierre told them there'd be a room for them at the Hotel Picard, booked under their assumed name Meijer. It was a mile's walk. He'd be in touch once he'd arranged a drop zone for a Lysander to get them out.

'A Lysander?' Nancy was surprised. She thought she'd be going overland.

'Airmen get priority treatment,' Pierre said. 'But if a Lysander's going to come in, we'll request a few small supplies – more ammo, explosives. I'll be sending to England tonight.'

'Any chance I could use the radio?' Nancy asked.

'Sorry,' Pierre said. 'Better you go to the hotel. We don't reveal the location of transmitters to anyone, especially not agents of other cells. Too many operators have been lost that way, through careless contacts. You do understand, don't you?'

'Of course,' she said in French, masking her disappointment. 'Ask them to send a spare radio, would you?'

'I'll add it to the list, and I'll have news for you as quick as I can. Don't go out at night. The patrols around the hotel are ruthless.'

She air-kissed Pierre on the cheeks in the French way.

'Be at that bench over there every day at eleven,' Pierre said, 'and soon as I can, I'll be back to tell you the details of how we'll get your man out.'

'What was he saying?' Edward asked, as she set off following the map Pierre had drawn on a scrap of paper.

She shook her head, meaning *not now*.

Edward sighed in annoyance but seemed to have understood the gist of the conversation as he strode on, carrying the suit-cases. Once they were on a quiet street, he said, 'What was that about a Lysander?'

Of course. The name 'Lysander' would prick up the ears of any airman. 'They'll send a plane for you,' she said.

Edward nodded and looked pleased, though he didn't look quite so pleased when they arrived at the Hotel Picard. A dilapi-dated sign hung above peeling double doors and the faded green curtains were tightly drawn though it was broad daylight. It looked derelict. They pushed through into the lobby where a man dozed in a filthy sagging armchair. A pungent Gitanes cigarette, instead of the usual black Belgian smoke, was burning away in the ashtray with a stick of ash an inch long.

'M'sieur and Madame Meijer,' she said. 'We have a reservation.'

The proprietor stirred and grunted through yellowing teeth, and hitched up his drooping trousers to under his armpits. 'This way.' He grabbed the Gitanes and stuck it between his lips, letting the ash drift onto his already stained shirt.

Up tightly winding stairs with threadbare carpet to the top floor. On the way, the insistent bang of a headboard against a wall couldn't mask a woman's cries of pain or ecstasy. Nancy dare not catch Edward's eye.

The proprietor pushed open a door with the key still in the lock and held it open. 'Curfew's at nine,' he said. 'No breakfast here. Get it at the bus depot.'

'But there's only one bed,' Nancy said.

The man shrugged and shut the door.

Nancy opened it again. 'Have you another room?'

'No. They pay me for only one room. You are lucky to have a place. It's a risk I take. Find somewhere else if you don't like it.'

He shuffled away down the creaking stairs. Back in the room, Edward commandeered the bed and lay back against the thin pillow, elbows out behind his head, crossed feet still in his brogues.

'Sags a bit,' he said.

Nancy sat gingerly on a wicker chair with bits of wicker poking out from holes in the seat. From beneath, the sound of banging continued.

'Someone's having fun,' Edward said.

She gave him a cold look.

'Aw, c'mon now. It was only a jest. Stop being so high and mighty. I was going to offer to share, but I wouldn't want an ice maiden like you in my bed in any case. Though I have to say, the room's so hot it might help.'

'Watch your mouth, or I'll leave you high and dry. See how far you get without me to negotiate for you.'

'I'd manage,' he said. Then he seemed to think better of it. 'It's just I'm used to doing things my way.'

'It's not just you though, is it? If they catch you, they'll torture you for the names of the rest of us. You fancy having your fingernails torn out, being whipped with a wire, or being strung up by your wrists?'

'They don't do that. That's hearsay. Wartime propaganda.' He was watching her reaction. She decided not to rise to it.

A few moments of silence before he said, 'You can have the bed. Isn't that what you were waiting for me to say? Despite your toughness, you still want to play the woman. Still want me to be the good man and give up my well-earned rest for you.' He stood up in a leisurely way. 'Go on then. I'll take the chair.'

God he was infuriating. Now he'd made her feel bad, when she was the one who was putting herself out for him.

He made a mocking bow and gestured to the bed, which was probably the most unappealing bed she'd ever seen. The floral cover with its ragged twist of braid was stained, and the sheets pilled grey flannelette. It stank of damp and mildew.

She kept her jacket on and sat down, feeling the springs creak beneath her weight. 'You can turn the light out and we'll get some sleep,' she said. 'With any luck, you'll be in England the day after tomorrow.'

She really hoped so. Something about Edward rubbed her the wrong way. She was desperate to be rid of him.

In the dark of the night, she began to itch. Restless, she sat up on the bed to scratch. She was still fully clothed. In the dark, she saw that Edward was also awake; he was just coming into the room from outside.

'Where've you been?' she asked.

'The john. Where d'you think?'

'In your suit and cap?'

'Feel undressed without them. And I needed some fresh air. This place stinks.'

The itching was worse, like needles on her back. She scratched furiously.

'What's the matter?' he said.

'I've been bitten,' she said. 'Probably bedbugs.'

'Well, you wanted the bed.'

She got off the bed and huddled on the floor, back to the wall. 'Could catch anything from that.'

286

A flare of a match as he lit a cigarette and sucked in to make a fierce red glow. He exhaled. 'Maybe the smoke'll kill 'em. Where did you stay in Amsterdam?'

She was about to tell him, but then remembered. 'Best not to say, in case something goes wrong.'

'What could go wrong? All we have to do is just wait here.' He blew a series of smoke rings, which wavered in the air and dissolved. 'Hey, beautiful, want me to get in with you, kill a few of those bugs?'

'No.'

'We could get more sleep, both in together.'

'I said no.'

He laughed at her in a mocking kind of way. 'You could be dead tomorrow, and you just turned down the offer of your life.'

She gritted her teeth and ignored him. The rest of the night she grew stiff and restless, propped up against the wall. Sleep wouldn't come because she didn't trust Edward not to make a move in the night. She wondered why she was so mistrustful, but then again, the training in Arisaig had made every man seem like an enemy.

Three more days they had to wait. Edward didn't proposition her again, but she caught him looking at her sometimes in a predatory way, and it made her cringe. In an effort to keep friendly relations, Nancy tried to get Edward to tell her about his life in the RAF, but he told her it was all classified.

'Where were you shot down?' she asked.

'Amsterdam. Dropped a few good ones though before my Lancaster got hit.'

'Were you the only survivor?'

He nodded and looked at his feet. She didn't want to press him; it must have been a harrowing experience. But he never seemed to want to talk, and after she'd longed for someone to share her experiences with, Edward never opened up a conversation. Sometimes she looked at him and he reminded her of a shop mannequin, handsome but hollow.

When they saw the stooped figure of Pierre finally walking towards them, Nancy wanted to hug him with relief.

'Good news,' Pierre said. 'We've found an approved landing site and the transport is on. Next full moon period is only a few days away so we have to get you out there as soon as we can. A butcher's truck will pick you up from your hotel in the morning. He'll take you over the French border into Belgium to a farm near the landing site.'

'Do I need to go too, or just Edward?' Nancy asked hopefully.

'The family only speak French. He'll need you to interpret. You need to look like farm labourers, there for the harvest.'

She nodded, though inside her heart sank. Edward turned away. Obviously, he knew they were talking about him.

'Don't be late,' Pierre said. 'And don't forget, there are still plenty of collaborators on the farms, so watch your step.'

When Pierre had gone, Edward said, 'I understood all that. And don't worry, I know you resent having to do this.'

'I don't. It's just . . . it's just not what I was sent here to do.'

'What were you sent to do?'

'Doesn't matter now. My contacts were already blown, and the Nazis got my transmitter.'

'That's bad luck.' He twisted his mouth in an expression of sympathy. 'How are your bites?'

'Bloody murder.'

'You could try to get something for them from a pharmacy,' Edward said. 'It's only one more day of walking around Brussels and one more night in that hotel, then it will be over.'

'Over for you maybe,' she said. 'I'll be going back to Holland.'

'You really think you can be of any use there? They've lost, haven't they?' His tone was sneering. 'At least England's still free. Got to admire the English. In Holland you're fighting a lost cause.'

'It will never be lost as long as there are people like me to fight for it.'

'You?' He gave a splutter of mirth that made her want to hit him, but she retained her dignity. She'd do her job, and then he'd be out of her life.

Chapter 37

Tom had taken to smoking more at Arkley View because the work was dull, and he couldn't bear to be cooped up like this, away from the hub of the SOE in Baker Street. He was taking a break from his headphones and idly doodling on a notepad when the door opened behind him.

'Bloody stuffy in here. You shouldn't smoke until your break time. I can hardly breathe.' Beauclerk was standing there, grey-faced, his trilby hat dark with sweat from the summer heat.

What the hell was he doing here?

'Lockwood, I need a word.' Beauclerk's voice was oddly ingratiating. 'Not here. Get your coat. In fact, bring all your things.'

What had he done now? Tom tried to stay as calm as he could as he gathered his belongings and followed Beauclerk down the road. Five minutes later, they were in a 'greasy spoon' café, at a table by the window, as far away from the counter as they could get. Tom stared out at the street through a blur of steam as Beauclerk ordered a fry-up at the counter. It would be cheap sausage and bread and a few country mushrooms if they were lucky, but Tom was puzzled to see that Beauclerk used his ration card for both orders.

So, it must be serious if he was paying. The woman continued to eye them for a few minutes before giving up and disappearing into the back, to the kitchen to cook.

Beauclerk toyed with the brown sauce bottle on the table. His eyes were rheumy, his skin sallow. If anything, he looked even more gaunt than the last time Tom had seen him. Beauclerk looked up. 'We'd like you to come back to Baker Street.'

'Why?' How dare Beauclerk demand that, when he was the one who'd moved him?

'Don't be like that. We've got a problem we need help with.'

'So now you need me, do you? And expect me to just tug a forelock and say, "Yes, your highness, anything you say"?'

Beauclerk sighed. 'Why do you always have to be so bloody awkward. If there was anyone else who could sort this out, we'd ask them. But there isn't, so we're stuck with each other.'

'What's it about?'

Beauclerk lowered his voice, leant in. 'We've got trouble. After the initial contact, we've now got an agent in two places at once. Obviously, one of them's the real agent, and the other must be a German plant. The trouble is, we don't know which is which. One of them's coding by the poem code, and the other by WOK. Agent Hockey, one of our most reliable men, asked for a new code for an agent who had lost the WOK so we sent a poem code. Now the agent is using both poem code and the WOK.'

'The WOK's the more recent method. Maybe the agent recovered it. But I suppose a German could have found the WOK and be transmitting, and our man could have reverted to poem code.'

Just then the meal arrived and all talk stopped. The woman plonked it in front of them without a word and whisked away back to the kitchen, where they could hear the banging of plates and pans.

Now he understood Beauclerk wasn't there to sack him again, Tom was massively hungry. In front of him was a slice of white toast, with an actual egg on it, and alongside it, a helping of mushrooms and a large slab of the ubiquitous beetroot. Not bad.

He tucked in, his mind whirring over the consequences of what Beauclerk had just said, while Beauclerk pushed his food lethargically around the plate. 'Would it make a difference if I told you the name of the agent?' Beauclerk said.

Tom looked up, stopped chewing.

Beauclerk put down his fork. 'N Section. Ludo.'

Tom swallowed. He tried to take in the implications, but it was as if his brain had stopped working. All he could feel was the thud of his heart. The food was instantly unappetising. He thrust the plate away.

'Nancy Callaghan.' Beauclerk confirmed what he already knew.

'I'll help,' he said hoarsely. 'What do you want me to do?'

'Come back with me now and we'll get you signed in.'

'What about my boss, Garrard, and the Signals ops at Arkley?'

'I spoke to him on the blower before I came and squared it with him.'

'Bloody cheek. How did you know I'd say yes?'

'Because I know you can't resist a chance to rub my nose in it.'

Tom gave a ghost of a smile. 'Let's go.'

Chapter 38

Tom inhaled the familiar smell of floor polish and cigarette smoke that characterised the Baker Street offices, as Beauclerk ushered him up the stairs. God, it was good to be back. He swanned past Beryl, whose mouth dropped open in surprise, as Beauclerk held open the door for him and ushered him inside.

Tom's mind was already chewing over it. Unlikely the same agent would be using two methods. So – two agents both sending as Ludo. One of them must be her. The thought that Nancy might still be alive buoyed him up, made him feel light. But it was unlike Nancy to lose her code, and this worried him.

'We need you to send something to agent Ludo that only she would understand,' Beauclerk said, plumping down into his familiar leather chair. 'Something to which she'd make a unique reply. It has to be something unmistakable, that only she and you could know about. Can you do that?'

'I'll think of something.' He wasn't sure how she'd receive it though. Given how they'd parted, she obviously thought him unhinged to have come to Tempsford to stop her flying.

'Code it to both agents sending as Ludo and then we'll see which one replies.'

'Right. Got it.' Tom frowned. 'It'll take a bit of time though.

I'll have to code two versions, the poem code you sent to Hockey and the new silk WOK. Who has Ludo's WOK?'

Beauclerk glanced at a typed memo on his desk. 'Alice Dobell's the decoder for Ludo. Once you have the codes though, you must swear only to send the messages we've agreed. If I find out you've sent unofficial messages again, you'll be heading straight to Wormwood Scrubs. And I mean it.' He chewed his lip a moment and sighed. 'You were spot-on about the fouling of the Dutch lines, Tom. I owe you an apology.'

Now Beauclerk had apologised, Tom felt able to be generous. 'No, you were right to be cautious, sir.' Beauclerk looked worn out, like he was being eaten from the inside – great dark circles like bruises under his eyes, and hands that were unsteady as he fiddled with his pen.

'I put too much trust in Neil Callaghan,' Beauclerk said, shaking his head.

'You know he's in hospital?'

'Yes. Bloody lucky, wasn't he? Family visitors only. But I had a word with the sister on the ward. She says he's progressing okay. Can't get out of bed yet, though, and it sounds like it was one hell of a blast.'

Tom didn't tell him he was there when it happened. He stood up, waiting to be dismissed, so he could get on with coding the message.

'Hang on a moment, Tom,' Beauclerk said. 'You'd better sit down again. Thing is, we have a little problem with Callaghan.' He opened the flap of a brown manila file to draw out a photograph and placed it on the top, then pushed the file across the desk.

Tom looked down at it. A black-and-white photograph of a balding, rather mild-looking chap. Tom recognised him straight away. Jack King. He was the man whose flat he'd been to, after following Otto to the Ritz. The man Otto was reporting to, who in turn was reporting to Giskes and Gestapo headquarters.

Tom did a double take. The photograph was labelled with a name he didn't recognise: Eric Roberts.

The unfamiliar name threw him, but all the same, it must mean Beauclerk knew about the Right Club, or why would he be showing him the photograph? Tom looked up warily. 'I've seen him before.'

Beauclerk seemed not to hear him. He tapped the photograph. 'This is one of MI5's agents. He's incognito as a Gestapo officer, code name Jack King. With me so far?'

Tom tried to take this in. 'A Gestapo officer? I don't understand. Then who's Eric Roberts?'

'A bank clerk from Epsom. Same man. He had right-wing sympathies once, before the war, but he's turned – and has re-invented himself as a Gestapo officer under the alias of Jack King.'

'You mean he's working for us?'

A nod. 'He's helping MI5 discover people who might aid a German invasion, should one arise.'

'Like an agent provocateur?'

'Careful. MI5 prefer not to use that term,' Beauclerk said impatiently. 'Any sense of provocation, of deliberately leading people down the route to fascism, would be deeply unpopular and against our British sense of fair play. But so far, Roberts has been amazingly successful, and he's keeping tabs on many of Hitler's civilian army of saboteurs over here. But we've run into a snag. One of the members of his little coterie was shot, a man called Oliver Johnson, and King has already told us Johnson was an agent for the Nazis. He spotted it when some of Johnson's backstory didn't add up.'

Tom swallowed, tried to take in what it meant. It seemed unbelievable that Jack King could be an agent for MI5. How much did Beauclerk know? Tom tried to sound casual. 'So, how does Callaghan come into this?'

'Callaghan's implicated in Johnson's death. We know this because King told us,' continued Beauclerk. 'He suspects it was Callaghan who shot him, though he has no proof. Callaghan and Johnson used to be friends, have some kind of history, but then Johnson started to lean on him.'

'Their families used to holiday together,' Tom said. 'Nancy Callaghan told me.'

'We need this shooting hushed up,' Beauclerk said. 'It's drawn far too much attention to Jack King and his contacts. MI5 are furious, and the whole fiasco is in danger of shutting down the SOE. We need you to remind Callaghan of his obligations – the Official Secrets Act – and persuade him to keep quiet while we invent a plausible cover story, and arrange a quiet burial for Johnson, out of the media limelight.'

A stunned silence. 'You're hushing it up?' Tom took a deep breath. 'But what will happen to Neil Callaghan? Won't he get some sort of punishment?' he blurted, his voice too loud and harsh in the small room. 'All those N Section agents lost because of him!'

Beauclerk blinked. 'On the contrary. None of Callaghan's intelligence ever got as far as the Gestapo or Giskes. Jack King made sure of that. And I admit, I haven't been quite straight with you. You were right, the Dutch lines were infiltrated by Giskes. Have been for years.'

Years? Tom felt outrage tighten his throat. 'How long have you known?'

Beauclerk raised his hands in a shrug. 'About Callaghan? We didn't. Not until MI5 told us. And proper fools we look too.'

'And the N Section networks?'

Beauclerk looked down at his blotter. His mouth worked, but no words came out.

Tom felt as if the rug had been pulled from under him. *So all the time they were fobbing me off, they knew.* 'So what happens now? You just let Callaghan go?' Tom's jaw tensed. On the one hand, Neil was suffering enough, and he'd grown to have some allegiance to him. On the other, the idea someone could just be a traitor and get away with it stuck in his craw.

'We'll be pensioning him off, of course,' said Beauclerk. 'And he did us a favour; Johnson was a dyed-in-the-wool Nazi, whereas Callaghan was just a man caught in the crossfire.'

He meant Callaghan was one of his own, and it was easier to brush it all under the carpet the way MI5 wanted him to.

'Of course, none of this conversation must go out of these doors,' Beauclerk said.

'Oh yes, the Official Secrets Act. A boat that leaks at your convenience. So, if I do as you ask, and try to shut Callaghan up, do I tell him about King or not?'

Beauclerk pushed the photograph of Eric Roberts towards him. 'When you visit Callaghan, you might need this.'

Tom took it. 'I get it. Damage limitation. You want me to find out which is the real agent Ludo, so MI5 will never know that you've known all along about the Dutch lines. And then you want me to show Callaghan this and persuade him to keep quiet so MI5 can continue their ruse with Jack King. We're just puppets of MI5, aren't we?'

'Don't think like that. I've been at this game long enough to know it's never black and white. Everything's shades of grey in war. Nothing ever stays clean.'

Tom could barely speak. 'You could have saved lives, and you chose not to. You sent good people deliberately to their deaths.'

Beauclerk's cheek twitched. He looked up and the expression in his eyes was haunted. 'A few men, yes. But can you imagine what it would do to all the other lines if it got out? For them to know there was no hub at all in the Netherlands? That the Nazis had won? It would destroy their morale. France and Belgium need to believe in the Resistance. We all need to believe in it. Without it, we would all just lie down under the Nazi boot.'

Chapter 39

Tom had been given a different office, one he suspected used to be a supplies storeroom, judging by the rack of dusty shelves and the single remaining box of rubber bands. He laid out the binders of transmission records on his desk. The desk irritated him; it was too low and made him stoop his back and cramp his knees.

He tolerated it as he pored over Ludo's WOK transmissions. He soon found out why it was so urgent to decide which of the agents claiming to be Ludo was real. One of them had asked for assistance bringing out an airman, what they called a 'Joe', and had requested an urgent pickup in a Lysander. Naturally, the RAF didn't want to risk losing another precious plane to the Germans. On the other hand, if it was a genuine request, then they couldn't leave the poor Joe in danger and they'd need to expedite a pickup as soon as possible. And they needed all the pilots they could get.

He closed that file and opened Hockey's file to track down Ludo. The agent sending as Ludo on the new bandwidth was after more cash and another long list of coded ammunition, grenades and plastic explosives – typical sabotage equipment. This one seemed more likely to be genuine, given that, from what Beauclerk had said, her mission was to liaise over supplies.

Just the thought that one of these messages could be from Nancy sent a tingle up his spine.

He began to draft a message. One that only Nancy would understand. It took him about half an hour to devise something short and foolproof enough.

WHAT TO EAT AT THE CORNER HOUSE QUESTION TOM

Would she answer? It looked a little bald out of context. Would she just ignore it, thinking he was playing some sort of crazy game? Or would she be glad to get it? He stared at it until the words seemed to twist into nonsense.

Enough. He grabbed it and set off to the coding room.

Doing something positive increased his energy tenfold. He relished being back in the heat of things again.

The coders looked up as he came into the room, a sea of heads in headphones.

'Alice Dobell?' he asked. Everyone looked to a small frizzy-haired girl who shot to her feet.

The others went back to work. He signalled her to come to the door. In the corridor he asked her, 'Beauclerk's orders – can you let me have the silk code issued to agent Ludo, please.'

'Oh, but I hardly use that now. Ludo's mostly on the poem code Hockey requested—'

'Then you won't mind if I take it for a little while.' He smiled at her and waited while she fetched the cardboard file from the cabinet.

She held it out and he slipped the square of paper into his pocket. 'Don't worry, I'll bring it back by the end of the afternoon,' he said. 'And meanwhile, if you get any more messages from agent Ludo, come straight to my office to let me know. I'm in room 17b on the second floor.'

'Okay,' she said and hurried away with the file.

Once back in his office, he took out the square, which reminded him even more of Nancy. Four rows had already been crossed out, so four messages. These numbers were a link to her.

He imagined her slim fingers tracing each of the numbers on her matching silk.

He took care with the coding, both with Hockey's poem code, 'The Owl and the Pussycat', and with the silk. It wouldn't do to make a mistake. If he chose the wrong agent, all ties with that agent would be lost.

Finally, both messages were ready.

He headed to the wireless room and handed both coded messages to Alice. 'Send them both at the next sked time for Ludo. Send this one to Ludo on Hockey's sked, at 11:00 hours, and this one to Ludo's new sked at 22:00 hours. Okay?'

She nodded and pulled both messages towards her. 'I'll see if I can get through,' she said, 'but there's no guarantee.'

Chapter 40

In Brussels, Nancy and Edward waited in the hotel lobby until a wood-gas-powered van with '*Lafage Charcuterie*' written on the side drew up outside and a man got out. Many tradesmen's vans were powered by wood gas, as fuel was impossible to get. Presumably this was Lafage, a balding, bow-legged man of at least seventy years of age. He opened the back doors to reveal a heap of dead rabbits and half a pig, along with buckets of blood and offal for puddings.

The smell of blood reminded Nancy of the man she'd killed when she first arrived and set off an instinctive fear which she could do little to suppress. Lafage pointed to a long narrow tank for gas which stretched back above the cab and over the load, and then he opened up the back of it and waved at them to get in.

'*Ici?*' Nancy asked. This was where they were to travel? But it was tiny. They couldn't possibly fit in there. Monsieur Lafage explained that the van was actually powered by a combination of petrol and wood-gas. The real wood-gas tank was much smaller and in a separate upright chamber sealed off from the big one. This big tank was merely a hollow space. Nancy understood it to be a good deception for carrying arms or goods, and an ideal hiding place for one person. But for two?

'Very cosy,' Edward said.

Nancy threw him a withering look.

'Heave ho!' Edward gave her a leg up and shoved her inside the cramped space. She pulled her skirt tight around her bare legs in an effort of self-protection. A few moments later, Edward was squashed up against her, too close for comfort. She tried to shuffle to get more room; she hated being pressed up against him like that.

'Don't wriggle like that, I might lose control,' Edward whispered in her ear. She ignored him, shrank away as far as she could, though it was too cramped to sit up, and all they could do was lie crushed side by side.

Every time they came to a checkpoint, the van switched from petrol to wood-gas from the small tank ahead of them, which got hot and released a stink of fumes. Nancy held her breath, keeping very still, as German voices echoed outside.

Then they were rattling on again, until finally there were no more checkpoints. The sun beat mercilessly down on the metal coffin they were in, and Nancy began to sweat. Only one small hole in the top of the tank had been drilled to let in air. She tried to turn but she was wedged tight.

'Most girls would give their eye teeth to be where you are,' Edward said.

'Does that include your wife?' she said tartly.

'Aww. Don't be so uptight. You have to take it where you can in wartime. Might be your last chance.'

'And my last chance to show some decency and integrity,' she said. 'Lay off, or you'll get no more translation from me.'

After another two hours of sweating and bad feeling made worse by the heat, the road turned into a bumpy track. Nancy's elbows and knees banged against the side of the tank.

When they came to a stop, both tried to move but found they couldn't. The back of the tank opened and a rush of air whooshed in. 'Got cramp,' she said, trying to free the numb arm that was underneath her.

Edward slid himself out first, and Nancy crawled out after, blinking in the bright sun.

Somewhere nearby a cow lowed. The farmer who came out to meet them was a weather-beaten young man, Remi, with sleeves rolled up to reveal wiry arms. Beside him was his pregnant wife, a blonde who introduced herself shyly as Nicole.

'My special delivery!' Lafage said.

'Ah, M'sieur Lafage, you are a treasure!' Remi said, kissing him on both cheeks. 'And is this our "Joe"?' They greeted Edward with awe, as if he was some sort of celebrity, which made Nancy grit her teeth. Full of smiles, they brought Edward and Nancy into the low-eaved farmhouse where they offered them earthenware cups of sweet cider.

When they'd drunk their fill and washed in a basin by the pump, Nicole pointed at a barn which had a hay loft above.

'You'll find the radio up there,' Nicole said in French. 'Under the second feed bucket from the right. The wire's linked up through the window. You'll need to set up a personal message on the BBC so my people know when to expect them and if it's definitely on. We usually get a good turnout of helpers.'

'You have a radio?' Nancy couldn't believe it.

'*Mais oui*. We are a long way from a town here. But only one or two messages a day, and short, okay?'

Nancy let out a long whistling breath of relief. Here in the country, there were no soldiers, and having access to England – well, that was the icing on the cake.

'Hey, look at this!' Edward was already opening the door into the barn, and she followed him through. Inside, it was airy and cool, the building being constructed from wooden lath on a base of brick. Stalls for cows were below, and a hay loft partitioned from a grain store above.

Nicole had waddled after them. She pointed up the ladder. 'You can sleep up there too, in the hay. There are blankets if you need them. I can't go up the ladder anymore.' She patted her swollen belly.

303

Edward was up the ladder before Nancy could even reply. He obviously understood more French than he let on. By the time Nancy poked her head through the trapdoor, he had already upended the bucket and was standing the radio set on it next to the window.

'Leave it,' she said, annoyed. 'It's my job.'

He held up his hands and ducked under the partition to the hay. When she next looked, he was lying back watching her through motes of dust. His scrutiny made her uncomfortable.

She glanced at her watch. It would soon be eleven and time to transmit. She slipped her silk from her pocket and hunkered down to code a message, resting her paper and pencil on the floorboards. She checked it over again.

'Does it always take you that long?' Edward asked.

'I can't risk a mistake. If we don't hear the right message from the BBC, we won't know if they're coming for you or not.'

'What's the message?'

'*The dog does not bark.*'

'Couldn't you think of anything better?'

She put on the headset and ignored him.

She turned the dial trying to find the connection through the soup of other frequencies. She tapped out her Morse send code, over and over into the frazzle of noise.

She turned to Edward. 'What's the time?'

He glanced at his watch. 'Nearly eleven.'

'Yep, that's what I've got too. Then there's a chance they'll pick me up.' She tried her send code again. Astonishingly, a reply came that she recognised. GO AHEAD LUDO OVER.

The thrill it gave her made her grin. She put her finger on the Morse button and tapped out the coded message.

She expected an over and out. But instead, immediately there was another message in code. She was ready to scribble down the letters. This one had no agent send code. Unusual. She Morsed, 'Message Received' and signed off, then bent over the paper to begin the transposition using the WOK.

'What did they say?' Edward asked.

'Don't know yet. More instructions, I suppose. Will take me a while to decode it.'

At first, she didn't know what to make of it. The first few words didn't make much sense, but then suddenly a name jumped out at her and the whole message made her heart thump before her mind could grasp it.

WHAT TO EAT AT THE CORNER HOUSE QUESTION TOM

She read the words again. Was it a joke? Was it really from Tom? It couldn't be. Could it? And if it was, how had he got the WOK from her decoder?

Edward, seeing her reaction, stood up and leant over the rail from the hay store. 'What have we got to do?'

On instinct, she grabbed the paper and pressed it to her chest before he could see it.

A mistake, because he immediately frowned and said, 'Let's see.'

'No.'

He clambered over the rail. 'Give it to me.'

She clung on to it until he took it from her hands and read the words written out in capitals. 'Who's Tom?' he asked. 'Why are you hiding it?'

'I wasn't.'

He read it again.

'It just means England,' she said, thinking quickly. 'Tom . . . Tommy. Get it? It's code for send a list of what you need. The Corner House is Baker Street. We use food as a code for arms. Pears are grenades, for example. I thought you knew that.'

His brow was furrowed. 'Something about it gave you the jitters though. Everything's all right, isn't it?'

'Fine. It's fine. It's just that I wasn't expecting to be able to get through and get such a positive reply.'

He handed the message back. 'What will you ask for?'

'I'll have to ask Nicole,' she said. The conversation had become ordinary, while inside a volcano of emotion threatened to derail her completely.

All afternoon she couldn't get the message out of her mind. The Corner House. It brought back so many memories. She imagined Tom on the other end of the message, carefully coding it using the silk they had devised together.

She didn't know what it meant, but she had to reply. After all, what was there to lose?

Later in the day more men came to be introduced to the 'visitors'. The men were swarthy farm hands, wiry, muscled, but old. She presumed the young ones had been forced into German factories like everywhere else. Only Remi was allowed to stay to run the farm and supply the Germans with their milk.

She asked Remi what else they may need for their network, and after consulting with the old guys, he gave her a list of ammunition and essential items like bicycle chains and tyres. Then the men all went off to inspect the landing site, taking Edward along with them.

Later, Nicole took Nancy to one side. 'The men never think of it,' she said, 'but cigarettes, chocolate, perfume for the ladies. Morale is low, and it makes a difference to have something good to share. Like hope, you know?'

'Leave it to me,' Nancy said.

'We get little reward for what we do,' Nicole said. Though her belly was large, she was thin as a straw. 'Our people risk death. A little luxury. It's not much to ask.'

Nancy spent a long time crafting the next message because her thoughts couldn't settle. She had so much to say to Tom, so much to apologise for, and yet the simple answer would have to suffice – to carry all that weight of emotion.

She knew Tom would understand it. The thought made her heart ache for him. She supposed this must be love; this terrible gaping hole inside that could only be filled by one person. She steeled herself to code the rest.

As she was coding, her pencil broke. Damn. She had no knife to sharpen it. She spied Edward's jacket hanging on the post of the partition; it was so hot up here he'd taken it off. Maybe he'd have a penknife or a pencil.

She felt through his pockets and brought out his pass, but she was surprised to feel another under it. Curious, she took a look.

Some sort of German pass. An eagle and swastika above it. A name – *Günter Sitz*. Her head began to spin. Was Edward German? She found the gun in his other pocket. She took it out to find it was already loaded. As she sent her transmission, she kept her other hand on the gun. He'd need to explain.

Concentrate, Nancy. She sent the message for Tom, but then requested a pickup the next day, and checked they'd got the personal message to give to the BBC. They'd broadcast it as a way of telling them the mission was on, on the night the Lysander would come. She asked for a replacement crystal set and added the list of requests from Remi's network, not forgetting Nicole's luxuries.

Edward came in as she'd finished the transmission and was slipping off the headset. 'Remi took me for a recce at the landing site,' he said. 'It's not very big. They've scythed it, as if they're haymaking, but I think they're crazy to put a Lysander down there. It's only about a hundred and fifty yards long, and really near—' His eyes went to the gun in her hand. 'What the hell?'

'Who's Günter Sitz?'

'Hey, what's all this? Put the gun down.'

She kept it pointing at him as she threw the pass across the floor towards him.

'I can explain,' he said. 'Give me a moment to explain.'

'It had better be good,' she said.

'Careful, it's loaded.' He took a step forward, his hands up. 'You don't know what you're doing.'

'Stay back! I know exactly what I'm doing. Now talk.'

'Just some random German who was in my way. I killed him and took the pass as a souvenir. Thought it might be useful if I had to pretend to be German.' His face was pale now, his eyes shifting side to side.

'When was this?'

'In Holland.' He swallowed. She saw his Adam's apple bob in his throat. 'It was how I escaped. Now put that thing away, it makes me nervous.'

'Not until you tell me exactly how it happened.' She kept the gun levelled at his chest.

'He was a sentry at a checkpoint on a bridge across the river. I needed to cross, get to a place I could get help. And I was panicking. I'd no papers then. I'd been shot down, remember? I slit his throat in the dark. Then I took his papers because it was easy. I was looking for cigarettes, anything useful. It was all he had in his pockets.'

Was this the truth or was it a lie? Nancy remembered the feeling of killing the man in the dark after she landed. She could imagine doing the same in his situation. 'Why keep his papers now we're here?'

'A souvenir. Something to show the men back home. Something to boast about, I guess.' He held up his hands. 'Come on, Mina, put the gun down.'

She lowered it gently. 'I'll keep it if you don't mind.' The fact he'd called her Mina, her cover name, had strengthened her resolve not to take risks.

He exhaled but watched her carefully as she put on the safety catch and pocketed it in her skirt. 'You can trust me, Mina,' he said. 'And anyway, I'll likely be gone tomorrow and out of your hair. Always supposing the plane can land on a space the size of a napkin.'

She paused to think. It was a plausible explanation and she mustn't do anything hasty. Edward was not her favourite person, but then he'd made no attempt to harm anyone, had he?

'If they say the landing place is okay, it'll be okay,' Nancy said, answering him at last. 'Stop fretting. I asked Nicole how many other men they'd sent home.' She held up two fingers. 'Two others,' she said. 'And you'll be the third. And maybe a few more after you.'

Edward turned away and gazed out of the window. 'Tomorrow can't come soon enough,' he said. 'Especially when someone on your own side points a gun at you.'

Nancy didn't rise to this barb. She went down the ladder, intending to go and sound out Remi and Nicole about Edward. She was still uneasy, but couldn't tell if it was sheer nerves, or something else.

Just as she got down from the last rung, Nicole came in to the barn looking flustered. 'Don't go outside,' Nicole said. 'A neighbour's boy's just been. He was crying. A big group of Germans arrived at his farm – it's only about a mile from here. Started throwing their weight about. They've thrown off all the farm workers, and taken it over. Ten of the bastards, a truck and four motorcycles.'

'Jeepers, that's too close for comfort. Where will your neighbours go?' Nancy asked.

'The women and children have already been taken in by my sister's family. But the men who were working there have been sent to work camps. I'm afraid they'll come here and take Remi next.'

'What's going on?' Edward appeared down the ladder.

'Germans,' Nancy said. 'At a neighbouring farm.'

'Sounds like bad news,' he said.

'What shall we do?' Nancy asked Nicole. 'Will the pickup still happen?'

'It has to. We have to get Edward out quickly. If they find him here, they'll shoot us all.'

'Can they see the landing site from the other farm?' Edward asked, and Nancy translated it.

'No,' said Nicole, 'God be praised.'

The thought of Germans so close was sobering.

That night they went through the final arrangements, sitting round the table in the farmhouse. Nancy kept her attention on

Edward, and now he looked scared. Perhaps she was being over-cautious. Just because she and Edward didn't hit it off, it didn't mean he was a traitor. He was trying to survive, just like she was.

Remi and another friend would take a cart down tomorrow morning as if they were simply labourers haymaking. They'd stash plenty of hay on the cart to disguise any supplies that might come in. Their other helpers would go at dusk by horse or on foot, a few hours apart. Edward and Nicole would go by bicycle, like lovers looking for a quiet spot. This idea made her skin crawl, but it was her duty. Country first. Besides, it would soon be over and he'd be gone. Remi told her everyone would be in place before full dark, and then it would just be a case of waiting.

Nancy translated all this to Edward, who nodded his approval, though he was jittery and couldn't be still.

That night in the barn, Edward stood at the window, Nancy noticed that the strain had carved lines around his eyes. The thought that the Germans had billeted themselves so close was obviously preying on his mind.

'Your wife will be glad to see you home,' Nancy said.

He turned, frowning. 'What?'

'Susan. She'll be glad to see you.' She wanted him to leave on some sort of positive note of friendship.

'Oh, yes.' A pause. 'Yes, she will.' He turned back to the window.

Edward waited until he heard Mina's breath settle. He was well aware she wasn't Mina, or even Gusta, the name she'd given at Ralf's. None of them were ever who they said they were. Still, the man who called himself Ralf, and his friends, would be in Gestapo custody by now; he'd telephoned Giskes from the hotel in Brussels to tell him where to pick them up.

Carefully, he tiptoed to the trapdoor. The moon was bright, even tonight, the day before the full moon, and it shone through the loading bay to the hayloft, illuminating the floor in a pewter slab of light.

The ladder creaked as he let himself swing down it to the ground. Within a few moments he was away, out through the barn door and loping down the dark lane towards the neighbouring farm. The night was peaceful, the countryside fragrant with recent haymaking.

A pheasant squawked and flurried into the hedge, and his shoes seemed loud on the dirt and stones of the track. Stupid bird, couldn't even fly. He glanced towards the forest that concealed the landing site. The site where two other English pilots had sneaked free; free to fly again and bomb his homeland. But not this time. This line would soon be broken. Giskes would be pleased, and maybe promotion might come, or a citation. It had been Giskes' idea to go one step further than impersonating English messages and to find an English speaker to impersonate an airman. And it had worked like magic.

He cut across the fields towards the neighbouring farm. There were lights visible there, even though it was forbidden, and he could see the solid shapes of the *Wehrmacht* trucks parked outside the front door.

Footsteps and a sharp voice in German. 'Who is it?'

Edward answered, '*Oberleutnant* Sitz. Greetings, friend. *Heil Hitler.*'

The man lowered his rifle. 'Ah, Günter. Come in, they're waiting for you.'

Inside the farmhouse kitchen, the men were playing cards, and several empty bottles of wine littered the tabletop. Major Schröder had his boots on the table, but he sat up as soon as Günter entered.

'What news?' he asked. 'Is it on?'

'Yes. The pickup's at 02:00 hours tomorrow, if we get the message on the BBC. But hold off until she lands, and with any luck we'll get the pilot and crew before we fire the plane.'

'Okay,' the major said. 'Here's the plan.'

*   *   *

Nancy was tired and let herself drift in the sweet smell of the hay. She must have fallen asleep, despite the fact she had one hand on the pocket with the gun, and some underlying tension made her always half alert. It was dark, and the moon almost full, so when she stirred there was enough light for her to see that Edward wasn't asleep in the nest he'd made himself in the hay. She sat up and peered around but couldn't see him. Probably nervous and gone out for a pee.

She settled back down, but he still didn't appear. Worried, she put on her shoes and went down the ladder and out into the yard. Everything was quiet. Not a whisper or a light from the farm.

In the distance, there was the plaintive cry of a goat or sheep bleating. She walked right around the yard, scanning gates and the track, but there was no sign of Edward. She was about to knock on the farmhouse door to see if he was there when she saw a figure moving up the pale stripe of the drive.

She sighed with relief. Edward. She waited for him.

'Couldn't you sleep?'

'No. I fancied a walk. I keep thinking about the plane landing on that tiny patch of ground.'

If he was worried, and he was an experienced flyer, it didn't bode well. 'The pilot'll be used to flying Lysanders. What did you fly?'

'Hurricanes. I flew Hurricanes.' Hurricanes? She could have sworn he'd told her it was Lancasters.

Just then, there was a squawking and a flapping. A fox ran by, a chicken flailing in its bloody mouth. Edward ran to chase it off but it was too late, it disappeared into the patch of woodland behind the house.

Chapter 41

Tom had been pacing the corridor, waiting for a response from agent Ludo. Between training new agents for F Section, he was supposed to be working on new silk coding squares, but every scheduled transmission time, he was there outside the wireless ops room in case Alice Dobell could get through. But he knew the problem – how hard it was for agents to keep to their times, and for the airwaves to be clear enough to hear their message. Finally, a response came from Ludo via Hockey's transmission code.

He pounced on it and with pulse racing decoded it in one sitting using 'The Owl and the Pussycat', He was immediately aware there was no send code on the message. He'd thought Nancy to be more careful.

SKED DROP SUPPLIES FOR NEXT FM STOP
WILL ACT ON REQUEST BUT NEED MORE INFO RE LAST
SKED STOP LUDO

The agent Ludo who was working with Hockey hadn't answered the question. In fact, was questioning the question. This wasn't her. Couldn't be. At the very least she might have told him to sling his hook. But no response? That was strange. And a demand for supplies on the next full moon. Should he tell Beauclerk?

No. He had to be sure. He had to wait for the WOK reply.

He was unbearable for the whole day, he knew he was, because he snapped at people when they tried to tell him the good news that Iran had stopped being neutral and had declared war against the Nazis. 'Who cares?' he said. 'When half of Europe is still under occupation?'

When the transmission from the WOK code arrived, he had to cadge a cigarette from Alice to calm himself before he could bear to decode it.

Feverishly he got to work.

The first words were SHEPHERDS PIE.

He shot upwards out of his chair and punched the air. Eyes wet with elation. It was her. Had to be. It was really her. She was alive.

It was several minutes before he could calm himself enough to decode the rest. She was confirming the drop zone coordinates of the plane so she could get an agent home.

His elation was short-lived. It wasn't Nancy who would be coming home, but the downed airman. But he could get news of her at least. He daren't message her again; Beauclerk's threat of a prison sentence had been serious.

Neil thrust the newspaper away. His father had insisted on ordering the *Standard* for him every day so he'd know what was going on, but Neil found it just made him angry. The Nazis were taking over the Greek island of Rhodes, and news had arrived of the atrocities they'd committed in Poland. He didn't want to look. It made him squirm to think he'd ever supported them.

He glanced at the bedside table, loaded with precious apples and a jar of honey. His mother had been every day. It must be costing the pair of them a fortune to stay in their London hotel and it made him feel guilty. And, of course, they still thought Nancy was bandaging the troops in Birmingham.

He lay back on the pillows and wondered what life would be like with two smashed legs. Both legs had survived the blast, but with broken bones. He'd be even more of a hobbler now. He was just thinking this when a familiar voice said, 'How's the wounded soldier?'

Neil heaved himself back to upright.

Tom was pink and cheerful and bursting with life. He dragged the hospital curtains around the bed with a rattle and swish, then pulled the metal chair nearer. 'I've got good news,' he said. 'First, they actually let me in! But better – news I'm not supposed to tell you.' His eyes were bright behind his glasses. 'Someone's sister is alive and well, and in touch with England.'

'Nancy?' Neil tried to sit up. 'How do you know?'

Tom leant in. 'I picked up a message from her myself.'

'How?' Neil flopped back on the pillows. 'Is she coming home?'

'No.' He glanced behind him, and lowered his voice. 'And you mustn't tell anyone. This is just between us.'

'My parents?'

'No. Have some common sense. She's in Birmingham, remember?'

Neil took a ragged breath. 'You wouldn't just be saying this to cheer me up, would you?'

'No!' Tom was vehement. 'She's alive, I swear it.'

Neil felt some scar in him crack and move. His eyes filled. 'Give me a moment,' he said.

Tom passed him a handkerchief. 'It's not the only news. Beauclerk asked me to have a word.'

'Go on.' Now it was coming. Tom's face was more serious. Neil prepared himself for bad news.

'You're a lucky devil. You're off the hook. They're hushing it up. Oliver Johnson never existed, and they want you to keep the whole thing under your hat.'

'What?'

'They're going to pension you off.'

Neil was silent. But he'd killed someone. Surely someone would want their pound of flesh? He twisted the sheet in his hands. 'No. They can't do that,' he said. 'Otto was my friend. I deserve everything that's coming to me.'

Tom threw up his hands. 'How many hearts do you want to break, Neil? Your mother's? Your father's? What would Nancy think?'

Neil pressed his lips together, tried to shut out Tom's words.

'For a long time, I was angry as hell,' Tom said. 'Thought you should be punished for what you did. But then I realised, war does strange things to us all. We turned a blind eye to all those men gassed or dying of dysentery in the trenches in the Great War. And if anyone should be punished, it's Beauclerk. For not running a tighter ship, and for keeping us all in the dark so long. And would it honestly help Otto's parents to know how and why he died?

'They're good people. Just like us,' Neil said. 'I don't know how I'll ever be able to tell them.'

'Then don't. He's gone. Nothing can bring him back. He was a bastard, but it's not their fault. Let's leave them to think their son's a war hero, right?'

Chapter 42

This corner of the dirt track was lit in the dim blue light of almost dark, the sun having just sunk below the horizon. Somewhere nearby, Nancy could smell a midden, but the aroma was overlaid with the unexpected sharp scent of pine. The summer nights were long and so there was only a limited amount of darkness. The Lysander would not only have to land on the equivalent size of a handkerchief, but do so in the small hours of darkness.

The bicycles were left exactly where Remi had said they'd be, and Nancy was relieved to see they were serviceable ones, and they'd thought to supply her with one without a crossbar. Edward had made no attempt to touch her and seemed preoccupied.

'This is it,' she said to Edward. 'You'll soon be home.'

'Can't wait,' he said. He flashed her a smile, but then again there was that slightly faraway, blank look. He took his time getting on the cycle, staring around as if to see the last of Belgium.

Nancy set off pedalling in the direction they'd been told to go. She hoped they'd meet nobody. She was wearing a cotton belted dress with a knitted cardigan over it, in the style of a Belgian worker, but the gun was in her skirt pocket and she was keenly aware of its weight against her thigh, and that she'd have to get rid of it if they were stopped. The suggested disguise of lovers in a clinch, should anyone come, was not a pleasant thought. She'd be glad to be rid of Edward; to go back to the job she'd been trained to do.

The drop zone the SOE had chosen was within a small wooded area of larch and pine, where they dismounted and thrust the cycles into a hedge. She noted the place well, for she would have to come back this way once Edward had gone.

'I say,' Edward said, 'let me have the gun now. Just in case something goes wrong.'

'I've had weapon training. I'll keep it, thank you. And anyway, you'll soon be out of here. It'll be more use to us in the network than to you.'

'There'll be guns and ammo in the drop, won't there?'

'Maybe.' But she still didn't offer to give it up. She was hoping for her own wireless set, but she knew there'd be little time to load and unload goods. The noise of a plane flying so low would surely bring the Nazis, who were now camped less than five miles away. She'd keep the gun.

Edward seemed more sure-footed here, as if he knew the way, crashing through branches and scrub. *Be quiet!* she wanted to say, but voices would be even more likely to draw attention, so she bit her tongue. A wood pigeon shot up before them in a flurry of wings, and Nancy's heart almost stopped.

She had a feeling, an uncomfortable feeling, that there were people watching. The occasional flicker of movement, or was it imagined? She glanced up into the tangle of branches and the thick canopy of leaves overhead, but could see nothing. Her nerves were getting the better of her.

As they approached the clearing, five dark figures emerged. Men carrying torches with game bags slung over their shoulders. Farmer's sons, hefty and broad-shouldered. These would be Remi's network, the helpers he'd promised. With surprise, she saw that one of them, wearing a man's coat, was Nicole, her belly sticking out like a balloon.

They came towards Edward and said a few words. He smiled and nodded, but he must have had no idea what they were saying. Remi took his men off to check the landing spot and clear any stones.

'Good night for it,' Nicole said to Nancy.

'God willing,' she replied.

They sat down at the edge of the clearing, by a pile of logs, to check their flare torches and to share some brandy from a flask. She let her gaze take in the scene. They were in a flat field, evidently used for grazing cattle and goats, for there were still a few dark rounds of cow dung they had to avoid putting their feet in. Nicole eased herself down onto one of the bigger logs. She had prepared thick slices of bread and butter with a soft cheese. It tasted like heaven after their meagre meals. Edward ate his, but he seemed nervous, his eyes scanning the skies, then swivelling to scour the woods.

Understandable, she thought. She too had that taut feeling in her belly.

Behind them, she heard another noise in the woods, a twig snapping. She whipped her head round to look.

'Fox, probably,' Nicole said, 'or badger. We've used this spot many times. It's hard to see it from the ground, or the Boche would have filled it full of stakes. Let's hope your pilot manages to avoid the flak on the way over.'

'Is that your cart?' Nancy pointed to a four-wheeled handcart by the gate.

'We always hope for supplies,' she said, 'and it's a fair way to carry them back to the village.'

Nancy nodded. The wireless set and battery would be heavy to lug on a bicycle.

The night grew denser, and all she could see now were the smiles of the men in the dark. A tingle of mist in the air and dew was falling, making everything smell fresh and new. In the distance, the bleating and bells of goats.

319

Again, the noise of something from the woods made Nancy startle. Nicole pressed her hand onto Nancy's. 'Don't worry. We heard the signal on the BBC. *The dog does not bark*. It's definitely tonight.'

At first, Nancy thought she was imagining the guttural purr of an engine. But Nicole's sudden grip on her hand made her jump to her feet.

At the same time, Edward leapt up and tilted his head back to look.

The men burst into activity, lighting the flares and running to set them out in the required triangular formation. Edward was stock still, eyes fixed on the opposite side of the field. Remi ran over to her and spoke in French, 'Get your man out of the way! Tell him to wait over there.' He pointed.

Edward was edgy, his eyes unnaturally bright. He refused to move to his appointed spot. 'I'll be fine here,' he said, moving a few yards to the edge of the woods, eyes fixed on the sky.

Nancy shrugged. She couldn't force him.

The men and Nicole had set out the five flares for the landing, glowing bright in the dark. The Lysander's drone grew louder until the big grey belly of the aircraft was so low Nancy felt she could almost touch it. Remi had told her the Lysander had a stalling speed of only sixty-five miles an hour, and that was why they used it for these pickups.

The wheels splayed from the undercarriage like giant feet. How could such a big thing land here, in this tiny space? The noise was tremendous. Surely every Nazi for miles around would hear it?

The plane tilted its wings, and winked the lights, before circling again.

'He's seen us,' Remi said. 'Get ready!' He waved his arms for everyone to clear out of the way.

In among the stars, the plane's lights were like two eyes, as it circled and came in again to loom nearer and nearer. 'You need to be on the nearside,' Nancy yelled to Edward over the noise.

He gripped her by the arm. At first, she thought it was nerves or excitement, but as she struggled, she felt him go for her pocket. He was after the gun.

'What are you playing at?' The realisation made her angry. 'Leave it!'

She slapped at his face to keep him off but he punched her hard in the chest. She doubled over, trying to catch her breath, but too late, he'd wrenched the gun from her hands.

The click of a cocking action. At the same time, the crack of a rifle shot from the woods. It echoed cold in her blood. She tried to run, but he caught her by the hair and yanked back her head.

A cold pressure to her temple. Too late she realised what was happening.

My God. He could be Günter Sitz after all.

Edward slid behind her, and this feeling of a gun to the temple reminded her instantly of Arisaig.

At the same time, the woods erupted with German soldiers, who ran forward from the dark of the trees. They were shouting, and it was a moment before she recognised the yells as, 'Hands up!'

From the fact they were surrounded, she knew, without doubt, it was a coordinated attack. 'You knew,' she said to Edward. 'You bastard. You knew.'

The Lysander was swooping in low, and the pilot could have no idea what he was coming into.

The men who'd lit the flares ran in every direction, looking for cover and to escape the German guns. Over the noise of the plane, she saw Remi fire and pick off two Germans, who jerked and fell. A rattle of machine-gun fire in reply.

'You will do exactly as I say.' Edward pressed the gun through her hair and into the soft nape of her neck. 'Move back into those trees while the plane lands, unless you want to be shot to pieces with the plane.'

Mind numb. Feet floundering over tussocks of grass, she let herself be led to the edge of the woods. Two bodies lay near the

321

flares. With a choke she realised one of the fallen bodies was the bulky figure of Nicole, a dark spatter across her chest. Remi had run to her, but now he was surrounded, a gun against his back, and he stood, head and hands hanging, his face white in the flare of the torches.

What a waste. Rage rose inside her in a flood. She could smell the sourness of Edward's sweat and hear her own heart pumping in the side of her neck. Her fingers fumbled for the edge of the belt tied around her dress. Out of reach. She tried again, fumbling to undo the knot. She caught the end and tugged. It slipped through the belt loops inch by inch. A sharp pull and it was free. With one hand she wound it around her wrist.

'Don't try anything,' Edward said, feeling her movement. He grabbed her chin with his other hand and pressed the muzzle of the gun harder to the nape of her neck.

The plane was a moving patch of black in the dark of the sky. She'd seen enough of the Nazis to know she was only alive because they'd want all her contacts from the moment she'd set foot on Dutch soil. She had to do something.

Edward had his eyes fixed on the plane. They were waiting for it to land. No doubt they wanted the intelligence and any supplies from the pilot, and needed him alive too. It might provide the diversion she needed.

With a thud of tyres and an almighty draught, the plane bumped to the ground and began to taxi in a circle.

Now! She stepped a leg back, hard and fast between Edward's legs, and threw the whole of her body weight backwards. He staggered, and it gave her enough room to turn and, while he was off-balance, to sweep one of his legs from under him. He toppled more easily than she'd hoped. A grunt as the fall knocked the breath from his lungs and the gun went off, the shot ricocheting into the trees, the recoil causing him to drop the weapon.

Instantly, he got to his knees and half crawled, trying to stand. On instinct, she grabbed a rough log with both hands. Using all her strength she heaved it up and brought it down hard on the back of his head.

He sagged but clawed for the gun where it had landed. Groggy, but not beaten. How could he still be conscious? In a flash, she unravelled the belt from her hand, crossed her hands to throw it around his neck, twisted it and pulled.

He did what any man might do by instinct, dropped the gun and his hands went to tear at the ligature around his neck. Nancy closed her eyes and pulled. Edward was weak and tried to speak, but she knew it was him or her. It seemed to go on for an age before he fell limp. Still she pulled, before the weight of him slumping, face into the mud, told her he'd lost consciousness.

Behind her, the plane had taxied and turned to face into the wind before it came to a stop. The door was on the other side and would be the Germans' target by now. She grabbed the gun from where it had fallen from Edward's hand and cocked it. Thank God his gun was a semi-automatic Colt pistol, exactly like the one she'd used at Arisaig, so there should be a few shots left.

Always make sure. Fairbairn's words. A carefully aimed shot through the head made sure Günter Sitz would never get up again.

She peered through the trees into the clearing where the Germans had backed off to give room to the plane which was slowing to a halt. It was a slim chance, but maybe she'd be able to disable one or two *Wehrmacht* before they caught her – allow the pilot time to get the plane away.

Shouts in German from the field, almost drowned by the rumble of the engine. Shielded by the plane, Nancy ran out of the cover of the trees and dropped onto her belly. Her chin prickled by grass stubble, and elbowing forwards, Nancy crawled beneath the plane. From that vantage, she made out two soldiers with guns trained on the portside hatch, and a barrel-chested *Wehrmacht* officer in a peaked cap, standing by to give the English crew his inimitable welcome.

Taking aim at the big man in the cap, she fired two shots in quick succession before lunging from underneath and up to her feet. She was in luck; the officer sagged and fell. Both soldiers rushed to his aid. It gave her the time she needed. She had to risk turning her back as she scrambled up the fixed ladder. Just in time. The Perspex hatch opened and a shot whistled over her head and ripped into the crewman's upper arm.

He was dazed, clutching at it, blood dripping through his fingers.

'Go!' she yelled. 'Get out of here! It's a German trap.'

The wounded crewman, a young chap with thinning hair and the airman's exhausted look, was wide-eyed with shock. He began to drag her inside.

'No,' she protested, pulling away, but a sudden jolt in the back of her shoulder made her scramble inside for cover. The crewman shut the roof again, just as a volley of machine-gun shots ripped through the fuselage.

The crewman shouted into the cockpit, blood dripping, and the plane engine roared back to life along with the churn of the propeller. More fire, but Nancy crouched low, as near to the wings as possible, making herself a small target. She felt the back of her shoulder, and her fingers came away wet with blood. It was at the front too, a sticky stain. She'd been hit. She was nauseous and her teeth were chattering with shock. Seconds seemed like hours before the plane bumped along the ground. Another row of smoking holes appeared in the side of the plane before, engine screaming, it banked and rose. The crewman, obviously a rear gunner, handed her an oxygen mask before he crawled to his post.

She breathed in the smell of rubber and canvas, and the plane tilted and levelled up into the night sky. Adrenaline made her breathless, but the oxygen helped. Here, clinging to her wooden bench seat, the petrol tank at her back, she watched the grey outline of the tail sink. Flashes of fire from below.

'We're clear,' the young man said as he disappeared behind his mask and gave her the thumbs-up.

A miracle to be up in the sky, and still breathing. Her shoulder throbbed, but she staunched the blood from the front of her dress as best she could with the hem of the skirt. The Perspex canopy cocooned her in a glass bubble high above the earth as it slid by, a black velvet tapestry intersected by silver-grey rivers. She glanced down to see near her feet all the supplies that couldn't be delivered; the stack of bicycle tyres, a wooden crate of rifles. And next to it a smaller crate with tins of Bournville chocolate and a pack of Yardley lipstick.

She couldn't help thinking of the roundness of Nicole's belly, now so still, the unborn child cut off before it had a chance to live. Of Remi, and all those others that would now be caught and tortured before they were sent to German camps. They'd risked their lives for the English, and an Englishman had betrayed them. She felt their pain like an umbilical cord dragging her back.

It seemed like madness that she was watching the war recede. Gunfire sparked in the distance as they flew towards the long flat expanse of the sea.

She must have dozed, despite the cold, for the next thing she knew, the English coast was approaching.

Lights flashed on the ground, red and white.

The plane bumped to the ground, each jolt from the wheels like a bite of pain into her shoulder. Finally, all movement stopped. Feeling she might faint, she unbuckled the mask and thrust the Perspex cover back to breathe in English air.

Was this really England? It was such a sudden transition, from danger to safety that she couldn't take it in.

Her legs shook as she climbed down the ladder to the ground, where two uniformed RAF men, a plain-clothes man and a car were waiting.

She approached them like a newborn colt.

'Are you hurt?' the plain-clothes man said.

'No,' she said in a daze, though her shoulder was now stiff and her dress thick with clotted blood.

'Where's the "Joe", Edward Lovell?' he asked.

'He was an impostor – I think, by the name of Günter Sitz. I suspect Edward Lovell's been dead since his plane crashed. They're using his identity to break the Resistance exit routes. But he's dead now, too, the German.'

'So there's no returning hero.'

'No. Only me. And I wasn't supposed to be coming home. There was just no other choice.'

'Sit tight then, we'll get you to the medics, get that shoulder looked at.'

'I was shot,' she said, stupidly.

'I can see that. I'm Major Hooper. I'll be debriefing you once you've been stitched.'

She let him lead the way. The strangeness of being in a place where she didn't need to watch her back made her light-headed. She was unsure who she was anymore. Was she Nancy? Or Gusta, or Mina?

They put her and the rear gunner in the car and drove through the night. At three o'clock in the morning she had a bullet removed from her shoulder and was given a sedative.

Her thoughts were hazy, drifting. She hung on to them as long as she could, the names. All the people she'd been in contact with. That long line which would now be broken like snapped twigs in a forest.

Remi and Nicole. Lafage. Pierre and the hotel owner in Brussels. Ambika, Danny and Ralf. The Van Hegels and old Anna who had first taken her in. The Germans were thorough; they would pursue every single one. She had the crazy urge to kill Edward Lovell who had betrayed them all. But then she remembered; she already had.

Chapter 43

After the debriefing, Nancy was told she was allowed to go home. The idea of going back to London seemed bizarre. If she thought being an agent was hard before, now it was even worse. She had to remember a new and more confusing cover story; supposedly her shoulder had been caught by shrapnel in a bomb blast in Birmingham, so she was allowed a few weeks' leave from the FANYs.

She was whisked off to be fitted with a new FANY uniform of a smaller size, because she had lost weight. And she had to pretend that she was a cheery nurse, not a woman in mourning for all the people she had met in Holland. She was no longer allowed in the corridors of Baker Street in case it blew her cover. She was sad and nostalgic that she would never see the inside of the cipher room again.

This morning she was to be issued with train passes.

'Change at Birmingham and be sure to destroy the other bus and train tickets from anywhere near Tangmere Aerodrome,' Major Hooper said. He was a bluff man in his forties, who seemed completely lacking in empathy. His stiff upper lip was well sewn on. 'We made some enquiries and it seems your London flat is no longer available. There was some trouble with looters and the landlord has reclaimed the rooms. There's apparently still some outstanding rent so—'

'What about Neil? My brother?'

'Oh. Didn't you know? He's in hospital. Marylebone. A bomb blast. But making a good recovery.' She had no time to take this in before he continued, 'You've got ten days' leave, but we've put you up at the London FANY hostel for now until you can find another place to stay.'

He handed her a piece of paper with an address on it, and a travel permit.

A hostel. She had expected a homecoming. But it seemed everything had changed in just a few short weeks.

Nancy went straight from the train station to the hospital. When she got to the ward, she could see two familiar figures sitting in one of the bays. She rushed past the rest of the beds.

'Mother!' Her mother turned and her face opened into a smile. Within a few moments they were hugging tightly.

'Nancy. Where did you spring from?' Her father slapped her on the back. She winced as it jarred her shoulder, but the gunshot wound was well-hidden under her uniform.

Her eyes went to Neil, who was sitting up in bed.

'I only just heard,' she said, hurrying to embrace him. 'I got here as soon as I got leave.'

'We didn't want to worry you,' her mother said. 'At least not until we had Neil home.'

'What's the damage?' she asked.

'Both legs broken,' Neil said, 'and a few cracked ribs. It'll take time before I can walk again. But I was lucky. Tom Lockwood helped to pull me out.'

'Tom?' The name had the power to make her heart leap.

'He's been a regular visitor,' her mother said.

'He knows about my work,' Neil said. 'Keeps me up-to-date with what's happening in the Inter-Services Research Bureau.' He gave her a meaningful look. 'And how's Birmingham?'

A pause. His gaze was slightly mocking.

He knew. She'd lay bets on it. She busied herself straightening the bedcovers and avoiding his eyes. 'Busy,' she quipped. 'With bomb blast victims like you. And I had a near shave myself.'

'The office has been so very kind to Neil,' her mother said. 'His boss Mr Beauclerk sent that basket of fruit. Imagine, an actual orange! We daren't even smell it.'

'About Tom – is he still living in the same flat?' Nancy asked.

'Aye,' Neil replied, reverting to the Scots now they were all together. 'His street's still standing. And he's still at Baker Street. He'll be glad to see you if you have time during your leave.'

'I'll make time,' she said.

He grabbed her hand and squeezed it. 'He saved my life. Fetched the medics when the building came down on top of me. You could do worse.'

From Neil, who she thought hated Tom, that was high praise.

Tom had resumed his tasks in the cipher room. He imagined Nancy sitting in her old seat, pencil pressed to her lips as she concentrated on the coding sheets in front of her. Beauclerk had shut down the suspect transmissions from Ludo, but it didn't prevent Tom worrying about the danger of every transmission Nancy made. He supposed that was why even friends and family never knew what agents were doing. The stress of wondering about her day after day was eating away at him. At night, he pictured her hiding in some attic somewhere, tapping out her message in Morse. Every night he sent up silent prayers that the Nazi detector vans would never find her.

He looked out of the window on to the grey pavement below, which was peppered with the first autumn leaves. Today, he might get news of her from the Joe that was supposed to have come back to England last night. If he could track him down. But it was a slim chance. No one would tell him his name.

* * *

329

Nancy looked up at the offices where she used to work. The outside of Baker Street hadn't changed, still the same tall white building with its ranks of blacked-out windows. The sight of its big doors and the name carved above the door, '83 Baker Street', sent a shot of nostalgia down her spine. There'd be women in the cipher room now, decoding indecipherables from agents like her. It didn't seem real.

She had no pass, so she was obliged to wait outside. Every person who came out of the side door made her stomach turn over. Finally, just before lunch, she saw him stride out. The same old Tom. He looked older somehow, and his expression lacked any joy. She wasn't used to seeing him without his smile.

She shouted his name, but the traffic noise drowned it out so she had to call again. He turned to look over and she waved frantically. He glanced over his shoulder as if she might be waving at someone else.

Then he looked back. Deep shock was etched around his eyes.

'Tom!' She waved again and ran towards him, dodging a taxi and a bicycle.

At the same time, in a headlong rush he was running towards her. 'Nancy? I can't believe it,' he said, stopping right in front of her. He put a hand out to rest on her arm, as if to test she was really there. 'I thought you were . . .'

'Sssh. Don't say anything until I tell you I'm sorry for—'

'You've got leave?'

'Invalided out for a week or two. Got hit by a bomb in Birmingham.'

He raised his eyebrows. 'And pigs might fly.'

'I have to stick to the story, you know that.'

'God, it's good to see you. I was afraid—'

She interrupted him. 'So was I. But I'm all present and correct.'

He was still staring at her like she was a mirage. 'You're thinner. You need feeding up.' His voice cracked. 'I can't believe you're here.'

The glassiness in his eyes floored her. It was a moment before she could get out any words. 'Have you eaten? We could go to the Corner House.' She looked up at him. 'I missed you, Tom. I should have listened to you. But then again, I'm glad I didn't.'

'Was it hell? No, don't answer that, just hold my hand.'

She put her hand in his, and it was warm and safe and comforting. Then she set off walking with him loping alongside. 'You know I have to go back,' she said, when they reached the open space of the park.

'Go back?'

'Of course, go back. It's what I trained for. And once you've seen how it really is for people in occupied countries, there's no question of sitting out the war.'

'You make me feel guilty.'

She stopped him with a tug of the hand. 'Never, ever, say that. Every measure you take to keep us safe is vital, Tom. The poem codes. The WOK keys on silk. And without the cipher room, we'd have no motivation. We think of London every day. It's all those brief contacts with home that mean so much, the link to friends and family. And the thought that there are people in England like you, people who believe in decency and freedom.'

'Sheesh, you've only just got back and you're talking of going again. You're a tough old bird.' They laughed, and it was like something breaking. His arm snaked over her shoulder. Even through the pain, the weight of it there felt good. She put her arm around his waist and they walked quietly to the Corner House. Once inside, they headed for their usual corner table. Around them swirled the cacophony of clattering cutlery, scraping of plates and hubbub of chatter.

'It seems like yesterday that we were here,' she said above the noise. 'And in another way like years.'

The waitress arrived to take their order. He ordered shepherd's pie for both of them.

'You've no idea how much your message meant,' she said. 'Food is scarce in Holland and the thought of shepherd's pie . . . well . . .'

'It had a purpose.' He leant in to whisper. 'The Nazis must have thought Hurling was you. They were transmitting Ludo's skeds as well. I had to test to find out which was the real Ludo.'

'Really? And I thought you sent it just for love.'

'I did. I mean, it was.'

There was a moment in which she saw that it was the simple truth, and it hurt in a beautiful way. 'Be careful, Tom. I do have to go back.'

'I know, I know.' He traced a circle on the table, his face in shadow, before looking up. 'I never stopped hoping you were alive . . .' He took her hand and pressed it to his lips.

'And I never stopped thinking of you,' she said.

They were silent, just holding hands across the table.

After a moment, she said, 'Talking about agent Hurling . . . anything?'

'No news. We suspect—'

'Don't say it.' She shook her head, knowing the answer. 'One thing I've learnt about war is there's always loose ends, and it's best not to think of them. Nothing's ever tidy or finished, every victory has a cost too blisteringly painful to think of.'

When they'd eaten, Tom suggested a walk up Primrose Hill. It was good to link arms with him and stride out in the open air, amid trees and grass, and to find space for her thoughts.

'Neil says you went to see him in hospital,' she said. 'You're a dark horse. I thought you hated each other.'

'He's grown on me. There's a lot you don't know about me and your brother, but I'm afraid most of it's classified.'

'Well, whatever you did, it worked, because we seem to have his blessing at last.'

At the top, Nancy gazed out a moment over the city. Dark clouds were massed over the skyline, which was dotted with barrage balloons and split by their criss-cross tether lines. Through the heavy rolls of cloud the sun began to glimmer through and pick out the spires of the churches in shafts of light, and she couldn't help but think of the people in Amsterdam for whom the sun would be a long time coming.

Tom seemed to read her mind. He drew her close. 'I'll be waiting when you get back. And you will come back.'

She was silent then. He would know, just as she did, that the odds were against it. That this might be their last reunion. It made every second precious.

'We've got ten days,' she said. 'Let's make them the best days of our lives.'

'Today is already the best day,' Tom said, and his fingers interlaced hers.

A Letter from Deborah Swift

Thank you so much for choosing to read *The Silk Code*. I hope you enjoyed it! If you did and would like to be the first to know about my new releases, click below to sign up to my mailing list. You will get a free WW2 short story when you do.

Sign up here! https://dl.bookfunnel.com/e6izwznl1e

The courage of women in WW2 – women who had to learn new skills and risk their lives in service of their country – is inspiring. Following on from *The Silk Code* I couldn't wait to write another book with some of the same characters, so do keep in touch so I can let you know more. I hope you loved *The Silk Code* and if you did, I would be so grateful if you would leave a review. I always love to hear what readers thought, and it helps new readers discover my books too.

Happy reading!

Deborah Swift

Website: www.deborahswift.com

Historical Notes

The characters in this book are fictional, but Tom takes on some of the roles played by the real Leo Marks during World War Two. Some of the names of the men in charge at Baker Street during the fiasco of *Englandspiel* have been changed out of respect for their still living descendants. The following notes explain some of the history and illuminate the real historical characters featured in the novel.

Englandspiel

Englandspiel – the English Game – was a name coined by *Abwehr* Major Hans Giskes to describe the way his team hoodwinked the Special Operations Executive and enabled the Nazis to run the Resistance networks in the Netherlands. It was also sometimes called Operation North Pole. After the war was over, a Dutch Parliamentary Inquiry Commission revealed that up until October 1943, more than forty of the fifty-six agents sent to occupied Holland by the Special Operations Executive were in fact met by the Germans. Thirty-six of these agents were captured and later executed at Mauthausen Concentration Camp in 1944.

While undertaking agent drops, RAF aircraft were often shot down with the loss of pilots and crew. The RAF suspended flights to the Netherlands in May 1943 after noticing that its flights to the Netherlands always arrived without opposition, but planes were fired upon during their return trip to England, suffering unusually high losses. In less than a year, twelve RAF aircraft were shot down during their return flight from SOE missions in the Netherlands.

The SOE ignored the absence of statutory security checks in radio messages, and other warnings from their chief cryptographer, Leo Marks, that the Germans had infiltrated the Resistance networks. Why this was so has never been completely clear – whether through incompetence, or a desire to hide their shortcomings from MI6.

Five captured men managed to escape, and two of them, Pieter Dourlein and Ben Ubbink, found their way to London. Anticipating their arrival though, Giskes sent a fake message, ostensibly from another SOE agent, that Dourlein and Ubbink were turncoats, having become German agents. Thus the two unfortunate agents were imprisoned on their arrival in London and were incarcerated in a British prison until after the Normandy Invasion in June 1944. They were later given medals by the government of the Netherlands.

Unsurprisingly, the Dutch government-in-exile and the British were condemned for their shocking negligence in not noticing the warning signs of the omission of security codes in the transmissions, and the fact that so many aircraft on missions to the Netherlands did not return safely.

The rather pointed message from Gestapo Major Hermann Giskes to SOE headquarters, dated 1 April 1944 reads:

To Messrs Blunt, Bingham, and Successors, Ltd., you are trying to make business in Netherlands without our assistance STOP We think this rather unfair in view of our long and successful co-operation as your sole agents STOP But never mind whenever

*you will come to pay a visit to the Continent you may be assured
that you will be received with the same care and result as all those
who you sent us before STOP So long*

British Fascists Fighting for the Nazis

Pre-war Britain had a small but passionate network of fascist
and pro-German groups: the main groups being the Imperial
Fascist League, the British Union of Fascists, which was led by
Oswald Mosley, and the short-lived National Socialist League, a
breakaway group from the BUF.

The Right Club (featured in this novel) was made up of anti-
Jewish and fascist sympathisers within the British establishment
and upper classes. It was formed a few months before World War
Two and was focused on opposition to war with Germany. Their
activities included sabotage and acts of treason – to the point that
many of its members were imprisoned for the duration of the war.

In response to fascism within the country, the government
rushed a new Treachery Act through parliament, which introduced the death penalty for any offences that might aid the enemy.
Anyone 'showing sympathy to enemy powers' could be locked up,
the BUF was banned and Mosley arrested.

An MI5 agent discovered after the war that the Right Club
had contacts in almost every government department – in the
police, MI5 itself, key government ministries and the War Cabinet,
and had been secretly compiling a list of Axis opponents to be
eliminated when the country fell to the Germans.

Jack King and the Fake Gestapo Cell

MI5's effort to thwart fascist activities was hampered by the
government's advisory committee on internment, whose members

frequently recommended the release of their upper-class friends and colleagues despite their fascist sympathies.

Determined to counter their influence, MI5 set about forming a fake Gestapo cell in London. It was led by Eric Roberts, a bank clerk and former fascist sympathiser who had changed allegiance and now was to become an undercover agent in the BUF.

Roberts was given a fake Gestapo identity card and assumed the alias of 'Jack King', supposedly a German agent recruited in Britain in early 1939 to compile information on those who would be 'loyal to the Fatherland' in the event of Nazi domination.

Over three years, Eric Roberts (under his alias Jack King) built a network of hundreds of Nazi supporters. The aim was to divert the information given to Roberts, duping its members into thinking that it was being fed back to Berlin, when instead it was sent straight to MI5 in London.

Central to the network were two ardent fascists, Marita Perigoe and Hans Kohout. Marita Perigoe made herself Roberts' deputy, and unbeknownst to her, MI5 housed her in a specially bugged flat in central London.

Agents provided 'Jack King' with maps showing the location of Britain's petrol and aviation stocks, top secret research on new types of engines for fighter planes, and reports on experimental tanks. Some recruits spied in their home towns for information on possible targets for German bombers, or for sites of military bases and civil defence. Some were happy to gloat over the death and injuries caused by air raids, incorrectly putting their success down to intelligence they had provided, when in fact none of the information ever got to Germany.

Kohout's attempt to pass details of the new Mosquito bomber was thwarted, as was the so-called 'Window' programme, designed to confuse German radar. This alone probably saved the lives of hundreds of Allied airmen.

Selected Further Reading

Between Silk and Cyanide by Leo Marks
No Cloak, No Dagger: Allied Spycraft in Occupied France by Benjamin Cowburn
Morse Code Wrens of Station X by Anne Glynne-Jones
Behind Enemy Lines by Juliette Pattinson
SOE in the Low Countries by M R D Foot
Hitler's British Traitors by Tim Tate
Covert Radio Agents 1939–55 by David Hebditch
London Calling North Pole: The True Revelations of a German Spy by Hermann J Giskes
SOE Manual: How to be an Agent in Occupied Europe: Official Manual of the Special Operations Executive

Acknowledgements

Thank you to early readers Tamsin Howe and Susan Paterson, and editor Richard Sheehan. A huge thank you too, to the team at HQ Digital, especially Belinda Toor whose excellent editorial suggestions made *The Silk Code* what it is today.

Dear Reader,

We hope you enjoyed reading this book. If you did, we'd be so appreciative if you left a review. It really helps us and the author to bring more books like this to you.

Here at HQ Digital, we are dedicated to publishing fiction that will keep you turning the pages into the early hours. Don't want to miss a thing? To find out more about our books, promotions, discover exclusive content and enter competitions, you can keep in touch in the following ways:

JOIN OUR COMMUNITY:

Sign up to our new email newsletter:
http://smarturl.it/SignUpHQ

Read our new blog www.hqstories.co.uk

𝕏 https://twitter.com/HQStories

f www.facebook.com/HQStories

BUDDING WRITER?

We're also looking for authors to join the HQ Digital family!
Find out more here:

https://www.hqstories.co.uk/want-to-write-for-us/

Thanks for reading, from the HQ Digital team

ONE PLACE. MANY STORIES